Praise for *Little Lovely Things*

"*Little Lovely Things* is a shattering adventure of utmost cruelty and impossible redemption. The scenes jump off the page as they hurtle toward a conclusion that the reader doesn't see coming."

—Jacquelyn Mitchard, bestselling author of *The Deep End of the Ocean*

"Combining the suspense and razor-sharp outlook of a Gillian Flynn novel, Maureen Connolly's debut sizzles. I finished *Little Lovely Things* in one heartbreaking, tear-batting gulp. Connolly takes risks that make the reader's heart start anew. Finding shards of hope amidst the chaos of tragedy is a testament to both the writer, and the characters she creates."

—Jenny Milchman, *USA Today* bestselling author of *Wicked River*

"Maureen Joyce Connolly's debut novel, *Little Lovely Things*, is a brave and uncompromising glimpse into child abduction and the fractured world it leaves in its wake. With an unflinching gaze, Connolly boldly juxtaposes the darkest crevices of a mother's grief against the all too human side of criminality and the forces that could drive one to the unspeakable. Yet in the midst of darkness, Connolly introduces Jay White, a well-rounded character of Lakota heritage. Through his own inner struggle, the natural and intuitive world becomes a living and breathing part of the narrative, providing light and hope. *Little Lovely Things* is an insightful and moving read that is well worth the journey."

—Vivian Schilling, bestselling author of *Quietus*

"Get ready—*Little Lovely Things* will take your emotions on a ride. Connolly skillfully places readers on a tightrope between hurt and hope from the opening pages until the very last sentence. This is a heartbreaking and compelling story about guilt, trust, and forgiveness that will stay with readers for a long time."

—Nic Joseph, author of *Boy, 9, Missing*

LITTLE

LOVELY

THINGS

LITTLE LOVELY THINGS

a novel

MAUREEN JOYCE CONNOLLY

Published by Sourcebooks Landmark, an imprint of Sourcebooks, Inc.
P.O. Box 4410, Naperville, Illinois 60563-4410
(630) 961-3900
Fax: (630) 961-2168
sourcebooks.com

Library of Congress Cataloging-in-Publication Data

Names: Connolly, Maureen J., author.
Title: Little lovely things : a novel / Maureen J. Connolly.
Description: Naperville, Illinois : Sourcebooks Landmark, 2019.
Identifiers: LCCN 2018026443 | (trade pbk. : alk. paper)
Classification: LCC PS3603.O54726 L58 2019 | DDC 813/.6--dc23 LC record available at https://lccn.loc.gov/2018026443

Printed and bound in Canada.
MBP 10 9 8 7 6 5 4 3 2 1

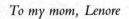

To my mom, Lenore

"Gory at thasp, keener fortha karabd."
"Laugh at death, but weep for those who die before their time."
—anonymous Irish Traveller saying

LITTLE

LOVELY

THINGS

PART ONE

1991

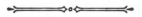

When Claire Rawlings thought of her family, it was more with the mind of a geologist than a physician—the sweeping drumlin of Andrea's collarbone, the narrow plain of Lily's sternum, the sculpted features of Glen's face. Her dreams, too, were crowded with images of rocks and continents gliding, meeting at ragged seams, and then drifting apart.

This night, the first Saturday in September, with a heat wave stalled over greater Chicago, Claire woke sitting upright, pillow crushed to her chest. A mosaic of impressions, foggy and frenetic, competed for clarity in her brain. Something vague about the girls. Her nightgown, twisted and damp, clung to her body, even as a chill ran along her skin. She turned toward the landscape of her husband, dark against the pearlescent glow of the window. Claire could smell him more clearly than see him, the musty scent of heated skin and sweat-tinged bedclothes.

"You were calling out," Glen said, shifting to his side. Their boxer mix, Gretchie, who was curled into a tight cashew between them, groaned at the disturbance.

Claire touched her hand to her temple. In addition to a minor headache, fragments from that dream were hide-and-seeking in and out of her consciousness. A yellow sky. A pond covered with treacherous ice. She'd go check the girls. But first, she leaned over her husband, peeking under the forearm that was thrown across his face as if he were shielding himself from an unseen onslaught.

"Room air conditioner," Claire whispered, as if a magical incantation would cause Glen to lose his frugality, his fear of falling short of money before she completed her medical program. She was in the final phase—all clinical rounds, with only five more months to go. Slipping carefully from bed, she left the sleeping duo in peace.

In the hallway, the house seemed to sigh in the layered light— darker near the ceiling, softer near the window. Built in the late sixties, pretty much everything inside, including the kitchen linoleum floor, remained original. In the surrounding yard, saplings had grown into mature maples and oaks. Claire often imagined this house longed for unfettered sunlight as much as it did for upgraded appliances.

Outside the girls' room, Claire's thoughts went to her pregnancies—the rich awareness of fetal cells inside her, dividing like wildfire, each one blossoming from a small bud into a perfect being. Two beautiful daughters, three years apart. As she entered the doorway, a snapshot from the dream flashed in her mind—this time, icy stalagmites gleamed in the distance and two small figures appeared on the pond. And then nothing. Momentarily losing her breath, Claire steadied herself against the dresser.

She could just make out near her hand a spray bottle where bits of plant material—most likely dandelion—hung in shadowy suspension. Monster repellant: jetted each night into every corner, the closet, and under the bed before lights-out. This was all four-year-old Andrea, in so many ways Claire's binary star—stubborn, feisty, and exhaustingly curious. She now lay silently on top of the covers, her valance of short brown hair matted with perspiration.

Across the room, fifteen-month-old Lily slept soundly in her crib under the window. Beneath her quartz-pink lids were crystal-blue eyes shaped like sideways teardrops. And that froth of yellow hair! Always a struggle to get into a ponytail.

Claire glanced again at Andrea's concoction slightly aglow in a thin shaft of light. A crescent of lemon peel was barely discernible in the murk. She smiled. These materials had been gathered and assembled with Andrea's characteristic attention to detail. *But could this be evidence that my daughter might be feeling insecure?* Even with in-home day care and Glen's teacher's schedule, the girls wanted

Mom. No. She shook her head. She wasn't quite thinking right. This was just the heat and the perennial lack of sleep, shifting her already active imagination into overdrive, scuttling her thoughts into frantic insects. Just last night she'd almost delivered a dose of Tylenol to Andrea before realizing it was Lily with the teething pain.

Andrea was fine; both girls were fine.

Claire wiped her hand across her eyes. They were moister than they should be. The headache was growing more insistent, and fatigue flushed through her limbs. She dropped quietly onto the rocker patterned with Mother Goose characters. The bedroom door squeaked open, and a square black nose followed by a sleek dog body padded in. Gretchie sniffled Claire's hand and then collapsed with a satisfied grunt next to her chair. Leaning back, Claire inhaled the clovery sweetness of her daughters. Her beauties. Still so much a part of her very body. Along with Glen and Gretchie, this family was the closest thing to a single perfect organism.

A shiver of contentment raced through Claire's veins, overshadowed only by a strange feeling left by that dream.

Chapter 1

Claire

*T*hwap, *thwap, thwap.*

Claire woke bleary-eyed to the sound of neighborhood sprinklers through the open window. Swords of sunlight cut through the tree cover into her eyes. Her back grumbled at the angle she'd struck in the Mother Goose chair: ninety degrees south for her lumbar region, twenty degrees north for her neck. The girls' beds were empty. A brief ember of panic stirred until Glen appeared in the doorway.

"Can you hurry, Claire? I have to be at the field in thirty minutes." He helped as assistant coach to the high school's football team on weekends for extra income. "Lily's dressed."

"Andrea?"

"Nope, but eating Eggos."

"One for two." Claire tilted forward and groaned. "I'm hurrying."

"You okay, hon?"

She nodded. It was her turn to take over their shared routine. She dragged herself to the bathroom and into the shower, where the hot water goosefleshed her skin.

Glen appeared in a cloud of steam to hand her a towel and then pointed to her stomach. "Claire?"

She looked down. A faint rash was splayed across her abdomen like a pink Canis Major.

"Might be," she spoke slowly over the din of the water, careful not to convey concern, "a slight reaction."

"Reaction?" Glen's voice tensed. "To what?"

"Hep C vaccine."

A new strain of the virus was invading healthcare facilities like mad, messing with patients' livers or kidneys. The residents had been put on an accelerated vaccination schedule. Two doses, back-to-back.

Glen's gem-blue eyes filled with worry.

"Don't do that, babe."

"What?"

"That oversensitive thing. It's nothing. I'll take a Benadryl."

"You should call in."

"You know I can't do that."

"Or you won't." He paused before smiling. "Laid a T-shirt and shorts on the bed for Andrea."

Claire dried off, dressed, and hurried into the kitchen where Glen blew three kisses before disappearing out the door. Sunlight blared across the worn flooring, promising another scorching day. Claire convinced herself she was feeling okay, even as a new ache spread into her jawline. It was now seven thirty, and caught in motion, there was no time to slow down and reconsider her schedule.

"Dog-dog!" Lily wriggled in her high chair, her unbrushed hair fluffy as a dandelion in seed. She looked at Claire and thumbed a mound of syrup off her tray, which threaded its way to the dog's waiting muzzle. "Ta-dah!"

"Lily, no!" Claire groaned. "You too, G. No!"

Gretchie's monk-brown eyes swam with guilt as she snuffled the amber goo with her blunt snout.

"Andrea, can you help?" Claire turned to find her older daughter standing next to the parakeet cage, still in her Curious George nightgown. Andrea wedged a finger into the gap of her missing front tooth and wiggled, attempting to loosen the remaining one. With her other hand, she stuffed a neat little triangle of waffle through the wires of the cage. Soldier-gray Butkus scooted along his perch, his right wing flaring awkwardly like misfolded origami.

Bau-auck! Bau-auck!

Claire rubbed her temples with her fingertips. "Andrea! Don't! He doesn't eat waffles."

"Why not?"

"It'll make him sick. That's why not."

"How?"

"Honey." Claire sighed. "It just will."

She almost said, *He'll choke on it, that's how. He'll gobble it down and it will glom into a wad in his gizzard and he'll end up at the bottom of his cage, feet pointing to heaven, Xs for eyes, strangled on a frozen pastry.* But she chose her words carefully around Andrea, the daughter with mercurial eyes and moods to match. You could never tell which way she took things: sometimes indifferent, other times overly concerned, like an old man in a little girl packet.

Butkus snatched the morsel—his sharp beak too close to Andrea's finger—and gobbled it down in one smooth motion. He then scooted quickly back to the center of his perch to stare at Claire accusingly with one white-rimmed eye.

Bau-auck! Bau-auck! His scratchy little voice pierced the air with a strain of verbal awareness. *Hurry up!*

"Okay," Claire responded in a falsetto tone, the one she used on Glen when he pissed her off. "Thank you, Butt-Kiss."

"What did you say, Mommy?"

"Nothing, honey. Please hurry!"

Claire lifted Lily from her high chair and grabbed the Benadryl from the cupboard. She took only one dose because, Christ, she had to function on rounds today.

Auck! Auck!

Damn bird.

Within twenty minutes, Claire was leading Lily outside across the driveway to their '91 Taurus wagon, a gift from Glen's parents to help in this final surge until Claire became a doctor. Smattered with the detritus of Happy Meals and Goldfish, the interior was now a disaster zone. She set the day care bag on the seat and rummaged in the glove box for her wraparound sunglasses, the kind that pretty much blocked all light. She slipped them on her face, then opened the back door.

Lily, bright as a button in her shorty overalls, climbed eagerly into her car seat. Claire barely registered the goofy-eared stuffed rabbit, clutched against Lily's chest.

"Good girl, sweetie." Claire lingered a moment, absorbing her tiny framed daughter, before turning to call through the open window. "And-rea-ah…we're in the car."

Behind her, the house door slammed.

"You're next, honey." But Claire's mouth rounded with surprise when she pivoted toward her older daughter.

"Charm dress today? Who said? Daddy?"

She could tell by Andrea's sheepish look that Glen had done no such thing. Claire ran her fingers along the soft, blue fabric. A childhood keepsake, it was sewn by Claire's mother, whom she had lost to pancreatic cancer in high school. The real charm was that within the hem, Claire's mother had hidden a small religious medallion—a depiction of the Virgin Mary—for protection and good luck.

Claire peered over her sunglasses and met her daughter's copper penny eyes. A remorseful pout appeared beneath the Milky Way of freckles across her nose and cheeks. She stuck a finger into her mouth and wiggled her wobbly front tooth.

"We'll talk about this later," Claire said and pointed to the open door. But Andrea stepped back and refused to climb into her booster seat when she spotted the turquoise bunny swinging from her sister's plump hand. Lily lifted him high and pulled one of his springy legs. *Boing.* His ears flopped in unison as he bounced.

Andrea's finger popped from her mouth as she jutted her bottom lip. "Jumpers is mine!"

Technically true. Glen had brought the bunny home, his face flushed with pleasure, after Claire announced her first pregnancy. But Claire wasn't about to mess with Lily after her recent bout with teething pain. Eyeing Andrea, Lily leaned forward against her shoulder harness and squeezed the bright-orange carrot attached with Velcro to his paw.

Crrrunch.

The sound of compressed cellophane ripped through the air.

Andrea stiffened.

"Honey," Claire spoke slowly. "If you don't mind Lily with Jumpers, then I don't mind the charm dress."

Andrea spent a full five seconds measuring the situation, shifting her gaze between Claire and Jumpers, back and forth—Mommy to bunny—and back again. Then she looked down at her dress. To Claire's relief, her daughter finally capitulated and climbed into the car. Claire strapped Andrea into her booster seat and quickly shut the door. She got behind the wheel.

It was almost eight o'clock. She'd need to step on it. Heading down sleepy Crestview, they passed bungalow-style houses and sycamores whitening with age. Claire grimaced at her face in the rearview mirror; even the dark lenses of her sunglasses couldn't disguise the shadows edging her slate-blue eyes. Her normally glossy brown hair seemed lifeless today, an unruly mass of dry tendrils left over from an aging perm. Only last week, Glen had expressed mild dismay at the attention and money spent on Claire's hair. Time and money. They were desperate for both. She wondered how he would do in this heat at the football field. Hopefully, they'd call practice early. This stress, this frenetic rushing around, would all be gone when she officially became an MD.

"Muh-uh-meee!" Lily cried, writhing against her straps. Only five houses down and already they were pulling to the curb.

"What, honey?" Claire jerked the Taurus to a stop and torqued around to face the girls. Jumpers lay on the seat next to Lily, empty-pawed, appealing with doleful eyes.

"Lily hurt Jumpers." Andrea kicked the back of the passenger seat.

"Where's his carrot?" Claire's stomach stirred. A sour taste surged in her mouth.

Lily sobbed as she pointed to the floor.

"Shh, shh. I'll get it."

Claire unbuckled and jackknifed over the seat. Her head thrummed and stars flickered at the edge of her vision. She managed to grasp the orange triangle submerged in a shadow and struggled upright with the toy in hand. Lily snatched the carrot eagerly back into the chub of her fist. Andrea's eyes enlarged as she fought back tears.

"Here, sweetie." Claire shuffled through the day care bag and extracted a Pop-Tart. "Take this." She held it out still in the packet. "It's strawberry, your favorite."

Andrea accepted the offering, but not without terms. She stared out the window as she tore at the package, giving her mother the back of her head. Within one bite, crumbs and gooey Pop-Tart guts dotted the front of the precious blue chambray dress.

"Oh, Andrea!"

Once on the expressway, Claire felt a bit better as they passed through the outer rim of the western suburbs. Wild Queen Anne's lace nodded at the edge of the road like a gathering of small cumulonimbus clouds. Knowledge of the natural world was important. She'd already begun pressing wildflowers and leaves into a scrapbook for the girls to study more closely when they were older. But that, like so much else, was back-burnered for now.

"Look, hons. Look out the window. Believe it or not, those pretty flowers are a type of wild carrot." She started up a childhood song, the girls' favorite. "Count the clouds, one, two, three..." But Claire remained a lone voice. "See the birdie in the tree!" She had never known them not to engage in their favorite ditty. "If he has a broken wing, he will never sing, sing, sing."

"Jumpers would eat them," Andrea announced over Claire. "Those carrot flowers."

Claire met her daughter's gaze in the mirror. She couldn't read Andrea's expression, other than a mixture of mirth and sarcasm beyond her years in her tight, little face. And then Andrea lifted the hem of her dress and all was hidden beneath a veil of blue.

Something like cold electricity shot through Claire and she gripped the steering wheel. The dream. It now returned to her with perfect clarity. The girls surrounded by white, playing on a frozen pond, dressed only in summer clothes. Frantic at the thinning surface, Claire called to them, but each crack running from their feet was a delight, another reason to press farther from shore. She watched her daughters grow smaller, tiny as seeds in the distance until finally they were swallowed into the silence of ice. And in that frozen landscape, both girls were outfitted exactly how they were now: Lily in her yellow overalls and Andrea in the charm dress.

Claire's hands, slick with sweat and shaking, almost slipped from the wheel. The next exit, she recalled, would be a cloverleaf. A slow banking loop and they could be heading back to Upton Grove. She shook her head. No, she needed to remain resolute. The driving force that had carried her this far in life would get her through this day. They were more than halfway to the hospital already. She'd get that nice attending—his name slipped away from her—to help her out, take a quick look at that rash on her stomach. Everything would be fine. She shifted to the middle lane and blew past the turnaround that would take them back home.

Not two miles past the exit, Claire's view of the road began to waver and seemed to pour beneath the car like an ugly asphalt river. An earwig of paranoia inched through her brain. What if the Benadryl was masking something worse than what she'd original surmised? A series of chemical reactions, potentially life-threatening, could be cascading through her blood. Was it really just the vaccine doing all this, or had she been standing on the cusp of a precipice and just slipped? This balancing act—mother, wife, doctor-in-training—seemed extreme enough to be against some law of nature.

Claire started singing again, her voice shaking. "Count the clouds..." But a quick glance into the back seat showed her she'd lost her audience, as both girls were now asleep. Andrea was bent forward at an acute angle in her booster, and Lily was slumped sideways, head tilted, her upper body forming a perfect S-curve.

Claire squinted through watery eyes as the Chicago skyline came into view through the windshield, then blurred into a smudged charcoal drawing. She blinked hard to clear her swimmy vision. Her heart galloped. There was no longer a choice; she needed to get off the highway. She slipped the Taurus into a line of cars merging down the next exit ramp. Following the traffic, they passed graffitied walls and shops with barred windows. A cop pointed right, then left, then right again—confusing as hell. Claire went right instead of left, or vice versa. Some guy in the other lane honked and flipped her off. Feverish blood rushed through her veins and she jerked the steering wheel hard.

Damn, damn, damn.

Luckily, neither girl reacted. Yet the nausea returned, this time with greater ferocity. Claire's breathing quickened and constellations flickered in her eyes. She needed to stop, collect her bearings. Approaching an intersection, she spotted a recognizable beacon in the wilderness of the rundown area: a bright-yellow-and-red Shell sign.

Pull over here. Catch your breath.

She feared she might pass out. This was drawn from experience, having suffered the same symptoms during her pregnancies, with Andrea giving her the worst of it. Crossing traffic lanes, Claire tried to divert her feverish mind with trees: gymnosperms first, then pines, firs, ginkgoes. Then, running short on those, deciduous trees, then plants in general, even cactuses. Cactuses? She'd never even been west of Iowa, and Iowa made her think of corn, which reminded her of the sensation of food in her mouth, corn in particular, round and globular. She gagged.

The Shell station thrummed with energy. People were at the pumps filling their tanks or grabbing coffee from the store. A bus emptied passengers nearby. Following the sign that pointed to the restrooms, Claire accelerated past the squat building, narrowly avoiding hitting something. Could've been a dog, it was so quick—almost a flash, only without light. Or a trick of her overextended brain. Still, she honked before jerking to a stop in the concrete-walled alley behind the building.

Next to the bathroom, Claire slapped the car into Park and rested against the arc of the steering wheel. The girls breathed heavily over the wheeze of the vents. Claire wished her unsick self were here. Or Glen. Or someone. She only knew she couldn't risk shutting off the car, having her girls boil in the heat, like a distracted mother at a shopping mall in the newspaper only a week ago. As she slid from the running Taurus, a light burst of wind, hot as a blow-dryer, ruffled her shirt. She gave the bathroom door, held open by a pneumatic arm, a test shove. It would clearly take a purposeful push to move from its moorings.

Claire glanced back to register her sleeping girls. Lily, behind the driver's side, her head connected with the window, glowed in a slice of sunlight. She had to stretch to see Andrea hidden from immediate view, still bent in half, the back of her head evident over her knees, sleeping nonetheless. They were at peace, protected from the vicious heat with the car running, the cool air circulating.

The gas station bathroom was a cell. A dark, filthy cell with deep, shadowy wells around the toilet. Leaning into the sink, Claire touched the faucet gingerly with the back of her hand. A forceful stream splashed against the porcelain, drowning out the labored growl of her Taurus outside the open doorway. She could feel her two girls, her babies, fast asleep in the car, angled like wildflowers toward the sun—in the direction away from their mother.

Water. And then more water. Some on her cheeks, some in her mouth. Passing her wrists under the stream, Claire froze at a smattering of crimson slashes on her forearms—the rash was spreading. Her legs weakened.

Dropping to her knees, Claire flattened one hand on the greasy floor like a kickstand. She couldn't pass out. Not now. She squeezed her eyes shut and inventoried the stuff she'd packed: Pop-Tarts, Goldfish for Lily, juice boxes. What about crayons? Did she remember to pack them? Andrea loved to color. Wasn't there a stash in the glove box? Exactly where the air-conditioning was certain not to reach. An image popped into her head: the rainbow-hued cylinders, wobbling into molten pools in the heat. The thought of their waxy odor sent a spasm through her stomach. She leaned over the toilet and vomited.

With her head suspended above the filthy bowl, a small quake traveled from the floor through her body. It took a moment for Claire to understand that it signaled the door had somehow shut, shivering tightly into its jamb.

That she was now in total darkness.

She tried to rise. But she could barely lift her head. Her only awareness was a surge of post-vomit relief like a tepid bath. She was not yet alarmed—her fevered brain had stopped working on overdrive the way it normally did. She imagined herself on her feet, wadding up toilet paper and wiping away the crap on her face.

And then another thought materialized in Claire's mind: her girls on that frozen pond, disappearing into nothingness. As she stood helpless on the shore.

Claire cried out.

Then all went black.

Chapter 2
Moira

Moira Kelly trailed a step behind Eamon O'Neill as they worked their way along a trash-strewn alley toward the Shell station for their morning washup. Slap, slap, slap. Her loose sandals clattered along the hot pavement in a merciless staccato that bounced off the heated brick walls.

Eamon slowed and turned his head. His sharp-angled features appeared birdlike from the side, similar, Moira had to admit, to her own.

"Jesu, Moira, you sound like a herd of elephants."

If only! She frowned at the comparison as she stopped to tighten her sandal straps. She and Eamon were both slim—not just because they were built that way, but because they were practically starving.

Eamon leaped onto a curb and crouched like he was surfing before moving on. While both were in their early twenties, Eamon's springy step and cocky demeanor made him seem younger. This often worked in their favor since it was easy for people to underestimate him. Might even prove helpful with the dine-and-dash breakfast they had planned for the IHOP later.

"Hurry it, Moira. The station's just ahead."

What she'd give for a decent bathroom. This city was getting to her, and she'd love a good splash of water on her face—one that came from a clean sink.

Approaching the building from the rear, they entered a

passageway between the restrooms and a concrete wall topped with razor wire. Moira noticed an unopened pack of Salem Lights on the ground. A welcome sign of good luck. She picked it up, leaned into the shadow of an overhang at the corner, and rummaged through her pockets for a light.

Eamon stood with his back to her, darkening the sun-whitened concrete with his name in pee.

"The toilet's right there, Eamon."

Moira inhaled the rich, lazy taste of menthol and laughed at his crooked attempt to draw an *E*. In pictures going back to their childhood, he was always the one with his hand on his crotch. And the not-so-funny ravenous look in his eyes.

Eamon zipped and turned. His chin was filling in with a pointy beard he'd been struggling to grow for almost a month. Dressed in a wifebeater and saggy black pants, he could be mistaken for a hoodlum except for his slight, almost girlish build. He was handsome, with eyelashes thick as fur and a pout that twisted Moira's stomach. He knew more about how to negotiate the world than Moira ever could. She was, in fact, lost without him.

His ropy arms were sleeved in tattoos, and one in particular troubled her. A leering wolf with glowing red eyes in the triangle of his left upper arm—their family insignia. A chosen symbol of wild roguery, it represented their clan's petty thievery and a taste for the drink, behavior that had plagued the larger group of traditional Irish Travellers' good name far too long. So they'd been forced out, formed a clan of their own of only three connected families. The image now served as another reminder of all Moira had lost. She wished the tattoo gone, or at least covered by a proper T-shirt.

K'erp'ra—liars, impostors. That's what she and Eamon had been labeled by her family in Shelta, the language of the Travellers. No longer recognized as one of their clan made them worse than *gyukera*—undesirable vagrants.

The first time Moira had come close to being kicked out of her family, she was pregnant and hid the identity of the father.

Her da took her back with reluctance after the miscarriage, but he had his suspicions. She miscarried the second time, too, but by then, her da knew for certain the father was Eamon. Moira's final remembrance of her family was that of her twin sister Siobhan's smug-ugly face as she and Eamon pulled away in the battered green Buick her da had provided as a shove-off gift.

Eamon stepped under the overhang and reached for Moira's lit cigarette with a quaking hand.

She glared. "You pinched from your stash again, didn't you?"

He'd promised when they first struck out for the city, not six weeks before, that he'd stay away from his own drugs. He'd deal, all right, but not indulge. Not in weed, not in coke, and not in the concoction he made all on his own. Twilight sleep, he called it. "Junkies can't get enough of it," he'd assured Moira. "Completely wipes their brains clean after a bad high. Expensive shite, believe me, like liquid gold. We'll be rich." By now, they were supposed to have droves of eager buyers—but so far, there had been no activity and they were flat broke. A taste from the stash was like stealing from themselves.

"Who cares if I'm trippin' a bit?" His words fell from his mouth with a thin line of spittle. "I can handle a buzz."

Moira frowned. She indulged in smoking pot once in a while but thought hardcore druggies the lowest form of life on the earth. They got what they deserved.

"Forgive me all things." Eamon bowed with a flourish. "My sweet."

Moira, as usual, softened at his puppy face and how funny it looked next to the inked lizard that ran up his neck. Reaching for another drag, Eamon weaved back onto his heels just as a station wagon, appearing from nowhere, wildly blew past them and curved around the corner.

He jumped and plastered himself against the wall. "Crazy fookin' driver!"

A vortex of air pulled the line of smoke from Moira's cigarette and every bit of her attention with it. A small blond head in the back behind the driver's seat flew by at eye level, wispy, young, perfect.

The car swung into the small alley and jolted to a halt at the bathroom behind the station. Touching his finger to his lips, Eamon made big eyes at Moira. They both peeked around the corner as a woman stumbled from the car and into the bathroom. She was obviously drunk or stoned, maybe both. The engine remained running with the child in the back seat motionless, unattended.

"Didja see that?" Eamon whispered.

They slid along the cinder-block wall soundlessly, well-versed in each other's movements. The guttural kecking of the woman vomiting caused Moira's stomach to twitch with revulsion. She glanced again at the golden head against the car window. What was a druggie doing with such a beautiful child?

Eamon moved close to the bathroom and placed his hand on the door.

"What are you doing, Eamon?"

"Shh." He rocked it back and forth, testing its hold.

"Eamon."

"Go. Now." He turned, whispering fiercely, "You head back to the garage."

"What? Why?"

"Never you mind. Do as I say."

Scanning the area, Moira slunk silently away from the gas station. It wasn't until she was close to the garage before she bothered to consider what Eamon might be up to. He'd probably steal the car—he was an old hand at moving hot goods. Or maybe they'd keep the Taurus and sell the Buick instead. The room in the back of a station wagon would be nice. They could spoon comfortably at night. But a sudden concern clouded Moira's thoughts. Even a knucklehead like Eamon wouldn't leave a child in the alley alone, would he? Maybe he'd leave her in the bathroom before taking off. But then, as each step melted into the next, a slight, sweet fantasy began to take hold. Her and Eamon living a real life as a family. She could feel the lovely blond child in her arms, the clean smell of Ivory soap on her skin.

Moira waited outside the garage, against the wall next to a clump of thick-bladed grass, the type that can cut your skin if you're not careful. A slick of leftover mayo on the cement reminded her that this was the same spot where they'd sat last night, eating sandwiches and poring over Eamon's treasured map by the light of a flickering neon sign. Running his finger northeast along markings, he'd continued into the far corner of Illinois before shooting north, just over the border into Wisconsin. Small print indicated trouble spots—an unmarked road here, a dangerous river there. It was a path they hadn't taken since they were kids.

"There." He'd taken a bite of his deviled ham sandwich and leaned over Moira's shoulder as she looked closer, following the details he'd outlined. "That's where we're headed tomorrow."

They'd leave the city and hole up in the rough-hewn cabin once used as a family stopping point to *foluigh*, or hide for a time, like wintering mud toads. Assuring Moira it was abandoned, Eamon intended for them to regroup, plan their next steps.

He'd sat back with the sandwich gobbed in his mouth. He'd stolen every ingredient from the mini-mart—the cheap meat, the small jar of pickles, the Miracle Whip, and a whole loaf of Wonder Bread—laughing at how easy it was to distract the Pakistani fellow by purposefully knocking over a candy display. At the time, Moira had laughed too. Because in her mind, with his new beard, he looked just like the little demon on the can of meat spread. But now she was growing concerned. His impulsiveness was fraught with uncertainty, even scary at times. She'd called him a *g'uk'ra* once, when they were twelve. The word came out of her mouth and then a fist was in her face, no time in between. He'd floored her. When she got up, still dazzled with pain and surprise, he'd said, "Don't care what ya call me, *blanog*—bitch. Just don't like that tone."

She'd forgiven him that. Like so many other things.

The heat-saturated cement made everything smell dirtier than it already was, including her clothes. She was cutting her own hair these days, and as she pulled it off her neck to cool herself, it curled wildly around her fingers, which hopped like angry spiders on her scalp. Damn tremors again. She'd been plagued with an unruly right hand since toddlerhood, since her mam left, and it popped up when she was nervous. She trapped it under her thigh but quickly jumped to her feet when the station wagon appeared in the street with Eamon behind the wheel.

He motioned frantically for her to open the garage door, which she did, and he slid the Taurus into the space next to her green boatlike Buick. She pulled the door down behind them, shutting them into the stifling dank of the garage. Cupping her hands around her face, she peered into the side window of the wagon.

"What? What is this?" She stared, wide-eyed. "What the fook?"

"Shh, you'll wake 'em!" Eamon motioned to the two shadowy lumps in the back seat as he slipped out of the wagon. "Two girls. Didn't see the other one until I was on my way."

"What in the name of Jesu are you thinking?"

"That woman was a druggie. Tossing her cookies. Even passed out."

"So what?"

He shook his head solemnly. "How could I leave them, with that sorry excuse for a mam?"

He'd know how this tugged at Moira's heart, having been abandoned by her own mother when she was so young and left to fend for herself with her drunken da and ill-intentioned twin sister.

"Eamon. This isn't funny."

He sighed heavily. "Haven't we always wanted a baby?"

Moira stubbed her sandal into an old slick of grease pebbled with mouse shit and bit the side of her cheek. It was what she'd dreamed of, in spite of her da telling her that her pregnancies had been mistakes. Terrible, vile, wretched mistakes. And while his words stoked a place of disgrace deep inside, she wanted them anyway, was brokenhearted when it didn't work out.

A jetliner rumbled overhead from nearby Midway Airport and shook the garage. It traveled through Moira's gut, slicing through this silly fantasy of instant family. She started at a movement inside the car. But it was only the shadow of a bird outside the slatted garage window.

Moira's breath tightened. "Take them back. The girls. To their mam."

The muscles in Eamon's jaw constricted. "Are you tellin' me what to do then? A clannie woman?"

Moira reddened. He brought his hollowed face, dotted with

piercings, next to hers and raised his voice in a veiled threat. "Thought you'd be grateful. Sweet *soobya*."

That word! Eamon used it as a mockery, as a reminder of their shame and the terrible control he had over her in the form of their shared dark secret.

Soobya. Cousin.

"Don't forget. If it weren't for me, you'd still be with that miserable sister and father," he growled.

"Your uncle." Moira's voice trailed off. The miscarriages. The shunning. So much loss on top of loss.

She looked again at the little blond—an innocent thing, so young and sweet. A trickling finger of pain ran itself along the edge of her heart. She'd grown up without a mam. With a drunk and disinterested da. In the shadow of Siobhan, the favored twin who shaped their world around her moods, her desires. Moira had lived with the understanding that she was somehow wicked, not worthy.

Sweat sheened across Moira's forehead. What to do? There were no sirens yet. There was still time to return those little girls. She'd be nothing but grateful, that mother; they could simply say they'd rescued them from some awful monster and then be on their way. Better yet, she might still be passed out. They could just leave the car near the gas station and be off.

She steadied her right hand and took hold of the door handle.

"I said, take them back."

Chapter 3
Claire

Claire woke to the pulsing of blood in her temple, bringing with it the slow awareness that her face was resting on greasy tile. Where was she? The muffled sound of what could've been a car engine echoed across the walls and then was gone. A wave of nausea surged through her stomach as she lifted her head. Managing to rise onto her knees, she walked her hands up her thighs to stand. She rubbed her eyes to erase the small bursts of stars in her vision.

Stumbling through the dark room, she reached for the faint rim of light around what she remembered as the door and threw herself forward, tumbling out into the glare. Hot rays of sun dazzled against the white concrete walls. The absence of the Taurus was simply an illusion at first, a trick of her mind. But then, within the flash of a synapse, Claire snapped into high-alert mode, registering that it was gone.

Galloping forward, she fully expected to find the wagon rammed against an alley wall. Perhaps Andrea had wriggled out of her toddler seat and hit the gearshift, allowing the wagon to roll forward. But what she found was only a clear view of an intersection buzzing with cars. It didn't make sense. Could Andrea have put the Taurus in Reverse? Still dizzy, Claire loped to the other side of the alley, stale vomit souring her mouth.

Again, nothing except a row of angled cars parked inside painted spacers. Bright-white lines against black asphalt. Something moved behind the dumpster. Thank God! The girls must've gotten out of the car somehow. She started toward the trash bin but froze and stared in disbelief as a cat with mangy orange fur strolled into view, glaring back with amber eyes as it sat to wash its face.

Claire staggered toward the front of the station before her right foot knocked into her left and she crashed to the ground. Forcing herself back onto her heels, she thought the outline of her palms looked like photo negatives in the gritty dirt. She managed to stand even as her legs liquefied beneath her, adrenaline alone keeping her afloat. She faced the pumps and cried out, "My car! It's gone! My girls!"

Three people turned in Claire's direction, their faces flashing a mixture of bemusement and practiced neutrality. She yelled louder, this time something incomprehensible, in a high-pitched tone of feral distress. Finally, one man reacted and moved toward her. She raced over to him. He was thin, about thirty, with sharp eyes behind wire-rimmed glasses.

"A blue Taurus," Claire sputtered at him. "My girls were in there."

"A station wagon?"

She nodded vigorously, causing her vision to swim. "Yes."

"I think it pulled out a few minutes ago." He pointed east down Hardwick. "That way."

"What?" Claire gasped. "That can't be. Who was driving?" Mixed-up thoughts flashed in and out. How could the car be gone? Had Glen somehow taken it? How long had she been out? The sky wheeled above her, even as the ground seemed to move beneath her feet.

"I'll get them to call the police. You stay right here." He dashed toward the mini-mart, where a small man in a uniform shirt leaned from the door, assessing the commotion.

Claire lurched to the edge of the street, scanning the cars approaching on one side, the blur of taillights on the other. The signal turned red and cars bunched to a halt, a mass of metal melting into waves of exhaust fumes. She clutched her chest as her heart banged against the fretwork of her ribs.

How had she allowed this to happen?

Several cars back, a blue wagon slowed as it approached the corner. Her car!

"Andrea! Lily! Thank God!" Claire couldn't jump, but she waved her arms frantically, calling their names. "Here! Here! I'm over here!"

The relief was overwhelming. She could sob with joy. As the car drew closer, a bumper sticker materialized where Claire and Glen had never put one. *Join the Marines!* And the license plate. That, too, was all wrong. In fact, this car really didn't look anything like her Taurus; it was much older, had a dent in the side. The light changed again. The traffic accelerated and the station wagon roared past, driven by an elderly man. Claire stopped breathing as the wrong Taurus vanished into the labyrinthine streets.

"Andrea. Lily. Dear God."

The man from the pumps appeared beside Claire in a cherry-red Honda and rolled down the window. Tires screeched as a van swerved around them.

"I'll drive down Hardwick to look." The man sounded calm, but he looked worried. "Stay here. The police are on their way."

"Thank you." She said the words, but it wasn't her speaking. The real Claire was in the Taurus with her girls, turning into the hospital parking lot. No. The real Claire was back in bed, this time with a girl under each arm and Gretchie draped across their legs.

The man in the Honda squealed away.

She spun on her heels to return to the place where her girls had been last. But sparks of light danced in her eyes. She willed her legs to move, to outrun the fever that was pulling her away to somewhere dark. She felt globs of something in her throat, drowning her from the inside. She doubled over and heaved, her churning stomach already empty. Then her vision again blurred, and stars clouded her eyes.

The next time Claire was aware, she was sitting half in and half out of a squad car, a cool, damp towel pressed to her head. Police cars and an EMS unit had colonized the area, their lights flashing like an angry mob. A media van, too, was identifiable in the mix. WKXK. She'd know it anywhere, even had the jingle in her head, a song the girls loved: *Sunshine-y day! Wake up in a new wa-ay...* Something sappy like that. She watched as if detached from her body, the scene unreal. Two EMS guys approached, but an arm halted them.

"Mrs. Rawlings?"

A woman's face came into focus. Copper-colored skin. Striking goldish-green eyes. On her head was a carefully arranged display of curls. Reflected lights from the many squad cars skittered across her white shirt.

"I'm Detective Hearns." The woman smiled, but her eyes were severe. "I know you've given the officers a lot of information already."

Really? When was that? Claire couldn't recall any of it.

"Mrs. Rawlings. You passed out. You're very sick. But EMS is right here. Please hang in with me a little while longer. We are doing everything in our power to get your girls back right away. Also, we think we located your husband."

"He's at the football field," Claire croaked.

"Yes, you told us. Upton Grove, right? Mrs. Rawlings, I'd like you to think if you remember anything at all, heard anything when you were in the bathroom? The more information we have, the better."

Claire shook her head. "No, nothing."

Wait. That wasn't right. Christ, what was wrong with her? Claire was suddenly back there, in that cell, fistfuls of sunlight punching through the open door, highlighting crumpled condom wrappers into fang-edged monsters. Framed within the glowing doorway, Claire recalled, the station wagon shimmering like a mirage in a cloud of fumes and heat.

"The door. I kept it open. I did..." Hot tears streamed down her face. "It couldn't have shut by itself. I checked. I pushed. It was closed by someone, something."

She'd honked at something, right? But nothing surfaced in her brain. The whole scene now was a hazy impression submerging under the weight of Hearns's urgent questioning.

"Mrs. Rawlings. Once again. Your children. A brunette and a blond—is that correct?"

The air crackled with the sound of radios and sirens.

"You mentioned an Afro. That's how you described your daughter's hair. Lily, I believe?"

"What?"

Claire sat stupefied, perplexed. And then it came to her. Of course! She must've struggled to convey Lily's distinctive froth of yellow hair. It would be visible against the car window. The old Claire would've supplied information with precision and accuracy, explaining its significance: Lily's unruly curls and Andrea's perfectly gapped smile. But that Claire was gone, consumed by this terrible reaction to the damn Hep C vaccine. Everything was happening so fast, and yet not fast enough. Claire heard a cop in uniform repeat the term into a mouthpiece. She shook her head and groaned.

"No... That's wrong... I meant..."

But Hearns was talking excitedly into her radio.

"Yes. Glen Rawlings. Great, good news." The detective turned toward Claire. "The Upton Grove squad has your husband. He'll be here momentarily."

Just then, a uniformed officer pulled at the detective's arm and spoke quietly. A group mingled around Claire, mostly first responders, but the man from the Honda stood close by, nervously wringing his hands. And a small man in a shirt with the Shell logo who Claire surmised was the cashier in the store shifted from one foot to the other, eyes large.

Hearns responded to the two cops.

"Six blocks south on Washington? Good. Great. Can you get me a direct line?" She turned to Claire and spoke loudly. "A squad car has sighted a Taurus with two girls."

Audible relief rippled through the group. Thank God. Hearns stepped back to allow the EMS guy to come forward. He set his bag gently next to Claire.

"Mrs. Rawlings, I believe you have a bad strain of the norovirus that's going around."

"No." She shook her head. He looked skeptical, as if he thought Claire were trying to do his job. "I need an EpiPen." Why hadn't she thought of this sooner? "I think it's a reaction."

He still looked confused.

She needed him to listen, to understand. "I'm a doctor." But that was in name only. She hadn't completed her program. Yet she didn't have the energy to repeat herself. Claire leaned her head into the metal of the car doorjamb. It was hot, not the relieving coolness she so desperately needed.

"Please. Just the EpiPen."

He opened his bag and pulled it out, preparing to inject her.

She couldn't wait. Instead, she grabbed it from his hand and plunged it into her thigh. A new, open-eyed world glistened sharply around her, and she jolted to attention. The sun overhead, the brightness of the sky almost overwhelmed her. This might be too much for her system; she had to get it together. Glen was coming. The girls were on their way back. She looked into the young man's face; his eyes were wide with surprise.

"I vomited a lot. Fluids. I need fluids."

He nodded, could apparently see that her awakening was harsh, verging on dangerous.

Just then, a cop car approached at high speed, jumped the curb, and screeched to a halt. The passenger door burst open, and Glen, as if a vision, emerged and dashed toward Claire. He was joined by Detective Hearns. Matching his pace, she yelled as they approached, "Sir, did they fill you in on the drive here?"

"Yes." Glen only half looked at the detective, keeping his eyes fixed on his wife as he closed the distance between them.

Thank God he was here, at this juncture, after they'd located Lily and Andrea. Moments earlier, he'd have arrived at a scene of disaster. But the girls were found, Claire had been treated; things were again starting to make sense. She wanted to say, *We'll laugh at this someday.* Like they did at some of their antics as undergrads together at the University of Iowa, when Glen claimed he fell in love with her beautiful, busy mind. But even as she thought it, she knew it wasn't true. This was too close of a call.

Glen bent down next to Claire. His hair was flattened with sweat and the whistle around his neck hung like a weird toy, adding a surreal touch. Over his shoulder, Claire saw the EMS guy preparing an IV bag for her.

"Are you okay, Claire?" Glen stroked her leg gently as if she were breakable and then stopped. It hurt to look at his expression, so full of disbelief and confusion. "Jesus, what happened? You left them in the car?" His head swung wildly from side to side. "In this neighborhood?"

Was it the fever or a terrible cocktail of fear and guilt that flamed through Claire? This couldn't be happening. "Glen, I—"

"Mr. Rawlings," Detective Hearns interrupted, "do you have a picture? That would help."

Glen scrambled to his feet and then turned to the detective.

"Yes, yes. Right here." He pulled his wallet from his shorts and extracted the photo they'd had taken at JCPenney the week before Easter in April. Lily was in a gingham dress, spring green with a yellow ribbon belt, and Andrea, as usual, in the faded blue charm dress. Claire and Glen were behind them, their arms encompassing both girls in a protective C. Moments before, she had been fussing with Andrea's bow, pinching it in place with an arsenal of bobby pins as her daughter squirmed and protested. Immediately after the flash, it had fallen out.

Claire wanted to scream *See, I am a good mother! Here's proof!*

Hearns looked at the photo and passed it to a nearby officer before lifting the receiver to her mouth. Her voice was broken by the percussive thump of a helicopter overhead.

"Repeat." She plugged one ear and grimaced, looking up. Her face went rigid as she spoke. "No, these girls are younger."

A wave of terrified quiet settled over the small group as the engines and sirens still blasted.

Glen left Claire's side and planted himself in front of the detective.

"What is going on?"

Claire felt as if she were watching a play on stage. Hearns dropped the radio and looked from Claire to Glen. She leaned toward them, half shouting over the din.

"I'm sorry. The children in question are not your daughters."

Claire shook her head. This was not correct. It was, in fact, absurd.

"What? Jesus God." Glen looked dumbfounded at this detective, who was now in charge of something so massively large it was close to inconceivable. Then he turned slowly toward Claire, and she saw an indescribable expression on his face. It came to her in a sudden burst of memory: shock metamorphism—a terrible force of nature that turns mineral into rock in tenths of a second. Only this wasn't some inert material. This was her husband.

Over Glen's shoulder, Claire saw a gurney approaching, the one they would lay her on to fill her with fluids and maybe even anti-nausea medication to help stabilize her. She couldn't allow this, couldn't allow them to take her away to the safety of the hospital while her girls were out there still, possibly with some monster. Glen was practically wrapped around Detective Hearns, pleading and demanding at the same time. A feverish heat tugged at Claire's limbs, but it didn't prevent her from standing up and stumbling away from the gurney, toward the street.

"Hey!"

"Mrs. Rawlings."

Voices rang from behind, as if from a tunnel. Still, Claire scrambled in the direction of her girls. Hardwick. They had gone down Hardwick. But in her jangled state of mind, she wobbled to the middle of the alley instead, pausing right next to the bathroom before she collapsed, crumpling like a wad of used paper in the exact spot where the Taurus had last been. A shadow stretched over the top of the cement alley walls, casting the image of long, sharp needles onto the pavement near her hand. Razor wire. People, strangers, surrounded her, their shadows consuming her in darkness despite the blazing sun. But Claire was unaware.

She had swallowed and was now digesting her own heart.

Chapter 4
Moira

E amon placed his hand over Moira's, which remained on the handle of the station wagon door. He squeezed her wrist. Hard. She fought to keep from losing her nerve.

"I'm taking them back."

"Are you daft?" His eyes glared with fury. "Do you think they'll be nicey with us then, after makin' off with their little ones?"

A single siren flared to life in the distance.

"You did this, Eamon. By yourself."

She could leave him here. Let him face the consequences. Yet the idea of two girls alone with Eamon was terrible.

"Your choice," he snarled before his expression shifted and his voice altered to a warm timbre. "Could be me, you. That wee one." He gestured to the blond. "Together against the world."

Moira peered through the window again, this time more closely. The little girl was asleep in a shaft of light, revealing plump cheeks and a rosebud mouth. Her knuckles, still dented with the chub of babyhood, were clenched sweetly into tight buds. Too young to remember her mam. Was it possible that this child could become her very own? Overtaken by an urgent desire to hold her, Moira murmured, "She's so beautiful."

"A family, Moira. We'll start fresh."

Moira's head went light. She struggled to hold her grip on the handle, but her right hand was giving in, full-out trembling, like an anxious toddler.

"But, Eamon. Stolen babies."

"No. Rescued babies." A slow, sugary smile crossed his face. "You will be the best mam. Truly."

He was right, of course. She'd be great. She dropped her hand to her side.

"We'll go now. To the cabin. You drive the girls in the Buick," Eamon said with excitement, like always, hashing ideas out loud, spur of the moment. "I'll follow later with the Taurus and supplies." He ran his hands across his sweat-soaked forehead. The high-pitched siren grew louder and quivered through the walls. Moira felt a fence closing around her, eclipsing any other options.

"A family." He drew her chin close to his face. "Of our own."

"Two kids…" Her mind crackled with conflicting thoughts. "But…we're broke…"

"Dunno, Moira, maybe we sell one off?"

What was this he was talking now? "Sweet Jesu." Growing up, Moira had heard dark tales about stolen children being sold for profit, but she had thought it nothing more than a myth. She'd never seen anything to make her believe such a thing really happened and shuddered to even consider it.

"Remember, I got connections."

She gritted her teeth. "Like what's got us this far, huh?"

"And what have you done for us?" He seethed. "Nothin' but…"

Just then, a shadow moved inside the wagon, followed by a sleepy groan. The older girl was resettling herself.

Eamon dashed to the Buick and, entering the back, grabbed a nylon bag hidden beneath the seat. He reached inside, pulled out a syringe along with a thumb-size vial, and hustled back to the Taurus.

"What? What is it you think you're doing?" Moira whispered hoarsely.

Ignoring her words, he jostled her roughly to one side and opened the car door. She grabbed his arm. He froze and turned slowly to face her. With his eyes narrowed into tunnels, he spoke through tightened lips. "You got a better idea, *soobya*?"

And then Eamon was bending into the car, casting a shadow over the entire back seat. Moira could see nothing beyond the sweat-soaked back of his shirt and arms. She imagined herself pulling him away, but the muscles under his skin sheened as definitively as a fist in her mouth. She tried to speak, to protest, but nothing came out. Instead, a terrible weakness overcame her as she visualized the amber fluid glinting inside the slim cylinder. Leaning against the garage wall, Moira slid to her knees. Her shoulders hunched reflexively at a groan from what must've been the younger child. And then her eyes squeezed shut and her hands flew to cover her ears at a truncated cry. The sound quickly diminished to a simper and then a soft mew and then, thankfully, quiet.

"Moira."

"Jesu!" She startled, finding Eamon's face hovering next to hers.

"How else we gonna keep 'em quiet?" he said. "Won't remember a bit of this. Get the trunk ready."

Moira shook her head. "I'm not helping you."

Another siren screamed. "You're welcome to go back now," Eamon mocked coldly. "To their lovely druggie mam."

The wagon remained quiet. Moira's eyes welled with tears. She searched Eamon's face. Flat. Determined. She understood there would be no other way than his.

Lifting herself from the floor, she wiped her cheeks with the back of her hand. Despite the shock of the circumstances, a thread of exhilaration climbed her spine as she considered the very real possibility that the enchanting little blond could be theirs. She'd make a home for her, one unlike what she'd had. One that was safe and caring. And the other girl, well, she'd put that out of her mind for now. She'd work to find a way to convince Eamon to keep her.

The quiet in the garage was shattered by the high-pitched whine of multiple sirens, reminding her it was life or death now. Hers. Adrenaline rushed into all the hollow spaces of her body as she hurried to the Buick to make it as comfortable as possible. As she popped the trunk, the latch wiggled in her hand.

"The latch, Eamon," she said, panicked. "It's loose."

"No time now," he responded flatly. "Just deal with it."

Moira set her jaw against the awful feeling in her gut. At least the trunk was deep and roomy. Along with a disposable cooler half-full of shoplifted food and the detritus of their previous lives, there was a dirt-encrusted stretch of burlap and a coil of rope from heisting and then pawning shrubs. She dumped the thick, greasy quilt that lined the back of the trunk onto the floor to make more room. She then hollowed a rough den with the remaining materials, using the Styrofoam lid from the cooler to keep the girls separated. Otherwise, they might get too hot.

"Get the blond," Eamon commanded. "I'm checking outside."

Moira gulped hard before entering the Taurus. She hovered momentarily over the smaller child, now perfectly asleep. Eamon was right. This wasn't so bad. Venturing her hand lightly along the side of the girl's head, she tilted the baby's face to meet her own, creating two pink indents in the soft, ivory skin of her cheek. She carefully lifted the girl's eyelid. Blue. Of course her eyes would be blue. But such a shade! Moira felt a rush of maternal affection.

"*B'in'ia*! You will be Bridget," Moira whispered softly. "My little Bridget."

Bridget was limp, her hands still in little balls. No trouble to move. Draped across Moira's arms, she was light and smelled wonderful, powdery, the proper scent of childhood. Moira could've buried her face in the little one's hair right then and lost herself. But the sirens outside kept her moving. Ever so gently, Moira placed the girl in the trunk and set her on her side, lining her legs up and bending them while curling her spine and head forward, like a small shrimp in its shell. She smoothed the material of her outfit along the small of the child's back, noting the color: sunflower yellow, in heavy cotton.

As she took a hurried step back, something on the floor caught her eye. A bright blue smudge in the shadows. A closer look revealed a stuffed bunny that must've dropped out of the Taurus when she pulled Bridget from the car. This would certainly help calm the girls once the journey was over. As she bent to pick it up, Eamon appeared and kicked the rabbit into a corner.

"What the fook?" Moira's voice rose with concern. "You can't leave that here!"

"No time," he said, grim-faced. "I'll grab it later. Let's go."

Returning to the Taurus, Moira momentarily froze when she saw that the older girl was still awake. Although groggy, she struggled with the seat belt circling her toddler booster. She stared at Moira.

"Don't be afraid," Moira whispered. "I won't hurt you."

The child's mouth ovaled, and then she screamed—a bottom-of-the-belly, bloody-murder scream.

"Shh! Shh! Sweet Jesu, shh!" Moira's mouth went dry.

The girl screamed again, the pitch higher, the volume louder.

"Everything will be all right if you calm down," Moira said. The girl, fixated on Moira's face, hiccupped into a terrified quiet.

Moira fought to control her hand, which looped in busy circles like a staggering drunk at the end of her arm, as if in protest.

The child stared deeply into Moira's eyes. Tears splashed down her face and onto the front of her faded blue dress, creating a necklace of watermarks. Moira pulled away, rattled. She needed a moment for them both to calm down.

The girl's eyes were darkened with dilated pupils, like a puppy or a seal. Of course, a *selkie*! From the legend every Traveller child knew, a seal caught in a net that, when brought home, transformed into a little girl. And what had the fisherman and his wife named their new daughter?

"Colleen." Moira held her attention on the girl. "That is your name now. Come here, now. Don't be afraid, Colleen. Come."

"Wonder how old she is," Eamon muttered.

A small yet sturdy voice rang through the air. "Four and a half."

Eamon practically fell back when the child spoke. Her tone was clear. Defiant. And from the look on his face, he found it terrifying. But Moira's reaction was different. The sound of the girl's voice sparked her into further action. After unbuckling the booster, she reached in to pull the child from the car. The girl stiffened and held firm. Moira then tugged at her shoulders but the child simply would not move. Fighting to maintain control, Moira spoke in a commanding tone that she hadn't even known she possessed.

"It's best for you not to cause problems."

Surprisingly, Colleen's body slackened and allowed Moira to

pull her free. Then, as Moira set her to stand between the two cars, the girl yanked her arm from Moira and slipped into the space between the wall and the side of the wagon, even as she wavered on liquid legs. Moira turned sideways and stretched enough to grasp Colleen's upper arm. But the child ducked and twisted wildly and managed, despite Moira's best effort to hold her, to squirrel beyond her reach.

"Christ! A fighter!" Eamon cursed from behind Moira. "That shite I gave her better kick in."

Moira stretched deeply, her jaw clenched in desperation as the chatter of sirens rattled through her head. She was finally able to snatch the girl's wrist and pull. When Colleen emerged from the narrow space, she sent a walloping kick into Moira's right shin.

"Ach!" Moira doubled over and massaged her leg, blinking away the afterimage of sharp pain. Her head pulsed with tension. The heat and unrelenting sirens were working her into a claustrophobic mess, approaching panic. It came as a relief when, weakened by the drug, the child collapsed just as Eamon grabbed her into his arms. He quickly lifted the floppy girl to the edge of the trunk and tipped her inside. The hem of her dress caught on the latch and it tore with a sound of heavy paper being ripped in two.

"Jesu, Eamon. Be careful."

He grabbed the chunk of material and stuffed it to the bottom of the trunk as Moira tugged the girl's legs into a deep bend, placing her awkwardly next to her sister.

With her body shaped into a question mark, the child was just aware enough to search Moira's face. Moira recognized a mixture of terror and incomprehension in the girl's eyes and pulled a stray strand of hair from Colleen's mouth.

"It's okay, little *selkie*," she whispered. "You'll have a new home soon."

The sirens were piling up on one another like a ball of angry hornets. The police would be on them in minutes. An abandoned garage would be the obvious place to look.

Moira stepped back. The two girls were settled so close together it caused renewed concern for Moira. "The heat," she said.

"They'll have plenty of air once you get this bucket moving."

Moira clambered into the driver's seat, as Eamon shut the trunk. She wrenched the car in Reverse, almost smashing into the garage door, which Eamon rushed to yank open.

"Calm the hell down, Moira." Eamon trotted beside the car. "Or we're in a heap of shite."

She stopped the car. "You're right." She drew air in deep gulps.

"Have you got the map? Remember the way. Logging road, bridge, slow at the ravine near the river…"

She nodded, her mind frantically reviewing the route they'd gone over last night.

"Eamon, the police…"

"Go now." His voice crackled with nerves. "There'll be a barricade soon."

And then he stopped and grinned, transforming into his jester-self, full of boyish piss and vinegar. Master of slippery calm. This was actually Eamon at his best, under pressure, someone on his tail; it was a high for him. Moira had seen it before in small scams they'd run. Always the big man out front. She knew right then that they would pull it all off somehow.

"You'll be fine, Moira. *Foluigh* in a few hours."

"Be there. Tonight. For Jesu's sake, Eamon. Please."

"Okay." He tilted his head in send-off. And then he reached through the window. He ran his finger along Moira's cheek and moved to kiss her as he whispered, *"Nus a dhalyon, mislt."* She turned her head away and responded under her breath more to herself than Eamon: "You too, with the help of God, go."

As Moira pulled the Buick from the garage, Eamon blew her that kiss through the air, and then mouthed *Soobya* with great exaggeration.

Moira headed toward the freeway, her hand flapping feebly. She drove carefully past state troopers, who were configuring a barricade, just as Eamon had predicted. One of the officers peered in the back of her car even as he waved her through. How could she warn Eamon? They'd obviously be looking for the Taurus. She forced herself to take a deep breath, recalling his talents; it was possible that in an hour the station wagon would already be a different color, maybe not even a wagon. A black police helicopter, swift as a dragonfly, rose in the side-view mirror and then disappeared.

Safely on the interstate, her heart racing with adrenaline, Moira felt she could levitate, car and all, right into the vibrant blue sky. A fresh start. The details would come later. With each mile behind her, time grew more fluid, and before she knew it, they were a full hour and a half away. Moira checked the map and turned onto the abandoned logging road. Yes, this was the path to her future. She'd barrel over every bridge, through every curve in the road. Nothing would stop her from having the life she deserved.

Chapter 5
Andrea

Andrea knew monsters. Two in her closet, one under her bed. Sometimes Gretchie slept in her room at night to keep them away. And now, they'd caught her. She'd finally been swallowed. She was only half awake. Enough to feel an awful pain in her head and leg where the monster had bit her. The air was thick. Some type of cover held her down. She'd scream. But her mouth was full of marbles. The world tipped and spun and bumped in waves—*bang, bang, bang*—smashing her legs, her head, her chest. Was she in the monster's throat or already in its belly? She couldn't tell. Maybe if she didn't move, the creature would forget it had swallowed her. She pictured it—a large wolf head with red eyes. But the smell, tinny like old coins, didn't match the nasty odor of what a monster should smell like. She held her breath. *Boom, boom, boom.* Her heart tapped in her fingertips. Ready to burst from terror.

She slipped again into darkness, back into her room, into her bed, under the covers, safe and warm. Andrea's whole family was with her, cuddling together. But the cyclone fence that surrounded their yard suddenly wrapped around them and was pulling them in, squeezing them closer—Gretchie, Lily, Mom, and Dad, even Butkus, all cinched up until they were choking. Andrea woke up again, coughing and retching. Everyone she loved had passed through the holes in the fence and drifted, one by one, away from her.

Sparkles appeared behind Andrea's eyelids. She forced them open, wide, then wider. The ache in her head was worse now. She was so hot. So very hot. Her stomach throbbed and she gagged up chunks of Pop-Tart and waffle mixed with grape juice, which added to the horrible smell.

She squeezed her eyes shut; if she fell back asleep, this would go away. She breathed through her nose, wheezing through the heat and slimy mess around her face. "Mommy! Mom-eee!"

It was so dark. She tornadoed like her dad had taught her when they played in the pool, twisting with all her might until she carved out a larger breathing space. A butterfly of light near her feet, shaped like Jumpers's bow tie, bounced and flickered like a candle flame. Was there a hole in this monster's stomach? She kicked, gaining an inch or two. She twisted, tingling with pain. Slowly, she made a small space for her arm by making circles with her wrist until her hand brushed against a tangle of fur. She shuddered and pulled back. Yet, there was familiarity to the texture. Fine and soft. Grunting with effort, Andrea swung her head just enough to see, within that small spot of bouncing light, a familiar patch of yellow-blond hair. Lily! Her mom and dad must be here too. A cold pit in her stomach grew until it almost gobbled her from the inside.

The monster would eat them all.

"Dad-eee!"

Andrea crooked her index finger around as many strands of Lily's hair as she could grasp and tugged.

"Hey!" There was no response. Their song. That would help. "Count the clouds…"

Andrea started to sing but then choked on the teary snot clotting her mouth. She reached hard, searching for her sister's hand. When she finally got hold, it was hot and limp. She squeezed. There was no squeeze back. A school of nervous fish swam in her stomach. She swallowed hard and sang louder.

"See the birdie—"

Lily's hand still didn't move.

"—in the tree…" Andrea sobbed.

Each breath was a gulp of hot, stinky air. She tried to straighten like a spring struggling to unfold. The world spun. Her head cleared a little, then fogged again back and forth. Monsters weren't real; that's what her mom said. She wasn't in a stomach or even underwater. The feel of this tight space along with the smell, like the smoke that came out of the pipe in the back of the station wagon, made her understand one thing.

She and Lily were in a trunk!

A stranger's face flashed through Andrea's mind—a woman, pale and thin with mud-puddle eyes—then was followed by a quick memory of a room like a garage. Then a bee sting to her arm. Somehow, the woman's face separated into two faces. There was also a man with sharp eyes and a pointy beard, just like the devil.

"Help!"

The car's jiggering became dips and heaves. And then the car swerved into a sharp turn. Andrea pinwheeled with the car's jolts, desperately trying to free herself—twist, push, dip, kick, push, scratch, dip, kick. The more she fought, the more the blanket twisted and tightened around her waist and chest, making it hard to breathe. Still, Andrea squirmed and clawed with ferocity greater than her fear.

"Lily. Lil-eee!" Andrea pinched her sister's hand. Why didn't she move?

The car switched from uneven bouncing to rough jiggling—*rat-tat-tat, rat-tat-tat*—like it was on sticks. The motion quivered into Andrea's stomach. She might throw up again. Tightening her mouth, she kicked wildly toward that small light near her feet, over and over, to open that hole. There was something next to it—a bar, or a latch, like the one on Gretchie's crate. She blew all the air out of her lungs and rammed that latch as hard as she could.

The car took a sharp turn and dropped hard to one side as if in a hole. The trunk lid bucked open. Andrea's hand was yanked from Lily's as she flew upward into a surprising whirl of fresh air. Crashing back down, the lid slammed directly into Andrea's face—*wham*—before bouncing open for good. Along with a rush of stars in her vision, the taste of metal filled her mouth, followed by the salty flavor of blood.

A wedge of soothing light, lemon-y and warm, danced across Andrea's face. She opened her eyes. This wasn't harsh like the sun—but inviting and seemed to wrap her in a hug, filling her mouth with a rainbow. She could taste the colors, like layered Jell-O: orange and lime, banana-strawberry mixed with orange. It seemed to swim right through her, as her body grew wavy and soft.

The car rocked to a halt with the open trunk lid waggling overhead. Stale spit surged into Andrea's mouth, along with a thread of blood from the crater in her gum. The trunk lid might fall on her, smash her throbbing head. All of the colors and tastes, given by the special light, drained away as quickly as water spinning down the hole in the bathtub, leaving a terrible dread in their place.

The slam of a car door shuddered through the metal.

Fear inched through Andrea's body, thick and hot like bad medicine. She almost peed. But it wouldn't come; it was bound up with everything else inside her. If she played dead, maybe the scary people would just go away. "Lily," she whispered but heard nothing back. She tightened her eyes shut and held her breath. When someone pushed against her, a small, frightened squeak came from her mouth.

A woman leaned over, blotting out the sky above Andrea. "Dear God!" Her voice, thin and shaky, rattled through the air. "No!"

Andrea felt the quilt unraveling from her legs and then hands underneath her, shuffling through lumpy stuff that pushed into her back. It seemed like forever before the woman found what she needed. Andrea dared to look up. This strange face wavered in her dizzy vision, yet she met the woman's eyes. They were dark, scary. Twisted with… What? Fear? Anger? She couldn't tell.

She gulped. Her mouth was so dry. The woman stumbled backward. She held a piece of rope in one hand and a brown bag in the other like the ones Andrea had seen around the roots of the bushes planted in the backyard of her house—her home, so far away.

And then the woman was gone. Andrea couldn't feel Lily near her anymore.

She started rolling, falling forward, even though she knew the car wasn't moving. The heat was grabbing the breath from her very mouth. Her mind blinked off and on. A picture of Gretchie panting flashed and then the picture quickly became Butkus and then Jumpers.

Hours, it seemed, passed before Andrea felt fingers brush the skin of her cheek. She jerked away.

"Don't be afraid, Colleen."

What? Who was Colleen? This was all a mistake! Despite the ache deep in her lungs, the impossible dryness in her mouth and throat, the whirling world overhead, she forced out words, clear and proud.

"My name is Andrea."

This took all of her energy, every last bit. There was a moment when the world went still. And then she was floating… No, she was being lifted! Ugh, she squirmed and tried to kick, but the woman's arms were so much stronger than her sleepy legs.

"It's okay, little one, hush."

Andrea arched her back, daring to look again into the stranger's face. Dark hair and pale skin melted away, and all she saw were eyes filled with tears.

A bird circled overhead, inky black against the sky. It landed somewhere in the trees and called, loud and angry. *Caw, caw.* Others joined. *Caw, caw.* Wild birds. Not like Butkus in his cage. Hot tears sprang from Andrea's eyes as she thought of her mother making waffles, of Gretchie next to her in her bed.

The woman set Andrea on her side in the back seat of the car. Its vinyl cooled her blazing skin, and she began to shiver and tightened herself into a pill bug. She slipped away again and did not move until the rev of the engine rumbled through the car. She would not go with this woman! She strained to work her arms under her middle, thrust her chest upward. She'd follow the sound of the birds still calling outside. They would lead her somewhere safe, wouldn't they? But everything hurt. Her stomach crawled with insects. She might throw up again.

"We'll be there soon." The woman spoke from somewhere far away.

"Mom-eee," Andrea croaked. Her tongue was so thick she could barely swallow.

The world rushed by in waving treetops as her vision grew smaller. Her head cartwheeling, she held on—fighting for Lily, fighting that horrible dark space, fighting to hold the memories that were now breaking into pieces, marching away like tiny ants.

Chapter 6

Claire

"Claire. Claire, wake up."

"What? Where...am...I..."

"You're doing it again, honey. Calling out."

It was the middle of the morning, and Claire was tucked infant-like on the sofa. Gretchie was stretched tight next to her, wheezing tornadoes of moist air onto her leg. She had barely slept in the two weeks since the abduction, moving through the days in a dark, magical dream state bordering on hallucination.

Someone jiggled her arm as she struggled to think coherently. Claire looked into familiar malachite-green eyes shining with tears.

"Honey, it's me. Vicki."

Her older sister's face came into focus. Unlike Claire's flat gray eyes, Vicki's were bright and beautiful, like their mother's. Vicki's caretaking was a pattern she'd stepped into when they lost their parents, when Claire was only a junior in high school. A one-two punch that had sent them reeling: their mother to pancreatic cancer, their father to a car accident—both gone within eight months.

"Lily. You were calling for Lily this time."

Claire squeezed her eyes tight. They would be here, in this room, when she opened them: Lily and Andrea, playing with Barbies or pink LEGOs—the large ones made for stubby toddler hands. "Mommy," Andrea would say, wearing her jean shorts with a patch. "Can you get the rubber band out of Barbie's hair?" It would be tangled in a mess, this new hairdo on her doll, and they would need scissors to work it out, and Barbie would end up looking butch or like a punk rocker or something that the manufacturer never intended. Claire opened her eyes and quickly searched the room. There was no one except Gretchie and Vicki, whose hovering, delicate face was fraught with concern. She rubbed Claire's back gently.

"How are you feeling?"

Claire didn't fully remember going to the hospital the day the girls disappeared. Apparently, she had spent three nights in the ICU, her kidneys coming dangerously close to shutting down. They said she was lucky—a resident in Milwaukee had died from the same reaction. But Claire didn't feel lucky. She had spent three critical days unconscious. While her girls were Out There, while the search was at its peak, she had been ensconced in a hospital bed, struggling for her life. As soon as she became aware, she felt the crush of guilt weigh on her chest, against her whole body like a lead apron. She'd tried to push it into the deeper recesses of her brain, as it seemed at the very least, self-indulgent and, worse, a handicap to the real focus, which was finding the girls.

"How's your stomach?"

She didn't answer her sister, since the reply was always the same—lousy, her stomach felt lousy. The terrible fever had sub-sided and the storm had cleared her system. By physical standards, she was now fine. So why was she still throwing up? Just the sight of food could elicit an explosive reaction. It was as if her guilt had shifted, had taken up residence in her reptilian brain, the one responsible for basic physical processing like sleep and digestion. Along with nerve-calming meds, she was gobbling the anti-nausea pills, Compazine, like candy.

"Vicki, where's Glen?"

"Another Staples run. Binders this time, I think."

Claire cringed. They'd argued earlier that morning about some-thing trivial. His face drawn and impatient, Glen had grumbled over how Claire accidentally knocked Vicki's contacts into the sink. She, in turn, snapped back. Why did he care about her sister's stuff anyway? She suspected that it was something else entirely, and that Glen was holding back from speaking his true mind. What he hadn't said was that Claire should be the one organizing, bringing the energy and determination to carry the friends, neighbors, and extended family through this search process. She'd always been the one with the busy brain and the big ideas—dreaming, pushing, reaching—while Glen was happy with his family and teaching and coaching high school. But now he was fighting for their children, organizing the volunteers. Now he'd converted the house into headquarters, had had an extra phone line installed to track tips, keep communication flowing. Meanwhile, Claire was still trying to summon the strength for the minimum necessary interactions with Detective Juanita Hearns, the reporters, concerned relatives, and friends.

Vicki brushed an eyelash from Claire's cheek. She'd arranged to stay with them as long as she could, to help maintain a semblance of order, leaving her job and Troy in California. But now it was time for her to go back.

The news from the police wasn't encouraging. In fact, it was close to nothing. No promising leads. No suspects. Each time Claire and Glen pressed the detective for news, Hearns went over every plausible reason for the abduction, searching for a motive, a starting point. The best scenario, a simple kidnapping, was fading as a possibility since there had been no ransom demand. This left only bleak alternatives, like schemers who sell kids for money on the black market. Of course, Hearns didn't say this was the best they could hope for. Worse scenarios were left to Claire's imagination in the darkest part of the night.

Bau-auck!

Butkus screamed from the other side of the house, his grating voice carrying all the way to the couch.

"Ugh." Claire groaned. "Make him stop."

"I've tried everything. A towel over his cage, the Mozart station on the radio…"

Butkus. A dumb name. Except it matched his bully disposition, his drab coloring. Other parakeets in the store had had bright shiny feathers, squeaked encouragingly. The one they chose—the one

Andrea chose—was hunkered in the corner, fluffed up in some form of bird misery. The last one Claire would've picked.

"How about him?" Claire had steered her daughter to a sleek azure fellow. "Truly beautiful."

"Nope, that one." Andrea had pointed as Butkus hunkered further into himself.

And that was it. Andrea got her way. Glen christened him and everyone loved it. The girls sang to him—"Count the clouds, one, two, three. See the birdie in the tree"—their voices chirpy with anticipation. But Butkus never attempted a single note, not once. Only chatted and *cree*-ed angrily, shifting as far from the family as possible in his wire cage.

Bau-auck! Bau-auck! His scratchy little voice pierced the air. Claire covered her ears and rolled away from her sister. It occurred to her that she could leave him outside. Tropical birds were susceptible to all kinds of problems once they caught a draft. But the thought of the girls returning to an empty cage, a squawk-less house, prevented such action.

"Come into the kitchen," Vicki urged, sliding an arm around her sister and pulling her to sit. "I brought you something from the store."

Claire placed her palm against the edge of her face as the room swam. Nonstop crying in the past few weeks had invited a permanent sinus infection. She was on antibiotics in addition to everything else. It took a moment to grasp her bearings amid the neatly stacked piles of papers in the living room. Glen's handiwork.

"What's my assignment today again?" Claire asked her sister.

"Phones."

A media van showed up in front of their house only every other day now, sometimes every three days. Glen made a point of bringing out coffee, chatting with the reporter.

"Oh yeah. I haven't missed any calls, have I?"

"No, honey, you took two before you dropped off. Remember?" Vicki smiled encouragingly.

Claire nodded, even though the answer was no. In fact, she frequently lost track of conversations and struggled to remember who she had talked to on what day, or even whether she had spoken to anyone at all. Time was measured from the last view of her girls, a dream moment now, growing ever more distant—Andrea doubled over and Lily wedged in a shaft of golden sunlight.

Moving toward the kitchen, Claire felt her sister's eyes scanning her ever-shrinking frame.

"You need to eat."

Gretchie paced around the kitchen, a soldier on duty keeping her eyes glued on Claire.

Vicki opened the remaining flimsy white shopping bag. "I don't know if this is good or bad for you." She pulled out a six-pack of 7UP. Claire almost smiled as she surmised what would emerge from the bag next.

"Okay. So far, okay."

"How about this?" Sure enough, with a flourish, Vicki extracted a bag of Fritos. It was always 7UP and Fritos, even—no, *especially*— when they were sick, a secret potion conjured up by Vicki when they were small.

"Hmm, let's see." Claire separated the top seam of the bag, releasing the corn-chippy odor. At first, the smell brought back old, soothing memories. Encouraged, she put a small piece in her mouth and let the salty goodness coat her tongue. And then she was dashing off with her hand over her mouth, running into the small bathroom, only steps away. The one connected to the girls' room.

Claire and Glen had agreed to close the bedroom off, in case any further evidence was needed. Even Andrea's monster repellant on the dresser remained untouched, although it had clouded with algae within a few days of the girls' disappearance. Now, hovering with her face over the toilet, Claire could see that the pocket door remained open an inch, revealing a small slice of the things left untouched since That Day: rumpled pj's, a pile of Dr. Seuss books, and Lily's large-eyed frog sandals, the ones she didn't choose the morning of That Day, stared from the middle of the floor.

Detective Hearns had requested items the police could use to match evidence, help with identification—did they perhaps have anything related at all to dental work? Claire and Glen worked together in silence to find what they needed. Each object selected became a dagger in Claire's heart. A small soft hairbrush with both blond and brown hairs had been handed over. Worst of all, Claire had stolen into Andrea's tooth fairy box and given up her front tooth, the first one she'd lost.

Butkus remained silent throughout Claire's vomiting episode, as if she and Vicki were now beyond his commentary, choosing instead to attack his cuttlefish bone with his scythe-like beak.

"So sorry, Claire!" Vicki pulled fine strands of hair away from Claire's face, her fingers soft. "I thought it might help."

Claire sat back on her heels and wiped the gunk from her mouth.

"I know." Awash in endorphins, she was, ironically, at her best right after she vomited. "It's okay. You were just trying."

Vicki helped Claire into the kitchen, where she settled into a chair. Vicki took Claire's hands into her own. The concern on her face reminded Claire that her sister would be leaving later that day. She had to. She had a life in California, a husband and a job.

"Ever since Mom and Dad died, you've pushed yourself so hard."

Both of their parents had been teachers and lived modestly. Claire becoming a doctor would've pleased them so very much.

Now her residency was on hold, as the University Hospital had generously provided a leave of absence for an undetermined amount of time. But losing her children and her job in one fell swoop meant Claire had gone from being frantically busy to quiescent. Her surroundings in the kitchen now seemed hideously amplified, the volume turned way up. The wallpaper—an aging pattern of red-and-yellow teapots—appeared to be closing in. The day they'd bought the house, she'd told Glen excitedly how she would tear it out and paint the room something cheerful instead. Maybe yellow. That was close to seven years ago.

Vicki stood behind her sister and pressed her palms into her shoulders.

"All this stress," Vicki said softly, "your poor stomach."

Claire knew there was also a deep place inside that connected this with her pregnancies. As long as she remained nauseated, her girls remained very much a part of her. Safe from the ugly forces of the world beyond her body.

"I need to pack now, honey."

Claire nodded. Vicki would be back once they heard something. Which was only a matter of time, right?

She followed Vicki toward the small bedroom where she was staying. But it was Gretchie who stopped and set her paw on the girls' bedroom door. Turning her square muzzle, she faced Claire and whined.

"No, girl, we promised."

But it hurt too much to stay away.

As Claire opened the door slightly, Gretchie pushed full throttle with her nose and they were both inside. Claire sat gently in the Mother Goose rocking chair, opposite the twin beds covered by chartreuse and yellow spreads. The one closest to the door was Andrea's. The other bed was untouched, ready for Lily when she finished transitioning from her crib. Claire moved from the chair, snow-angeled onto her back in the tufted chenille, and inhaled, trying to remember the perfect smell of Lily. A hint of flower petals along with sun-bleached shells and unspoiled skin. No, that really wasn't close at all. But it would do. And Andrea, what did she smell like? Claire couldn't remember. But she forced it, something that fit her personality—Elmer's glue and the bold fruitiness of powdered Jell-O.

Gretchie pressed her muzzle into Claire's leg and appealed with worried eyes. Claire found the top of her dog's head and stroked, the warmth of her fur a small comfort.

Butkus cackled from the adjoining room.

"Count the clouds…" Claire called, waiting for it, for the girls to chime in. "See the birdie in the tree." All she needed was one small sign, a tiny foothold of hope. "If he has a broken wing, he will never sing, sing, sing."

Glen stood in the doorway.

"Hey."

She looked up. He didn't seem to mind that Claire was there, had breached their agreement to stay out of the room. He had an orchid in his hand, the color of soft lavender.

She smiled. "Hey back."

His eyes were bright with purpose, yet his skin was pallid.

"Glen, I'm so sorry about the girls." She wouldn't cry. It wasn't fair to him. "I…"

He looked past her. "Don't Claire…not now…" He cleared his throat. "I think we may have another shot at *Chicago Live at Five!*" The local show did interviews that could be picked up by national news programs. They'd been featured once, but only as a quick vignette as part of a larger story on kidnapping. That was the first week the girls were abducted. Now they were lobbying for a full-on interview with a live audience. They couldn't let people forget. Someone out there had to know something. "The station called earlier, when you were asleep."

"That's really great." She sat up and swung her legs over the edge of the bed. "Glen, I don't want to change the girls' room, ever, promise me that."

"Claire, the girls are coming back." Impatience creeped into his voice. "We have to think that way."

"I know. But promise me. It needs to stay exactly as it is right here, right now. Regardless."

"Of course." He set the flower, wrapped tightly in a cone of florist paper, on Andrea's dresser.

"C'mon, let's help Vicki pack."

Just as Claire set her feet onto the floor, the telephone rang. She followed Glen into the kitchen where he answered it.

"Yes?" He pointed to the receiver and mouthed *Detective Hearns* at Claire. "Oh man, oh God!"

What? Claire wanted to scream.

"Yes, yes. Immediately." His face flushed bright pink. "We'll be right there."

He hung up. "Hearns has some information."

"What kind of information?"

"She didn't say. She wants us down there right away."

Claire turned to Vicki, who along with Gretchie, had blown into the room, caught up in the new energy.

"Go. You two." Vicki dropped her bags to the floor. "I can't leave now. I'll reschedule my flight."

Glen touched Claire's arm gently as he moved past her to grab the keys hung near the bulletin board. She hurried after him, snatching her coat from the back of a chair.

"Her voice, Glen. What did it sound like?"

"I don't know." He stopped and shook his head. In that moment, Claire's husband looked like a small child, a little boy filled with hope. "Cautious, I guess. But not dismal."

Claire locked her eyes with Glen's as if holding him in a non-physical hug, and then set her jaw with determination.

"Let's go."

They were at Cook County Headquarters in twenty-eight minutes. They raced through the industrious atmosphere and straight to a room where Detective Hearns stood over a table, examining an array of papers. She was as impeccably tailored as cut crystal, her curls still tight as snails. Her expression warmed when they entered.

"Let's shut that door. The noise in this office sometimes! Sit, sit. I have a lot to show you."

Claire and Glen found chairs and sat side by side, rigid with anticipation.

"It's all a little rough right now. Not super solid, but still…a possible suspect is good news."

A suspect! Claire could barely breathe.

"As you know, we've been re-canvassing the neighborhood behind the Shell station."

Claire and Glen nodded.

"We've heard hints, rumors, of a strange man…"

No! This should be a woman. Claire had willed it. She must've gasped, because Glen grabbed her arm in a gesture to hush her.

"I'm so sorry. Do you need a minute?"

Glen sighed as if his lungs were deflating. Of course they did, but a minute longer was too long. Claire shook her head.

"Please, Detective, continue."

"As I said, a man, a junkie or pusher, one even said *gypsy*, appeared and then disappeared just as mysteriously. Possibly squatted in an abandoned garage two blocks west of Hardwick. Might've been nearby on the day of the abduction. So we knocked on every door, talked to every junkie, to find out whatever we could about this possible suspect. I want to emphasize here that we don't know anything for sure, but a drifter does seem to have been in the area of the Shell station on the day in question."

Claire sat further upright.

"But first…" Hearns looked at them. "I didn't want to bring this up on the phone. Physical evidence is difficult for the family."

Huh? What does she mean? Claire's blood contracted in her veins. *What on earth does she have?*

"We were able," the detective continued, "to get a search warrant for that garage near the gas station. Found it in a corner, under a pile of sawdust. Please hold on." Juanita Hearns's voice trod gently. "It might be a little tough."

The detective reached into an oversize envelope and then held out a sealed plastic bag. "Is this the little bunny you described?"

Jumpers!

Claire reeled back in her chair as if punched in the chest. Glen made some sound that defied categorization, like a cry, only dull, as if he, too, had been hit.

"Yes. It's…" Glen started but just shook his head.

"Detective," Claire whispered hoarsely. "It's Andrea's rabbit. It was in the car when—" She couldn't finish, couldn't say *When our daughters were abducted.* She quietly took the sealed bag when Juanita held it to her. Claire knew it couldn't be opened. But, oh, how she longed to touch Jumpers, run her finger along the outline of one of his long loopy ears. No longer a lovey, he was evidence now, an item to be catalogued, tested in a laboratory.

Claire kept her voice steady. "Did you find anything else with him?" She pointed to a spot on Jumpers's right paw. "There was a little felt carrot that went right here. Lily had it in her hand when…" Claire's voice wavered. She set the bag on the table and smoothed it over Jumpers's foreleg.

"No, nothing else. I'm sorry."

She set the bag back onto her lap. Jumpers looked two-dimensional inside, like some cartoon rabbit that had been steam-rolled or punched with a mallet. He was dirty and twisted too. But his eyes were clear enough. Overlarge, surprised. Still goofy. If only he could talk. She wanted to apologize to him, tell him how sorry she was about his carrot, how sorry she was about this whole unbearable thing. Hearns gave them a moment.

"We have a sketch we are releasing today." Hearns's voice stayed even. "This is what we do know about the suspect. Two witnesses—I'll be honest, both junkies—said an outsider, some lone wolf, was trying to peddle drugs. Takers were slim, since the area is pretty well covered and suspicious of newcomers. So far as names go, he's possibly Brian or Eamon."

"Eamon," Claire whispered to herself. Rhymes with *demon*.

"Keep in mind," the detective said, sliding a large piece of thick paper across the table, "this is a work in progress."

Claire looked into the sketch of a dark-haired man's face. Memorizing and then rememorizing each contour. A chill worked its way slowly along her spine. The tight features and the long thin lines of a goatee. And the eyes. Just a shadowy smear of charcoal in each socket. She imagined the sound of his voice, high-pitched, irritatingly percussive. Could smell him too—stagnant pond water covered in velvet scum.

"The day the girls went missing, our mystery man disappeared too."

Glen pulled the sketch toward him. The disbelief in her husband's face frightened Claire.

"I... We...uh, don't know what to say, Detective." Glen's voice wavered. He pulled Claire's hand into his own and squeezed.

"Remember, a suspect is a really good thing." Hearns was trying to help, to soften this blow. But it was a bad thing too. What in the goddamn world was in that man's—no, that creature's head?

"Anyone else? An accomplice?" Glen squeaked. This face was too ugly to contemplate being alone with their girls.

"No. No one so far. He was always seen alone."

Thick silence.

"Motive? Do you... Can you imagine a motive?" Glen asked. Of course, they'd gone over every plausible reason for the abduction ad nauseam. About predators, predatory behavior. Pedophiles.

Desperate people or schemers who sell kids. Yet somehow, this face changed everything.

"As we discussed before. Could be so many things. I mean, if he's a junkie, which he fits the profile, then maybe he's just trying to get money… Probably an impulse when he saw the car running."

Why did Hearns have to say that? Glen dropped Claire's hand.

"So maybe he's not a pedophile?" Claire said, her voice thinly veiled with hope. "But how do two little girls help him buy drugs?" She knew this answer somewhere in her head. But the information flow had changed direction inside her. She could barely measure out granules for a simple cup of instant coffee much less hold the notion that her girls were being bartered.

"There is a market for children, Claire."

"What's next?" Glen's voice rose. "What do we do next?"

"We'll get this out there, to the media. Reactivate their attention. We're continuing to follow our leads, of course. Details can make all the difference. Did someone suddenly remember something they'd seen that day? We go back and talk. And search. I'm asking you to keep working on the TV stations, reporters. As you know, right now that's key. Keep going with it. Get the information out there."

Glen squeezed Claire's arm. "It'll be all right." But he stared forward. "The girls will be home soon."

Claire forced herself to look again at the two-dimensional face flat on the table. She swallowed hard against the bile rising in her throat, fighting the urge to throw up. *You're not getting the best of me right now, you bastard.* She tightened her grip on the bag with Jumpers in one hand and grasped the top of Glen's forearm with the other.

They could do this. Build on this little bit of hope together.

Chapter 7
Jay

Jay White inched his '72 El Camino, fitted with a camper shell, onto the shoulder of the interstate in rural Illinois. Squinting into a shadowy notch of trees, he searched for the entrance to an old logging road that appeared as a mere broken line on his map. *Ah, there it was. Perfect.* Nobody to mess with him here. Still, with October tapering to a close, time was running out for this type of camping. At thirty-five, Jay was feeling old and stiff-limbed from nights in a truck bed.

Entering the canopied woods, he shrugged off an immediate sense of foreboding. "Feelings," his mother had simply called them. He'd had them often since he was a young child, and just as often tried to ignore them, pretend them away. Profound impulses, they were "passed through blood," his grandmother told him as she worked fry bread dough through her floured hands. Jay knew she was referring to his mother, whose angular face; dark, straight hair; and willful jawline Jay shared, the stony features of the Sioux—a warrior tribe. But while his mother's eyes were black as obsidian, Jay's were a startlingly gray-green, the shade of lichens. Jay had no memories of a man in his life, other than his mother's boyfriends—all seedy drunks with oily gazes.

His gut tugged again. It had been a long time since he'd experienced this sensation, a pull from inside, like self-generated gravity.

He cranked the radio. His musical preference, especially on dark nights, tended toward ballads, sappy stuff. Stumbling onto

Patsy Cline was a stroke of luck. He sang along as much to take his mind off a growing uneasiness as anything else. He almost decided to turn around at the first bulge in the road. But he was determined to keep his forward momentum, toward his new life, through these towering jack pines blackening the hurry-down dusk.

Seemed like half his lifetime he'd been working through some deep subliminal pathway on a slow migration away from his roots in North Dakota. And yet, he never got quite far enough away. Always, even among this flat terrain of northern Illinois, he imagined the severe hills that loomed in the distance just outside the border of Devil's Lake Reservation, where he and his mother, Sioux members of the Lakota nation, lived as outsiders. It was time for "the big change"—to settle permanently somewhere, anywhere. Just after leaving jail a week ago, he'd opened an atlas. After blocking out the Dakotas with a book of matches, he closed his eyes and swept his hand gently over the map. And then stopped. There. Opening his eyes, Jay discovered the western edge of what looked like a mitten trapped under his thumb. Michigan. Far enough away to start a new life. Hopefully, a decent place to nurture his fragile sobriety. He'd head east—his first firm decision since putting that last drunk and disorderly charge behind him.

"Just you and me now," Jay said to the dirt-filmed mirror. He tried to laugh at how ridiculously like a stereotypical Indian he looked, with a scar to boot—a thick furrow that ran from his forehead, barely passed over his right eye and ended in the hollow between his cheekbone and jaw. The angry red raised skin on his face served as a reminder of home, the Badlands etched in his flesh like a geological fault line. Seeing himself backlit by moon glow, he grimaced. How many days since he'd showered? He'd lost count. His hair, falling just below his ears, slicked back a little too easily. The hole from the gold stud he'd pawned six months ago looked like a tiny crater on one ear. *Hey, Moon Man. You'll need to clean up as a short order cook*, he thought. He was smart enough not to risk bartending again. Too close to the bad stuff. He'd been out a week now and made himself a promise: this time would be different.

This time he was facing up to himself.

The El Camino swung along a curve in the road, which ran parallel to a creek. The presence of water nearby comforted Jay, as did the reflection of the moon in the braids of icy liquid on the tops of the rocks. He cracked the window, and the windshield misted with moisture from the densely packed trees. The creek dropped from sight, but he could hear it and smell its tannic crispness. Maybe he should rethink this path, return to the interstate. Crash instead at a truck stop or rest area. But he pushed on, even as the stirrings of an old familiar longing began to deepen in his gut. He sang louder, trying to suppress the feeling. But it only intensified, like some ancient creeping instinct that was beckoning to be explored.

The path narrowed quickly as the dark bruise of the September sky deepened into thick purple overhead. A gibbous moon rose over the treetops, cutting a swath of light. Jay had never known just one moon. Aside from the phases, there were also different lunar personalities for each season: heat moons in summer, mud moons in spring. Tonight was a monster, low in the sky—a big orange-gathering or harvest moon. He knew it well. It pulled him back to his childhood, to the small kitchen of their tar-paper home with the pilot light in the stove glowing. It was always warm there, despite being cold throughout the rest of the house. His grandmother had looked over at him, pleased with a question he had posed.

"The winter moon again?" she had teased, knowing his obsession with all things celestial. "Jay, you already know the legend."

"C'mon, one more time, please."

"When earth grows cold, the moon's face pales, looks tired next to autumn's beautiful gold…"

"But she's not tired…"

"You want me to tell it, or you?" His grandmother had a wide, flat face, a huge smile. Most of her bottom teeth were missing.

Twelve-year-old Jay couldn't help himself. His hair was slick and shiny and crow-black. His eyes shone with excitement. "It's where the bright white snow geese and swans migrate when the ponds and lakes freeze over."

Jay's mother remained absorbed in beading Jay's new vest.

"Mr. Know-It-All." She laughed. Jay had become her apprentice in the traditions of their ancestors, beginning with learning useful plants and the Lakota language. It was a slow process, might take an entire lifetime.

His grandmother was pleased. "There's hope for him yet," she had said to her daughter, who nodded and winked.

Alone on this dark path, Jay swallowed hard against this memory. Both women would be dead within the year. His grandmother from complications related to diabetes, his mother—well, that remained unthinkable.

The road grew worse. Stuff in the back rattled. Most likely a liter bottle of Pepsi had banged loose and was rolling rogue through the array of things that constituted his life: a sleeping bag and some tin pans, along with some bent aspen twigs, dried broomcorn—stuff he'd learned to gather as a kid when his mother taught him to make dream catchers. He just hoped the Pepsi bottle didn't leak or he'd really have a mess.

His gut jerked again. It was almost annoying, like a taunting. He peered over his steering wheel and through the windshield. Blackness. Jay needed some reassurance. He snapped the glove box open and rifled through an array of misfolded maps and bottle caps, an old empty flask. Brushing against his shaman's rattle surprised Jay; he'd forgotten it was there, a remnant from his past life. He pushed it away, straining for something else: a small Petoskey stone. Someone had left it in the pocket of a vest Jay bought at the Goodwill in North Dakota before leaving. From the unusual look of it, he had known right away that the stone was something special. Polished to a smooth gloss, it was spotted with small astroblemes, as if inscribed by some great cosmic event. Learning that this was in fact a fossil found only on the shores of Lake Michigan, he knew it was meant for him to find, as some sort of guide, a talisman to help lead him to a new place. He also found it gave him strength when he was tempted to drink. He slipped it into his quilted vest pocket, took a deep breath, and immediately felt calmer, reengaged with his intuition, which pulled him along this course like a sailboat in an ill-fated wind.

About three miles down, Jay halted the El Camino at a plank bridge studded with gaps—like rotted teeth in a smile. Now it truly was time to hit Reverse—jam the El Camino ass-backward down the road until he could swing it around. But the sensation returned, this time more powerfully than before. Like a sharp wing flapping in his chest, pulling him in one direction. Forward.

Oh Christ.

He touched his hand to his chest and the small bump of the stone. Then he shut his eyes and pressed the gas. A dangerous groan rose under the truck's weight. Jay peered out from half-closed eyelids as he inched tentatively forward: one-one thousand, two-one thousand, counting the seconds until the front tires met solid earth. He opened his eyes.

Whew, that wasn't so bad.

Maybe the feeling, the encroaching fear, was all about the bridge crossing, which was now behind him. Tapping the accelerator, he spotted something in a small depression near the road. It wasn't much, a flash of orange caught momentarily in his high beam, a smudge of color in the otherwise colorless landscape. An intense chill crept over Jay's scalp. He trained his headlights onto the object and brought the El Camino to an idle.

After snapping the radio off, he sat for a moment in unsettling silence. He took a deep breath, opened the door, and stepped out into the clear lunar cold, which wormed through his ratty Nikes. Goose bumps rose along his arms under his flannel shirt, puckering his skin into tiny mountains. The moon tossed mottled pools of light between the dark branches and onto the road.

With a few cautious steps, he approached a small triangular shape chinked with shadows in the harsh light of the high beams. He crouched down low to the ground. Lifting the item carefully onto the palm of his hand, he drew it near his face. Although grimy with ochre mud, it was still identifiable.

Some kind of toy carrot. Just longer than the bridge between his two knuckles.

He held it up and squeezed its fat middle. A surprising little crackle snapped through the air. Curling his fingers, he blew into the hollow of his hand, clearing some of the dirt. "Where did you come from?" he whispered, keeping it close to his lips.

A burst of wind crawled on Jay's neck. He shuddered and placed the carrot in his vest pocket, next to the stone against his heart. Something else was here. Something wrong. Eyes keened, he walked away from his car, ignoring his numbing ears and feet. Searching the edge of the road, he kicked clumps of dirt and small pebbles into the depression that ran where the shoulder should be. Within moments, the heel of his boot caught a soft spot and the edge of the road cratered beneath his weight.

"Shit!"

He slid into a small pool filled with cold water, immediately soaking both his feet. Flailing for a handhold, he smacked a clump of cattails, a plant he knew well from his childhood. He'd shredded their tight brown heads for pillow stuffing, dug their rhizomes for food and poultices. Now, grasping a handful, they gave way easily, nodding forward as he pulled himself Tarzan-like out of the mud. As if they were telling him something.

Behind the bowed stalks, an unnatural shape materialized in the moonlight.

Probably some garbage dumped from a car. He looked closer. Nothing more than a pile of leaves under muddied burlap and a small reach of rope.

But Jay knew better.

Ignoring the clammy wetness crawling up his lower legs, he crouched over the filthy heap. Barely visible, on one end of the soil-crusted material, was a matted clump of blond hair.

His stomach somersaulted. The air stung his face. Christ, this must be a mistake. The alternative was unimaginable. He could run away right then. Put the little toy back, get in his El Camino, and be gone. Who the hell would believe he wasn't involved in this ugliness, this terrible scene? A transient—an Indian, no less—with a blighted history? How could he even explain how he'd found this hidden place? He looked up at the moon. Its face was bright, splotched with the ancient markings he'd studied all his life.

Yet Jay knelt, slowly, reverently, and brushed against the tattered edge of the burlap, scattering a clump of dirt. A slim stretch of yellow materialized, bright as butterscotch candy in the moonlight. He pulled the covering away but only several inches.

Exposed, almost luminescent in the ghostly moonlight, were the first finger and thumb of a small hand.

Jay fought convulsions in his abdomen and the heated fear now screaming for him to turn away. But he stayed strong and removed the burlap.

Forcing himself to look down, Jay stared into the remains of a child's face.

The past that he'd fought so long to suppress rose and surrounded him like an encroaching mist, one that smelled like burned pine and singed juniper. The only other dead person Jay had ever seen outside of a funeral parlor was his mother, her face blistered by heat, her long hair crimped into frenzied matchsticks just short of the flashpoint. An image he'd been running from since he'd left the Devil's Lake Reservation at sixteen.

The feeling fully overcame him, this time pushing him against the membrane between the past and present. He was twelve again, stepping off the school bus to a great black tenterhook like a curled finger in the sky. Smoke. From the direction of his house. He ran. Until his side ached. He ran. Embers rained on him like small fiery birds as he drew closer.

Jay remembered his helplessness when he arrived at the fire in the shed. If only he could've swallowed the yellow flames with his eyes and the dark smoke with his mouth. By the time he got to his mother, after pulling off a stick buttressing the door closed, it was too late. The sky sank into the earth where she lay. Jay had fallen to his knees. He was silent then. There was no prayer big enough.

Later, he'd learn it was an ex-boyfriend. A quiet, unremarkable man whose face haunted Jay's dreams. A man who'd latched the shed from the outside, destroying Jay's world at the age of twelve.

"*Wakhán Thánka!*" Jay cried out loud, releasing an ancient prayer learned from his mother. One he'd held inside for so long.

He hated how desperate it was to inhabit his story at times. And unfair. This man shivering in the cold, filled with fear and lack of destiny, wasn't who he truly was. The real Jay was a seeker, endlessly circling to find his true home, his life's purpose, all of which had been taken away so young.

"*Wakhán Thánka*," he repeated, calling to the Great Spirit, to the souls of his mother and his grandmother, because what he had just found was beyond understanding with the mind and soul of this world. He momentarily lost himself and, leaning back, swayed in rhythm with the growing wind, the sweeping of the tree branches—echoing the long-ago motion of his mother as she etched a ceremonial circle with bare feet in the sandy dirt outside their small home—the Black Hills beyond, inking the sky.

A sudden whiskbroom of cold snapped him back.

Time to stop running.

He returned his focus on the child.

Be precise, Jay, capture every detail.

This was important. His breath amplified in the damp air. His emotions were gaining on him. He covered his mouth with one hand and looked as closely as he dared. Strands of yellow hair partially covered the young girl's face. Her eyes were eerily intact and startlingly clear—pure and vacant as crystals. He found himself reconstructing her features. A beautiful little girl, angelic even. How old could she be? Maybe two.

Jay tenderly recovered the child's remains with the burlap. He needed to get to the police right away. The prospect sickened him. A bad mix, Jay and the authorities. They'd be suspicious. Unfortunately, he had a great alibi for whenever she died. How ironic that the drunk and disorderly charge that landed him in jail for three months could now be helpful.

How had he ended up here? He'd never been near this place before, never even heard of it. Yet he could practically hear his mother—"There are no coincidences, Jay"—followed by his grandmother—"Each person, each event, is a thread." She had touched the hoop of an unfinished dream weaver. "An interwoven spoke in the wheel of life."

The wind whispered in conspiratorial voices. Jay pulled at his hair, trying to decide what to do next. Should he turn around, go back the way he came? The known path meant the risk of the El Camino getting stuck. And then there was the bridge—would it hold this time? Pressing forward seemed his only option. From what he recalled of the map, it was at least ten miles until the interstate. Christ only knew what else lay in that direction on this godforsaken road. But he felt he must go forward. Deep down, he truly believed he was somehow meant to find this child.

First, he memorized the spot—a clump of cattails just near the bridge—and then clambered into the cab, stiff with cold. Trembling at the wheel, he fought against imagining the girl's family or how this happened. *Don't think, just drive.* The only way he could help that child now was to get to the police. He couldn't recall ever wanting a drink so badly in his life.

As Jay kicked the engine up, he heard the wind screeching through the bridge behind him and shuddered. Nails on a chalkboard. He couldn't afford an accident in this unforgiving place. He gunned forward, faster than good sense allowed. Yet he pushed the truck well beyond sixty on the rutted, twisting dirt track. The looming forest closed in; to Jay, it was now a scene of horror. Bumps in the road created a landscape of small, half-buried moons, tossing the El Camino like a Wave Runner in a storm. The Pepsi bottle boomed from wall to wall in the back. It occurred to Jay that he really had no idea where he was.

Thick forest slowly turned to scrub, and then field. The Big Dipper hung in open sky guiding him like a welcome friend. Within minutes, Jay was back on the interstate, the hidden road diminishing behind him like a spent nightmare.

After twenty long minutes, the blaze of neon and sodium lamps directed him to a truck-stop diner. Entering, Jay was punched back by a wave of grease-heavy air and bright lights. It occurred to him how important it was that he hadn't been drinking. A plump, graying woman behind the cash register looked him over suspiciously. He was accustomed to this, the way people shifted, held close their possessions, their little ones, when he was near. A constant reminder that he was unworthy.

"Can I help you?" the woman grunted. Her skin was pallid in the chrome-reflected light.

"No. Just the phone."

She pointed to a shadowed alcove out of the glare. Jay picked up the receiver and dialed 911.

As the phone rang, his throat tightened and he feared he might sob. But then a soft warmth emanated from his pocket and sifted through the material, through the wall of his chest, and gently loosened the tight fibers of his heart. He ran his hand along the small bulge in his vest and replayed the scene—dirty burlap, and the perfect, haunting blue eyes.

Someone picked up. Jay cleared his throat.

He could feel the earth stretching toward its equinox.

Chapter 8
Moira

Moira was losing track of time. How many days had it been since she'd left Chicago? Over a week for certain. For Jesu's sake, it seemed like an eternity. Where the hell was Eamon? Somehow, she'd managed to keep the older sister alive. So far.

The cabin, no more than a two-room shack, was nothing like the large space Moira remembered as a young girl when it was packed with aunts, uncles, and cousins, their caravans parked outside colonizing the surrounding yard. She'd managed to scare up a box of matches and an old Coleman lantern. Thankfully, it was saturated with fuel and lit immediately. The smell of rodent filth on the solitary bed, combined with her concern for the child's condition, was powering a deep panic.

The first several days, Moira scavenged for supplies. Using an empty coffee can, she scooped water from the creek and boiled it in the outdoor chimney. Colleen slept through all of it, didn't react to a thing. But each day after, she awoke for a few minutes at a time. Her eyes were far away, that was certain. Moira took the chance to dribble a drop or two of water into Colleen's mouth.

The morning of what Moira imagined was the fourth day, she fashioned a makeshift dress from a pillowcase she'd discovered in a jelly cupboard. Kneeling beside Colleen, she mopped the child's skin good as she changed her clothes and tried to untangle the matted hair that clumped into dark splotches along her forehead.

She balled up the soiled blue dress and tossed it into a corner. The panties, soaked with urine, couldn't be helped.

Please come soon, Eamon, while this girl is still alive.

She intended to offer a sip to the child's parched mouth, but the coffee can was dry.

"Don't worry, little one," Moira whispered as she stood. "I'll be a wee moment."

Outside the cabin, Moira was greeted by a sea of thigh-high weeds, which she waded through past the fieldstone chimney that loomed over the landscape like a sinister giant. Beyond it, the creek ran like a dark slash along a line of slim-trunked cottonwoods as delicate as a child's eyelashes.

When Moira returned, she splattered droplets along Colleen's arms with her quaking right hand.

"Please open your eyes."

Fear and exhaustion were claiming Moira's energy. That whole first week she ate granola bars and chips. But now she was down to crumbs. And twilight was just around the corner. Waiting for Eamon in that godforsaken place was bad enough during the day, but nights were filled with dread and terrible sounds: howling owls and switch grass wind-fiddling in a high-pitched shriek.

She hadn't actually slept more than three hours at a time and her thinking was growing cloudy. She lit the lantern, keeping the wick low to save what little fuel was left. Turning toward Colleen gave her a startle in the gloaming.

Jesu!

The child's features appeared frighteningly slack, verging on lifeless. And her skin was a shade Moira had never seen. Grayish, approaching blue. Squeezing her eyes closed, Moira leaned her head close to Colleen's chest where she detected the faintest rise and fall of breath. Slow, and with great effort, but present nonetheless.

"Thank you, Lord."

Moira dropped to the floor next to the bed and set her hand on top of Colleen's. It fit beneath her own like a small turtle fits into a shell. Maybe if she said something familiar, her name? This felt terribly dangerous to Moira. And yet…if it helped.

"Andrea, wake up. Please..." She repeated it several times, louder until she was close to yelling. No response. The flame in the lantern flickered, then died.

Darkness slowly claimed the cabin. Moira kept her hand on Colleen's, no longer certain if blood pulsed in the girl's veins. Hours melted into lumps of clay. Slippery and thick. Menacing figures appeared in the shadows. Wasn't that her da's face on that wall? She shook her head. *Stop this.* Yet her whole body trembled.

The wind gasped and rattled at the door. She could swear she heard Siobhan calling in mockery from the other side. She rushed across the room, stumbling in blind fear, and kicked a broken stool against the doorjamb.

"Nothing, Moira, you heard nothing!" She screamed as if the sound of her voice could chase away the terrors. Covering her ears, she turned around and gulped in shock by what, or rather who, was now joining her.

Her long-gone mam.

She was sitting, real as daylight in the cabin, with a phone receiver to her face, near a playpen with two small raven-haired girls. Moira recognized herself in that playpen, a toddler, arms uplifted, filled with expectation. She now felt the anticipation in her own chest, and it pushed her backward, directly into the wall next to the door. A mess of spiderwebs tangled in her hair, but she barely felt it. Her younger self was appearing as if it were a movie before her.

Mam, Mam, she called to her lovely mother, who was coming to pick up young Moira, whimpering in the playpen. But the moment her mother's soft hands reached Moira's rib cage, Siobhan whined dramatically, so that their mother flew past Moira and over to her sister instead. Siobhan was lifted up, her unruly hair bouncing, and the scent of cloves and the creaminess of her mother's precious skin all gone as well. This very memory was Moira's last clear image of her mam—button-dark eyes, eager smile. She had been, Moira would learn later, only sixteen at the time. Moira was so much older than that now. And childless. No one to care for her, no one to care for.

Moira dropped to the floor, her knees clutched against her chest. Through the window, a skeleton of clouds blew near the moon. She waited for hours without moving until through that same window, the muddy blush of sun announced morning. Moira wasn't sure if she'd awoken or just stirred from a sleepless limbo, wide-eyed and crampy. When she stretched her limbs, she was weak, her thirst maddening.

She stumbled to the creek and plunged her hands into the cold water, the right one first in the hopes of shocking it out of its tremors. She drank straight from the stream even though she knew better. Head down, she started at a percussive splash several feet away. The same sound as a seal slapping the water. A seal? This was a sign, a message to her. The selkie! Of course, the girl was bluish for a reason. This was the true, natural coloring of her skin.

Ignited with fresh purpose, Moira ran back through the weeds still ruddy in the scant morning sun. She burst into the cabin and rushed to the child's side. Her features were engulfed in shadows and difficult to discern.

"Andrea, Andr—" Moira began, but then she stopped short. The idea of a new life, a fresh start, might reverse this dire predicament. "Colleen. Colly." Moira's heart raced with excitement. "Maybe you'll make it, huh? If so, I'll take good care of you. I promise. Be like your own mam."

There it was, as clear as any commitment spoken. And if Colleen didn't or couldn't hear her, well, God certainly could.

The bass drone of a large insect filled the cabin. Moira jumped to her feet and then realized it was an engine growing nearer, higher pitched as it approached. Moira dashed to the window. A station wagon appeared on the road about a quarter mile down from the cabin. The Taurus. It was now black and banged in such a way as to look years older. Moira's eyes narrowed as Eamon parked at the edge of the clearing, just beyond the shadow of the chimney that reached like a black finger toward the tree line.

Within moments, he was entering the cabin, disheveled and wild-eyed, pulling damp air and car exhaust in behind him.

"Where, in the name of Jesu"—Moira caught her voice at the edge of a sob—"have you been?"

But he ignored her and pushed past to search around, assessing.

She swallowed a gasp as his eyes rested on the girl draped on the mattress. He stomped over and lifted Colleen's arm to pinch above her elbow before letting it drop in a flaccid wilt. "What the fook did you do?" His expression hardened into something beyond anger. "She's done. This whole thing was a bad idea, Moira."

"You." Her voice dropped to something hard and raspy. "You covered those little girls with that quilt."

He ignored her. "Her brain's fried. She won't remember a thing. If she lives."

"Dear sweet Jesu…" Moira clutched her chest. "She still has a chance."

"Chrissake." Eamon shook his head. "Look at her color, then!"

In the stray bits of early light, they could see her blue-gray skin as if it were melting in the rays.

"She's a selkie, Eamon!" Moira straightened with excitement. "That's why she's blue!"

"What the shite's gotten into you? Selkies aren't real." He spun around. "Where is the blond?"

"She's gone." This hurt so much to say, her mouth went dry.

"What are you tellin' me?" Eamon's voice narrowed. He took a step closer, growing monstrous in the shadows. A glowering giant to Moira's shrinking figure.

Her tongue slipped into rapid Shelta, heavily accented by fatigue. The story ran forward in a river of words rushing over rocks and through gorges. It all came so fast: how the latch on the Buick came undone, the one that she'd begged him to fix. *Remember, Eamon?* Moira continued, even as the image exploded in her head, little Bridget limp on the ground. She finished with resignation in her voice. "Covered her as best I could."

"As best I could." Eamon repeated in a mocking falsetto before grabbing two dust-covered mason jars and heaving them at the wall, where they shattered like angry rain. Moira jumped and shrieked. Colleen didn't flinch. He raised his hand next to his ear and leaned into Moira's face. She recoiled at his breath, a rotten cloud gobbling her breathing space. "Do ya think that little one won't be found, then?"

"Go ahead." She closed her eyes. "Beat the shite out of me."

He dropped his arm. "Not wastin' the energy." He moved to the door. "I'm going back."

"What?"

"Make sure no one finds the body."

"I'm going with you. I'll show you the spot."

"You said by the bridge." He gritted his teeth. "I'll find it myself, for God's sake."

In that moment, the thought of being left in the cabin with this child was too much to bear.

"Don't leave me, Eamon. Not alone. Not here." Moira grasped his arm.

He yanked away. "I'm goin' alone," he growled. "In the meantime, you do as I say."

Moira began to sob.

He grabbed her shoulders and shook. "Didja hear me? Do as I say."

"Yes, Eamon. I'll do it. Whatever."

"Burn everything from the trunk. It all has to go. Any extra burlap, the quilt, and this." He pointed to the dress, balled into a small heap.

"Eamon." Moira followed with her eyes. "What if she doesn't wake?"

He sighed heavily, conveying his irritation. Moira knew what he was thinking. No wonder her da had rejected her. Nothing but trouble.

"Then," he said slowly, deliberately, "you burn her too."

She gasped. "I'll do no such thing."

"Right, *soobya*? Do you want me to come back then?"

Moira nodded, horrified. The choices were impossible. Continue with Eamon's horrific plan, or be abandoned here, alone in the world.

"When I get back," he spoke with the deliberateness of one speaking to an idiot, "this one's either running around this place, just fine, ready to be sold off, or she's gone for good. Got it? No use to me, to us, otherwise."

"Eamon…I want…to keep her…"

He glowered. "Do it. Or else."

Moira groaned, as if her own *gradhum*, her spirit, was shifting into nothingness.

Eamon ignored Moira's reaction. "We'll bury the ashes." He headed toward the door. Moira's entire body, beginning with her hand, quaked. Her nerves were like severed wires firing at random.

"Eamon. Be careful near that ravine, huh," she said, but when he turned, she involuntarily backed away. His eyes were strangely dark, as if they'd gobbled all the light.

Moira waited through the heat of day outside, among the bugs, hovering on the edge of disbelief. Where now was Eamon? He was probably still searching like mad on that godforsaken road. As afternoon shadows lengthened into evening, a slow, pulsing panic grew inside her, along with an urge to wash the filth off her hands. The right one, for some reason, had quieted a bit, twitching only infrequently as if exhausted by its own rogue behavior.

She'd eaten nothing that entire day and her head felt stuffed with cotton. When the sun dropped behind the jagged pines, she knew she could hold off no more. Time to build the fire in the outdoor hearth. She used a stick to clear leaves and old soot from the chimney where generations of field mice had settled. And then started the fire slowly, with dried weeds and small sticks—each pass giving Colleen more time to wake.

Ach, c'mon, girlie…

Finally, with the addition of thick logs, the fire grew into a roaring ball of heat, big enough to consume the items from the trunk. The quilt went in first, the bulk of it almost smothering the flame. But once the dried grease caught, it blazed into a large hungry beast, melting and crackling enough to singe Moira's nose.

Anything and everything went in. One by one. The Styrofoam flashed a bright orange and was followed by the extra burlap and rope. With each toss, the flames grew hotter. Moira's face felt as if it, too, were aflame. After each item, she walked out to the creek to rinse the soot from her hands.

Saving the blue dress for last, she bunched it up before tossing it into the flames. A haunting sorrow filled Moira as she fed it into the hungry fire, knowing what was to come next.

Eamon would be here soon. When Moira entered the cabin again, shafts of twilight spilled into pools around Colleen's ghostly body. The last time Moira had checked, she kept more distance, afraid of what she'd find. Now, she stood even farther away and narrowed her eyes to stare. Not a single motion in the child's chest, not the tiniest rattle of breath. She was certain the girl was gone. At the very least, she could deliver something close to last rites, for God's sake.

She'd bring some water back in her cupped palms, anoint the child with it—a fitting gesture for the little, lost selkie. She walked slowly parting the thick grass with each step. Crouching at the edge of the icy creek, Moira stared into a swirl of blank water, then dropped her head in sad resignation.

Chapter 9
Claire

T he morning of Lily's funeral was achingly brilliant. The maple, half-leafless, did not block the sun, which poured into the windows on the east side of the house. A navy dress Vicki had brought from her own closet in California was splayed like an empty shadow across the lumps of Claire and Glen's unmade bed. Claire couldn't help notice the irony: something borrowed, something blue, a ditty for a time of celebration.

Standing before the dresser mirror in her slip, Claire pulled the hair back tight from her face. The perm was a memory; her hair, neglected and limp, was whitening at the temples. She had continued to lose weight as her stomach symptoms still plagued her, teasing her with a reprieve, only to be set off once again. It could happen anytime, at odd moments like brushing her teeth or when thoughts of the girls overtook her. She had vomited all over the living room the day after Hearns had come by to tell them Lily had been found.

Lifting the dress, she noticed a small split in the seam under the arm. She reached into the drawer of the bedside table for the sewing kit, forgetting momentarily that this was where they kept a copy of the police sketch. Although Glen requested she stop, Claire opened the drawer most every night to look at the suspect's evil face, always creating more detail than was offered by the crude lines. She needed something to sink her teeth into. Charcoal Man: that's what she called him. And next to the picture was another document. A copy of the police report with details provided by Jay White. It was excruciating, and yet she read it over and over, obsessively. In places where there was only a line or two of space provided to write, this man, this Jay White, had included an arrow and continued on a separate page. Paragraphs emerged rather than simple phrases. And from it, Claire conjured the scene, the reality of that moonlit night, when he'd found himself on a dark road and, apparently urged forward by some type of intuition, discovered the ruined body of her lovely Lily.

Even as Detective Hearns reassured Claire and Glen that Jay was not a suspect, the detective seemed wary of him, describing him as shifty, a one-time drunk. The proximity of both documents, the sketch and the report, along with the detective's comments, jarred Claire. Though she'd never seen Jay, she often confused the two faces in her mind; she imagined Jay with a pointy beard and the Charcoal Man as Native American.

Ten long days passed between the awful discovery and the burial. The police needed to talk to this Jay, collect evidence. Run forensics and perform an autopsy on Lily. What they discovered horrified Claire. Drugs in her system. A mixture of sedatives preferred by junkies who needed to erase bad trips. But the official cause of death was much worse. Heat stroke. Suffocation. Unbearable.

Claire sank onto the bed and opened the small sewing kit, but choosing a needle and thread felt like a monstrously large task right then. And who was she fooling anyway? She never sewed. On Halloween, the girls wore store-bought costumes. Clothing with rips was placed in the Goodwill pile or simply overlooked. But things were different now. It was the carrot that had brought Lily back, saved her from being forgotten on that deserted road. As soon as they found Andrea, Claire would sew the stuffed pieces back together. She couldn't—wouldn't—accept the idea that Jumpers was never made whole, separated from his carrot forever.

"Claire," Glen called from the kitchen. "We've got to leave in five minutes."

Claire threw on the navy dress, her emaciated frame offering no resistance, and, shoes in hand, joined Glen in the kitchen. Noisily, Butkus scrambled perch to perch in his cage.

"Sorry, my man," Glen whispered, lifting the birdcage into a far corner. "We have people here later."

The wire bars suddenly felt wrong to Claire, a violation, recalling a conversation she'd had with Andrea in January when she turned four. "What would happen if we let him out?"

"Nothing, honey. He has a broken wing."

"He won't fly away?"

"No. He can't."

"Then why is he in a cage? Did he do something wrong?"

Claire recalled struggling to explain how it kept Butkus safe or something like that, how birds were always in cages. But Andrea's face had remained perplexed, unconvinced. "What about Gretchie and her crate?" Andrea had been insistent. Claire remembered she had been rushing at the time, hurrying off yet again to day care; the roads were slick and she couldn't find one of Lily's boots.

"C'mon, Claire." Glen broke her reverie. "Let's go."

They looked at each other. In that moment, Claire felt they could've dissolved onto the linoleum floor, absorbed by grief so great that they would disappear. But they needed to push through. For Andrea, still Out There.

"C'mon, G." Glen opened the door to the dog's aluminum crate as he patted his leg. "Get in, girl."

"No!"

Glen startled, then stared at Claire, questioning.

"I can't...today. It feels...cruel."

Glen hesitated before stepping back, leaving the door open. "Be home soon, G." He tugged at the dog's ears.

Claire offered a kiss on the top of her soft head.

Claire made it to the car as Glen locked up. It was an old Cadillac, a permanent loaner from Glen's parents, who had gone one winter to Florida and never returned. Others—friends, cousins, even the funeral director—had offered to drive. But they had chosen to travel alone to the church and afterward to the cemetery, ten miles north, in acres of ex-pastureland dotted with evergreens and artificial ponds.

They drove in silence with Claire keeping her eyes closed. Maybe this was just a bad dream. In her imposed darkness, the car bounced and weaved, moving forward, it felt, because of Glen's sheer willpower, the same energy that was allowing her to believe Andrea could be alive somewhere. They just had to find her.

Opening her eyes, Claire could see the spires of Holy Redeemer, the church where she and Glen had married, where both girls had been baptized. The service was mercifully short. Claire sat in a fugue with the organ music vibrating through her like a small earthquake. At the end, passing through the crush of family and friends, she saw Detective Hearns standing in the back, a looming reminder of Andrea's absence.

At the cemetery, the grave site was ringed with people who parted solemnly when Claire and Glen approached. Those closest to the family, Vicki and Troy, Glen's parents, and various cousins from both sides, huddled tightly as if trying to encase them in a protective cocoon.

During the ceremony, Claire dug her hands deep in her tightly cinched trench coat. Beneath a moist wad of tissue, she held between her thumb and forefinger a small cellophane bag. Jumpers's carrot. Hearns had arranged this kindness, which was against all form of police policy. Made Claire swear that it would remain in the bag. She manipulated it as tenderly as possible through the plastic, surprised to discover that the cellophane within the soft orange felt remained crisp enough to crackle.

Final prayers were said. Once the respectful lingering was over, the outer tier of mourners, which included Claire's colleagues from the hospital, Juanita Hearns, and several uniformed police officers, drifted back to their cars. Glen stood in a small circle of relatives, with his parents closest, as if binding themselves to their son.

Claire's elderly aunt May approached, holding Vicki's arm. "I'm so sorry, dear," she said, and Claire detected the faint scent of lily of the valley as they embraced. "You are so strong. Always have been. Ever since you were a little girl."

"Thank you," Claire whispered. "For being here." Managing to hold herself together, to speak, seemed like some kind of miracle.

She'd collapse later at home, after everyone left. "Vicki, can you help Aunt May off the lawn?" As always, she found comfort in her sister's sympathetic eyes. "I need a moment right now."

"Of course, honey. C'mon, May."

Claire needed a last goodbye. Approaching the grave, her eye caught a small rose-colored square set near the freshly disturbed dirt. She lowered to one knee and picked it up. It was an envelope. Just then, she spotted the figure of a tall, slim man in a jean jacket and boots walking away. He turned and bowed his head toward Claire, exposing the part in his long, black hair. He was unmistakably Native American. Jay White. Claire felt a sudden, searing pressure along her ribs.

When he lifted his face, she found herself staring, but he didn't notice—he was focused on something else. She followed his gaze past a line of neatly planted arborvitae to the west and discovered something remarkable. A small white flame seemed to emanate from the sky and hover over the greenery. The light pulsed, catching Claire in an astonished blink. She blinked harder. It didn't go away. Could this be retinal flashes brought on by stress? Was she so far gone she was now seeing things? But it was real. Jay White could see it too.

Was this an offering of some kind, possibly from heaven? Claire felt momentarily luminescent, uplifted.

"Claire?" Glen was now at her side guiding her arm. "We need to leave now."

She started to speak, to draw Glen into this amazing sight. But the flame burst into a small explosion of otherworldly light. As quickly as it had come, it slipped away, swallowed by a line of fast-moving clouds. And yet it left behind a remnant of sensation that surged through Claire's entire being like a cool drink of water. There was a small but palpable easing of the sailor's knot that was her stomach. She slipped the envelope into her pocket.

"I'm driving," Vicki said firmly. Troy ushered Glen's mother down the slope with one arm while his dad followed behind. "Troy's taking your parents."

Climbing into the car, Claire turned toward the place she'd seen

Jay White. What on earth had happened? Who was this man? He was many yards away, pulling his jacket closed as he fought the wind, a mere outline against a now darkening sky.

Vicki set the car in motion.

"Glen, I found an envelope…" But his thoughts were somewhere else.

They took off. As they passed through the iron gates, Claire pondered the impossibility of this event, all of these terrible happenings, the abduction, losing Lily forever. But a slight warmth, as if a small ember had landed on her chest, brought back that same feeling she had experienced when she saw that incredible light in the sky.

They arrived home to an intimate group of family and friends who set out food and filled their house with comforting words and gentle touches. Gretchie, effusive at the house full of people, bounced from one person to another, being rewarded with pieces of cheese and crackers that snapped satisfyingly in her mouth. Claire didn't bother to interfere with this gorging, even though a bellyache later was a foregone conclusion.

Butkus could be heard across the house, squawking his usual disapproval. Vicki draped a bath towel over his cage. "There," she scolded. "Now keep quiet for a change." He remained boisterous but muffled.

Claire slipped into the hall for a moment alone. Autumn twilight was sifting through the house, blurring the faces of her friends and relatives as if seen through cataracts. She leaned into the wall with her head on her forearms. A hand met the small of her back from behind. Glen. She turned into his embrace.

"I'm so sorry," she whispered through tears, trying yet again to apologize. "For all of this…"

Glen released her and moved to assist his dad in getting out of a chair, even though there were plenty others rushing to help.

Claire wiped her face before treading softly into the girls' room. She'd placed the envelope Jay had left at Lily's grave on the dresser when they first arrived. She ran her fingers over the soft, pink surface before opening it. Slowly and carefully, she lifted the contents from inside. A dream catcher. Lovely and delicate as spider webbing, it filled the shape of her palm. She almost smiled. Lily would've liked this. She took the small string attached and threaded it through the hook of the old mobile that still hung over the crib. When she stepped back, a delicate wreath of twigs and feathers spun softly in an unseen current of air. Once again, the feeling given to her by the light she'd seen at the cemetery returned. Briefly this time, but unmistakable.

She needed to talk to Jay White.

Chapter 10
Jay

T wo days after Lily Rawlings's funeral, in the wake of a cold front that brought early snow, Jay got off to a later start than he'd planned. The engine in the El Camino cranked but wouldn't turn over. He was lucky to get a jump from a passing trucker and then was finally on his way. *So long, Illinois.* He couldn't wait to see the state line sign in his rearview mirror. On the drive, slowed by traffic, he fought to replace the trauma of the past ten days with fantasies of his new life along the northwestern shore of Lake Michigan: cherries ripening on trees like small moons and crisp, rainbow-trout-laden streams crisscrossing through pristine dunes.

In the evening, close to the Indiana border, he pulled into a half-deserted campground outside Calumet City for a fast-food dinner and a quick nap. When he roused himself to get back on the road, the El Camino's engine didn't make a sound. It was just plain dead. October nights closed in early, so Jay settled into his mummy bag, tightening up against the cold. He could feel weather coming in his bones.

The next day he walked up the main road, to Danny-O's garage, just past a strip mall. He learned that the tow alone would be forty bucks. All Jay had was twenty-seven dollars and some change. He offered to work it off. The manager said that he'd check with the owner when he got back, maybe later that day, maybe tomorrow. But he didn't sound enthused.

Small pellets of snow and thin needles of sleet accompanied

Jay as he returned to the campground. This probably wouldn't last long so early in the season, but still a pain in the butt. He pulled his collar tight before lifting the hood and bending to take another look at the decrepit battery. Maybe if he stared hard enough it would charge. He laughed at himself.

An engine revved next to Jay. Startled, he banged his head against the hood. A local police cruiser had slipped up beside him with spooky stealth.

"Jeez, you scared me." Jay rubbed the back of his head.

The guy inside was young. A block of granite. Kept his sunglasses on even though it wasn't sunny. What now? What on earth had Jay done this time?

The officer dropped the window a quarter open. Did the same with his opaque glasses down his nose. Then a slow scan of Jay and the El Camino.

"I have a message from a Detective Juanita Hearns."

All along, Jay had had a feeling about Hearns. Her suspicions about him. The disapproval on her face. That Hearns was able to find him in the campground felt like some kind of breach. Like he was being followed or something.

"She said you have her number."

Jay nodded.

"She'd like you to give her a call."

"About what?"

Jay was sweating. Standing next to the squad car did this to him.

The cop shook his head, shifted his car into Drive. He lifted his glasses above his eyes but kept his face forward.

"Just need to know you're going to do this, buddy. There's a pay phone up the street. Don't want to be back here for another visit."

"You don't need to worry."

The cop rolled up the window and moved the car slowly forward as if navigating a trash heap.

"Thanks for the lift, man," Jay murmured. Not that he would've taken it.

He made his way back up to the main road and to the phone booth, an egg-shaped fixture at the edge of Danny-O's parking lot, and dialed Hearns's number, which was written on the card he kept, on the side printed with the *Help Find Andrea!* hotline.

"I hope you didn't mind the visit from the squad car."

"How did you know where I was?"

"Let's just say I had a hunch you'd be camping."

"If my car were working, you wouldn't have caught me."

Why did he say that? Made him sound like a suspect all over again.

"This message is actually from the Rawlings family. They asked if you would meet with them."

"Why?"

"I'm not entirely sure. I just offered to reach out to you on their behalf." Her voice remained cool, edged with disapproval. "Three o'clock at the Tin Drum Diner. On Tenth and Harmon. Half a block from the station. There's a train station within walking distance. Brings you right downtown."

Ugh. Train tickets cost money. And near the police station. That rattled him too. But mainly what shook him was that the last time he was with Hearns to review and sign his statement, Jay made the mistake of filling her in on a little too much of his history. He was tired, raw, distraught about the whole thing, and Hearns seemed comforting, almost maternal. In addition to the details of finding the body, he'd told her about his drinking and, foolishly, about his ability to sense things beyond what others could, even how his mother had been training him to be a shaman before she died. He cringed.

"Do me a favor." Hearns's voice slowed. "Take it easy on the family, huh?"

Jay was baffled. What was the detective talking about?

"Sometimes we see things, imagine things, that aren't there."

With a change in trains, followed by a five-block walk, it took Jay two hours to get to the diner. His jean jacket, the same one he'd worn to Lily Rawlings's funeral, was damp from a clod of sleety snow that had fallen from a roof and smacked into his shoulder. What he'd do for a hot shower right then. A low-grade sense of embarrassment about his dirty clothes and slicked-back hair almost made him turn around. But this was important.

The Tin Drum. It was an old place—dim, all linoleum and gouged tabletops. Smudged windows. Jay slid into a booth with cracked vinyl seats that pinched the back of his legs like a crawfish. The Rawlingses were late. Jay's head started to fill with second thoughts. What could they want from him? The idea of sitting across from this distraught family unnerved him, but it was too late now to bow out. A mother with little kids entered the restaurant. A boy and a girl. They were young, two and fourish. They chose the table next to Jay. The mother set out crayons.

When Claire Rawlings finally appeared, standing at the table, Jay was surprised. He'd expected her to have the frayed edges of someone in shock, a person diluted by grief. But she wasn't that. Besides being thin—thinner than a person should be—she had a presence about her. What was it? Quiet strength.

She sat across from Jay. "I can't thank you enough for this."

She touched his hand. Her skin was pale as a ghost pipe, a plant that grows in sunless woods. Christ, she'd better gain some weight. The kids one table over were making a small ruckus. Claire looked at them quickly and then back at Jay.

"You must think I'm a terrible mother."

The skin around her eyes was lined with creases. Her coloring was sallow. And then, in turn, he wondered, what did she see when she looked at him? He must be strange to her. As he was to so many.

"I'm sorry about everything," he said.

That was a dumb thing to say. The waitress approached. Claire ordered coffee for them both in a no-nonsense manner indicating they didn't want interruptions. Clearly the in-control type. Or used to be.

"Are you working?" she asked.

"No. I'm just waiting to fix my car."

"And then?"

"I plan to move on to Michigan." He briefly touched his hand to his chest pocket, where his talisman remained safely tucked away. "Plan to sell my crafts, maybe start a landscape business. I'm pretty good at that. Who knows?" He shrugged. "Maybe get a place of my own. A trailer or something." What was he doing, yammering on about himself? "Will your husband be coming too?"

"Huh?" Claire Rawlings was there but, at the same time, she wasn't. "Oh. No. *People* magazine called on our way out." Claire's voice grew slower, quieter. "Glen stayed on. He's hoping for an interview."

The waitress returned with two coffees. Jay stirred, even though he didn't add cream or sugar.

"Please tell me," he said. "What is it you need me to do?"

"The information you included in the police report." Claire cleared her throat. "It was very detailed. You mentioned something about having feelings...what did you call it—an urge—that helped you find Lily... Can you tell me about that? Are you..." She struggled for the right word.

"Psychic?"

She nodded.

"It's not really like that. Sometimes I sense stuff, but that doesn't guarantee anything. It's not like I can control it. Well, not anymore."

"You could before?"

"There was a time." Jay felt himself redden. "I was, well, training, sort of. To be a shaman." He was doing it again, oversharing. And yet Claire somehow seemed safe. "I had a connection to things. Nonphysical things, sort of like signs. As did my mother. Probably sounds ridiculous to you, a Western medical doctor."

"Doctor-in-training," Claire corrected. "It doesn't matter how I feel about it. What matters is you found my daughter. And my other daughter is still out there. Still with that crazy man." She set her jaw and met Jay's eyes strongly. "I'm not looking for guarantees. We are, as you can imagine, desperate. We will pay you for this. Compensate you for your time."

Jay cleared his throat. "I just...I don't want to disappoint you."

He caught the sharp pain in her eyes before she glanced away. "I'm already disappointed," she murmured, more to the window than to Jay.

He wanted to say *You're killing me, Claire. Stop it.* He wanted to say he knew what it was like, what she was going through. But even after the terrible loss of his mother—he couldn't imagine what it must be like to lose a child.

"I brought something that might help. Pictures. Of Lily, how she really looked." Claire drew air quickly, as if something sharp had hit her chest. "And Andrea. I thought, I don't know, I'm hoping it might stir things up in your mind…"

She opened the envelope and set the pictures on the table.

The black-and-white photograph of Andrea was the same one the Rawlingses had chosen for their search campaign. It was less grainy, more defined than on the missing persons posters. The little girl's bangs were parted slightly. A clear, impish look lit her eyes.

God, she looks like a great kid.

Moving to the photo of Lily, Jay tried not to, but he shuddered. Before him was a perfect headshot of a beautiful, shining child with fluffy yellow hair like an angel's halo. Nothing like that face he'd uncovered that horrible night two weeks ago.

The waitress approached, but Claire held up her hand to keep her from intruding. One tear made its way down her cheek before she wiped it away.

"Please. Take your time."

Jay nodded. He scrutinized each photo, moving back and forth between the faces of the two little girls, willing himself to feel something, sense something. There was a stirring in his stomach, but only when he looked at Andrea. He struggled to clarify his thoughts, connect the dots from his head to his gut. And yet the overwhelming sadness he felt about Lily was messing with him. He was trying hard for this woman. Her desperation was filling his brain so he couldn't think clearly, much less let his feelings flow. Jay briefly touched his hand to his chest pocket and bumped against the Petoskey stone. A slight warmth, maybe? Or maybe just his imagination. There was nothing concrete. Certainly nothing to raise Claire's hopes.

"I…I'm sorry. I'm not…I can't just turn this off and on…"

"I'm not trying to be pushy… We're just so…" She looked out the window. Jay followed her gaze. The pane was thick and dirty and everything beyond looked wavy, unreal. "Can you tell me, Jay, what it was I saw? In the sky."

"You mean the light."

Just the mention of it and Jay felt something inside, a comforting warmth followed by the slightest tingling in his gut.

"Yes." She circled her hands around the mug in front of her. They were trembling. "Did it make you...well...feel anything?"

"A sensation. Of being soothed, maybe...not really sure how to describe it..."

"That's it!" Claire almost knocked over her coffee in astonishment. Even as she looked in his eyes, he was back at the graveside, catching sight of the indescribable glow just above him. "What does it mean?"

Jay remained silent and searched her face. It was more animated. He chose his words carefully. "Well, I grew up believing, being told really, that there are no coincidences."

"Like you and I were meant to meet?"

"Uh-huh, and that light...in the sky. Might be a sign. From Lily." He cleared his throat. "That she's okay. And that..." Claire's eyes widened as Jay continued, "Her sister, your other daughter, Andrea..."

There it was again, a tight sensation when he spoke her name.

"Yes?"

He smiled. "A really pretty name. I think, not certain, but maybe it was a message."

He wasn't making this up. He had the beginning of a feeling, nothing full-blown, but an inkling, about Andrea. And then Hearns's voice was in his head. *Sometimes we imagine things that aren't there.* He stopped himself from saying more.

"Please." Claire drew air quickly. "Keep the pictures. Maybe something will occur to you, or you will have a sensation like before."

"I promise. I'll let you know if anything...well...arises..." He looked again at the image of Andrea, her bright open face, her windswept bangs. The constriction in his gut returned.

"Claire...I..."

Her eyebrows rose in anticipation. "Yes?"

Hearns's voice once again ground through his head. *Take it easy on the family, huh?*

"Um…it's just that the last train to Calumet City is in fifteen minutes."

Claire exhaled and then slowly nodded, as if deflated.

They sat in uncomfortable silence. The waitress slipped the check on the table. The family next to them finished up and the mom started gathering their belongings, jackets and gloves, backpacks, typical kid stuff. They paid and made their way noisily out the door. It was a relief they were gone.

"I'm driving you."

"The train station is just around the corner."

"To the campground."

"No way. It's too far."

"I insist."

Jay figured it might be best to walk outside with Claire and then let her know he wasn't going to drive with her. When they stood, she set a few small bills on the table to cover the coffee and tip. Jay realized that neither of them had taken a sip. At the door, Claire placed her palms firmly against the glass and gazed at Jay with a determined look.

"I'm taking you back to your car. Don't say another word."

"Okay." He wanted to make her happy.

Outside, it was cold but not biting. Claire looked at Jay's jean jacket with disapproval.

"Do you have something warmer to wear?"

"Don't worry about me, I'm fine."

They headed out against an asphalt-colored sky. Pockets of snow along the road looked dirty and old, marked with holes like a kitchen sponge. The proximity to Claire in the car made Jay nervous. He wasn't accustomed to this type of intimacy, side by side for miles. He wished he'd taken the train now. He was sorry as hell for her but scared of her too, scared of her emotional need and his own inadequacy.

Forty minutes later, they passed the small strip mall with a 7-Eleven and Danny-O's garage. Near the entrance, the phone booth glowed in the late-day gloom. The campground was only several hundred feet away, the entrance unmarked.

"You can just drop me here. I'm good."

"No deal. I'm taking you all the way in."

The Cadillac dipped and hawed along the small road that led to where the tents and "car people" were. Jay wondered what she must be thinking about him. When they came to a small fork, he instructed Claire to loop around the long way since a group of kids were playing in the dirt and didn't look too interested in scattering. After passing scrubby lots, they encountered a contingent of strange-looking trailers. Five of them, huddled close together in a crescent shape—they hadn't been there when Jay left earlier.

"What are those?" Claire said.

"Traveller caravans," he answered without hesitation. "They still look the same as when I was a kid."

Smaller and rounder than the other mobile units, with wood siding, they could've been comical in a stuck-in-the-fifties sort of way. But nothing was funny here. Jay thought he saw a set of curtains open and then quickly draw closed.

"Are you having a *Children of the Corn* moment?" Claire whispered.

Jay smiled, understanding her reaction to people who were less settled than the norm.

"Travellers," he said.

He knew them from itinerant summers spent with his mom peddling dream catchers in Oklahoma and Missouri. Overall, they were wonderful, caring people. But isolated bands like these raised alarm bells. There was a reason they were separate from the larger groups.

"They move around a lot, sometimes call themselves Irish gypsies. Have an interesting language...um..." He furrowed his brow, attempting to recall. "Shelta. Never knew them to come this far north. Or east—"

"Gypsies?" Claire interrupted. "The suspect, that revolting man... in the sketch...that word was used by the detective to describe him. I think it was his tattoos or something. You know a lot."

She looked at him with a new curiosity. Jay wasn't sure if she was surprised because people like him shouldn't know much, or if it was just that the Travellers were an oddity. He wanted to tell her that he was no dummy. That he'd taken night classes at a total of three different community colleges over the years while working at restaurants or doing shifts at small packing plants. That he'd set a goal for an associate's degree, but it never quite worked out. That his real loves were history and astronomy, and that he could probably still quote Poe's "The Raven" by memory. That in a strange way he understood the clan identity, similar in so many ways to his own. Yet while they seemed so self-certain in their world, he had a love-hate relationship with his Indian-ness and wanted, after all these years, for it to be all love.

"Is that your car?"

"Yup."

Claire slowed and then stopped. Trailer park smell flooded in as he opened the door, compost-y, dank. Jay glanced at Claire. There were Styrofoam cups and other litter strewn through the park. A dog barked in the distance. Scenes from the poverty line. Jay knew it well.

She handed Jay an envelope. "I want you to have this."

He could tell it was thick with bills.

"I'm good. I don't need any money," he lied.

"Please. It's important to Glen and me."

"On one condition," Jay said.

"What's that?"

"Whatever's in here, I split in half and give the rest back to you, since, you know, I didn't come up with any information for you."

Claire shook her head. "No deal."

"What? Why?"

"Just because."

"You're pretty feisty."

"Do you mean to say pushy?" Claire half smiled.

"I guess so, yeah."

"You know what? That's the nicest thing I've heard in a long time."

Jay waited a minute before he said goodbye, because Claire was crying. He felt his own tears gathering at edge of his eyes. He stopped himself from losing it, though, because he didn't want to make the moment worse for her. But when she finally spoke, her voice was clear and strong.

"Thank you," she said. "For doing this with me."

"I'm kind of worried about you, driving back to Chicago and everything." What was going on here? He barely knew this woman and yet he was feeling the type of connection he once was open to, the kind that was so big and deep and overwhelming that he'd learned to fight it off lest it consume him.

"No, I'm good," she said. "Need some alone time."

She looked away from him. The air had warmed, forming a layer of mist over the cold ground.

"Are you sure?"

"Jay, you're going to send me a forwarding address and I'm going to send you stuff, okay? Like a jacket and maybe even home-made food or something."

"You don't have to do that."

She spun around, to directly face him. "I know this is weird to you. But you give me some connection to Lily and…well…Andrea too…"

Jay got it. After his mom died, all he cared about was blow-ing out of the reservation. When the chance came at sixteen, he made sure he brought a bunch of stuff with him to sell and trade away—silly "Indian" things that white kids used when they played cowboys and Indians, like plastic beads, feathered ankle-bands. But he'd kept his mother's ceremonial garb and held it dear. Until he didn't. A flare of shame shot through him as he recalled how he'd gambled away her doeskin vest and moccasins when he was drink-ing. He understood more than anyone wanting to stay connected to something lost to you. He opened the door, got out, and went to the driver's side. Claire rolled the window down. The cold air swooshed in and around her, gobbling up all the warm stuff.

"Claire." The stirring in his gut sent a small buzz toward his heart. The fear that gripped his heart—what if his instinct betrayed him and he roused false hope in Claire?—momentarily receded. His feelings had never before failed him. "Your daughter, Andrea."

Her eyes looked like she was half a foot underwater, drowning. "She's alive."

Claire caught her breath like she'd been punched. Should he have done this? Given hope in such a raw moment? But he didn't stop. "I know it. I feel it."

Claire's face flushed. With what, relief? He couldn't tell.

"I believe you, Jay." She almost smiled. "I really do."

She handed him a slip of paper with her name, address, and phone number.

"Promise to call me anytime with any information." She swallowed hard. "Or just to keep in touch. Please. Don't forget. It's important to Glen and me."

"I promise."

Jay watched the Cadillac pull away and followed the red embers of her brake lights into the mist. The sun stayed hidden behind a veil of clouds. It took him a minute to swallow the lump in his throat, the hard ball of emotion stuck right in the middle of his life, where it couldn't be ignored. He was sorry as hell for Claire and her husband and their little girls.

He stood next to the El Camino. Outta here in twenty-four hours.

"*Ri-midril!*" A woman's voice jarred him from behind.

Jay hadn't heard the odd language since he was eight or nine years old. The quick cadence, the guttural overtones, it all came back to him as if it were yesterday and not thirty years before. He turned around.

A small woman in her early twenties stood about ten feet away. She was petite, her features severe. An angular nose. Dark eyes full of suspicion. A small, hard mouth. When she started to speak, a toddler with a peanut butter and jelly face appeared from behind his mother, clambering on her legs until she reached down and swung him onto her hip.

"Need to move this car." She shifted the dull-faced toddler on her hip. "Blockin' our path." Distinctive brogue combined with a southern drawl. Like fried chicken and soda bread in her voice.

"Would be nice," Jay responded, "but it's dead."

"Push it then."

Jay almost laughed.

The woman's eyes flashed in warning. "We don't want trouble..."

A window creaked open from the caravan. A male voice, gruff and slurring, called out, "Siobhan! He givin' you shite?"

"No. He'll be movin' it soon," she called back. Then she locked Jay into an uncompromising gaze. "Won't you?"

Her eyes fixated him. They flashed restlessly, disturbingly impersonal. And there was something else. An unsettling far beyond his stomach, as if some kind of dissonance occurred in the great wheel of life his grandmother had spoken of.

"Relax. It'll be gone first thing in the morning."

The woman turned her back and returned to her caravan. Jay remained riveted in place as she disappeared into the little doorway. The longer he stood, the more troubled he became. Beyond her callous attitude was that face. Those unforgiving features.

Soon it was dark. One last night in this messed-up car. It was cold. Jay added an army blanket to his layering, but he didn't sleep. As soon as the moon slipped fully into the sky and the sounds of the park settled in, his mind began to churn and twist. Something wasn't right. He took out the photos that Claire had given him. They were barely visible in the gloaming light. Was that a flutter in his chest? An urge? It went away as quickly as it had visited. Probably the chill working on him. And then it happened again. This time it was unmistakable, a slight constriction of the skin under the stone in his pocket. He wrestled his way out of his car.

Standing stiff-legged, he looked up at the smattering of white stars burning through the velvet blue sky overhead. Moonlight illuminated the scrap pines and leafless saplings. Jay listened for an owl and sniffed the air, drinking in the bright night odors. Still too Indian, he thought wryly. There it was again, but this time stronger, an almost painful pulse that ran just beneath the stone in his jacket to his skin.

He started walking to the egg-shaped phone booth. It must've been close to midnight, but he no longer owned a watch. Feeling through his pockets, he came across the edge of the *Help Find Andrea!* card. He'd call the hotline and leave a message. No questions asked. Best that it be anonymous. It would be more believable that way.

Jay's heart pulsed wildly as he dialed. A crease ran through the numbers on the card. Was that a four or a one? Shit. He only had enough change for one call. He gambled on four.

It rang. Clearing his throat, he prepared to speak to the recorded line. But someone picked up.

"Hello? Hello?"

He hesitated.

"Look, I know someone's on the line. It's okay. Say anything. It's safe."

"Detective Hearns?" Crap. Why was she working this late?

"Jay?" She sounded weary. "Jay White?"

"I…I was…just gonna leave a message."

"What is it?" Maybe she was just tired, but Jay felt impatience creeping through the line.

"I think… I don't know for sure, but I have a feeling it's a woman."

"Who are you talking about?"

"The suspect."

"You think that the kidnapper"—Hearns's voice rose with incredulity—"is a woman?"

"Yeah…" He hesitated. "Yes, I do."

"And how's that, Jay?"

"I saw someone, felt something. I believe a woman took both Rawlings girls." There. He said it. "And that she still has Lily's sister." He spoke slowly, the cold numbing his lips. "What I mean is that Andrea Rawlings is still alive."

Silence.

"Have you considered the Irish Travellers?" Jay continued.

"Look. I appreciate your help. Really. But we have looked into that community, and we know they never journey this far north."

"That's not true. They're here in this campground. I saw them today."

He could hear a quick sigh.

Jay's urgency and confidence were waning. Why didn't she believe him? *Because I'm not credible*, he thought. *That's why*. That was fine. He'd call Claire in the morning, offer his hunch to her, and then be done with it. This whole situation, the entire scenario, was wearing him down. It was a good thing that he couldn't buy anything to drink.

"Jay, I just have to ask, and I don't mean to sound rude. Have you maybe had a drink tonight? This whole thing has been hard on you, I know."

Why did I ever tell her? He pressed his lips together to keep his teeth from chattering.

"Do you want to come in and file a report?" Hearns offered. "I'll need more information."

Based on his car situation, she had to know this would be close to impossible. "No."

"We'll keep this on file. And we'll look again into the Travellers, I promise. And the woman thing, well, here's what. I'm gonna ask you something really important." She sounded like she was talking to a fifth grader. "We have a strong lead. And as you know, it's a man. A real SOB."

"A sketch. All you have is a crappy sketch." This was so ballsy for Jay. And right away, she'd knocked him down for it.

"Jay." She drew his name out with a condescending lilt. "The family, Claire and Glen Rawlings, real nice people. They are both clearly a mess. Really struggling."

Jay didn't think of Claire as a mess. She seemed incredibly strong, considering. But Hearns continued.

"Let's not go upsetting or confusing them right now, hey? I mean, I think you understand. I'd appreciate it if you don't say anything about this to them. I'll follow up. I promise. But please, please, don't go contacting Claire or Glen about this."

Jay hung up. He'd be out of here first thing in the morning. Bright and fucking early.

Chapter 11
Claire

T he early weeks in November stirred with restless winds and occasional sleet. Claire and Glen stood in the wings of the late-afternoon broadcast of *Chicago Live at Five!* set underneath a large clock with iridescent numbers. The backstage lighting defined Glen's features along with the newly noticeable wrinkles at the edges of his eyes. He took Claire's hands into his own.

The staticky sound of people milling about echoed through the hollow space as the audience settled into their seats. They brought a warm energy, this audience. Claire could just tell. She and Glen had prepared for this moment. Ever since they had received word that the Taurus had been found submerged in a river at the bottom of a gorge twenty miles northwest of the deserted road where Jay had found Lily.

Claire had seen pictures of her car hoisted onto the slim road, repainted black and mangled from the crash. Full-color police photos. But Claire's mind changed the entire scene into something older looking, pewter-toned, as if everything was covered in fine, dull ash—ash everywhere—the water, the car, the severe landscape. It helped soften the harshness.

The police and FBI estimated it was immediately after the abduction that this crash happened. They theorized that Charcoal Man may have panicked, left Lily hastily, and sped off to hide in the dense woods. Probably drove too fast along the narrow road and skidded down the ravine to his death. The big news was that his body was found in the car. Alone. The authorities were now canvassing the area carefully, fanning out in an ever-widening circle that encompassed the lower part of the river as well as the neighboring countryside. Claire secretly hoped they found no clues. Not there. It meant Andrea wasn't involved in this horrible scene at all. Had maybe gotten away earlier. Somehow escaped using her resilience, her clever mind.

The moment Hearns brought the news to them, breathless with the update that Andrea had not been found in that car, Claire and Glen blazed with renewed purpose. The search was on full force. And the story was once again hot locally. Finally, a solid chunk of evidence. The two of them called together the old volunteers to man phones. They contacted *Chicago Live at Five!* and set up this interview with the hope that it would be picked up by the national news, morning shows in particular—the meat and potatoes for daytime viewers: women, mothers. They'd been warned by Hearns and the police media consultant that the live show was a tough format. Crying was okay, but too much muddied the message and too little risked them seeming cold, uncaring. They practiced their on-air personas together in front of the bathroom mirror. Glen, of course, with his sympathetic eyes and open expression, was a natural.

"Remember what they told us, hon," Glen offered. "Eyes on the camera. Keep calm."

The timbre of his voice warmed Claire. This discovery had created a slight crack in the shell of their grief, brought them back to working together, to moving forward as a couple. Most importantly, it seemed to have tempered Glen's disposition, which was prone to moody silence since they'd buried Lily.

Claire glanced at a small cosmetic mirror set in place for the anchors. The nervous look on her face perfectly mimicked the feelings churning inside. She had convinced herself that if she did a good job, there would be credible sightings and calls within hours.

Motioned by a man in headphones, they took seats onstage and settled side by side into molded plastic chairs. The backdrop lit up. A computer-generated image of Lake Michigan ebbed and flowed behind them, the waves lifting in a gentle pattern. Music followed.

A moisture mustache broke out on Claire's upper lip. And then the voice of the female host, Jodi, surged through the speakers in an excited tone.

"Goood day, Chicago! You are with us along with our studio audience on *Live at Five!*"

Applause.

"We have Claire and Glen Rawlings here with us today with an update. This is the family, you will recall"—her voice slowed—"that had their two beautiful children stolen three long months ago."

The audience simmered to a hush. Jodi's coiffed blond hair remained impeccable, her green eyes earnest as she spoke into the camera, explaining the events relating to the abduction. When Jodi got to the part about Lily, Claire's head grew light. She feared she might pass out. Glen took her hand into his own.

"Mr. and Mrs. Rawlings." Clive, Jodi's cohost, joined in. "Today we have some new information." He was a large guy with a surprisingly high voice. "Only a few days ago you learned that your station wagon, the one that was stolen along with your children, was discovered to have been part of an accident."

A picture of the crumpled Taurus flashed onto the large-screen monitor next to the camera. Claire could see the car and the audience at the same time as her mind involuntarily reconstructed the evil Charcoal Man. She scanned the faces in the audience for sympathy, rage.

"My understanding, Mr. and Mrs. Rawlings, is that since this discovery was made, you've worked every phone line, every muscle, to gain more information because you are hopeful..." Clive hesitated for dramatic effect. "Hopeful that your daughter Andrea may still be alive. Can you tell us, Mrs. Rawlings, what leads you to believe this?"

Other than the absence of her daughter's body, there was nothing. Except that Claire felt Andrea was alive, almost in her very bones. It was as if a ray of what Claire now termed Lily's light, the one she had seen at the graveside, had returned, lifting her desperation. Her stomach, too, had become tolerable since learning about the Taurus. And they had support today. Detective Hearns and Vicki sat in the third row, a unified army of two. That felt good. Vicki, once again in from California, offered eager eyes. Claire knew all this travel was a strain, and was doubly grateful she'd come.

The detective's violet blouse accentuated the deep bronze of her skin. As always, Claire kept a read on the detective's movements, her facial expressions. When she'd delivered the news to Claire and Glen in person at their house, she seemed downright buoyant, even as she urged keeping their expectations from running wild. She now smiled encouragingly.

"Mrs. Rawlings?"

Claire cleared her throat. "There is no evidence of my older daughter at the scene of the accident. She may have escaped. Or been given to"—Claire paused momentarily—"sold to someone else." A quiet gasp rose from the audience. "We believe she is still alive."

Jodi took over. "We have someone joining us today, a child psychiatrist from Northwestern University Hospital, Dr. Howard Fisher."

They had been told an expert would be phoning in, not sharing the stage with them. Somehow, the idea of a child psychiatrist seemed terribly unsettling. This Howard Fisher wrestled onto the stage with a three-footed cane. He was thick and short, grandfatherly. But shadowed by the lights, his deep-set eyes were unreadable. His presence seemed to give lumpy shape to the scarier emotions clamoring inside Claire. She needed positive information, good news.

"Can you tell us your thoughts from a professional perspective, after reviewing the circumstances?" Jodi was referring to Lily's autopsy report.

Clive looked down at prepared notes. "Weren't there drugs involved?"

Dr. Fisher's deep steady voice echoed across the stage. "Aside from a traumatic brain injury—possibly heat stroke—traces of some pretty powerful chemicals were found in the little girl's body. Lily and most likely her older sister, Andrea"—he paused before continuing—"were exposed to mind-altering drugs, drugs that can effectively erase memory. At least in the short term."

The audience was riveted. Claire's eyes flashed over to him, searching for sympathy. But he was either too far away or too focused on the camera to notice. She suddenly despised this man for making a spectacle of her children.

"Please continue, Dr. Fisher." Jodi's voice radiated concern.

"From a therapeutic standpoint, there's something else as well." He paused and cleared his throat. "According to research, traumatic memories in children have a number of unusual qualities. They are not encoded in a verbal linear narrative as they are in adults. Rather, they may take on the form of vivid sensations and images. These often override memories of cherished events in the past, or even of loved ones."

"In other words"—Jodi turned to Claire—"if your other daughter is found, she may not know who she is? May not even recognize you?"

This was Claire's fear realized, brought to life in words. Beyond death itself, or even—God help her—sexual abuse, the worst thing possible would be that Andrea, when found, would somehow no longer be hers, that her memory and thus all ties to her family had been destroyed. She moved her mouth to speak. Nothing came out.

Glen cut in. "We don't care if she remembers us right away. We just want our little girl back. We hope to find her quickly. We will look everywhere. The longer this goes on, the slimmer our chances…"

He didn't finish.

Claire was losing momentum. She could feel it. She needed someone to stand up for her. To announce to the viewers that, at one time, she had been superwoman, managing it all: med school, a happy marriage, and most important, being a really great mom.

Discussion droned on, with the expert forming words that Claire could simply no longer perceive. Finally, Clive looked into the camera.

"This is why it is so important for us all to memorize this little girl's face."

Andrea's picture filled the screen; it was the one Claire had given Jay White. Claire dabbed the corner of one eye, but there were no tears. Not now. The intensity of this public situation was wringing her dry.

Thankfully, Jodi kept her attention on Glen. "Turns out he may have been a transient, a vagabond of some sort. The FBI is still sorting this out—trying to ID him, locate his family."

"Turns out he might be a transient, a vagabond of some sort."

Glen focused on the police sketch, now flashing on the monitor, which was in turn replaced by a live shot of Claire. She was stunned by her appearance. That very morning, she and Vicki had gone through a hundred changes of clothes together, trying to get this right.

"How about this one, hon?" Vicki had held up a mauve blouse with mother-of-pearl buttons.

She tried that. And then the olive-green turtleneck after. One by one, her closet emptied of outfits. Nothing looked right. Because Claire no longer looked like herself. The weight loss had drawn her face into something severe and her coloring was sallow. She finally decided on a navy knit sweater. It seemed like a good choice at the time, but now she was concerned it might make her appear harsh to the people at home watching. The very same people who would magically divulge where Andrea was last seen. Thankfully, Claire detected murmurings, small bits of sympathy palpable in the room.

Clive was out among the studio audience, weaving up and down the aisles to field questions. A large man with thick silver hair stood to express support. A retired teacher, he loved kids. "Just wanted to say"—he removed and wiped his glasses—"that I'm sorry for what you've been through."

Claire glanced toward Hearns. She gave a thumbs-up look. Not a hand gesture—that wasn't Hearns at all. But a look. Claire flushed with appreciation bordering on love for the detective, for the audience. This was something, right? Something good. A woman waved Clive over to her seat along the aisle. She was thick, frumpy. It took an embarrassing minute to lift her heavy body out of the chair. But Claire liked her face. She liked the faces of everyone assembled today. They were going to help her find Andrea.

"If you don't mind, Mrs. Rawlings, I'd like to know, as a mother, I mean, do you feel any guilt about leaving your girls in the car?"

"Excuse me?" Clive rocked back on his tall man-heels, acting like he was aghast. But he wasn't. This was good drama.

Claire was stunned. How could this woman, or anyone for that matter, understand the burning guilt that was nibbling her apart piece by tiny piece, in a very literal sense consuming her body. She looked frantically at Glen, who responded with a confused expression of his own. Sensing his hurt, Claire quaked with outrage and leaned forward tightening her voice into a defensive weapon. "That is the most inapprop—"

Glen squeezed her hand, meaning: *Stop it, Claire.*

"Ma'am…" Glen cleared his throat and squinted a little. He gushed with understanding, diplomacy. "This was no accident. This…this…predator would've found a way to get our girls." His voice dropped lower. "We—I—am convinced of it."

Claire knew this wasn't true. Any of it. Glen wanted to strangle this woman but instead chose to manufacture the emotion he needed for their daughter. Claire loved him for that, hated that she couldn't do it herself. But the worst thing was that this woman's question had exposed the truth that Glen refused to name, the thing that was driving his swingy moods: this was her fault and they both knew it. Her stomach laddered upward toward her chest, and she feared she might be sick.

Jodi gestured to Clive. "We will be back in one minute."

A commercial break. The momentary respite her stomach needed to settle back down. A quick signal was given and Dr. Fisher lumbered from the stage and disappeared into the wings. That, too, was a relief. But now Claire found it awkward to sit in silence in front of the naked lights while the audience stared.

"I feel like a salamander," she murmured under her breath.

"What?" Glen turned to her, barely hiding his exasperation.

She wanted to tell him that if you touch a salamander, the acid from your hands will literally burn it. And she now felt as if she were being touched by a thousand hands.

The cameras flared back up, and urged by a stage manager, the audience started clapping again. It was short and tense. This wasn't the time for perceived joviality.

C'mon, we need more support here.

Claire scanned the crowd. Hearns was looking down at

something. Maybe at her pager? Vicki's head darted from side to side as if in disbelief. Her hand shot into the air. She'd straighten this situation out.

But a petite woman with a generous face beat her to Clive's attention. "This is such a terribly sad story. It just breaks my heart. I've been watching, you know, following along since August. You're in my prayers. I take care of little ones and…"

Clive pulled the mic back. He engaged another person and then went on to someone, and then someone else after that. But Claire had faded, was almost dizzy. She felt she could tell what these women were thinking, could easily read it in their tight, little expressions. What kind of mother would've done this?

Jodi cut in. "So sorry, but time is close to up. One last statement from our parents?"

It was Glen who had the final word, bringing the discussion home with a plea.

"Please help us. Find our Andrea. Her fifth birthday is in two months. We'd like to celebrate it with her at home."

Claire's heart swelled at how Glen was able to do this—talk about Andrea in the present tense with no hesitation.

Glen continued, "She has the most beautiful brown eyes and"— his voice wavered, then strengthened—"we will look forever, as long as it takes, to find our daughter. Anywhere…in the world… We just want her back."

Andrea's picture and the hotline number came up on the monitor. Try as she might, Claire couldn't muster tears. Not public ones. Hers were rough-edged, internal, grinding through her very bones.

Claire turned to Detective Hearns for support, but her chair was empty. A small panic ignited inside. Probably someone else's emergency. *Silly Claire.* That woman was busy. There were other people in the world with problems, other crimes to be solved.

With the show concluded, Vicki met her backstage. "You did great," she said, but her eyes suggested otherwise.

"Where's Detective Hearns?"

"Dunno. She got a message. Said it was urgent and left." Vicki glanced at her wristwatch with a worried look. "Sorry, hon, I have to stop in at Troy's mother's. I promised. I'll be home later. Hopefully before the bad weather."

Claire hugged her sister, grateful for her presence. "Be safe, Vicki."

Glen came out of the bathroom, his expression granite, eyes averted. They walked to the parking garage without a word.

In the car, he finally spoke.

"What the hell, Claire? You almost went off on that person in the audience. I mean, I'm always the one picking up the pieces. And…"

"What?"

He pulled his hair from his forehead and then slammed the gearshift into Drive. "Nothing."

"Glen. Can you just say it?" Claire felt herself wilting. "Can you just say that you blame me?"

He didn't reply. Yet his face rippled with tightened muscles. Claire waited until they were on the highway to bridge this gulf between them, to break through the terrible tension. "Glen. Andrea is…"

"Don't say it. I already know. Out there somewhere. We just have to find her. The goddamn thing is this: I've looked into private detectives. International ones. They cost money, Claire. A lot." His voice deepened with controlled rage. "My salary doesn't come close to covering such a thing. It barely makes the house payment. You need to finish med school. You could be done in, what, half a year? Then we'd have some leverage. I asked at the bank. We can get loans until then—but only if you're back in the program. We'll be buried otherwise, Claire. Buried alive financially."

What was he talking about? Return to work? How was that even possible? Of course, she knew they were facing an avalanche of debt. Med school tuition was equivalent to buying three new BMWs a year. For four or five years. It was beyond imagining when they had signed for the loans. But at the time, they could easily guarantee that they'd pay them off, no worries. Unless, the loan officer had chuckled, some untoward disaster or act of God occurred.

However, what Glen was asking felt inconceivable. What Glen didn't say was that Claire owed him this. She locked her jaw and made a promise to herself. She didn't care how much Glen pushed; she wouldn't go back. Not until Andrea was found. Otherwise, it would be as if she were abandoning her girls a second time. She kept silent, with her eyes on the road.

Two exits down, they were forced into a detour and ended up going the wrong way when they got back on the highway. By that time, rush hour was gumming up the roadways and the storm Vicki mentioned was kicking into gear.

Once in their neighborhood, Glen brought the car to a crawl among drifts rising like bread dough. Cones of light from the streetlamps were shaggy with falling snow. Andrea could be out in this somewhere. *Please God*, Claire prayed, *keep her warm*. They managed their way into the house and sealed themselves in. There was no talk of dinner. Claire only remembered to feed Gretchie when she found her licking plates in the open dishwasher. The boxer looked up with generous coin purses for eyes, as if to say, *I'll be okay.*

Butkus was a different story. He cackled angrily and shuffled along his perch, demonstrating his displeasure at their return.

Just as Glen switched on the TV, headlights danced across their picture window. Claire rubbed a spot of condensation and peeked through the pane expecting to see Vicki's rental car. But a different vehicle materialized through the strobing precipitation.

"Glen. It's Detective Hearns."

Claire watched her husband as he met the detective at the door. He would, she knew, be trying to read her expression quickly, trying to discern the reason she was in their house, off duty, in this weather. Hearns entered crackling with snow and cold, her mood subdued.

"I wanted to tell you something we just learned. In person. Maybe we should all sit down."

The detective half crouched awkwardly in a swivel chair, an old piece of furniture donated by Glen's parents. Gretchie had claimed it recently after they'd somehow misplaced her dog bed. Hearns's face went from solemn to distressed. Claire and Glen waited on the couch. Catatonic.

"Remember I told you about the search effort supported by the FBI? Near that ravine where we discovered the Taurus?"

Claire pictured it, desolate, menacing trees naked in the season. "Is the storm causing a problem?"

"Actually…" Hearns slowed her speech. "I got the call during the show today. They found more evidence."

The room filled with phantoms, ghostly creatures dancing in the weirdish glow of the TV. Glen got up and snapped it off. The gray outside spilled into the room. Claire was glad he didn't switch on a lamp. More light would make it all worse, would define Hearns in contrast to the things around her, the drapes, the end table, the plastic plant. Not seeing Hearns's face made her a free-floating voice. Somehow less difficult to comprehend.

"Not too far, five miles maybe, from the car. Just over the border into Wisconsin. The FBI found a hidden plot of land with a small cabin. Looks like the kidnapper may have been there after he left Lily. And then in an attempt to escape, took off and the car ended at the bottom of the river."

"What?" Claire couldn't make sense of any of this. First, Lily half-buried along a roadside. Then, months later, the Taurus emerges some forty miles north in a ravine. Where was Andrea?

"Claire, Glen, there's been a discovery." Juanita hesitated and then continued. "Fibers. Blue chambray. They match the description of"—she swallowed—"the charm dress."

Claire gasped.

"I'm sorry. This is so hard." The detective proceeded with words that seemed as though she were stepping through broken glass. "Apparently…apparently, there was a fire of some sort near this cabin. Like a bonfire. Materials were burned—charred—pretty bad. Found in a crude outdoor…well, oven. A goddamn outdoor oven."

The windows were whitening by the minute. It could easily bury them alive, this snow.

Glen groaned.

"I'm so sorry," Hearns continued. "And—"

"That's it?" Claire interrupted. "Fibers? Some material? That's nothing. I don't care about some burned fabric. Andrea's alive. I just know it."

"There's more—" Detective Hearns spoke softly.

But Claire cut her off again. "My daughter is alive," she said, as if Andrea were hers alone; Glen somehow didn't factor into this now that she could feel his belief slipping away. "Out there somewhere." She made a grand sweeping gesture toward the window.

"Cut it out, Claire," Glen said flatly.

How could this be true? What about Lily's light? The certainty with which Jay White had said Andrea was alive? Claire choked with anger, disbelief.

Glen looked at her with disbelief of his own. Only his was directed at the ridiculous woman who had caused all this pain.

"Calm down," Glen barked. "Calm the hell down."

"Claire." Juanita struggled to hold her voice steady. "I know this is hard. But I need to tell you more…"

Hearns could say what she liked, but Claire knew her daughter. She'd escaped that car accident. She'd run away from that Charcoal Monster. Remained hidden all these months.

Claire stood up. "We need to go look for her. In those…those woods… She'll be cold." She faced the door. "Freezing… She's almost five. She can do this…"

"A fragment, too." Juanita raised her voice. It was necessary in order to speak over Claire. "Of a tooth. In the ashes. It matches Andrea's." The detective's voice wavered. "The one you gave us when the girls were abducted."

"God." Glen put his head down to his knees. "Oh God."

Claire rocked backward. She pressed her hands to her face. "My little girl…"

Gretchie, tail down, crawled to Claire and whimpered as she licked Claire's arm.

Glen groaned again.

The detective was openly crying.

They sat, unmoving, like creatures caught unaware and frozen in place. The detective stayed with them as long as she possibly could before standing and gathering her coat closed.

"I really have to go. Before it gets worse. I can't tell you how…" She wiped her eyes. "I'm just so sorry, Claire and Glen."

Claire didn't get up. Glen did, though, and walked Hearns to the door. The wind practically carried him away, as though he were standing near a hole in the wall of a plane at cruising altitude. He slammed the door behind the detective and then fell forward, pounding his fist into the doorframe.

Vicki arrived not much later. The scene must've looked like some sort of a massacre had occurred. Two people drained of blood, drained of life really, yet somehow still alive. She cried with them, but Claire remained stiff during her hugs. She wouldn't accept any comfort she didn't deserve.

The snow kept coming and then abruptly halted at midnight, leaving gleaming piles and drifts throughout the yard and driveway. Claire didn't know how, but she ended up alone on her and Glen's bed with Gretchie stretched longitudinally against her, touching her with as much dog as possible. Glen stayed in the living room with the TV on low volume, droning through infomercials. Claire must've fallen asleep because she dreamed. She was in the sky, floating. Miles above the earth. And then she began to drop like a stone through inky black silence. The earth, rushing closer, was the most sparkling shade of sapphire blue. In her dream, she closed her eyes and prepared for the inevitable, the terrible impact.

Claire whiplashed awake.

The clock on the nightstand read 3:00 a.m. She went to the window. The backyard was blanketed in white, layered like a torte, the top crusted like sugar. What was that she was seeing? Snow angels! Fifty in total, maybe more—the yard was covered with them. It would've taken her girls half the night to make these, their small bodies pressed into the powder like footprints in sand or bottle caps in clay. Claire wrapped herself in a short terry-cloth robe and stepped out onto the porch, then down into the yard, touching each indentation, each perfectly fan-shaped crater where one of her girls had laid flapping her legs and arms like wings.

How clever of Andrea to give the angels personalities! Some looked frantic, edged with mounds caused by the kicking up of hastily removed snow, while others were luxuriously delicate. And then there were Lily's, shallowly pressed into the fluffy powder.

How her girls loved to play in the snow.

Claire felt an arm at her waist and a hand on her shoulder. Glen. He led gently, turning her toward the house.

"No, no, I can't leave. They're so beautiful. So very beautiful."

But her bare feet burned with an icy fire, and as she stumbled into the house, they were numb. Vicki appeared in the living room surrounded by night silence. She and Glen sat on either side of Claire.

"The angels are a sign from them, from Lily and Andrea," Claire said. "Don't you see? She's still alive, Andrea is alive."

"Jesus, Claire," Glen said. "Be real. Both girls are gone."

"No, no, it can't be," Claire moaned.

"Honey," Vicki said softly, wrapping her in an afghan and rubbing the circulation back into her feet. "What you saw were little drifts. An illusion created by moonlight on the fresh snow."

Claire sat, unmoving.

"Glen," Vicki whispered. "I have an idea. Can you open a window in your bedroom?"

They escorted Claire to the bedroom, one on either side of her. Vicki coaxed her to the window and helped Claire to place her head out into the freezing night air. Claire coughed. Her breath surrounded her like a cloud of white ash, and her nostrils stung.

"See?" Vicki urged. "It's a trick of the eyes."

Claire looked around at the quilted mess in her yard, the jagged footprints going forward and then back—large, boxy chunks of snow displaced by some kind of skirmish with one or two people, maybe three. Her sister was right: bodies as small as her girls' couldn't create such deep indents in that type of snow, thick as cotton batting yet unforgiving as cement. But still…

"Claire, look at the moon." Vicki's voice was encouraging. Claire understood this was an effort to anchor her back into the world as everyone else saw it. She searched the sky and found what Vicki was calling the moon, a large, gleaming spot of milk on a dark wood tabletop, spilled in June by Andrea when they'd celebrated Glen's father's birthday at his parents' soon-to-be-sold condo in Evanston. The shape wavered in the air. Yes, she saw it now; it really was as Vicki said. Gretchie licked the back of Claire's leg with her soft warm tongue. But it did not console her.

Claire pulled away from the window and looked at Glen. His eyes were enlarged, shining.

"Tell me, Glen. Is it true? Are both of our girls gone?" A long minute past and then Claire's voice broke. "Did I do this to us?"

Glen dropped his head into his hands and responded. Not with words, but with guttural sounds that grew into an aural storm, as deep and marred as the snow outside.

PART TWO

———◦———

Four Years Later

Chapter 12
Colly

A ch! Out of that tree!"

Aha! Colly just knew she was being spied on. And from her own room no less. When she and Moira first moved to this part of Indiana, she'd discovered that the towering jack pine next to her room was the perfect spot for practicing sleight of hand tricks, only with acorns instead of coins. In the lower branches, she could keep a watchful eye on her new Barbie who was sunning on a rock in her neon-pink bikini. An internal alarm rang when she saw weeds parting at the edge of the yard. This was the preferred pathway for that nasty neighbor kid.

"You'll kill yourself, Colly."

Colly looked over. She could see Moira's face behind the screen, strained with concern, piercing eyes deep in their sockets surrounded by dark hair tumbling around her head like a mess of coils. Her voice, tinged with brogue, rang through the curtains. They weren't real curtains, of course, but pillowcases tacked over the windows to help screen the bugs, the biting kind with black bodies and shiny green heads, that seemed to find every little snag in the wiry mesh to pop through. The kind that left tiny volcanoes of itchy skin when they were done.

"Please, *serku*."

Serku meant *daughter*. Moira only used that word when she was really scared—as in anything to do with heights—or really happy. But she wasn't Colly's mother. Had actually rescued Colly from druggie parents that tried to sell her. And then they died in a crash. But Colly didn't know more. It upset Moira too much to talk about.

Colly went a branch higher.

She hoped Moira wasn't messing with her stuff. In addition to paints and drawing material, she had a number of collections: wild berries from the woods set out to dry on the TV tray she'd scavenged on garbage day. A shoebox of pinecones sorted with greenies on one side, fully opened brown fans on the other. Acorns, a particular favorite, hard shelled and rigid as clams, were stored safely in a hinged cigar box under her bed, only to "magically" appear on the bathroom floor, giving Moira a surprise or two when she stepped out of the shower. Now Moira never went without sandals. Colly, for her part, abhorred anything on her feet, which were calloused like exoskeletons, a term she had gleaned from the *National Geographic* magazines she devoured.

"Jesu, Mary, and Joseph. Come down now."

"Oka-ay."

Aligning for a dismount, Colly set her stomach to the trunk, dug her fingers into the corduroy-like bark, and wrapped her legs around the tree's girth. She needed to come down anyway, confront that pudgy booger before he caused trouble.

"Don't jump, Colly. By God, don't do it!"

She imagined Moira crossing herself as she hitched her shoulder blades into wings and let go, free-falling the eight or so feet, bringing Moira's stomach—she was certain—along for the ride. Twisting in midair, she landed in a swell of pine needles, soft-pawed and flushed with accomplishment.

"You're giving me a heart attack!" The rusty window grated along its track. "Come in now and help me gather the laundry." The window slammed shut like a resounding period at the end of a sentence.

But Colly wasn't bothering with Moira. Chubby had gotten his grubby mitts on Barbie, snagged before there was time to fill her in on the hazards of trailer park life. Colly wiped her palms, smeared with dark pitch from the tree, onto her cutoffs and faced the kid.

"Give her back."

"Sure," the boy sneered. "For a dollar."

"I mean it."

"One dollar." His eyes ran up and down. "What are you, some kind of freak? You and Barbie with the same hairdo!"

Despite Moira's protestations, Colly managed her own hair, had chopped it short so it stuck out like porcupine quills. Today, it was purpled from a paste of Kool-Aid powder she'd run by the fingerful through the stubby strands. Along with two missing bottom teeth, it gave her a clownish quality. Colly didn't mind his insult. At eight-and-a-half, she kept her own counsel, followed up on her own ideas.

She eyed her doll, suspended cruelly by her bright-toned hair that Colly had dipped in food coloring the moment she'd been brought home. It was almost a weakness, Colly's love of color. Behind her, tree trunks were patterned with enormous swaths of pastel chalk, her work from earlier that day.

"*Gort muilsha sik*—I said, give her back."

"What did you just say?"

Colly bit her lip, angry with herself for this breach. The deeply engrained rule was to keep their lives, especially their language, a secret. Avoid attention at all costs. The authorities might take her back to the people who'd paid for her.

"Weirdo. Ha-ha."

Colly could see gapped teeth inside his mouth, which was ringed with grape juice and dirt. Barbie remained prisoner in his unrelenting grip, stiffly holding her own.

She briefly considered calling to Moira for backup but knew she needed to handle this on her own. Moira hated anything to do with neighbors or people in general. Besides, she disapproved of this Barbie, a cheap purchase at a garage sale the day before.

"You don't want that doll, Colly," Moira had said. "Look, she's damaged. Someone's been at her face with a knife!"

"Moira." Colly spoke with insistent authority. "I'll make her good as new. You'll see." She dropped two quarters on the table, a bargain as far as Colly was concerned.

While Barbie's nose indeed had been gouged off, Colly planned reconstructive surgery later that day with a pinch of dried Play-Doh and glue. She'd done this type of thing before and found the results passable, admirable, even. But now, Barbie was close to losing her bathing suit as she dangled from the creep's hand, creased at the wrist with dirt and chub. He was one of those whose mother shouted at dinnertime from rickety aluminum porch steps, his name joining the others that bounced among the trailers, rattling like tin cans, the syllables spread thin as margarine on toast.

"Toh-ho-mmy!" or "Roh-hob-bie!"

The kids, one faceless mass to Colleen, dashed off in a mad scramble to get home, eat their supper, and laze in front of the TV until bedtime. Colly had no official bedtime or suppertime. There were days when it was only Wonder Bread and watery milk from powder. She fended for herself. Because they stayed on the move—Moira's jobs only lasted a short time, and never paid much—it meant grabbing what you could when no one was looking. Always careful to, as Moira put it, "avoid pryin' eyes."

Aside from remaining wary of outsiders, Colly was free to do as she pleased. And it pleased her to be in the trailer as little as possible. The black-and-white TV provided little interest anyway. Colly had better things to do: sift through the woods and fields near their trailer, rifle through her beloved secondhand *National Geographic* magazines, or draw the landscapes that lived in her head, putting them to paper with crayons, chalk, water paints, whatever was handy. It was these treasures, carefully hoarded and sorted, that she feared Moira might mess up. But right then she needed to liberate this new Barbie. She hadn't even had time to name her. A name was a shining coin, a precious medal to carry with you. Barbie's would have to be properly considered.

"What do you have to say, Skinny Minnie?"

Colly caught a glimpse of herself in the chrome edging on the trailer. Pale and thin to the point of bony, with dark serious eyes, she was aware she sported dimples when she smiled. She faced the boy straight on. He began circling, swinging the doll wildly. She sized him up. He was a head taller than her, but he'd be slow with all that pudge. She ignored his taunting and focused on his back pocket and the small bulge in his dirty beige shorts. Probably a pocketknife. His best treasure, no doubt.

She couldn't wait too long to make her move. Today was one of her sluggish days; she was wracked with sporadic light-headedness. When it happened, it was as if her very blood lingered in her veins. Moira said it was Colly's picky eating, but Colly sensed it went deeper. She shook her head, sweeping away the stars that danced in her eyes.

Squinting into a shaft of sunlight, Colly made an awkward move forward and stumbled right into the bully. He clawed frantically to break free of their awkward dance. As they floundered, Colly seized the opportunity to slip her hand into his pocket. He staggered onto his heels and then shoved her away.

"Get off of me!" the bully cried. Barbie swayed and a bikini strap slipped down her slick plastic arm. The worst thing would be that her private parts would show, and the disgusting brat would see it and leer.

But Colly sighed loudly with satisfied relief and fixed her gaze at his pants.

The boy suddenly stopped. Looking down, he could see a smudgy handprint of black pitch from Colly's palm outlined near his pocket.

"Ew! You touched me!" His eyes narrowed as he held Barbie aloft like a football. "Fun's over. Prepare to launch!" Arm cocked, he took aim at the towering treetops. "Get ready." He hesitated dramatically, preparing to spiral the hapless doll into oblivion. "'Cause thar she blows!"

Colly smiled. A big, gaping, disarming grin. Running her tongue over her teeth, she tasted a full mouth of warm pancakes. With strawberry jam. The bully stopped and looked at her, confused by this change in her demeanor. Colly extended her right arm, hand tightly fisted. Turning her palm up, she opened her hand to reveal a small pocketknife, no bigger than an Indiana grasshopper. It was smudged with pinesap from her hand.

"Hey, how did you get that?" The boy's eyes widened and he

bit his bottom lip. His grip on Barbie loosened as he groped at his pants pockets.

"Magician's trick. Now you see it." Colly wrapped her fingers around the knife and pulled both hands behind her. "Now you don't."

The kid dropped Barbie into the dust. She landed with her head tilted at just the right angle to stare, unblinking, at Colly with her tiny blue points of eyes. Colly's stomach stirred with butterflies.

The boy's chin quivered.

"Hey. That's mine. Give it back!"

"You need to say the right word."

"Er, I'm sorry?"

"Nope." Colly waved both fists magician-like in front of his face.

"Please?" he pleaded. "Thank you?"

"Nope and nope." Colly opened her left hand, gave him a glimpse of the weapon, and then, just as quickly, closed her fingers again. "I guess it's mine to keep, huh?"

The screech of the window sliding on its tracks cut through the tension. "That's enough," Moira called through the screen. "Give him his knife. You've got what you wanted."

Colly cocked her head, considering Moira's interference. Had she been watching all along?

"Ach…what did I say?"

Colly hesitated before dropping the knife into the dirt. The boy immediately grabbed his property and scampered off. She considered chasing after him.

"Come in now," Moira said, defusing the charged energy. "We're off to the laundromat."

Colly picked up Barbie, wiped her hair, and arranged her bikini properly with gentle hands. Looking into her rescued doll's face, Colly's front left tooth suddenly ached and she touched her finger to her lip.

What if Moira was wrong and her real parents had somehow lived?

It was a thought she had more and more. The pain of it scurried down her throat and poked at the edge of her rib cage. What was her real name? The one she was given when she was born? She drew air sharply. Colleen shortened to Colly. A name that somehow had never fit. She was already clever with cursive—homeschooled by Moira when she had time, her signature carefully executed with the two middle *l*'s rising tall above the other letters, like bunny ears high on alert—yet she was reluctant to write *Colly* with conviction, holding back on her best penmanship, saving the careful strokes instead for her artwork.

The sky pressed down. Even the beautiful rich scent of pine seemed unwelcomingly heavy as if sap, too, were in the air. Every time she imagined her birth parents, confused thoughts came like urgent crickets in the last of summer. She tried to pull a curtain against the hidden chorus, but they kept singing as if they didn't have a season. What if her parents had just somehow lost her?

At night, when this longing ran deep, she could swear something brushed against her in the darkness, just after she'd cried herself out and sleep was settling in. It felt like reassurance, the softest of touches—like a true mother's caress.

"I have to say, Colly"—Moira's voice was polished with pride—"you are something clever. A true clannie."

Moira loved explaining her family traditions: not only the myths about selkies and wee folk in the woods, but the "rules" about how people were untrustworthy or how—*for God's sake, Colly, at least try*—to dress, act, and speak without drawing attention. So where were these people? Moira's family? Only phantoms to Colly. Knowing that she didn't really belong to Moira, Colly sometimes felt like an uninvited guest in the stories. When she turned toward the window, the glass was filled with a blank curtain and nothing else.

Once inside the trailer, Colly set Barbie against the pillow on her cot. "You stay here today," she whispered softly. "You need a little time off."

Then she pitched in to help assemble several baskets of clothing and towels. Colly and Moira enjoyed their trips to the laundromat. Moira got to relax while the machines tumbled their clothes and Colly loved freshly laundered things, all of which she carefully arranged into stacks by color and size. It created a small oasis of calm and orderliness in the chaos of their household.

General Hospital, Moira's favorite show, blared over the blur and snow on the TV until she snapped it off—reaching to the switch with her long fingers. To Colly, she looked like something close to a cartoon scarecrow, all thin lines and angles.

"Take this out to the car for me, eh." Moira set a bulging plastic basket at Colly's feet. "I've opened the trunk."

Colly staggered down the front stairs with the bulk. She stopped at the car and set the basket heavily at the edge of their ancient Buick. Closed, dark spaces in general were scary enough, but there was something about the trunk in particular that made her heart pound. She heaved the load up and forward but the flimsy weave caught on the latch, spilling the contents unceremoniously into the deep well.

"Good thing it's all dirty," Moira called from the doorway.

Colly gathered up the scattered towels and clothing. She needed to dig into the deep recess to retrieve them all. The taste of hard, dry licorice filled her mouth.

"I can see you missed some. Can you get in deeper?"

Colly groaned.

"Remember, good workers get rewards." Moira's voice sifted through the air. There was only one reward in Colly's mind. Root beer. From the machine at the laundromat where you reached in and grabbed an ice-cold bottle.

She stood on tiptoes and leaned into the trunk, reaching with all her might. One item in particular, a troublemaker, was much farther down than the others. She struggled to wrench it free from under the spare tire. When she finally held it in her grasp, she almost laughed. All that work for nothing. While Colly kept rags to help with her painting and art projects, this one was practically useless, nothing more than a square of torn fabric. She held it eye level in a shaft of sun punching through the leaves overhead. Heavily spotted with grease, she couldn't even make out the color. Light blue or white, it looked like it might have been torn from a small stretch of hem, an old dress maybe.

"Hey, Moira, where's this from?" But Moira had disappeared inside. She returned a moment later with a second basket of laundry.

"Help me load this one too. Let's get on!"

Colly tossed the small rag into the first basket of clothing without another thought. She grabbed the other one from Moira and hoisted it carefully to set beside the other. After slamming the trunk closed, she hopped into the car. As usual, Moira's hand fluttered awkwardly when she tried to insert the key into the ignition. It took three tries for her to finally get the engine going, and no sooner had they headed out when she cursed and swung the car into a parking space alongside a neighbor's double-wide.

"*Blanog.*" Moira slapped her hand against the steering wheel. "Forgot the detergent."

But her tone brightened as she peered through the windshield. "By Jesu, Colly, do ya see that?" She pointed to a box, stowed behind the porch in a blanket of shade. It read *Sunny River Citrus* on the side in taffy-pink lettering. A delivery notice flapped on the door.

"You sit tight and give a little honk if you see anyone comin'."

Moira dashed out and, stealthy as a badger, grabbed the box. She stumbled under the load as she scurried toward the trunk.

"Oranges, Colly! Hurry. Pop the latch," she ordered, scooting past the open car window.

Colly climbed forward into the front seat, did as she was told, and then scaled back over while Moira slipped the crate into the trunk. Colleen felt a small thrill at the theft, followed by a wave of concern. Wasn't this wrong?

And who'd eat all this? Moira knew that Colly had a specific relationship with fruit. She preferred it in a can. Was, in fact, madly in love with the neon-red cherries in snack-sized fruit cocktail. Oranges stuck in her teeth and made her mouth feel fuzzy. But she had her sights set on root beer today. She kept her mouth shut.

Moira retrieved the detergent and they were finally on their way. Passing the trailer park office, a little red building no bigger than a shack and just as rickety, the manager, a woman with a squarish face and a stump nose, flagged them down.

"Hiya in there."

"*Bider a hyna krish blandg.*" Moira slapped her game face on as the woman approached.

"That's not very nice, Moira, calling someone a cow."

"Hush, she'll hear us." Moira snickered, batting her hand in Colly's direction. "And Jeezus if not a cow, then a piggy for certain." She rolled down the window and smiled. "Is there a problem?" Moira spoke nonchalantly. Yet she had placed a foot on both the gas and brake. Colly knew this trick; it kept the car idling high, and the whining sound gave people a sense of urgency.

"No, just wanted to ask ya something's all." She leaned into the car and nodded to Colly. "Was wonderin' 'bout that picture."

She pointed to a small painting leaning against the side of the plastic chair where she had just been sitting. One of Colly's creations. A doodle fest really. Some vegetables she'd sketched out and then filled with fluorescent markers. Ruby-hued radishes and an eggplant, purple as a bruise. She'd copied it from the cover of an old *Good Housekeeping* magazine pilfered the last time they visited the laundromat. The real fun for Colly, though, was the things she'd hidden in the vegetables and their leafy tops. A tiny world of fantastical camouflaged creatures, some scaled, one feathered in bright green. A topsy-turvy world filled with dogs with wings, birds with wagging tails. You had to look close to see it. This picture was one of her favorites, and Colly was hurt that Moira had thrown it out.

Moira held her breath. Colly could almost hear her saying, "What's it to ya, lady?"

"It's real good. Saved it, as you can see. Hope ya don't mind. Got any more like it? There's a craft store in Michiana, 'bout two hours north of here, in Michigan." Colly felt Moira's relief. "You can get 'bout seven dollars for that picture."

Moira's face lit up. She pulled her foot from the gas. "Really? I mean, oh yes, that was a mistake by the way—throwin' it out. We have plenty more where that came from." She turned to Colly with big eyes. "Don't we, Colly?" Moira threw a look into the rearview mirror. Colly nodded. Colly could tell Moira was already counting money in her head. "How many of those can you do in a week?"

The woman wiped the sweat gathering at the edges of her face. "Course, I wouldn't mind a bit of a finder's fee."

A pickup glowered on their rear, its engine revving impatiently. "I'll stop in later," Moira said to the woman with exaggerated pleasantness as they pulled away. "You hear that, Colly? Sounds like you'll have some work to do, *serku*."

The whole car percolated with Moira's excitement. Colly didn't mind the idea of painting pictures for money. It actually sounded like fun.

"This works out, maybe hot dogs for dinner more often." Moira winked into the mirror.

In the laundromat, detergent in hand, Colly felt the humidity and sweet odor of fabric softener enfold her like a burrito, a favorite food and rare treat. A lone rotating fan shook its head slowly from side to side as if to indicate the futility of trying to move the thick air.

"Root beer!" Colly held her hand out greedily. "It's still fifty cents here!"

"I swear, Colleen, you are addicted."

"You promised," Colly said sweetly and yet with authority.

"Okay, okay." Moira handed Colly two quarters to use in an old-fashioned soda machine just outside the door. She returned with an opened glass bottle in one hand, the crimped cap in another.

Waiting for the wash cycle to complete, Moira fanned herself with an ancient *People* magazine left lying at the far end of a folding table.

Colly approached, grinning.

"Do you see the bottle cap?"

"Mmm-hmm." Moira nodded, too distracted by the magazine to show interest in the item Colly presented in her palm.

"Now you see it." Colly closed her hand, bumped her fists together. "Abracadabra! Now you don't."

"Okay, Houdini. Let's get the dryers fired up or we'll be here all day."

Colly wandered off to explore the crannies between the machines. She might find a dropped coin or two. But there were only lint balls the size of mice. Behind the garbage can, she discovered a box half full of dryer sheets. There was a time when other people's laundry stuff had fascinated her and she'd approached Moira, inquiring about fabric softener after opening and smelling the empty bottles rich with the remnants of perfume-y liquid.

"That"—Moira sniffed—"is the smell of money. Wasted money."

Colly ran her hand along a rough, square dryer sheet. A furry odor filled her nostrils, fake, heavy, unpleasant. Moira was right. She tossed it in the trash. It had been over an hour and she was bored. The heat and gauzy air kicked Colleen's thirst up again. She circled over to Moira.

"Look, the first dryer is done, Colly. You get started on those towels. I'll do the sheets when they come out."

"There's shirts in there too, Moira." The well-worn clothing they got mainly from the Goodwill.

"Yup."

"Just saying that they require a little extra effort folding…"

"So?"

"So it's a tough job when you're thirsty. A bit more root beer might help move it along."

"You little rascal. We'll just see what kind of a job you do before I decide to spend more precious money on your habit." But Moira struggled to contain her smile stoked with pride.

Colly tended dutifully to the basket, focusing first on the warm towels, wrapping the rectangles into thirds like fat, stuffed sausages. Moira remained several feet away sorting through steamy sheets. Colly grabbed a washcloth and found the small rag that she'd retrieved from the trunk earlier. It clicked with static as she separated it from a towel. Although still stained, it was clean enough to now see that it was blue, almost like jean material, only softer. She held it arm's length in front of her. A sudden tingle of energy rushed from her fingertips and up through her spine. For a moment stars flashed, then vanished.

Colly instinctively turned her back to Moira. The rag had clearly been torn, as three sides were tattered. But a small hem remained on one side. She fingered the edge and discovered a surprising little lump. When she squeezed it, she could make out a smooth oval shape no larger than a dime hidden within the hem. She hunched a little, a small gesture of privacy, and pinched against the lump in the fabric. It moved.

She continued to work it, pushing it behind one edge in the way that a boa constrictor swallows a pig. Within a minute, a small item, shiny and flat as a coin, popped through the frayed opening. Only it wasn't a coin. Colleen's eyes widened with discovery. A medallion.

"What is that?" Moira materialized next to Colly.

Startled, Colly closed her fingers around her palm.

"Show me."

It was no use trying to hide it. Moira narrowed her eyes and thrust her good hand out, demanding. Colly set the item reluctantly into the center of her outstretched palm.

Moira peered down and then hastily closed her fingers and crossed herself. "The Madonna!"

"What?" Colly looked more closely. There was a woman in a veil surrounded by stars in the middle of the medallion. "What's a Madonna? Who's that?"

"For God's sake, it's the Virgin Mary, Colleen. Don't you know anything?" She crossed herself again. "Where did you get this?"

Before Colly could respond, Moira's gaze landed on the scrap of blue material now lying on the folding table.

"*Grafsa grat'i!*"

"What? A haunted dress? Was this someone's dress?"

Moira clutched the medallion in her right hand and snatched the scrap from the table with her left. But her bad right hand jerked violently, flipping Colleen's new treasure into the air. It glinted in the light and landed on the filthy tiles next to an unattended machine groaning through its spin cycle. Moira sank to her knees and groped along the floor. Colly watched, stunned. Normally Moira seemed so in control, but now she was frantic. Colly wanted to say it was hers and hers alone. She wanted it to be hidden under a machine where Moira couldn't reach and Colly could explore later.

But Moira, sweeping her hand along the floor, found it near her own bended knee. She sat back and held it out on her flattened left palm. Tilting her head, she examined the medallion with a look of reverence and fear on her face.

Colly couldn't contain herself. This was her treasure. There was only one way to get it back.

"Now you see it." She swooped in, quick as a squirrel, and snatched it from Moira's palm. "Now you don't!"

"Ach, you little demon!" Moira scrambled to her feet alongside the quaking washer. "Come here! Give it back."

Colly's choppy bangs flew in the wind from the fan as she dodged between the washers and a long line of folding tables. Moira chased behind.

A pear-shaped woman turned, her rump bucking up with surprise.

Moira lowered her voice. "I mean it…"

But Colleen was off into the restroom before Moira could reach her, upending a cart and a bottle of fabric softener, flooding the air with boozy lavender. After darting into the bathroom and slamming the door, she hastily engaged the rusty latch, which screeched over the thumping of the dryers and the rotating fans. She shifted in discomfort in the closet-sized space, huddling near the toilet under a swinging bulb. This was a great game.

But hearing Moira outside the door changed it from fun. "Open it!" she demanded. "*Blanog!*"

Uh-oh. She'd provoked Moira enough to use Shelta in front of a stranger.

"Open," Moira hissed with her mouth close to the door.

Colly stood tiptoe on the toilet and peered through a crack in the wall. The expression on Moira's face, twisted and ugly, was different from anything Colly had seen. Like something dangerous and deep had been disturbed. Like a snake caught exposed on a rock. Colly shuddered and sat momentarily on the toilet, all wind and energy pulled from her. Her heart beat frantically, and yet her blood seemed still. She tapped the side of her head with her fist, the medallion closed tightly within.

"Can't hear you," she called. "I'm peeing."

Moira wiggled the handle, then banged on the door.

A shiver ran down Colly's spine.

She set her foot against the toilet handle and pushed down, creating a loud boom followed by a sucking swirl. Colleen caught her breath and nonchalantly opened the door, but not before carefully tucking the medal into the change pocket of her cutoffs under a hard, little knot of lint. Moira yanked the door open all the way.

"Sorry, Moira." Colly held out her hands. "The medal fell in the toilet. *Ke nytpa hu*—what can I do?"

Moira pushed past Colly and snooped around the bathroom like a dog missing its bone.

"Ooh, you little…" She turned and pinched Colly's arm.

"Ouch," Colly said, loud enough to draw Mrs. Pear's attention once again. The woman waddled over.

"Is everything okay?"

"Fine," Moira said. "We're fine." Her voice was overly sweet, like those sugar dots on paper strips, and it almost made Colly's jaw hurt. "Aren't we, little one?"

They gathered their things quickly. Moira even pulled a half-finished load from the dryer, for once not bothered by the wasted coins. She pushed her way back to the car, then tossed the steaming basket into the trunk before she slammed it.

Colly climbed in and they drove in silence, with Moira steering hard around the pits and dips in the parking lot.

Once on the road, with Moira's eyes set forward, Colly produced the edge of the medallion from her pocket. It glinted in a bar of sun. She quickly ran her finger over the image, of this special woman surrounded by stars, before pushing it back into the deepest fold of the material.

Moira grabbed Colly's eyes in the mirror. "Do you remember, Colly girl," she spoke slowly, "what I told you about where selkies live?"

Colly nodded.

"The good little ones go to rocks high above the waves in the sunshine and fresh air, but the naughty ones…" Colly stared ahead blankly. She knew the story. Only too well. Still Moira continued. "They end up in deep caves underwater, filled with tangles of kelp and angry crabs and black water and…"

Moira kept going but Colly didn't hear her anymore. Instead, she shuddered, imagining the horrible tight space filled with grasping seaweed and vile creatures and suffocating darkness.

Chapter 13
Claire

Claire was amazing. Everyone told her so. The doctors and nurses at Northwestern University Hospital. Her mentor, Dr. Margaret Christner. The card on her office desk, attached to a vase of richly hued freesias, testified to Vicki's thoughts as well. *You go, sis!* The bouquet reminded Claire of the scrapbook of wildflowers she'd begun for the girls. Left unfinished, it had been tucked away in their bedroom, along with so many other cherished items.

Claire now stood next to a patient's gunmetal-gray bed in the ICU. In the four long years since That Day, she had not only finished her primary program, but a specialty too. She was now a radiologist, and in the throes of Northwestern University's doctorate program with a focus on radiologic treatment for cancers.

Life without Lily was terrible. But the way Andrea had died, the fact that there was no body, had remained inconceivable to Claire, troubling to her very core. The only thing that helped to quiet the nonanalytical parts of her brain was the laser beam focus required by her work. She cared deeply for her patients, attending to them with loving concern. They, along with her research, allowed her to mole away from the rest of the world, provided a barrier from her guilt and grief. Kept her from the repetitive wheel of self-recrimination. If she'd only done something different That Day. And her marriage—considering how much she'd hurt Glen fed into an ever-widening distance between them. Some days it felt as if she were straddling a seismically active fault line. One of her making.

She must indeed appear like superwoman to everyone. Everyone but her husband.

A shadow flitted past the frosted window. She grasped the edge of the bed as a memory descended with fresh immediacy: Andrea in the kitchen, next to the birdcage, watching Butkus fluff his feathers and stretch his misshapen wing.

"Mommy, how do birds fly?"

"Their bones are hollow inside."

"Like straws?"

"Well, sort of ..." Claire remembered taking a pause.

"How was that possible? And where, then, was their marrow?"

She'd intended at the time to look it up. To make notes and tell the girls all about it. Another small thing left undone.

Claire offered a smile to her patient, even though the elderly man's eyes were closed. Connected to multiple tubes, he reminded her of a displaced sea creature, pale and struggling near the ocean's surface.

"I'll check back after your radiation treatment tomorrow, Mr. Lyman."

Had he heard her? She couldn't be certain. Still she patted his hand before leaving with his chart. Returning it to the nurse's station, she moved to a computer where she brought up his chest X-ray. An image flickered on the screen—healthy white lung tissue surrounded by shadow, like an eclipsing sun. Mr. Lyman's incurable cancer. It was cases such as these that drew her deeper into her research. Maybe she could save someone. Searching for any post-treatment changes in the tissue, Claire drew closer to the monitor where she encountered the eerie reflection of her face superimposed on the screen. Ashen skin, gray canyons for eyes. *Jesus, Claire, you look like a patient yourself.* She blinked and turned away.

She'd return to her office and pack up since she was leaving early today. She headed toward the back elevators, the ones rarely used by patients. While immersion in the medical culture turned out to be a blessing, the hospital remained fraught with emotional hazards. Having spent so much time dramatizing and imagining the growth of her daughters since the last time she saw them, she was still startled whenever she spotted a patient, particularly a girl, in close approximation to the age that either of her daughters had been, or would be.

Some days, it was only the remembrance of Lily's light that gave Claire courage to continue, filling her with a twinge of comfort at particularly difficult moments, which still occurred far too often. She often caught herself looking for a possible sign from Andrea, searching the patterns of clouds outside her office window, the arabesques of frost on the windshield in winter.

Stepping into the elevator alcove, she hit the up arrow.

"Dr. Rawlings?"

Claire turned to face a petite woman with white hair and serious eyes: Margaret Christner, head of radiology and a sitting member of both the PhD admissions and the grant committees. Admission to the program meant a dream realized. A grant meant no more loans to worry about.

"I read your proposal," Margaret said as they entered the elevator together. "I have comments, of course."

Claire pressed the button for the fifth floor.

"The committees have agreed"—Margaret's eyes twinkled—"that your presentation in October will be a key moment."

October! Claire's head spun. Only five months away. There would be barely time to breathe. How would Glen respond?

"That's too much, Claire," he'd replied when she'd mentioned her research project six months prior. "For you. For us." There was resignation in his tone that matched the shadow of sadness tattooed into his expression. It was only a month later that Claire proposed the idea of her temporarily moving away from their place in Upton Grove to a housing unit subsidized by the hospital. She'd be home on weekends. It would eliminate the exhausting commute and allow Glen's schedule not to be so disrupted by her wild hours.

Glen had been visibly stunned. "This is ridiculous."

"Residents do it all the time." Claire had continued, "It's only for a short while. Until everything is wrapped up at the hospital."

He had finally agreed to the plan, with reluctance. Since then, they'd had no meaningful discussion about the future, had made no arrangements to reunite. Was she really just using the program as an excuse? Because coexisting in the house, close to Glen, hurt too much? Weekend visits became bimonthly. She hadn't spoken to him in close to ten days.

"I understand the effort that goes into these proposals," Margaret said. The elevator stopped and the door opened. "Take the rest of the day off."

Claire nodded as the door closed.

Leaving early had nothing to do with the reason Margaret had cited. Entering her office, Claire's gaze moved to the calendar. May 12. Lily's birthday. If her daughters had lived, Lily would be five and Andrea eight and a half. Claire closed her eyes tightly. It still seemed impossible to her that the landscape of her life no longer included motherhood.

This was the first milestone for which Claire and Glen wouldn't be together. Last year, they'd spent the evening together on the couch, fingers intertwined into a tightly woven basket. Thinking of him now filled her heart with ache. He'd kept busy in his own ways—joining a support group, maintaining the house with careful attention to detail. Panging with the urge to call him, she checked the clock: 3:45. He would be getting home from school.

She lifted the receiver on her desk phone but wavered. She dialed Vicki instead.

Out the window, Claire could see her unit, in a line of town houses, situated just on the other side of the hospital parking garage. The buildings looked like aging dorms. Along with grass in the courtyard, she would've appreciated working appliances. But the rental agreement allowed for dogs. Glen had agreed that Claire and Gretchie couldn't be separated. Butkus, growing ever ornerier, stayed at the house.

"Hi, honey," Vicki answered.

"Hope I didn't wake you." Vicki had started working odd hours as a volunteer counselor at a shelter.

"No, no, it's fine." She was using her overly chipper voice. The one held in reserve for special occasions specifically hurtful to Claire: holidays, either of the girls' birthdays.

"I'm taking your advice."

"Oh?" Vicki's relief was audible. "You're going to find a new therapist? And stick with it this time?"

"No. I'm leaving work early."

"Okay. Good. That's a big step. What are you going to do?"

"Hang out."

"What else?" Vicki hated that Claire was alone when she wasn't working.

"Dunno. Maybe take G to the beach." She had discovered a secret little spot on the shore with rough chop and no swimming allowed, perfect for a dog to run.

"And Glen?"

Claire sighed.

"You know how concerned I am about you two. I wish you were together."

"This is a common—"

"I know, I know," Vicki interrupted. "You are so busy, I get the pressure. But it isn't good, you and Glen in separate places this long."

Silence flooded the phone line.

"You need someone, Claire. To help you through all of this… Listen, honey. I'm running out to pick up the car from the shop. Call me later if you need me. Promise?"

"Okay."

Claire began to gather some papers and her purse and then stopped. One more time she dialed. On the fourth ring, he picked up.

"Hello?"

"Glen. It's me. Is this a good time?"

"It's fine. I'm just…um…sitting here." She could see him in one of the kitchen chairs, the vinyl seat worn.

"I wanted to, you know, touch base."

"I'm glad you did."

Claire felt herself dissolving into the comfort of his voice, wishing the emotional distance between them could somehow magically disappear. That first year after returning to her program had been shaky. Aside from adjusting to the demands of her new routine, Glen remained overly reserved, with the issue of guilt never discussed. By year three, the broken energy in their home had built up like a snowball rolling downhill, keeping them bereft. Their bedroom, too, had become a desert—a place only to undress silently and swiftly so as not to spark intimacy—aside from Claire's body being numb, anything that smacked of joy or abandon would be a betrayal, unfair to the memory of her girls. In response, Glen circled cautiously, as if she were somehow strange to him.

"You okay, Glen?"

"God. I keep thinking about…" His voice grew soft. "About all the things we would've done with Andrea and Lily…"

Claire felt herself spiraling, could easily lose control. When he spoke about both girls, it was in a final, definite past tense. In Claire's heart, they were as alive as any children could be to a mother. Blood rushed to her face as the experience of Lily as a newborn was suddenly present, her soft, fresh skin as fragrant as pastries. She knew right then that she would never have forgiven Glen for being so careless with their babies. Even if he was as sick as Claire had been That Day. Never.

"Glen. I have to see a patient now."

"What? Really, Claire?"

"It's an emergency."

"This is why—"

"I have to go. I'm sorry. I'm being paged…"

Claire grabbed her things and left the office. She'd take Gretchie to the beach. And then, she didn't know. Probably call Vicki. She was immediately ashamed of the way she'd cut Glen off. Ashamed of how her emotions controlled her. Hurrying through the hall to the stairs, the sound of the elevator dinged behind her.

"Excuse me, is this radiology?" An urgent voice carried along the walls. "My daughter. She's in pain."

Claire turned to face a woman, thirtyish, with blond soccer-mom hair, her features wrought with concern. Next to her stood a young girl. No older than three, maybe four. She leaned into the woman, cradling an arm wrapped in an Ace bandage. She, too, was blond, with a stick-straight pixie cut. But when Claire closed her eyes, she saw soft hair as ethereal as cotton candy. Opening her eyes, the little girl's dress, covered in bright sunflowers and sunflower buds exploding with possibility. An acute ache triggered in Claire's chest.

"We've been sent to radiology."

"I'll…I'll get someone for you."

The woman clutched the girl closer. The girl's chin quivered and she whimpered. The sound swam through Claire's veins like minnows in a wave. Claire step-fell backward, knocking into a service cart.

"Are you all right?" The mother reached forward to touch Claire's arm.

Steadying herself, Claire scanned the area, looking anywhere but at the young patient before her. She fled into the stairwell and descended the stairs two at a time to the lobby. Clearing the front entrance doors, she broke into full gallop into the bright afternoon, tearing past the cement urns bunched with pansies, then bee-lined directly to the parking garage. She'd drive to Upton Grove. Apologize to Glen for being so abrupt on the phone. They should spend what remained of this day and evening together.

In the driver's seat, Claire leaned her head on the steering wheel hard enough to conduct a purposeful pain along the bone. Without motherhood, her life seemed so terribly meaningless. She squinted into the rearview mirror, blurring the imperfections, the tension wrinkles in her face. A red mark like the storm on Jupiter was growing above her eyes. There was that look she knew too well. The expression she'd seen on the faces of terminal patients. Holding back the flood of tears, she managed to spiral her way to the exit of the garage and set off west toward the highway. Overhead, the sky loomed clear and endless.

The very same shade of blue as the young girl's eyes.

On Crestview, Claire counted the houses. One, two, three. Theirs was the fourth one down. Her stomach puckered when she arrived, hoping this wasn't too great a surprise. And then she was the one who was surprised when she found Glen's car gone. He'd probably run to the store. She'd wait for him inside.

Entering through the back, the familiar sound of hostile squawking greeted her. Butkus. She smiled and approached his cage, mindful of his boundaries. He fluffed up and scuttled to the far side, turning his back to Claire. Just then, she noticed his cuttlebone had fallen to the floor. Claire bent and lifted it into her palm. The bone, feather light like false ivory, was a sudden bright reminder of the terrible gap that separated Claire from the girls' childhood. A flood of tears was heating up. She fought it back. It was too hard to cry alone.

Still, she began to whisper-sing "Count the clouds..." before catching herself. No, nope. None of that. Claire shook her head and moved quickly into the kitchen. Water. That's what she needed. She turned on the tap in the sink and reached for a glass. That's when she noticed a business card near the phone. She held it up to look closer.

Dwight Emerson, Esq. Divorce & Family Law Attorney.

Claire stumbled and sat in a chair. Then she stood. And then sat again, her thoughts so gummed up in her head that she couldn't shake them loose. Reflexively, she called her sister.

Claire squeezed her eyes shut when she heard her sister's voice.

"Claire? I haven't seen this number in a while. You at the house?" Vicki's voice rose with anticipation. "Is Glen with you?"

Claire held her breath a moment.

"Hello? Claire?"

"Yes. And no."

"Are you okay? You don't sound okay."

"Vicki. Do you remember our giant?"

Vicki hesitated.

"Our backyard pool giant?"

"Uh, yes, of course."

"Dad was on the bottom. Then you, then me." Stacked up, all three of them, in their aboveground pool that had been placed too close to the maples so that it filled with helicopters in the spring.

The last time they made the giant was the summer before their parents died. Their dad was the legs. Vicki the torso. Claire, the youngest and smallest, was the head and flailing arms. Their dad got too close to the edge and slipped and Vicki went down okay but Claire chipped her tooth on the hard rim of the pool. The giant broke into three. That was Claire now, all split up, no hope of recovery.

"What happened? Do you want me to call someone?"

"Vicki," Claire said. "Glen and I are over."

"Honey…"

"I'm okay, really. It's okay."

Getting up to leave, she felt a hard jab in her gut. The realization that she could now lose Glen, too, sank into her like a slingshot stone.

Chapter 14
Moira

S tay inside this time." Moira jerked the Buick toward the gas
station air hose alongside the cinder-block building. "I don't
need you wandering around like always."

"You mean exploring." Colly cracked a mischievous smile.

"And no messing with the dials either." Moira attempted to
be stern but then shook her head and smiled back. That child! So
curious, and by God was she smart. Sometimes too smart for her
own good.

The Buick heaved and sputtered before turning off. Clearly,
the end of its lifespan was fast approaching. Moira got out and
crouched near the wheel well, turning her face to avoid the foul
smell of hot rubber. Anchoring her shaky right hand, she twisted
the snake-headed tube into place.

This was a hard life for sure. Living hand to mouth. Almost
twice a week now, she was filling these near-treadless tires. But
she'd kept her promise to Colly, tried to be just like a mam to her.
Thank Jesu she was so independent. That girl knew everything—
how to cook oatmeal, how to keep vermin at bay, and always, the
last place where Moira left her cigs.

But recently, with Colly getting older, keener to wisecrack,
Moira found her patience buzzing in alternating current. After all
of Moira's sacrifices, she was beginning to wonder if that child
wouldn't abandon her the way everyone else in her life had.
Her mind went to Eamon. She bit her trembling lip against the

surfacing distress she still suffered. Despite everything, she missed him so.

And part of Moira still longed for the feel of a larger family around her. Life as a Traveller had been like living in a pile of hamsters, always one on top of the other. The shock of sudden isolation after the shunning was gone, but a deep wound still festered inside. This life with just the two of them seemed beyond lonely; it felt unnatural.

Tap, tap. Moira looked up. Colly's face was plastered against the window like a fish in an aquarium, her hand gesturing, finlike, toward the outdoor soda machine.

Moira shook her head. Did that girl think they were made of money?

Colly sank from view.

The tires took longer to fill each time. She yawned and glanced around. Nothing for miles in the slow Indiana landscape except acres of furrowed fields under a hazy sapphire sky. It was late spring and the heat, thank God, wasn't yet razor sharp. She followed the robotic blink of lights on the outdoor soda machine, and then counted the rows of cinder blocks on the wall. Fourteen in all, from the roof to the tops of some shaggy-headed grasses, stiff and upright as sentinels. A quick breeze swept them to one side. Moira froze at what she thought she'd seen on the wall behind those weeds.

Could it be?

"Colly." Moira banged against the fender. The top of Colly's hair appeared in the window, like a thatch of green sod, followed by her thin face.

Moira swallowed hard, choking with emotion. "Come out."

"Really?"

Before Moira uttered another sound, the car door flew open and Colly's bare feet hit the ground.

"Here." Moira motioned to her side. "Take over."

"Do I get a root beer?"

Moira didn't answer. Colly slid next to the tire, and Moira guided her grasp to the nozzle. A blast of air blew through the tube and across her wrist.

"*Blanog.*" Her hand quaked with wild energy. "Keep it steady."

"Okay, okay. Am I doing it right?"

"Yeah, it's fine. Great." But Moira's attention was on that spot on the wall. She had to be certain what she'd seen was real. She hustled away from Colly, leaving her to struggle with the hissing hose.

When Moira drew closer, she almost fell over. What appeared as nonsense graffiti to the untrained eye—a hastily chalked triangle with three slashes run through—was a clear, unambiguous sign to her. Jesu! It was the ancient Gaelic symbol used to indicate a stopover. Travellers were in the area.

"Moira, I need—"

"Go to another tire." Moira barely turned her head.

"This one isn't done."

"Just do it."

Moira ran her hand below the symbol, just above the dirt line, searching for a crack or crevice that should be there. Could it be her clan? No, not possible! She continued to search with great caution, because the anticipation actually hurt. If it was indeed her family, what would she do? A small piece of Moira's heart swelled. She clutched her chest.

Don't break. Not again.

"Hey!" Colly called.

Moira clenched her teeth and leaned back. "What is it?"

"This one too?" Colly pointed to a rear tire, clearly low and saggy.

"No. And shush now."

"But you said—"

"Just get back in the car." Moira's mind clattered with the voices of family members, their laughter across the caravan park, the aroma of the simple meals prepared inside the little homes. The display of exuberant rowdiness, life fully lived.

Hearing the car door slam behind her, she placed her hand into a fissure in the wall. There should be a pencil in that hollow and scraps of paper. A crude mailbox system for messaging, most likely checked once or twice a day. And each piece of paper would have an insignia on it—a deer's head, or a shamrock, or, dare she even think it, her own clan's symbol.

She reached deeply and then brought a lump of folded paper into the light. Her whole body trembled as she opened it.

"Ach!"

There was no mistaking the simple lines, rudimentary as a child's design: a wolf. With red chalk eyes. Her family was here. Somewhere. Nearby.

Her right hand lurched uncontrollably as she worked to smooth the creases against the wall. A series of straight lines—| | |—with one crossed out. Three days total they were here. With only two remaining. Her legs weakened. Was it, could it be, Siobhan's or her da's writing? She couldn't tell for certain. But one thing she knew was that they'd be gone soon.

Pearls of sweat gathered at her temples in the now overbearing sunshine.

"Moira!" Colly yelled through the car window.

Toppling from a squat onto her bum, Moira's bones nearly leaped through her skin. Anger bordering on rage welled in her throat. *You little...*

"I've got my own money for root beer."

She ignored Colly, just as she now ignored the fact that she had lost her family well before Colly came along. That child now seemed the reason Moira lurked on the edges of life—the tedious cash jobs, the operating under fake last names, the dull but nagging fear of discovery.

Clutching the pencil in her good hand, she positioned it over a clean scrap of paper. This moment, this simple decision, meant so much, almost too much. The weeds rattled in another swipe of breeze. Were they encouraging or warning?

She'd know that answer soon enough.

That night, the temperature plummeted, and Moira tossed beneath two meager blankets as thoughts of Eamon crashed through her head. She had seen the mangled Taurus on TV and now imagined his body swept away in the cold river, trapped somewhere miles downstream, disintegrating in the muck. It troubled Moira that he'd not had a proper burial, and she made certain she said a prayer every August in his memory. Even now, she barely wept. Life was too difficult for sentiment. Pulling the covers to her chin, she shuddered, thinking back to the cabin and those very first months with Colly, the effort it took to get her talking again. The one thing Moira was grateful for was that the girl remembered nothing of that day and of her previous life.

There had been, of course, no one to explain to Moira how things went with a child. She had to make it up as she went along. She had dreamed of it all so different, fresh smells like baby powder, wiping sweet drool from chubby cheeks and padded chin. Instead, she got this rambunctious creature, half child, half adult, running barefoot until the snow fell.

She thought again of the selkie myth. She'd never told Colly the whole story. The way the changeling child eventually swam away into the wild, returning to its creature shape without so much as a glance backward. Her legs thrashed against the covers, as if in defiance, as if suddenly acknowledging the uncomfortable parallel to the way Eamon had left her.

Hours, it seemed, passed before Moira drifted from restless anxiety to sleep. In her dream, she saw Eamon. But only his back—not his face. He was walking and she fell in behind, unquestioning, for miles on end. Exhausted, she finally sank to the ground. Eamon stopped and slowly began to turn, the tattoo on his arm apparent at first, then his rough profile.

Just as his face came into view, Moira startled awake to Colly's voice. Crying. Many times, she had gone into Colleen's room in the night. Her eyes were always closed, but she moved and made sounds as if she were in some far-off place awake. Some nights it was singing. A bright, lively tune about clouds and birds. Other nights she frowned and whimpered. Colly never knew the next morning that anything unusual had happened, and Moira never said a word. Tonight, once again, she called for a mother. "Momeee, Mom-eee."

This time, Moira stayed put. It burrowed into Moira's head, this terrible longing, and hurt like a betrayal after all she'd sacrificed for the girl. Soon she heard her own voice, echoing through her head, pleading for her mam. Like a silly little child. Moira clamped the pillow over her head. *Shut up, Moira. Shut yourself up.*

Colleen resumed louder. "Mom-eee, Mom-eee," she called, in a high, lonely wail.

Sweet Jesu. Moira pulled the pillow down over her face. *Make that child stop!*

The morning sun brought air sheepishly warmed, as if recovering from a spanking, and yellow light mottled by the dirty kitchen window. Moira chipped last night's dinner of dried SpaghettiOs from a pan. Rinsing the bowls, she pulled her hands from the water. They were red and chapped from the harsh detergents she used in her job cleaning rooms at the Motel 6. Everything about her, including the reflection of her face now stretched across the chrome toaster, looked older than her twenty-four years.

She turned toward the tiny TV set on the counter. Images from a commercial danced in black and white. With the volume button perpetually stuck on high, the voices blared. This time it was a man trumpeting about the world's most versatile knife. As she brought a cup of instant coffee to her lips, Moira's stomach teeter-tottered against the lukewarm liquid in her mouth—had she made the right decision about leaving a message?

Scree, scree.

Moira whipped around. Colleen was scraping her dry bowl of cereal with a plastic spoon. The sound shot through her like a loud demand. Instead of flesh and blood, all Moira saw for an instant was a stick figure with a mouth. And crazy blue hair. She blinked hard.

Scree, scree.

The man on the TV roared a toll-free number. Even the spring day was bursting through the trailer, tapping at cracks, imposing inward. Moira walked to the window. Birds everywhere, as if trees were nets that caught them. She drew a skewed blind tight against this chirpy season. She could just choke those damn trilling birds.

"Moira. We need milk."

Empty milk cartons, broken TV dials, leaky tires. The list was endless. Exhaustingly so.

"You have Pop-Tarts," Moira snapped. What a pretty penny they were too. "Here's what you'll do until I get back." She held up a poster-sized photograph of trees she'd gotten at the dollar store. Maples and ashes in the height of autumn brilliance, scarlet, flame yellow, colors normally irresistible to Colly. "You'll paint that exact, got it? Just a simple copy."

That manager woman was right: they were making decent money off this stuff. Up to twenty dollars apiece. The woman also proved most helpful, kept taking finished canvases to flea market heaven, Michiana. The understanding was clear from the beginning; tourists only bought bright, sun-filled pictures. Lately—no matter how Moira cajoled—Colleen's paintings were becoming abstract and desolate. A frozen creek here, stark stands of wintry birches there.

"Exact copy." Moira held the door handle.

Colleen blinked back her surprise at Moira's tone, which Moira softened as she continued. "I'm off, little one. Can't be late for work."

Climbing into the Buick, she felt Colly's eyes on her from the window, eager and, as always, questioning. She backed away without a glance and gunned past the trailer, a great fatted pig of aluminum, kicking small tornadoes of dust in her wake.

Passing the exit where she should turn for the Motel 6, Moira's anxiety rose each minute she grew closer to her new destination, the one she'd outlined in the note she'd left for her family. So many things bounced through her head. What exactly was she doing? Did they know about the abduction? Had they heard about Eamon's death? While they weren't ones for watching TV news or reading papers, bits of information easily became wild gossip.

And the most consuming thought of all—did she even dare to ask them to take her back? It was the *soobya* situation, consorting with her cousin Eamon that had gotten her into this mess. And that was now ancient history. If her family agreed, then what about Colly? How would she make them understand what Eamon had done and how she'd stepped in to help this girl and to keep her safe from a bad mother? Her mind crackled until she almost missed the exit and had to careen over a lane to catch it. At the end of the ramp was the meeting place. A Big Boy restaurant. Her heart smacked wildly against her ribs.

She prayed it would be her da and not Siobhan who was there.

Moira circled behind the building, parked and waited, drumming her fingers as she scanned the area. Only a pickup truck and a sedan sat in the lot, both empty. Ten minutes passed. No one came. The sun, too, was playing games, drifting behind a few striated clouds thin and wispy as harp strings. Moira picked one to track to keep her mind in place.

She checked the clock again. Almost twenty minutes now she'd sat past the appointed time. Disappointment began to froth in her soul, setting her thoughts to fester. She'd been a fool to get her hopes up, to even try for this. Leaning to start the car, she detected movement and a person appeared alongside as if from the very air. A slip of a woman, pale and thin with sharp dark eyes. Moira shoved the car door open to stand before a mirror image of herself. Siobhan.

"That damn Buick still, huh, Moira?"

Aside from the tiny mole to the right of Siobhan's mouth, they were identical. But Siobhan's eyes were steely and hard as bullets.

"Sister. It's good to see you."

An expression ran across Siobhan's face, one that Moira remembered so well. The satisfied look of one more favored, one closer to their mam's heartbeat, one whose actions pleased their da. Then she narrowed her eyes. "What have you been up to then, Moira?"

"Oh, workin' here and there." Moira's throat constricted.

There was quiet between them. The noise of the highway grumbled in the distance.

"So, what do you want? We're on the move again tomorrow."

"Can you talk to Da?" Moira's breath caught as she spoke. It took so much courage to continue. "About, dunno, maybe letting me travel with the clan again." The question came from such a deep, hungry place inside her that the words hurt when she spoke them. She rose up on her toes and then back down again. She'd kill for a cigarette.

A police cruiser pulled into the parking lot and curved past the two women like a shark, hesitating momentarily before moving on. Moira felt her expression go flat. Her hand kicked wildly inside its pocket.

"When was it?" Siobhan asked. "The last you saw of Eamon?"

"Um…dunno." The image of that river, the rushing water, the crushed Taurus flashed in Moira's brain. "Years."

"Hmm. What do you think was in Eamon's head, Moira?" Siobhan kept her eyes steady. "Makin' off with two girls like that?"

Moira felt blood flooding her face. She fixed her gaze onto a line of dark clouds crawling over the horizon. Just past Siobhan's head.

"Look at me," Siobhan demanded. "I mean in the eyes."

Moira's heartbeat battered like a ramrod in her ears.

"Tell me it was madness. What Eamon done."

Blanog! It would be impossible to explain how things went down. That it was all Eamon's idea and Moira was an innocent victim. Moira felt she was dueling with not only her sister but with Eamon as well, listening from wherever he now was, preparing to curse the words she was about to speak. "It was beyond horrible."

"Tell me right to my face you had nothing to do with that devilish plan. Stealing and killing children!"

"I don't… I didn't…" Moira squeaked, dry-mouthed. "Maybe he thought he was saving them from some druggie of a mother."

"Let me see your hand. The one in your pocket."

It was always Siobhan's way, measuring Moira's feelings by her tremors. An ugly little game she played when they were small. Moira fought to hold ground. She kept her hand, writhing madly, hidden.

"You can fool the world. Maybe even yourself. But I'm pretty sure you had something to do with this fooked-up situation." The squad car continued on, passing through to the adjoining parking lot. "I have a good mind to give a shout to that cop."

"But…"

"Or call the station. Anonymous tip, Moira. Think you'd check out okay?"

"What are you sayin'?"

"Be grateful you didn't get caught for whatever you and Eamon done. And be grateful we don't carry on with cops. I'm warning you. Don't trouble us again." Siobhan began to turn away and then stopped. "You know the rules. As far as Da's concerned—the whole family, in fact—you're good as dead."

She set her back to Moira and walked away.

Moira almost ran after her sister, fell to her knees to beg forgiveness, pled for her old life back before Siobhan disappeared behind the building. It was pathetic, really. She was pathetic. But she remained frozen, searching the area for proof of what she'd just experienced. It was as if Siobhan had never been there.

Moira did eighty-five on the way back to the trailer. The Buick shook and rattled, but she didn't care. When she arrived home, Colleen was in a tree, swishing branches in greeting. She was now an Indian. In addition to the chunk of old rag mop woven into braids, she'd cut a paper grocery bag into a fringed vest and used crayons to decorate it with bold symbols that signified nothing. Moira entered the trailer, slammed the door, and sat on the sagging couch where she smoked three precious cigarettes in a row, one after the other.

There was no way to process what had just happened. That she could never return to her family. It wormed within her like an ugly maggot in a rotten apple. Through the window, she could see Colly shimmy down the tree trunk like a monkey. The distant roar of a bus accompanied her through the door, followed by a whiff of spring air.

"Why can't I go to school too, Moira?"

Moira clenched her teeth. "I told you why. I teach you things." Other than the fact that she had no papers for her, she withered at the questions that would form in Colly's head if she went to school.

"You never do anymore. I learn on my own."

Moira's eyes narrowed into a "watch it" look, cutting through the crap all over Colly's face. Why did she want to be away from Moira so bad anyway? A clear yet ugly thought inched its way into her brain. Maybe this was the beginning of Colly's smooth pathway right out of this life with Moira.

"Are you talkin' to kids around here? Didn't I say you're not allowed?"

Colly shrugged.

Moira suddenly noticed that the aluminum easel, set up on the table, was turned toward the wall. She'd invested quite a bit of her hard-earned money in art materials ever since the trailer park manager had started selling Colly's paintings on a regular basis. Working with a man at the craft store, she'd purchased colors that he'd assured could be coaxed into pastels—lemon yellow, rose madder, cerulean blue. Lately, Colly had been leaving these tubes untouched, opting instead for brooding colors with exotic names like alizarin crimson, phthalo green, and titanium white.

"Show me the picture."

Colleen hesitated. Moira circled the table to get a full view of the painting. It was the same picture as she had asked Colleen to copy, all right. The trees. But instead of early fall, she'd advanced the scene by many weeks so that the trees were bare and the leaves, wet and sodden, were scattered in a lifeless apron around the trunks. The sky overhead was dark and threatening.

"This isn't worth the cost of the paint you used." Moira leaned into the gas range to light up another cigarette. Her last. She faced the wall and exhaled, teeth clenched. "We need this money."

"Could save a little," Colleen said, "if you didn't smoke so much."

Moira spun around. "What did you just say?"

"Nothing," Colly responded in a small voice.

Moira went still. A slow, angry calm came over her. The type that tested boundaries. "What have I told you, little one, about the naughty selkies?"

Colly shrank back.

"About being trapped in a dark, scary cave? No way out. Nothing but old seaweed, and savage crabs—white as ghosts."

Colly sidled to the front door and then she was gone, dashing off the porch to who knew where. Probably to rummage in the woods, find a new climbing tree, Moira didn't care. She needed cigarettes. Badly. The 7-Eleven wasn't far away. Maybe she'd get milk after all. She drove to the store and entered as if in a trance. Finding herself in front of the dairy cooler, Moira scanned the items half-shadowed in the fluorescent lights. A man in a suit appeared next to her.

She was careful not to make eye contact.

He pointed to the wall before opening the cooler. "Terrible thing, eh?"

Moira fixed her gaze at the cartons inside, arranged into a small village with pointed roofs. But the angle of the door, covered in condensation, reflected the image from a missing persons poster on the wall as if in a mirror. As the man leaned into his search, Moira came face-to-face with a young girl in the glass who had two teeth missing and a swatch of brown hair. Laura or Lori, her full name undecipherable, last seen near Detroit. She looked startlingly similar to Colly. Moira stepped backward. This was beyond unsettling; it was a sign.

"Miss? Did you want milk, miss?"

Moira hurried from the store, milk and cigarettes be damned. Once in the parking lot, the breeze worked a cyclone of litter onto her feet, and then quickly whisked it away. Scrambling into the car, it was all clear to her now. Only a fool would've stayed this long in one place. Moira opened the glove box and pulled out Eamon's old map. She placed a fingertip over a small stain formed by a glop of mayonnaise that had fallen from his sandwich all those years ago. The greasy mark seemed the very texture of betrayal. She was close to numb with pain: a snitch sister, a shyster for a lover. And Colleen, what loyalty did she actually have to Moira? That damn selkie was given love and attention, yet it turned its back on its human family, its only thought to return to the sea.

You've been too careless, Moira.

Paled by the sunlight curving hungrily through the windshield, she stared at the blue veins in her wrist. Her right hand was uncharacteristically calm. She lifted it slowly and then slapped herself across the face. The hot sting brought tears, but she was able to hold them back.

Scanning the map, she searched for a new place, one where it was possible to disappear in plain sight. Biting her nails, her eyes darted along the edge of Lake Michigan, where it arced northward from its dip into Indiana. There it was. Michiana. What did that trailer park manager call it? Flea market heaven. Tourist community.

Less than two hours north. Yet a world away.

Chapter 15
Claire

C laire?"
      The wheels in the tape recorder answering machine spun.
"Please pick up."

Round and round. Claire could hear them softly squeaking,
like conspiring mice. Two weeks it had been. Two weeks since
Lily's birthday. Since going to the house.

"I've spoken to Vicki. I understand why you're upset."

Ooh, I'm going to kill my sister, Claire thought, grabbing the
receiver.

"Is this what you want, Glen? Attorneys and all that bullshit?"

"I tried to talk to you. But there was never a time. Not a
moment that you could spare. So I…" And then he stopped. "Just
forget it." He hung up.

Claire exhaled and set her hands flat on the kitchen counter.
Feeling a gentle tap on her foot, she looked down and found
Gretchie searching her face with questioning eyes. Claire stroked
the fur of her hankie-soft ears.

"C'mon. Let's go to the beach." Gretchie was allowed to romp
along the shoreline but not swim. Her thickly muscled body was
the opposite of buoyant, slow and heavy in the water, the way
Claire felt she was navigating the world. She grabbed the leash and
an old hand towel she used to wipe down G's sandy paws.

"Let's go, girl."

They walked to the parking garage. Once inside, Gretchie

pressed her nose to the floor, keen on the greasy odors. Claire unlocked the car, opened the passenger door, and patted the seat.

"Bye-byes."

Gretchie obliged eagerly and jumped in, minesweeping the dashboard with eager sniffs. Claire circled around and climbed inside.

"Here, hold this." She tossed the towel onto G's back, watching as her dog shimmied out from under it. Any other time Claire would find this comical. But now she just stared at the cement walls and floor of the garage. Details jumped out at her. Water and oil stains like continents, small, secret worlds unto themselves. A fine webbing of fissures as if spun by intricate spiders. *Step on a crack, break your mother's back.* The game of little girls.

Claire started the car. Maybe she should drive to Upton Grove, talk to Glen face-to-face. Reversing the car out of the parking space, Claire stopped abruptly, noticing an empty storage unit the size of a small garage alongside the car to her left. She could easily maneuver the car around and pull it into that unit. Glide right in there, close the door behind her, plug the exhaust, and be done with it. All the grief and struggles gone.

She met Gretchie's eager stare, her eyes, round and bright. Claire was no coward. She deserved the distress of living each quiet moment regretting her ambitions, her actions on That Day. Sighing, she reached over to explore the little indent just behind G's right ear, the spot that got her leg thumping, when *Bang!* The car lurched forward and then fell back into place.

"What the hell?" Claire sucked in air and reached over to steady her dog as she struggled to understand what had just happened. The clap of a car door echoed and a short, heavy man appeared in the driver's side window.

He said something, but the glass muffled his voice.

"What?"

"Can you drop it down?" He made circles in the air with his hand. "The window? Down?"

Claire hit the button robotically as Gretchie lunged over her lap to investigate the new person, sniffing wildly. Claire looked at the man. He had a beard. He was small and rotund with round glasses, probably pushing seventy.

"Hey, nice boy!" He reached a hand toward Gretchie. "So sorry I hit you! Didn't you feel it?"

Claire sank low in the car, hoping to hide herself in shadow. She didn't respond. His voice sounded familiar, but she wasn't sorting thoughts well.

"Say, I think I know you. From the hospital."

Claire's mind remained blank.

"Do you work in the hospital?"

She nodded.

"Me too. I'm on the eighth floor."

Psychiatry. Just fucking great. She still said nothing. She looked in the rearview mirror. A BMW.

"Anyway. Looks like some paint's chipped. That's all. I think. We should have it checked out. Give me your number. I'll pass it to my insurance…"

A sudden rush of emotion overcame Claire. Hot, unfettered tears sprang from her eyes and ran down her face. What was happening here?

"Oh my gosh, so sorry. It's okay, really. It's only a small scratch." She shook her head.

"Hey, you're…uh…Claire Rawlings…"

Oh God. Glancing in the side-view mirror, she saw a cane, and suddenly, she put it all together. The voice, the beard. Dr. Howard Fisher. He was the expert they'd dug up to appear on the *Chicago Live at Five!* talk show that day of the horrible interview. Before Claire could react, this Howard Fisher was hobbling around the front of her car and then he was in her car, on the passenger side, with Gretchie wedged between him and Claire, her tail going to town, beside herself to have a friendly human to destroy with licks and kindness.

Claire cried harder.

"Look, I don't know what's going on here. But I remember your story. I'm really sorry about your family. I'm wondering if maybe—"

She cut him off.

"I'm fine. Please…" Meaning *get out*. But she only sobbed harder, and it came out garbled. More like a turkey than a human. She bent her head into her hands.

"Here, take this."

Dr. Fisher pulled Gretchie's towel from under his leg. He barely fit in the front seat with his cane, his girth. But he was kind.

She took the offering and mopped her face.

"Who can I call for you, Dr. Rawlings?"

"No one." She suddenly felt ridiculous.

"Your therapist? A friend? Your husband, maybe?"

More tears.

"Why don't we take a walk to my office and sit for a few minutes? It's not two blocks from here. I'm an amazingly good listener." Gretchie gave her best I-want-attention whine. "Your dog. What's his name?"

Claire swallowed to slow her tears. "He's a she."

"Of course, sorry."

"Her name's Gretchie," Claire said, her voice wavering. "I call her G sometimes."

"Great name!" He held out his palm, which she snuffled with relish. "Okay, G, you stay here. Don't let anyone steal our cars. Your mom'll bring you a treat."

Gretchie lifted her paw onto his arm as if in agreement. Pathetic.

Claire shook her head. "I can't leave her here. Alone." She was pretty close to being fully cried out.

"No problem." Fisher patted Gretchie awkwardly on the head. "She can come with us."

And then he was out of Claire's car, shutting the door and maneuvering his BMW into a parking slot before she could think, before she could stop from being caught up in this unexpected momentum.

Ugh. She pressed her palm to her forehead. She looked into her dog's generous expression and almost started bawling again. But Fisher was already at her window, looming like a large, lumpy shadow. Gretchie yelped a happy little greeting at him. Claire sighed and climbed out as G whimpered madly through the window crack.

"Dr. Fisher?"

"Howard."

"What about your patients?"

"I mainly teach. Have a seminar later. Besides…" He stopped and held Claire in a fierce gaze. His eyes weren't creepy like she'd surmised when she saw him onstage. They were filled with compassion. "You are more important right now."

She nodded slowly.

"Your dog can sit with us in the office, or outside in the yard. Your choice. My home office is no great shakes. Don't see patients there anymore." His voice shifted back to serious. "What is your decision, Dr. Rawlings?"

This was his way of telling Claire that he was adamant. That she would not escape him. In fact, he was already moving in a slow, lumbering way, leaning into his cane.

"You two coming?" he called over his shoulder.

Howard's house, on Lakeshore Drive, was square, with pillars and a flat roof. It might have been charming, but it needed paint, and the landscaping, even to Claire's poorly trained eyes, was out of whack. Big trees with too many leaves and not enough sun.

His office was an extension on one side, which they entered through a small waiting area. Claire found herself surrounded by pictures of turtles. Serious-looking prints and framed bookplates of various species labeled in Latin script. Aside from a coloring book and a few old *Highlights* on a table, not much kid stuff. That was a relief. He went into an adjoining room and motioned Claire inside.

"Come in here, where we can talk." He moved a stack of papers from a chair. "Sit, please sit."

Other than the oval neatness of a large Galapagos tortoise shell shellacked and hanging on the wall behind him, the room was pretty close to shambles, as if an emanation from a disheveled mind. Claire looked around. On a different day, under different circumstances, she would've rolled her eyes.

Howard must've followed her gaze.

"Like I said, I don't see patients here anymore." He pointed to a ceramic pitcher and paper cups that sat, along with a box of tea biscuits, on a tray behind a yellowing plant. "Water?"

"No. Thank you."

He poured a cup for himself and slipped Gretchie a butter biscuit. Claire frowned. "Only one."

"Of course," Howard said and tossed one more in the air.

Gretchie leaped and snatched it with doggie precision.

"Sit, girl." Claire motioned Gretchie near her. "And pay no attention to that man."

G flopped to the floor beside Claire's chair. Claire reached down and patted her dog's thick hip.

"Dr. Rawlings." Howard settled back a bit, but his size kept him from leaning much farther. "I'm going to pry a little. Are you in therapy?"

Claire shook her head. "Too busy."

"Hmm…that's interesting." He said this with an air of gentle sarcasm. "Especially since Northwestern has a great mental health department. You have access to anyone on staff."

"Okay. Once. I saw someone once. Didn't work out."

"Why are you so hesitant to talk to a therapist?"

A general suspicion of the breed of professionals who thought they knew so much, combined with the fear of exposing her deepest feelings, and a dash of flat-out stubbornness—she didn't bother to explain right then. How could anyone plumb her depths, offer her advice, unless they had been through what she had?

An urge to test this man, to needle him, surged through Claire. "In my professional opinion, they're all idiots." She added, "I hope I didn't offend you."

"Not at all. Between you and me, I think all radiologists are moronic. But I'd still go to one if I broke my arm."

Claire allowed a weak smile. "Touché."

Howard met her eyes. His broad, bright face was filled with wrinkles. A Santa Claus face.

"Tell me." Claire met his eyes. "Do you have any tragedy in your past?"

"Not in the way you've had. Only normal loss of loved ones. Aging, cancer…this." He pointed to his leg. "A childhood accident. Barely even remember it. Nothing like what you've been through."

"Then how can you presume…" Her voice rose with agitation.

"To understand people with problems, real tragedies, is that what you mean?"

Claire narrowed her eyes at him. This was an unending challenge she'd had with well-wishers, colleagues. People who tried to help by saying they knew what she was going through. Her swallowed response was "No, you damn well don't." The only person who seemed to have any type of a clue, ironically, was Jay White. They'd kept in touch as he'd promised. The shared light they'd seen maintained a bond between them. She actually sent Jay money at times, and he sent her postcards of the tourist area he'd settled near. Simple pictures. She kept them lined up against a mirror. Bright, sunny images of impossibly clear days, dunes, and shots of lakes touched up so the water sparkled like turquoise jewelry. It made the familiar seem far away, exotic. It made her, in an unexplainable way, feel closer to her girls.

"I don't know."

"What kind of answer is that?"

"An honest one. I just always wanted to do this. Be a child psychiatrist." He lifted the cup to his lips, realized it was empty, and then set it down again. "I see you're disappointed. I wish I had a better answer. Sorry."

"Do you have children?" Claire only half believed she was being this bold. This response was important if there were to be any trust between them.

"So this is an interview then?" His expression hinted at bemusement. "I suppose I should tell you that my wife and I tried and weren't successful. That we always wanted kids and it was a real heartbreak when we couldn't. But the truth is I never wanted them."

Claire tossed him a searing look.

He didn't flinch. "You see the stuff I deal with every day can be, is, difficult. My patients, kids, need so much. Other specialties, they see ugly things. Horrendous skin rashes, broken bones. But me, I get broken little souls. Abuse. Kids that cut themselves from a sense of worthlessness. I have an eleven-year-old anorexic in the ICU. I take the cases labeled hopeless or without financial means. I have a decent home, love my work. That's my reward."

As he spoke, a small knot of tension released in Claire's neck. She got this man. In so many ways, it paralleled Claire's own story. Overly driven. Not easily understood. His kindness settled in around her like a soft blanket. They sat quietly for several long minutes and then several minutes more. It was strange to Claire that she didn't feel awkward or hurried. That it was okay to just sit.

"Do you know"—Claire looked toward the single window moving with shadows from overhanging tree branches outside—"that fetal cells remain within the mother's body for up to a quarter century?" She closed her eyes while picturing the phantom passengers, microscopic reminders of the most intimate connection.

"Dr. Claire Rawlings." Howard spoke softly, stretching forward to place his hand over hers. It was dry and warm and comforting. "It's time for us to get you some help. Someone terrific to talk to."

Claire cut him off. "I know you are a child psychiatrist…but… do you mind…" She spoke softly. This was hard, so very hard. "Would it be possible if I schedule with you?"

Howard sat back. "It's a little unusual, and, in fact"—he crinkled his forehead—"I'm not sure if I'm the right person in this situation."

Claire's heart sank.

"But," he continued, "considering the circumstances, I would be honored. And you know what? I've got time. Now."

"What about your seminar?"

"As I said earlier. You are more important. And," he added, his eyes twinkling, "far more interesting than a bunch of stuffy academics."

Claire nodded slowly and caught her hands together, feeling the bony angles of her fingers where fat padding should be.

"I want to hear things from you," Howard continued. "The things that circle through your head and"—he placed his hand on his chest—"around your heart."

A clutch of starlings soared past in a small triangle of sky through the branches. Could she do this? Any of this? She'd held so much inside for so long. She dropped her head. "I just…I can't talk about what happened…the situation…my two daughters…"

"Then let's not. For now."

She told Howard Fisher instead about her sister, Vicki. How she relied on her love and support, and the comforting friendship with Jay White. About Gretchie. About how her ears perked up when Claire spoke to her, even when it was nonsense. She looked at her dog, softly shaped into a brown crescent. Claire's very heart. She touched G's back lightly, her fur warming in a band of sun.

"Your husband?" Howard asked when she finished.

"And my husband… Well, he's contacted a divorce attorney."

Howard kept his gaze focused on Claire's, urging her to continue.

"This whole thing with Glen has just filled my head with more—" She stopped abruptly.

"More what? Please tell me."

She sighed. "I cling to these memories—the texture of Lily's hair, the sparkle in Andrea's eyes, they are still so present to me… and then…"

"Go on."

"I saw something once. A light. I know it was from Lily. But there has been nothing from Andrea, and…" She spoke through a growing lump in her throat. "It reminds me that…that this terrible situation…is all my fault." She placed her hand over her mouth.

"Claire." Howard smiled. "Earlier, you told me you couldn't talk about your girls. But you just were."

She gulped and stared into his face. His eyes were strong and sincere.

"All this pain," he said, "gives me hope."

"What?"

"That you haven't shut down."

She shook her head. "I have, though. Don't you see? I locked myself away in my work, abandoned my husband."

"And he responded pretty harshly." Howard let that sink in. "Claire, I'm going to allow you to do something. Go ahead and be mad at the world. Be really pissed. For a moment or two."

"I…I can't."

"Not everything is your fault. Anger can be very cathartic. I think you need some directed away from yourself."

He left a silence. This moment of reprieve brought Claire comfort and allowed her to regroup a little. When she once again spoke, Howard's face remained animated, absorbed in every detail, yet calm. He did not push her or lead her in any direction. It was a relief that she could say anything without him responding in surprise. She was all over the place, bouncing from all the unresolved issues between her and Glen to hoping to make a difference in the lives of cancer patients. Everything but her daughters. She wasn't sure if it was the free flow of thoughts or a catharsis caused by her sobbing when she first met Howard in the car, but she felt like a load of cargo was sliding off her back.

It was Gretchie who ended the session when, after three and a half hours, she stretched and yawned with great drama, strode to the door, and whined.

"Thank goodness he's here," Howard said. "He can come anytime to remind us when to stop."

"He's a she." Claire smiled.

Howard wrote a number on a slip of paper. "I'm available for you. Day or night." He handed it to Claire and then escorted them to the door where Gretchie was scratching. "You did a great job. Go home. Rest."

"Okay."

"And then I will call you later. To begin scheduling and also"—he raised his eyebrows like a worried parent—"just to check in."

"Okay."

"And you will promise me that you will call me too. In the middle of the night. Or whenever. If you need me."

Claire nodded and leashed up Gretchie. She left shaky for certain, but also amazed. An accidental appointment with an accredited therapist was behind her, and she was still intact. That was something at least. A block away, she heard waves rise and fall, and the wind carried the distinctive scent of Lake Michigan; she'd know the fragrance of blue sky and glacial meltwater anywhere.

Claire pulled G closer and kept walking, one step at a time.

When she returned to her place, she settled in on the couch, exhausted, and drifted to sleep with her dog warm and solid against her leg.

Within minutes, Claire was floating under deep, hyacinth-colored water, acutely aware that it was her turn to drown. Overhead, she heard the roar of a voice, far off but approaching. Charcoal Man. His tone was different from how she first imagined—not high-pitched, but a low, angry rumble. She flailed her limbs, to propel herself away from the voice. Beneath the black undersides of lily pads, she hovered just above the muck and remained still until he was gone. Suddenly she heard a faint calling, and though it was warped through the water, it was familiar.

"Mommy! Mommy!"

Andrea. Even muted, Claire knew it was her daughter. She knew it in an indecipherable way, the way millions of animal mothers through the canyons of time have recognized their babies by smell, sound, mere presence. The voice became louder, clearer; Claire thrashed around, looking for her child in the murk; the cries grew closer still and then suddenly stopped. Claire desperately tried to swim to her but was not able to move, mired in muck, useless in the deep.

Chapter 16
Jay

J ay had just secured his hands on the pruning shears when something struck against his glove. Searching the fan-shaped tips of the arborvitae, he found himself in a stare-down with a praying mantis. Forelegs extended, it was itching to fight.

"Hello, little warrior."

Jay offered his hand for it to climb and laughed as the creature tickled his arm. He'd recently had a strong feeling he'd be meeting someone new soon. The insect stared at Jay with garnet-colored eyes and then scampered into the deeper branches, blending perfectly with the yellow-green foliage.

"You just reminded me." Jay chuckled. "I gotta move it."

He skimmed through the hedge quickly, keeping one eye out for a stick-thin insect appendage, and the other on his watch. Today was one of the most important in his life. Today he'd sign the papers to close on his very own place. He'd finally found a home. After leaving Illinois, he'd headed straight for Michigan as planned, but he'd never made it as far north as his Petoskey stone had urged because the El Camino gave out one last time. The alternator. The accidental location turned out to be fortuitous. Right next to the Great Lake, Michiana was a tourist town that swelled with seasonal visitors, some of whom were interested in dream catchers. Jay soon realized that being close to this amazing body of water was just the thing to lift his spirits. Most importantly, the locals and businesses here were in need of landscaping services, and after a few years of searching for clients, his business was coming along nicely.

Within the hour, Jay was seated across from the real estate agent and the mobile home park manager, putting his signature on a rent-to-own agreement with the rent part crossed out. After saving up for almost five years, he could now call the trailer where he'd been living his own. Outside the window, his new truck gleamed. Okay, not quite new, but a damn good used one. The best part was the sign on the side, *J. W. Landscaping and Snow Removal*. It had started simply enough, small jobs here and there, that grew into longer-term contracts. Eventually, with luck, perseverance, and sobriety, he'd made it. He was now both a business and property owner.

There were two checks to hand over today. One from his own account and one from Claire Rawlings. True to her word, she'd stayed in contact. They'd grown to be some kind of long-distance friends, bonded by their shared understanding of unimaginable loss. He'd send her a postcard, a quick note once in a while, checking in, updating her on the status of his business. Claire, in turn, sent him packages, things like sweatshirts and baseball caps, fudge around the holidays. As soon as he informed her about his big purchase, she stepped up; Jay hadn't even asked.

He felt a nudge of longing looking at her handwriting, receiving her generosity. Thoughts of her older daughter still got to him. He'd even made a dream catcher for Andrea. A small, unadorned one. Just like he'd made for Lily. But he didn't have the heart to send it to Claire. Not after instilling hope by telling her Andrea was alive when she had probably already been reduced to ashes. How could he have been so wrong? He no longer trusted himself, his feelings. Even as they persisted to dog him that there were pieces of that story missing. Something about the tragedy and its devastating outcome left him with a lingering uneasiness, a sense that things didn't quite line up. Whenever he recalled that freezing night in the campground, just after he'd met with Claire, he could swear over a thousand Bibles that it was a woman who had stolen Claire's girls and that Andrea was alive. Now he was consumed with guilt. And the fact that Claire was so nice to him made it worse in some ways. But he'd keep the bond going. As long as she wanted.

The manager, a blond guy with pockmarks, smacked his gum. "Getting a bargain for certain with that adjoining land. Keep you really isolated back there."

"Yeah, except for that rental across the street."

With his trailer set apart from so many others, the old broken-down mint-and-chrome unit, directly in his line of view, was a sore spot for Jay, a blight on his seclusion. Management offered monthly leasing on that place and so drew short-termers, transients—people with problems.

"No worries, man." The manager again smacked his gum. "A woman and kid moved in last week. They seem harmless enough."

Jay had seen an old Buick coming and going at odd hours. Whoever they were, they were quiet, elusive.

"A kid?"

That made Jay nervous. He'd lived in enough mobile home parks to see his share of punks, adolescent males with a full-on rage button. Usually started with BB guns, shooting out windows, and then escalated to smoking pot, drug dealing.

"A little girl. Eight, nine maybe. Like I said. They seem fine."

The real estate agent shifted in his chair. He was overweight, with a buzz cut that looked like a five o'clock shadow on his head. "Sign, please, Mr. White. I gotta hit another showing."

Jay's tranquility was restored as he took the pen in hand. This was partial fulfillment of his dream. A nice double-wide with a garage. He could keep his mowers and other equipment stored comfortably through the winter. The open-air shed offered plenty of space to work on his dream catchers. In fact, the best part was that the property abutted scrubby open land, which led to woods, then to dunes, and finally to the lake, where he scavenged all kinds of cool materials to use in his craft—freshwater shells and local plants. The trees here were mostly familiar from his childhood, quaking aspens, hardwoods, even ghost pines. But no cotton-woods. For that, he was grateful. Didn't need that reminder of his home in North Dakota.

Jay completed the paperwork without flourish and left. He had one more client scheduled and now a mortgage to pay. He arrived at the site and worked with enhanced stamina, clearing brush and spreading mulch, and by the time he finished, he was spent. Eschewing the highway, Jay rattled along the rural route that hugged the lake. The late-afternoon sun almost blinded him with the pulsing richness of a chemical fire flowing onto the waves, phosphorescent orange and sulfur yellows. His clothes smelled of gasoline from the equipment, a strong, sweet odor that reminded him of whiskey. He cracked his window.

Passing through the entrance, he laughed when he saw the sign: *Flamingo Nest Mobile Home Park*. Flamingoes. Here in Michigan. And sure enough, each trailer came with at least one iconic plastic bird. The people up front took it seriously, kept theirs out near the mailboxes or next to their doors. Even in the winter, he'd see pink heads peeking through the snow. Most of the people seemed friendly, waved as he passed. Jay would have to talk to them more once he was less busy. This was his community now, and he intended to be part of it, quit his loner status.

Darkness settled in as Jay traveled the U-shaped path toward the back of the park. Jay's place was at the apex of the curve where the units were farthest apart. Swinging through the bend, his headlights skittered along brush, mailbox posts, and tree trunks. One large oak surprised him with a pair of bare feet hanging from the skirt of the canopy. Small ones, a kid's, dangling like someone had suspended a body there. As soon as the light hit, they disappeared into the leaves.

Pulling into his drive, Jay noted with mild disgust the unit across the road. A bloated, submarine-looking thing, it was propped up on cinder blocks. Might've been funny if it didn't look so sad. There were no lights on, except a faint glow in what must be a bedroom. Otherwise, it looked unoccupied. Something about this place was causing an uneasiness he had come to recognize as a pre-feeling. *Stop it, Jay. Keep the focus on your own life. No reason to look for trouble.*

He let the truck idle and touched the deed left faceup on the seat next to him, the ink of his signature still fresh. He'd need to store it in a safe spot, at the very least waterproof. He took a moment to survey his property as if for the first time. Among the lawn equipment, about a dozen dream catchers twisted in the open air shed. In the dwindling light, Jay could just make out shapes of piles on his workbench—one for lichens and mosses, another for shells and dried lake grasses. The shutters on the trailer could use a touch of paint. And the bare rough circle of dirt, several yards in diameter, he'd need to decide about that. An attempt to re-create a ceremonial dance ring that his mother had made outside his own childhood home. Now it would remain an on-again, off-again work in progress. He stepped from his truck. It was chilly for June, with a cold evening to come, and he shivered slightly. Among the pines, spindly oaks darkened in a ring around his yard. They wouldn't mature here; the soil was too sandy. But he gave the acorns credit for trying.

He grabbed an armful of arborvitae trimmings from the truck and dropped them onto the earthen floor of the shed. The branches were pliable and released a slow, heady odor of green that would last long after drying. Starting back for another load, he knocked into the workbench and heard the sound of glass rattling. A bottle. Southern Comfort. An insurance policy that Jay had hidden when things were real shaky, back when he first learned the story of Andrea Rawlings. Ever since, his dreams were often infiltrated by cattails and long endless roads, all in a monotone of haunting crystal blue, just like Lily Rawlings's eyes.

He'd spent plenty of nights awake in a bath of sweat, staring at a stain the shape of Madagascar on the ceiling directly above the nightstand next to his bed. The pictures that Claire had given him at the diner in Chicago, those of her two girls, had been kept in the top drawer of that nightstand. Water droplets, slow and stealthy, had leaked through a crack in the roof, and made their way into the drawer. By the time Jay discovered it, the damage was done. Lily's picture was only slightly messed up, but the water had fully saturated Andrea's photo, bringing her face to ruins.

The pictures were now on a shelf in his main room, in a folder wrapped in plastic. But Jay couldn't bear to look at them. At what had happened to their images by his foolish neglect.

He held the bottle up. It felt smooth and lovely in his hand. The topaz liquid inside winked at him in invitation, an old familiar gesture. Why not celebrate? He opened the bottle. Just one sip—a yes or no sip, as he used to call it—would hurt nothing.

He thought of his early job in the morning. Plantings and cleanup at a convalescent home in town. He'd promised the manager he'd be there by six. This new client had taken hard work to land. He thought, too, of his mother. She'd be proud. But she'd been gone so long he couldn't recall her face. A dull ache inched into his chest.

Go ahead, Jay, loosen up a little.

He looked into the darkening sky.

"What moon are you tonight?" he whispered. A rich, thick crescent beamed soft white rays down to earth. "A tattletale moon, huh?" Jay turned his face away, and with the bottle firmly in his grip he sat on a lichen-covered stump and filled his mouth with an entire gulp. He held the liquid in the hollow of his cheeks. The first tasting should go slow. Fiery warmth blossomed in his mouth. He allowed a trickle to seep down his throat.

But the moon was having none of it. A gust of wind swept branches overhead to one side, unveiling a relentless beam of light, which angled across the yard and up the side of his trailer, illuminating the windows like a movie screen. The shape of a man's face appeared with a leering grin, his eyes darkly hollow. It could've been that devil in the police sketch, or the man that murdered his mother. Didn't matter. They were all takers. Jay shut his eyes. No one was taking from him now. He turned his head and spit. The liquid cratered into the soft dirt. Grimacing, he poured the rest of the bottle onto the thirsty ground. A sweet burn stayed in his mouth and he had to spit a couple more times to clear it.

He stood and slipped into the circle of bare dirt in his yard. While he didn't have his shaman's rattle, or the twigs of juniper carefully gathered by mindful hands, he did have the drumbeat of his heart and the soft mournful Lakota prayer to the Great Spirit. The wind carried itself off the lake and over the dunes and swam among Jay's legs, urging him to dance. But he resisted. It had been too long, dragged up too many memories.

Instead, he lay with his back on the ground. A cluster of firs stood out against the last band of light in the sky. Black and slender, they rose high above everything else. He traced his finger along their steepled tops all the way across to Orion's Belt.

This was his place, his moment. Basking in the night air, the cool light from the stars, he closed his eyes, allowing the sky above him to spin away. But a sound in the bushes pulled him upright. A fox maybe? Looking toward the trees, he spotted a figure, with a thatch of flame-colored hair, dash from his yard and across the street. *What the hell?* But Jay didn't have the energy to investigate. Not this night. He went inside his trailer and opened every window, to soak in the comfort offered by the lake, the sweet scent of clear water, the hush of waves.

Morning brought bad news. Today's job was canceled; the owner had changed his mind, would do the work himself. Dry weather encouraged other clients to space their cuttings longer. Damn. He couldn't afford that now. He'd have to focus on his craft today, his other source of income. Walk the shore for things to collect, bring new ideas. Looking out the kitchen window, he watched the dream catchers, hanging from the lattice rafters over his workbench, spiraling slowly. He'd accumulated quite a collection. Among the assorted shapes, near a quiet corner in the back, hung a small, simple circle twisting softly in the breeze—the one he'd dedicated to Andrea Rawlings.

He set out toward the shore, along a half-hidden path next to his trailer through bracken and trees. Within fifty feet, the lake shimmered before him. Each encounter was a surprise, and each time he remained startled by its beauty. Yet today a tiny hint, more like a pinch of something, was troubling him in a way that was not definable. The waves were choppy, topped with meringue-like foam. Limp weeds and detritus lined the shore along with the faint smell of storm drain. He scoured the high-water mark before heading onto the crest of a dune. Soon he discovered a vernal pond with all kinds of new treasures: bladderwort and water hyacinth that would dry nicely. As usual, he lost track of time until his stomach grumbled for lunch.

Arriving back at his shed, Jay could tell right away his work area had been disturbed again. A small pile of carefully sorted stones was missing.

"Damn!" Two days before, it had been a clutch of sandpiper feathers. At first, he figured he'd misplaced them, or the wind had taken them. Now he reconsidered. Someone was stealing.

From the corner of his eye he caught sight of a small figure darting jackrabbit-style along the edge of his yard and then across the street. Maybe a girl, but Jay couldn't be certain. Whoever it was had kelly-green hair, like a cartoon leprechaun. The kid dove underneath that infernal rental across the road.

Jay marched over and bent down, peering into the dark space between the cinder blocks.

"Hello!"

No answer.

He dropped to his hands and knees.

"It's not like I couldn't see you." Bending deeper, he rocked his knee directly onto a sharp stone. "Ow, shit!"

"You shouldn't swear." A girl's voice. "Go away."

This was the kid the real estate agent had mentioned and the owner of the pair of dirty feet he'd seen dangling from the oak. She was young, but definitely not meek. The little sneak had waited for Jay to leave and then raided his stash.

He crouched farther, angling his head to one side. He couldn't actually see anything, since whoever was under there was hiding behind a makeshift wall of stones.

"Are you going to make me come under?"

A quick shuffling noise, then silence.

"I will, you know." Who was he fooling? He'd never fit.

"I can't talk to strangers." The voice echoed along the dirt.

"I'm not a stranger. I live across the street. I know you've been messing with my stuff."

Nothing.

"Do you want me to tell your mom?"

"She's not my mom."

Jay rocked back onto his haunches and rubbed his pebble-dimpled knee. A crow parachuted onto a low sumac nearby and cocked a suspicious eye directly at him. He had a mind to grab it, pluck its shiny black feathers.

"I caught you red-handed stealing from me." He sighed. "Look, I won't say anything if you promise not to do it again."

Jay heard stones scuttling. He peeked underneath. A largish rock moved, just enough to reveal a slice of a young face. A single brown eye sparkling beneath a thatch of lime-colored bangs. There was a Lakota term for her eye color. What was it again? *Ghi.* That was it, a certain brown like the beauty of autumn leaves still flecked with gold. And why was he thinking like this anyway?

"Really?" Her voice softened. "You promise?"

"Scout's honor."

"Okay, then I promise too. To stop."

"Looks like we have a deal."

Jay's joints cracked as he stood.

A foot protruded from under the trailer, adorned with a toe ring with a plastic flower, brightly colored, gaudy. The girl followed, scrambling out from the impossibly narrow space. She stepped fully into the sunshine. Her hair was choppy, clearly a do-it-yourself job. He suspected hair dyes didn't come in that shade. A mischievous light in her eyes glinted like mica in a rock. For a moment, he thought there was something familiar about her face, as if he'd seen her before. Maybe that candy commercial on TV—Skittles—one of the girls in a pack of the kids running in circles. Jay's fingers worried the Petoskey stone in his pocket.

The girl pointed to Jay's shed. "I know what you make over there."

"You do, huh?"

She nodded solemnly. "Uh-huh. Dream catchers. Are you Lakota?" Her eyes widened with fascination. His hand went to the scar on his face, amazed that so far she'd shown no fear of him. Instead, she actually jumped up and down. Her bare feet smacked onto the sharp stones and she hopped from one to the other. Jay cracked up a little. She was comical, with the hair, the uneven cutoffs, that attitude—the whole look.

"Yeah, that's right." He offered, "Are Indians your hobby or something?"

"I have a lot of hobbies. I know all the constellations."

"All of 'em, huh? That's pretty impressive. What else you got?"

She shrugged. "Too much to say, actually."

"Oh."

"So you're a real Indian?" She was completely enraptured, all pretense gone.

He shrugged. "Yeah. I am. Cool, huh?"

"Yeah, but you're not Chippewa. How come?"

"What do you mean? 'Cause I'm Lakota, that's why."

A tribe of warriors. A joke. Jay was the least brave person he knew.

"No, I mean, your tribe is from the Dakotas, right? Chippewa, that's from around here."

"Look, I find the feathers in the woods behind my place, and the rocks are from a pond near the lake. I can show you where I get everything." This offer suddenly felt too much, too intimate. What if she took him up on it? Jay cleared his throat. "Okay, then. Well, I gotta go…"

He began to walk away.

"Wait. Do you mean it? You'll show me where you find things?"

Jay stopped and turned. "How 'bout we make a different deal?"

Her face flushed with anticipation.

"I let you keep the stuff. And you tell me what you do with it."

Her face grew serious. "You'll think it's weird."

"Really? I make contraptions that catch dreams, and I'm gonna find something else weird?"

He was really talking to himself when he said this, some great rhetorical comment, because he had been stuck, it seemed, for so long, and now his life was loosening around him—which was good and, he realized, terrifying at the same time. Jay pulled the hair back from his forehead. The last time he'd bothered to look, there were streaks of ash white amid the jet black.

"Well, okay." This was clearly a concession on her part. "I do art with it... I paint and draw, stuff like that."

"Sounds like we're kindred spirits, eh? By the way, my name is Jay. Jay White."

She looked disappointed. "Is that it? Do you have an Indian name?"

"No. It's just plain old Jay White."

"Oh."

"Tell you what. I can sense..." He put his fingertips to his temple and closed his eyes. "I can sense a name coming on, into my brain. Yup, it's one for you, though."

"Wow, really? You can do that? What is it?"

She bounced up and down and then hooted at gouging her foot on the sharp gravel.

"Yup, here it comes. It's...it's... Crazy... Wait... That's it! Crazy Hair." He opened his eyes.

"Hey, not funny." She tossed an imaginary rock at him. And yet her eyes were shining.

"Actually, that way you hop around reminds me of a little bird. What is your name, anyway?"

She hesitated. "Colleen." Her face darkened. "But I like Colly."

"Yeah, okay, come over sometime and I can show you how I make the dream catchers. In the meantime, keep the stuff you took." It wasn't gonna kill him to share this with her. He was actually enjoying the company.

"Goodbye, Jay White."

"Goodbye, Little Bird."

Jay returned home happy for the encounter, the few moments of company. But as evening slipped into night he began to feel unsettled. What was it about that girl? There was a look on her face, something he couldn't pin down. Not fear—but there was something. While she was funny, there was also an unnerving maturity about her. Yet Jay wouldn't allow his thoughts to remain long on his most-likely-transient neighbor. He had too much else on his plate. Like finding more clients.

Around midnight, the rhythm of the waves rising from over the dunes woke Jay. He'd been dreaming about his childhood. He fully expected to see his mother and felt the sensation of her hand on his forehead. But there was only the quiet of deep night in his room. Rising, he listened for an owl and then stepped out onto the porch where moonlight illuminated the plants around the trailer like a soft web. In the brightness, with the press of the trees surrounding him, Jay sensed a feeling coming on. But he willed it away and sat down on the metal porch. The grating bit into the back of his legs, but he ignored that too. He was afraid of this odd stirring inside him.

Afraid of trusting a feeling that was coming like a change in weather.

Chapter 17
Claire

On the way to her office, Claire took a shortcut through the hospital gift shop. Ducking along an aisle of teacups, she encountered a new display of small plates featuring birds—robins, finches, and blue jays. She was instantly reminded of Jay White and the money she'd sent him from her new personal checking account—another divide between her and Glen. She made a mental note to reach out to Jay again, see how things were going since he'd bought his place.

Taking the stairs, Claire's mind buzzed with the unlikely people in her life, Jay and Howard Fisher. Could these relationships, in fact, be some type of message? A shaft of sun fanned along the broad window causing her to squint through the brightness. Even turning her head didn't help much since the whole stairwell, painted enamel white, seemed to glow with insistence. Like her dream last night. That same one was visiting regularly. At least once a week, Claire would be moored underwater and hear Andrea calling. Was it her imagination, or had her daughter's voice been growing louder, stronger?

She ascended the five flights to her office. Small distractions like counting steps allowed her a diversion from waiting to hear if she had been chosen to present her findings at that critical seminar in October. This was more than about personal accomplishment; she truly loved the idea of helping others—Howard had pointed out that it was part of the path forward for her own healing. It also allowed her to push aside the anxiety of the status, or rather nonstatus, of her marriage. It was August, and she and Glen had not spoken since their fight. It was something Howard urged her to address in their twice-weekly sessions: to clarify her feelings about Glen and their marriage. He hoped that Claire would be the one to initiate conversation between them. But her emotions were betraying her, swinging wildly from stubborn anger to deeply felt pain. In truth, she realized she wasn't sure what she wanted from Glen.

Once in her office she settled at her desk.

Knock, knock. The frosted glass in the office door rattled.

Claire stood up. On the other side of the block letters of her name, she read the profile of Glen's face before opening the door. She stiffened. She wasn't ready to see him. Not yet.

He stepped inside. "I hope this is okay. I remembered you don't see patients today."

"Of course." She tried to remain casual even as she was pinned to the wall by his eyes.

"Claire. We need to talk."

She nodded, then pointed to a chair across from her desk. He remained standing.

"I'll get right to the point. You jumped right into this research program without considering me. Our marriage."

Claire exhaled loudly. "You were the one who insisted I finish medical school."

"We needed you to go back. You know that. Besides"—an air of sarcasm entered his tone—"you seem right at home here. And now a possible PhD. I want you to be happy—but there is not time for anything, anyone else in your life."

There was something different in his eyes, a new type of sorrow. When had she become so dissociated from her husband? She remembered when they were in college, Glen would watch her study during spring term, her skin pink, his biscuit-brown from the rays they caught lounging outside the dorm together, and how she felt special, sexy, encircled in his gaze. She wanted to tell him that she was happy to see him again. That they should try to fix this terrible gulf between them for the girls.

"I felt…" he began, his voice slow and earnest. "I still sometimes feel, Claire, that you buried our marriage with our daughters."

A boulder, rolling downhill, knocked her flat. "You have never said that you blame me. But I know it's there. Between us. I mean, how could you not?"

He looked down. "I want the old Claire back, the ferocious woman I married. The one who would fight for us."

She looked closely at her husband. They had once possessed the ability to read and respond to each other's thoughts, moods. There was a hollowness in his expression beyond the drawn quality that had taken hold after the abduction. Defeat.

"That's why I think it is best to separate. I mean, we already live in different places. Different lives." He hesitated and then continued, "I don't mean to hurt you. I just think we need to move forward."

Claire felt, in this bright room, as if she'd suddenly been engulfed by shadow. As if the light she was harboring from Lily was now all but gone.

"I want this to be as low stress as possible." He dropped his voice so that it was almost a whisper. "Take some time to think about what we each want to keep…what to do with the girls' things."

He looked at Claire, and his eyes grew moist. It was almost as if he were pleading, it seemed, for some indication of hope in this seemingly hopeless situation. Glen deserved a life. And, selfishly, she didn't want a life fully without Glen. She realized she still loved him. Why didn't she tell him that? There was a prickly sensation at the back of Claire's throat, where words stuck like a half-swallowed cactus. Because the woman he wanted, the one he'd married, was gone.

Even though her heart was splintering, Claire held steady and nodded.

Glen stepped back and remained in the doorway for a moment, shifting awkwardly. "I want the best for both of us," he said and then left.

She watched him walk down the hall, the back of his blue shirt and khaki pants, the gloss of his hair. After he disappeared around a corner, she tried to return to her work, but her papers were now full of hieroglyphs. She buried her face in her hands. The hospital suddenly felt like a rabbit warren and she was surrounded—offices, rooms, labs, all filled with people and more people. Her pulse raced. This was something more than normal anxiety. And it was cresting out of control. She needed to get out, grab a few gulps of fresh air. She left down the back stairwell.

Outside, she was surprised to find it was still morning, because it seemed as if a whole day had passed. She wandered aimlessly, each step like a small swell in a sea of emotion. Life without Glen was terrifying, life with him unbearable.

Each thought generated more confusion until she could barely breathe and move at the same time. Each step brought increased angst, more confusion. Without being aware how she had done so, she found herself on the same street as Howard's home, and then she was inside his waiting room.

He was on the phone with the door closed. So she stood, rubbing the tops of her arms as a slow-burning irritation blossomed inside. Could it be a sham? The feeling of comfort here? A quick look in a small mirror—why did he have a mirror here anyway with all these damn turtles? Her face was chalk-white, with two round spots of red on her cheeks. Clownish, that's what she was. Especially in this place designed for children. She noticed the threadbare patches in the mustard-colored carpet. Why didn't Howard pay more attention to this shabbiness? It was off-putting. No patients here, he'd said. But wasn't she a patient? Didn't she matter? She heard Howard shuffle up to the door and then it was open.

"You are a surprise." He smiled warmly. "Come in."

She blew past him without even a grunt and sat stiffly in the chair across from his desk. Was it her imagination or did he take his time getting to his seat? Already she was thinking what a mistake it was to be here. She should've called Vicki instead. She felt as if she were on a train, on a slope, facing downward, and there were no brakes.

"Claire, you seem very upset."

Howard's tone suddenly struck her as patronizing.

"Don't analyze me." Ridiculous, of course. She was sitting in the office of a therapist she was paying to analyze her. But what she needed was simple empathy, to have her feathers smoothed.

"I'm just here," she said, shifting the conversation, "to tell you that I'm staying away from Glen for good."

"Because?"

"Because you said I should blast him."

"I never said that, Claire."

"Yes, you did. That I was entitled to my anger." Realizing that she sounded like a little kid tattling stoked even more irritation.

"A slight misinterpretation of our discussion at our first meeting. But go on."

"He came to my office today."

"Oh?"

"All I can think is that I wish I were someone else. The person Glen used to love. And I can't be her anymore." She dropped her head into her hands. "Can't do it."

"What?"

"This!" She motioned wildly with her arms, indicating the surrounding office. Why was Howard so slow on the uptake? Why didn't he simply read her pain and help her without questions? "Therapy. Life. Any of it! It's too hard. Just too damn hard."

"I'm here to tell you that you can, Claire." Howard asked gently, "What do you want from Glen?"

She sat up and leaned forward.

"A tantrum. That's what I want." Her voice rose in pitch and volume. "To hear he either despises me for what I did or—"

"What if he doesn't blame you?"

"What?"

"At least, not in the way you think he does. Maybe he blames himself."

"How is that even possible?" She was incredulous.

"He's the man of the family, the protector..."

"Stop! This isn't helping. It's making me feel worse. Now I'm responsible for his guilt too?"

"Have you and Glen ever talked about how you actually feel toward each other since the abduction?"

Of course not. That was absurd. She'd thought Howard understood how grief went between couples, how it became its own little world of gestures and heavy pauses and assumptions—this strange current of their lives, molten and subterranean. But then, how could he? He was a doctor for children.

"Why are you agitating me like this?"

"Claire, you are agitating yourself. It isn't a bad thing. You need to do this—to let the junk out. I'm just trying to understand the trigger that brought you here."

She felt as if she were onstage behind a thick velvet curtain, and whatever she said came across as muffled gibberish to the audience. It was stifling. Unbearable.

"You are not listening to me."

"Claire, I get it. You're afraid."

"Of what?"

"That you can't hide from your grief and the feeling that…if you talk about the girls, then maybe you are giving something away. Your very motherhood perhaps."

Claire covered her face. Why didn't he stop?

"Maybe, too," he added softly, "you're angry that Glen accepted their deaths before you were ready."

Claire dropped her hands to her sides. She kept her arms stiff, her muscles tense, in a purposeful gesture of disgust. "Enough!"

But Howard continued. "I know you feel overwhelmed. But you are strong."

She squared her shoulders and stared directly at him, as if the power in her expression could make him stop this prodding, this exploring, teasing this wound.

"You can do it. You can rescue yourself. But not by hiding."

Her face reddened with anger. "You don't know anything." She wasn't strong enough. For this. To continue forward. To make her marriage work. She stood and swerved toward the door.

"Please feel free to leave if you need to," Howard said evenly. "But I invite you to stay. And work at this. Work hard, Claire, at reclaiming your life."

She took two steps, then hesitated in the doorway between the rooms.

"We'll start with your marriage. You are avoiding the tough

stuff. With your husband. Who…" Howard paused. "Who is still alive."

Claire reeled. This ambitious plan for putting her life in order was nonsense, a farce. She despised Howard, everything about him and his precious presumptions.

"You were right." She pivoted to face him. "Your instincts, I mean. I need an adult doctor. You are designed for kids. What was I thinking?" She chortled. It was an awful sound. Everything was awful. Most of all Claire. She wanted to cut into him with words, make him hurt, make someone hurt as much as she did. All she could see in that moment was a plump, aging figure behind a messy desk.

Howard remained irritatingly calm. "This is the first time you haven't been sad here."

"Oh, so this is better?" She threw her hands in the air, as her voice seethed like a kettle boiling.

"Just different."

"Well, whatever the hell you are trying to do to me is not working."

And then she was gone, stomping across the room, slamming the door behind her and pounding along the pavement.

No longer a wife. No longer a mother. Who was she, truly, now?

Chapter 18
Colleen

Colly slipped through the narrow window of her room just as the sky was opening its door into morning. She barely fit—if she were wider, even by a fraction of an inch, this would be a no-go. Even Crow, her boisterous companion, wasn't up yet.

Silent as a cat, she darted down the path next to Jay's trailer, through the bushes along the edge of the dunes, until she came to the lake—gloriously blue and shimmering like magic. It had stormed last night, but you'd never know it by the sky. She sat in the moist sand at the edge of the water and lifted her face into rays stretching like waking muscles. Each sunrise was like visiting an old friend. She lingered in the warm hues, melon and Popsicle-orange and the scarlet-rouge of a clown's cheek, as long as she dared before heading back. Her secret wanderings had to stay just that. Plus, she needed to wake Moira.

The light inside the trailer, dulled by the small windows, made the place feel unfinished, as if it were in its pj's instead of fully dressed. It seemed to wobble with flimsy sloppiness, from the patches of plywood flooring to the walls that were mere pieces of paneling tacked to studs. Even the bathroom door was backward—the lock was on the outside so someone could walk right in, surprising the person inside.

She scooted to Moira's bedroom and stood in the doorway, watching as Moira slept openmouthed, studying her tangled hair, the slick of saliva at the edge of her mouth, her eyelids buried deep in her sockets. She'd be mad if Colly let her sleep in. The storm had knocked the power out, messing up the alarm. Still, Colly hesitated before moving closer.

The shadowy room seemed to close in around Colly, trapping her like an animal, giving her the same feeling she got when Moira talked about the selkie's cave. The thought of it made Colly's breath come quickly, her knees threatened to buckle. A person lost things in dark places, like those cave-dwelling fish that no longer had eyes.

She comforted herself by holding the medallion, running her fingers over the soft curve, the toothed edge she'd worn smooth. It was the very same one she'd discovered in the seam of that scrap of material from the trunk. Madonna—so similar to *mother*. The word felt soft and full in her mouth.

"Moira."

Nothing. Colly pulled at the frayed cord hanging near the foot of the bed, careful to open the blinds no more than a quarter inch.

"Moira." She wiggled the bed. "Get up."

Moira bolted upright, dazed.

"What the—?" The sun slapped stripes across Moira's faded T-shirt and men's boxers, clothes she'd dug from a Goodwill box left for pickup in the last park where they'd lived. Or was it the one before? Didn't matter. The clothes had started out grayish and only got worse over time, so now they looked like she was wearing some sort of bad weather.

She pulled thick tendrils of hair back from her face. "What time is it?" Heavy smoking made her voice crackle like a mouthful of Grape-Nuts cereal without milk.

"It's seven thirty."

"Colleen?"

"What?"

"Come closer."

Colly hesitated, then did as told. But only a step or two, executed with caution, as if there were glass on the floor. Moira's wild appearance was scary.

"Promise me." Moira breathed deeply. "That you'll never leave me. That you'll stay with me until I'm old. Take care of me, eh, *serku?*"

Colly didn't know what to say. She could've promised, made Moira happy. But a wicked tingle surged through her, and she shook her head. Being alone so much, she'd come up with her own language. Spoke it to herself. A mixture of Shelta and something mysterious and wonderful sounding. She used it now, fully expecting its impact.

"*Mook savatto.*"

"What's that you're sayin'?" Moira waggled her head, clearly disturbed by the sound. "Bastard words. Translate."

"Okay. No way, Moira. Not lookin' after anyone. *Blanog.*"

Colly strummed her fingers in the air, said it in a certain tone, a sassy Traveller voice. But Moira was pained; Colly saw it in her eyes, her pupils expanding with hurt. Her mouth tensed into a grim line as she reached over an ashtray to grab a fresh cigarette.

"Go light this for me."

Too cheap to buy matches, Moira swiped them from restaurants they didn't actually eat at. Now she was out. Colly went to the stove and got the burner lit, puffing just enough to get the cigarette started. A cloud of smoke enveloped her head, dizzying her steps back to Moira's room.

"You don't look so good," Moira said, standing in front of the dresser mirror. She steadied the trembling right hand with her left, took the cigarette from Colly and inhaled deeply. Peering into the mirror, Colly could see what Moira meant. She was paler than ever; her earth-toned eyes and softly sculpted dimples seemed diminished by the purple half-moons under her bottom lashes. Her hair, ratty from sleep, needed a touch-up, as yesterday's cherry-red dye job was fading into streaky auburn.

In the few weeks since they had moved here, Colly sometimes felt like she'd swallowed something heavy. While being near the lake was like a tonic, thoughts of a "true" home kept popping up, not places that she knew they'd eventually leave. Indiana was the longest they'd stayed anywhere. Not that it had felt like home. When Moira had announced they were leaving, Colly was foolish enough to be hopeful. Instead, they'd ended up in a drab shoebox of a trailer similar to the ones before. Only the pressure was on now. Colly was expected to produce more and more pictures to sell at flea markets and craft shows. Summer landscapes and sunsets over the lake, all painted to Moira's specifications.

Still, in this place that smelled like musty earth and cigarettes, Colly found herself working on private paintings with a strange urgency. She squirreled them away behind the thin wall paneling. Colly noticed that her artistic skills were sharpening. After seeing something once, even briefly, she could reconstruct the image in detail, capturing even complicated tones and values. But usually she ended up changing the reality into something more dramatic. Like the walls in her room. As soon as they'd arrived, she'd gone to work with chalk, sketching, replicating things she'd seen in *National Geographic*, circling the stains and pockmarks, exaggerating them into exploding nebulas, or single-celled radiolarians, or amphibian eggs in late stages before hatching. Things she'd learned about that now seemed part of her, looking for expression.

Moira met her eyes in a watchful gaze.

"You need to get your work done. I know what you're up to at night. Chalk everywhere but on a canvas."

"It's washable."

"Ach. That's not what I buy it for!" Moira rolled her eyes as if Colly were the most impossible creature in the world, then turned away and slipped into her jeans. The outline of her bent body seemed thinner than ever, sharpened into harsh edges and angles.

Colly bit her lip. This place felt different from the others in a way she could not describe. Strange dreams were visiting at night. A piece of the sky appeared in her hand, soft and blue, like fabric. Willow trees weeping, their branches like strands of blond hair. Blue everywhere and yellow. On good days, she tasted lemon. On bad, she swore there was tar in her mouth. Or what she imagined tar to taste like, anyway. And then there was this thing, this memory, deep inside, the sensation that something, she had no idea what, had slipped away from her. The urge to paint was growing ravenous inside her. Things that Moira would never approve.

Moira tugged at Colly's hair before leaving. She was letting it grow a little longer, but tufts along the top weren't keeping up with the sides.

"Really, can you do something with this?" She cackled. "You're lookin' like a rooster."

"What time will you be home?" Colly needed to gauge how long she had to work on her "real" stuff. Moira still only had part-time jobs: the graveyard shift at a foundry and cleaning cages at an animal hospital, or, as Moira called it, the "fookin' animal hospital."

"Ugh. I'm off to both places today."

When Moira opened the door, Jay White's truck roared into his driveway, kicking up dust and rattling equipment.

"Colleen. That man over there is off in the head. Daft or something. I can tell. Stay away from him. Hear?"

Colly swallowed. She'd felt a kinship when she and Jay had met, a connection. Moira's eyes narrowed with suspicion.

"Of course." She crossed her fingers behind her back. "I would never even talk to him." Another secret. Secret visits to the beach, a secret language—what was one more?

After a bowl of off-brand cereal and watered-down milk, Colly sat at the cramped kitchen counter that doubled as a table. She swept a dusting of crumbs away with the back of her forearm to make room for her work. Another beach picture. All pastel sky and water and sand. She sprinkled salt into the wet paint. Add some texture. Customers couldn't get enough of that type of thing and Moira loved how fast the pictures sold. The whole thing took half an hour with minimal effort. Could've done it with her arm pinned behind her back. That was enough of that. She fished out a clean canvas and started fresh. The blank space shifted her into happy mode. Like pure, white snow. Filled with possibility. Setting the canvas in place on her collapsible easel, she felt she could soar. Her tongue tingled as if her taste buds were open to new sensations. She carefully arranged her oil colors by hue, light to dark. She'd begun naming days—sometimes after colors, sometimes sounds or tastes, depending on her mood, the weather, her frame of mind. Today was an azure day—bursting with promise.

She started slowly. This picture was coming from a different place. And, like building an onion, it was appearing in layers, a mystery even to her. In the light from the window over the sink, she stopped often to examine each stroke closely. The image emerging from the tip of her wet brush felt almost propelled by something beyond her control. She swirled lemony pigment across the middle, creating what seemed to be hair, and heard a low, distinct murmuring, faint as a sleeping hive. It was friendly, nonthreatening—the sound of happy industriousness and hot summer days.

Rat-tat. A sharp beak tapped Morse code on the window. Crow.

Colly understood his pushy nature. Like her, he was new to the neighborhood. Had pilfered his space from a vesper sparrow. She'd seen him circling overhead for days, as if carving the sky into patterns. He probably lived in that white pine across the street next to Jay White's trailer. That's where she'd live, anyway, if she were a bird—in the safety of the staggered branches, breathing in the sweet odor of pine resin.

She stood on tiptoe and leaned toward the window over the sink, meeting one black patent leather eye tilted in her direction.

"Shoo. Got something for you later. Busy now."

He cawed and flapped away, but she knew he'd be back soon.

She worked for an hour, then two. The more she attended to the yellow, the louder the buzz thrummed in her ears. Opening the tube of cerulean blue, she laid a stripe onto the palette. This was indeed becoming a girl's face, and the incredible shade of blue would be her eyes. The vivid hue made Colleen feel light, almost as if she were floating. A touch of dizziness threatened, then passed. She stepped back. The eyes were the taste of peppermint on a perfect sky day. As if she were touching, smelling a memory. Yet the emerging image still felt flat, needed something. A small mat of moss or crumbled lichens saturated with paint and worked into the canvas would do nicely.

All these things were stashed in her secret lair underneath the trailer. Colly rubbed her eyes when she stepped into the brilliant sunshine. She brought with her a piece of Pop-Tart and set it on the railing for Crow, who was hanging out on a low branch nearby.

The bird stayed silent and cocked his head.

"C'mon, you little monster. You know you're safe with me."

He popped onto the rail and gobbled the chunk into his craw.

"You still need a name," she said softly. But it couldn't be a silly one, and nothing substantial had come to mind, so she left it alone for now. She poured out a pitcher of clean water into an old birdbath forgotten by a previous tenant at the side of the trailer. Just in case he needed it. Flamingoes, too. Plastic ones bleached white by the sun, lay flattened into the dirt. She'd get to those later.

Lowering herself onto her stomach, she shimmied under the trailer along the cinder blocks that held the unit up from the ground. Sunlight landed in darts around the edges of the metal skirt. She could still see Crow's pitchfork feet in the gap as she inched her way forward, commando-style. She held her breath, and moved quickly, holding thoughts of the medallion as she fought through her fear of cramped spaces until, relieved, she reached the hollow in the middle where she could sit up on her knees.

The air was rich as a tidal pool, or how she imagined a tidal pool might smell, filled with clammy damp animals, shelled creatures, and seaweed. She opened a plastic bag and surveyed her plunder: fragile twigs, two brown feathers, and a clump of moss. Also, a lump of beeswax she'd found, empty of honey and confettied with dirt—yet it was the work of bees and therefore magnificent. And then one clean white bone she'd discovered under a bird's nest. She ran her finger down the length of it. Its fragility took her breath away. Who had done this? A cat maybe. But she hadn't seen any in the area. She chose a pinch of club moss, as the spongy texture held paint nicely.

Crow disappeared, replaced by two boots. Colly held her breath.

"Knock, knock."

Jay White's voice boomed through the crawl space.

Colly stiffened. Her fear of exposure overtook her, even as she recalled that he was friendly and seemed trustworthy.

"Hello? You in there—uh, under there?"

She touched her pocket to be certain the medallion was still safe and in place and then, quick as a minnow, she wriggled back out into the sun, which was warm and bright and caramel flavored. She hadn't seen Jay up close in the week since their first meeting but still kept a keen eye on him all the same—his comings and goings, making his dream catchers, working his craft in his shed. She recalled the friendly details of his face, now framed by a wide-brimmed hat. She could see how the scar might be scary. But it wasn't to her.

"Hi." He smiled. "Accidentally got some of your mail. Here."

He handed her an envelope from the manager's office. The rent bill. Moira wouldn't be happy to see that.

"Are you guys the..." He lifted the name up, scanning the smeared ink. "Is that an *R* or a *K*?"

"*R*. Reilly." This time. She didn't mention how many versions of their last name Moira used—Reilly, O'Reilly, once in a while O'Keefe. Moira said it had something to do with strangers taking Colly away if they weren't careful. She pointed to a long rectangular box across the road on Jay's porch.

"What's that?"

"Oh. Just came in the mail. Ordered it weeks ago."

"Can I see what's inside?"

She was already galloping over to Jay's trailer, like a Labrador chasing a stick.

"Do I have a choice?" He followed, chuckling.

She squatted next to the box and ran her hand along the stiff, brown edge.

"You can open it."

"Really?"

"Uh-huh."

Colly didn't ask twice. She tore the box open, revealing a colorful label that said everything wonderful at once: meteors, comets, Saturn's rings bright as rainbows. A telescope.

"Cool!" they said in unison.

"It's a cheap one." Jay removed the pieces from the box. "But it'll do the trick."

He assembled the tripod. That alone was a wonder. All tipple-jointed like the legs of a walking stick insect. He set the long tube in place and began leafing through the instruction booklet. The delay was killing Colly. She couldn't take her eyes off the picture of the giant gas planet. Was it possible to see something, a faint glimpse of Saturn's rings maybe, in the daytime?

"Stop hopping around like a bird on a hot plate." Jay laughed. "You're distracting me."

He leafed through the pages of instructions. Mostly boring black-and-white diagrams. "Make yourself comfortable. Take a look around the place." He added with careful sarcasm, "Seeing as you're already familiar."

"Ha! Good one." Colly skipped over to the shed to check out the dream catchers suspended like woven, open-air moons. "Wow."

Up close, she could make out the intricate webbing entwined with the treasures Jay had gathered nearby. She drank it all in, as they dangled magically overhead like some great cosmic constellation of feathers, small stones, and delicate shells.

"Tell you what," Jay called to her. "It's gonna take me a while to figure this out. But you can come back tonight or tomorrow night or whenever you like. Deal?"

Colly didn't respond. She was too taken with one dream catcher in the corner, set off by itself, simpler than the others.

"So beautiful."

Jay made his way to the shed.

"You can pick one, if you like."

Colly didn't hesitate.

"How about that one?"

"Over there? The plain one in the corner?" Jay's face darkened and he shook his head. "That one is special. Belongs to a family. A little girl, actually. Been keeping it for a long time."

"Friend?"

"You could say that."

"What's her name?"

Jay didn't respond.

"Names are important. They're given to people for a reason."

Jay shook his head. "She was just someone I knew. That's all."

"What do you mean, *was*?"

"She's no longer around." Jay turned and went silent.

Colly felt something. She couldn't say what it was, but this other girl was a curiosity, possibly a threat. She flushed with jealousy.

"I want my dream catcher to be really different from hers now."

"Why?"

"You looked sad when you talked about her."

Jay took off his hat and rubbed the back of his neck as if a sharp hot whip of sun had burned it. "Hey. Now it's your turn," he said softly. "I want to see your paintings."

She hesitated. If Moira ever found out…

"We had a deal."

"Okay, but you gotta promise me something."

"What?"

"If for some reason Moira ever talks to you, you don't know me. Got it? Swear." Colleen felt her knees weaken just thinking of what would happen. "She can't know. That I talk to you. At all."

"Okay. That's fine. But I'm a neighbor. I'm safe. I'm thinking I should introduce myself to her. You know, be friendly…"

"No! It's not like that. I mean it. If she knew I was over here, we'd probably move again."

"C'mon…"

Colleen desperately tried to hide her distress. "I mean it. She really doesn't like neighbors. She's very private. Got it?"

He nodded. "Okay."

"Now." She spoke with determination. "Let's do this fast."

Crossing the road, Colly threw in a long jump and marked her landing with a rock. Jay followed suit with a jump of his own. She beat his by a hairbreadth.

"Need to work on that, Jay."

"Gotcha, Boss."

The sun was high and hot. At the trailer, Colly placed her hand on the door and turned. "You can't come in. You have to stay there."

Jay waited on the steps while Colly went to retrieve her picture. She was embarrassed at what he could see when he looked in: dishes in the sink, finger marks on the walls from previous tenants, an open Doritos bag under the sofa. He leaned forward.

"Close your eyes." She didn't want him to see her hiding place. "For real. Not fake closed."

She turned her back, hesitating before prying aside a loose wall panel and extracting a painting she'd worked on the day before. It was not yet fully dry, so she held it by the edges. She returned to Jay, still in the doorway.

"I did this one from memory. Well, sort of. I have this special medallion…"

Jay's mouth dropped open. Colly couldn't tell if his reaction was good or bad.

"What the…?" He spoke more to himself than her. "This is… Oh my gosh. You did this?"

She saw it, too, with new eyes. The Madonna from the medallion was just an outline, really, a lifeless depiction. But Colly had transformed her. Instead of a face, the woman had a tree growing from her head with the branches formed by the slim fibers of Jay's feather quills, the hairy parts torn off. And the stars around her were Jay's own stones, which seemed to emanate a flow of meteoric light.

"It's so strange. But beautiful." Once again, as if he really couldn't believe what he was seeing, "You did this?" Jay whispered from a place of reverence. His eyes squinted and then grew wider as if to help him see more clearly. "It looks, I can't describe, almost electrified."

Colly couldn't help but beam.

"I've never seen anything like this."

"Moira wants me to paint touristy stuff." She pointed her finger down her open mouth and made a gagging sound. "Sells them at the flea market and gas stations. Those type of places. Sometimes I hide things in the picture. It's fun, and"—her eyes sparkled— "Moira hates when I do it." She twitched at an engine sound that rumbled in the distance. "I have to put this away now, okay? I have work to do."

"What about that one there?" He pointed to the painting propped on the counter, angled away, so only the white backing was visible.

She shook her head.

"Not ready for anyone to see yet. I'm kinda just figuring it out as I go."

"Will you show me when it's ready?"

She hesitated. "Dunno…maybe."

"Promise?"

"Okay, okay, I promise."

As Colly watched Jay cross the road, she felt a sudden sadness. It was hard to be alone so much. She tried to return to her paints, determined not to let this day be swallowed into an exhausted stupor, which she feared might happen if she stopped. But it was so hot and her blood felt sluggish. She set the rotating fan near the couch to high. A nap would be good, would bring her energy back.

She lay on her side, legs tucked. A fly smacked her in the face and then on her calf like an annoying metronome. *Pop. Pop. Pop.* She began to drift, flickering in and out of sleep. Images stuttered off and on. Different faces: Moira's, unsmiling; the Madonna from the medal, open-armed, beautiful. And then it quickly changed and became a pretty woman with brown hair, her face severe and worried.

Suddenly, she was trapped in the dark. Where was she? She thrashed as the odor of exhaust fumes choked her, followed by the sweet, rotten smell of syrup and vomit. She fought to wake up, but something held her in this place of not asleep and not awake. A small flame of light seemed to float at the tip of her feet and she felt the presence of another person. Someone with softly glowing skin and yellow hair who disappeared as quickly as they came. She felt, momentarily, a soft touch—a mother's touch—one filled with love and answers. And then it was withdrawn. Just like that. Colly kicked around on the couch. She heard a voice she didn't recognize at first as her own.

"Mom! Mommy! Mom-eee!"

Her heart teeter-tottered in her chest, followed by pain near her breastbone, sharp as a jagged piece of glass. She awoke on the floor next to the couch, not aware whether she was in Indiana or Michigan. What was that dream? It felt so real. She slapped her palm against her head. The air was just as hot, but the sun was lower and reached onto the couch as if searching the faded pattern. *Move it, Colly.* There was work to be done.

A dog barked somewhere in the trailer park. She ran her hand through her hair and wiped sweat from her upper lip and forehead. The Kool-Aid had run all over. She went to the bathroom to wash up. The mirror told her that Moira was right. She looked ridiculous.

It was almost four o'clock! Moira would be home soon. She returned to the kitchen. The mess, the half-done canvas. She felt so overwhelmed. As if by instinct, her hand went to the coin pocket of her cutoffs. She pulled the medallion out and laid it on the counter near the easel. Crow eyed her through the window. And then she remembered. Tuesdays, Moira worked late. She returned to her special canvas, lost in a strange new energy as she pieced together pieces from the dream. Blue, black, yellow, brown, bright white. Over and over it spun in her head, propelling her to spread the colors in fine and broad strokes. She painted for two hours, then three.

It wasn't until the light was leaving the sky that she stopped, realizing she hadn't eaten since her Pop-Tart that morning. She wolfed down a can of tomato soup, not bothering to heat it, then stepped back to look at the picture she'd spent so much time on. What she saw astonished her. A beautiful little girl with lemony hair and perfect cerulean-blue eyes was looking back at her. There was more work to be done. Yet it was time to wind down. She finished by washing a thin film of white, translucent as a delicate sheet of mother of pearl, over the pale complexion. If Colly didn't know better, she would say the girl was smiling.

The Buick crunched outside. A prickly fear fired into Colly's brain. For some reason, she knew Moira must never see this picture. Colly hurriedly slipped it into the space in the wall next to the one she'd shown Jay earlier. If she kept this up, the walls of the trailer would explode before fall. Moira walked in seconds after Colly popped a half-painted beach scene into the easel.

"How was your day?" Colly asked, swallowing her nerves. She checked the table for any evidence of her secret activities. Knowing Moira, she could find something as simple as the arrangement of colors to be suspicious.

Moira stretched her arms over her head as Colly scrambled the paint tubes on the table. A bright, shiny object fell to the floor.

The medallion!

Colly skirted around Moira and dropped to her knees, practically knocking her off balance.

"What in the—?"

Nervous crickets jumped along Colly's skin. She slapped her hand over the oval treasure, where she felt it stick to her palm.

"What's gotten into you, Colleen?" Moira doubled over and glared suspiciously.

Colly's stomach flipped. "Bugs."

"What bugs?"

Colly swallowed and then counted one, two hard heartbeats before answering. "An ant. That's all."

"Lemme see"—Colly held her breath and tightened her grip— "if you made dinner." Moira glared at the cluttered sink, the smudged counter.

"Uh, sorry, Moira." Colly sighed, slipping her hand into her back pocket. "We have soup or Pop-Tarts."

"I'm tired." Moira yawned and collapsed on the couch. "And not hungry." She twirled an unlit cigarette in her fingers, keeping her jumpy hand busy. As if the effort were too great to fire it up.

Colly retreated to her room and quietly shut the door. She listened as Moira shuffled around and settled in to watch TV. It wouldn't be long before Moira was asleep and Colly was hoisting herself onto the edge of her bed and squeezing back out the window.

The dunes shimmered in the moonlight and the *hush-hush* of the water was as comforting as a hug. She thought about what Jay had said and how she knew by the look on his face that her paintings were good—really good. She thought, too, of the painting and the feelings that were sifting into a pattern—but what? The stars seemed to crackle like cellophane and the sky was full with a moon etched in the same design as her medallion. A Madonna in the silky colored sky.

PART THREE

Chapter 19

Jay

"My turn!"

"Again?"

"C'mon, Jay. See if you can stump me this time."

Jay and Colly stood side by side at the telescope, like two owls brightening in the evening air. Yesterday she had been over. And the day before that. In the weeks since Jay had met her, they'd formed some type of bond. Moira was working the late shift at the foundry. Twilight had drifted into early darkness and the stars shone crystal beams through the clear air.

He'd been super busy with his business, which was exhausting: the heavy lifting, the relentless sun. But it felt good too, being successful. It was nice to relax in the evening, enjoy the night sky alongside a fellow armchair star traveler.

"Okay. What landmark is this?" Jay crouched with a small flashlight in one hand and the celestial atlas in the other with a page opened to a luminous picture of the moon. "In the southern hemisphere. You'll see it as a whitish area."

Colly, bent like a paperclip, peered through the eyepiece. "Tycho Crater!"

Jay chuckled. "Pretty good."

She lifted her head. "Does it feel like lemonade to you?"

"What?"

"Nothing."

"No, tell me what you mean."

"Well, lemonade is bright and happy."

"And?" Jay trained the flashlight beam at her face.

She reddened.

"You are turning purple. Hey, maybe that should be your name instead of Little Bird. Little Chameleon."

She ignored his chiding. "Go ahead, ask me my favorite."

"But I already know that you know it."

"Don't care, ask me anyway."

"All right, settle down. The large pale feature in the southeast quadrant?"

"You mean the one that can be seen with the naked eye?"

"The very one."

Colly looked into the night sky at the perfect round circle of the full moon. "Sea of Tranquility!"

"You got it. You win!"

"*Mucho pilámaya!*" She bowed with exaggerated flair. "Thank you."

He laughed. "You don't stop, do you?"

She'd been insistent on learning everything Indian he knew—the little bits of language, the customs and stories from his childhood. They played guessing games. Just yesterday, he introduced a new Lakota word and she'd been trying to figure out the meaning since.

"*Tiyospaye.*" She mimicked Jay carefully. "Is it 'cat'?"

"Nope. Nothing like that."

"Hmm, I'll keep working on it."

"I know you will," Jay said. It was amazing how her interest in his culture stirred him, brought him back to something terribly important and deeply hidden all these years. She was a force of nature, this girl. Casually offering him yellow Post-it Notes with reminders of things he'd offhandedly promised, things like: lessons in his native tongue, how to smoke fish, even though, to Jay's knowledge, she'd never even caught one in her life. And, of course, her insistence that they make the perfect dream catcher together. To that one, he always replied, "When you're ready, Little Bird. Not a minute sooner."

Now he asked, "Moira on double shift again?"

"Yeah, there's some rumor the foundry might be cutting back soon, so she's working extra."

Jay glanced at the rundown trailer across the street. It bothered him that Colly was left alone so often, although he had to admit Moira didn't seem like much of a parent even when she was home. Occasionally he'd see the glowing tip of her cigarette through the kitchen window, a shadowy figure rifling through cupboards. Sometimes he'd catch her outline, her hair like Medusa, swirling in wild tentacles around her head.

"Colly, did you say you were adopted?"

It was, Jay knew, a strange question, considering Moira wasn't Colly's mother. But an aunt maybe. That would make him feel better.

Colly shrugged. "I guess so. Yeah. But I don't think officially. Moira says my parents didn't want me before they died. Were druggies or something." She went quiet for a moment before speaking again. "Sometimes it's hard."

"You mean with Moira gone a lot?"

"No." Colly shook her head firmly. "Work is driving her a little crazy lately. I mean, I think it's that…" This was more to herself than him. "Can we get back to the good stuff here?"

The sky was full and rich and together they explored the heavens, from the asteroid belt to the twinkling Pleiades. While Jay could never get enough of the moon, Colly gravitated to the planets, the gas giants, revisiting the great red storm on Jupiter each time. Always saving the magical glowing rings of Saturn for last.

"Wow." She sighed. "There it is."

Jay didn't have to even ask to know what she had located. "And how many moons does Saturn have?"

"Eleven."

"And what are their names again?"

"Can't remember."

"I don't believe that."

Colly pulled back and looked at Jay. There was a faint circle around her eye where it had been pressed into the eyepiece.

"Like I said before, names are important. I want to get them right." She straightened her back. "I mean, take Jay. Were you named after the blue bird?"

"Not sure. How about you? Colly?"

"I'm named after a selkie."

"What's that?"

"Oh. It's an Irish thing. A mythical creature. Half girl, half seal. I used to think it was real. Along with the tooth fairy. Sometimes"—her voice went solemn—"I think Moira believes it is…"

Jay eyed Colly. "Is what?"

"Real. Like she really thinks I'm a selkie. And the problem with that is…" She stopped.

"Go on, Little Bird, please."

"The selkie always runs away. And Moira, she thinks that makes it bad. Jay…I need…want…to tell you something."

"Okay."

"About a cave. Not a real cave, something made-up. You know, to punish kids."

"Sounds scary, Little Bird."

"Yeah. It's like being locked in a room or something. For a really long time."

"Colly? Did this happen to you?" He looked at her. He must've seemed overly surprised, too tense, because her confiding attitude dropped away.

"No…no… I heard about it on TV."

Engine sounds at the entrance of the park spooked Colly into sudden silence, and she dashed through the thin darkness back to her trailer, leaving a wake of uneasiness. The more Jay had come to know her, the more confused he'd grown. Like an old-fashioned mood ring, she presented something different every day: a new hair color, a bright, open face or one narrowed with curiosity. Lately, he'd seen an underlying tinge of restlessness. No, anxiety. And it was raising his concern. What was really going on here?

He wished he could talk to someone about Colly. But who? The nerve it would take to face the police again, and what would he say? Even social services. What would he report? There was no evidence of abuse. And neglect? Welcome to the crappy lives of trailer park kids.

Jay understood that the options weren't good for parentless children. After his mother died, he'd ended up at an orphanage.

Catholic Home for Boys. A redbrick building off the main road just outside the reservation. His memories of the starkly geometric place remained clear. High rectangular windows with metal grates. Triangle-shaped nuns treading down long, dark hallways. Birthdays were a group event. Once a season the kids were gathered in the big hall. Summer birthdays were the winners. They got served a slab of sherbet with vanilla sheet cake. The winter kids got shortchanged, overshadowed by preparations for Christmas, which was focused on prayer and quiet meditation. Jay's birthday was in February, or was it March? He had to look at his driver's license to remember.

At sixteen, he ran away. Maybe this was his and Colly's bond, the reason they seemed so easy in each other's presence: they were both unwanted in some form. Still, something else nudged at him, tickled his antennae. Maybe things were all right, would be okay, if he just stopped worrying, seeing problems where they didn't exist. Ever since he'd gotten things wrong about Andrea Rawlings, he'd fought off his deeper urges. Part of that was simply for survival; he needed to establish his business, get on with life. But there was more: self-doubt. Probably self-loathing. A bad combo for a recovering alcoholic.

A set of headlights cut through the tall grasses, followed by the green Buick that curved into the makeshift driveway across the street. Moira. Despite how Colly had pleaded, Jay was resolved to go over and talk to this mysterious woman. Too many unanswered questions that fed into the slow burn pulling at his instincts about Colly. But not tonight. It was already past ten. He'd do it in the morning and spent the rest of the evening stargazing alone, until a ceiling of clouds chased him inside.

He clicked a lamp on and sat on his sagging couch. In the dull light, his trailer, with its uninteresting furnishings, seemed so lifeless. Maybe that was bothering him. He really needed to spruce things up a bit, add some color. Colly could help with that. He chuckled at what she'd come up with. Apple green and bright orange, no doubt. But her talent was very real—he'd seen it for himself. Why was this Moira such a tyrant about it? Couldn't she let a little girl develop her skill?

The only item in the room that spoke about Jay as an individual was a rough-hewn shelf of cherrywood. Jay had cut and finished it himself. It now held an old hornet's nest, his shaman's rattle-frayed feathers, and a perfectly shaped fir cone, long and tight like a scaled stalactite, that Colly had given him. It anchored a slim folder, set flat, underneath. This was where he now kept the pictures of Andrea and Lily.

He turned on the TV. Reruns of stupid sitcoms he hadn't liked the first time around. He turned it off. Why was he so restless? A drink, he knew, would settle him down. Pinching his eyes shut, he gritted his teeth. *You know better, Moon Man.* He couldn't even allow such a thought. Claire popped into his mind. She was strong. If she could manage the way she had, he could too.

Had he thanked Claire enough for the money? He'd sent a note right away. But a phone call was in order as well. He lifted the receiver. He knew her number by memory, even though they rarely talked. Dialing, he lost his nerve. It was too late to call.

Instead, Jay felt compelled to stand and visit that shelf. To look at those photos again. He lifted the fir cone. It was a substantial object, heavy in his palm and sweetly scented. Setting it to the side, he grasped the folder and drew a breath before opening the folder. Lily's picture was on top. Other than discoloration on one edge, the photo was fine. He spent a good long moment scanning her face. As always, it was her eyes that got him. The very image of innocence.

Andrea was next. The water had stolen the original glossiness from the photo and the image was nothing but an amoeba-shaped blot now. But he remembered having once seen so much life in that little girl's face. Looking closely, he could just make out the edges of bangs that he recalled were swept to either side as if she were running in the wind. Jay's stomach twinged. He closed the folder with the photos inside and returned it to its place back on the shelf. It was important to keep his focus forward, just as Claire Rawlings had done by becoming a doctor.

Around midnight, it stormed heavily and rain pelted his roof. Jay fell asleep with the moon hidden behind a veil of clouds.

In the morning, the sun attempted to show through a punched-tin sky. But its effort was weak and Jay found himself idle, waiting for the ground to dry out. As he was stirring a packet of Swiss Miss cocoa into his cup of instant coffee, he caught sight of red taillights backing out from across the street. He ran outside barefoot to meet the car. Finally, a chance to grab this Moira. Maybe talk to her about a babysitter or something.

"Hey!" He waved. But the woman only accelerated and blew right past him.

For the first time, Jay caught an actual glimpse of her, even if it was just in profile. Hard edges and a thin mouth. Watching the car disappear around the corner, his arm hairs stood up as if magnetized. He brought his fingertips to his temple to ease a sudden throb. Before his head cleared, Colly jetted out from her trailer and stood next to him.

"Huh? How'd you get here so fast?"

"Can I help you in the shed today, Jay? Please?"

Jay looked up. The sky was clearing. There were bushes to be trimmed, lawns to edge, but it would be a while before everything dried enough to work it.

"Sure. Why not?"

She skipped to the bench, dodging large droplets of leftover rain that a quick breeze shook from a maple. Jay followed.

"It's time, by the way," Jay said, "to get started on your own dream catcher."

Colly's eyes widened with disbelief. "Really?"

"Yup." He nodded. "And I have a surprise."

She grabbed a handful of sycamore twigs from a bundle on the ground. "I want these."

Jay shook his head. "Not that type, Little Bird. Got something better in mind. Follow me." He led her through the trail to the lakeshore.

"Bet you can't surprise me."

"You'll see."

The sun was fat and high, and the clouds stayed out of its path. Jay pointed to a small jut of land covered in low trees and wild ramblings. "That, we can only get to by water. Take off your shoes."

"Don't have any. Remember?"

He sat on a log. "Okay. I'll take mine off, then."

They waded through the shallow water where Colly fell into formation behind Jay. They kicked through waves flecked with high noon diamonds and splatters of tangerine and every bright luscious color imaginable. "You remember, Little Bird, that to my people this great water is sacred?"

"Is that it?" she answered from behind. "The meaning of *tiyospaye*—sacred?"

"Nope, but you're getting a little closer." Jay smiled openly. The warm air, the clear water, this moment with Colly were deeply satisfying. As they approached a steep incline clotted with slippery roots, he realized she was too short to climb it. He'd need to lift her onto the ledge. He held his hands wide.

"Ready? Here we go."

She felt so fragile in his grasp. He placed her gently onto smooth dry land and then scrambled up behind to meet her. He then knelt and tilted the branches of a small bush with maroon bark. Jay scratched a twig exposing the green wood beneath.

"What is it?" She peered closely.

"Sand cherry. Can you smell it?"

She nodded. "What is it?"

"Sort of like licorice, Little Bird. Do you catch that?"

Her eyes grew round. "Yeah, kinda like root beer!"

Jay laughed. "Let's grab some and go back. We can get started right away."

They worked quickly, returning to the shed with bundles of thin branches in their arms. Jay pointed to his assortment of shells and other treasures.

"You can choose what you want. But first"—he handed Colly a small saw-bladed knife—"we need those about twelve inches. Be careful. That knife is sharp."

"I know. Sheesh."

Colly leaned over the bench, meticulously planning each stroke.

Jay studied her face as she disappeared into the pleasure of her work. With her eyes focused downward, her lids were pale lavender, the color of a weak shadow. Another reminder of his concern about the situation across the street. He pictured Moira zooming past him this morning, leaving him in her dust. Beyond being elusive, she was clearly strange. *Stop it, Jay.* Colly was completely independent and seemed happy enough. Maybe it was better Moira hadn't pulled over earlier. What if his involvement only made things worse?

Colly moved the knife with precision, but her hand slipped on the second cut. She pulled back, exposing small crimson beads blooming on the edge of her knuckle.

"*Dalon stk sudil!*"

"What did you just say?"

"Nothing." Aside from wincing from the pain, a look of alarm flushed across her face.

"But it sounded like…"

"Made-up words, Jay." Colly quickly stuck the joint of her thumb in her mouth. "That's all."

Jay's brain flooded with many things at once: the smell of sand cherrywood, the heated moist air, and now a made-up word that sounded vaguely familiar. Feelings of wrongness were piling up, like gristle on a smooth bone, combining into a tightening that resonated through his chest and into his gut. Something he could not simply wish away. Still, it remained vague, nothing full-blown. Yet.

"What else do you make up, Colly?"

"What do you mean?"

"Don't see you going to school."

"School's out. It's summer. Remember?"

"When do you start, then?"

"I don't. I'm homeschooled."

"Right. By who? Can't be Moira. She's gone too much."

"Books. I do my own reading. It's not illegal, you know." Her face darkened. "Besides, she can't teach me anything."

"Tell me more," Jay said, his eyes tense, serious. He wanted to get her to talk about that cave again. But Colly seemed intent on something else. He'd have to work up to it.

"Well, ever since we moved here, I'm painting a little differently and I've had some crazy dreams. What do you know about dreams?"

"All I know is the legend of the dream catcher, Little Bird."

"Can you tell me?" Colly's face grew calm and sweet. As if the very thought of his story was a lullaby. She settled onto the ground right where she was, next to the bench.

"Again?" Jay dropped to his haunches. "According to Lakota legend, good dreams pass through the center hole to the sleeping person. The bad ones are caught in the web."

"Like a spider's web, right?"

"Right…just like that…and once the bad dreams are trapped, they perish in the light of dawn."

"Where are you supposed to hang them?" Her eyes were large and round, searching.

"Near a child's bed. Or best, near a sleeping baby, next to her crib."

"And why is that?" Colly was whispering, along with the breeze that filtered through his legs and around his neck. He felt as if he were in his own dream, protected by the warmth of this girl's lovely soul.

"Because if you do it when someone is a baby, it can protect them from bad dreams forever."

There was a long, luxurious silence between them and Jay felt his worries ease. Things were all right, would be okay, if he just listened harder. It was clear he needed to tune in deeper to this girl, to himself. He was afraid, he knew, of opening too wide, of letting too much pain back in. Jay drew his knees to his chest, tenting his legs, and etched tight circles in the dirt with his feet.

Colly's eyes were closed. She sat for a long moment, breathing in the moist air. The afternoon sun played shadow hide-and-seek with a handful of acorns scattered on the ground.

"I wish," Colly said, "I had a dream catcher when I was little."

"I wish," he responded with his throat lumping up, "you did too, Little Bird."

Later that night, after Colly had gone home, Jay began to settle in. Get some sleep for the busy morning to come. But just after he took off his clothes, he remembered something. *Crap. My shoes.* He'd left them down by the lake.

He slipped on his pants and dashed out to retrieve them. At the shore, the moon on the horizon sent playful winks along the waves. He returned to his trailer, shoes in hand, to find his yard illuminated in milky white light. A sudden breeze tossed his hair and chilled his bare chest. He sensed his mother's presence, strong and clear.

A rhythm started deep inside and he began to sway. He moved stiffly at first, shuffling along the edge of the circle he'd carved in the dirt. But muscle memory from his childhood took over and he danced as if he were no different from the wind, the sighing lake, the phosphorescent stars. There were no worries, no attachments to his tormented past. He lifted his arms upward and then raised his voice to meet the sky.

"*Wamakaskanskan. Wamakaskanskan.*"

Jay called to the Great Spirit for himself. He called, too, for Little Bird, his new friend with a confusing story. Drifting somewhere past the clutches of time, he felt the caress of his mother's, then his grandmother's, touch in the wind. When he finished, the pattern drawn by his feet in the shadowy dust looked like the craters and seas on the moon. He spent the rest of the night in the open air, escorted by the stars into dawn.

Chapter 20

Claire

Exactly one week after her blowup at Howard's office, Claire sat at a table in a quiet corner of the hospital cafeteria moving cold macaroni and cheese around on her plate. A familiar shuffling sound approached. She looked up.

"Howard?"

"Room for one more?" Struggling with his cane in one hand and a tray in the other, he came precariously close to tripping. Claire grabbed his tray and set it on the table as he lowered himself into a chair across from hers. Along with a plate of food, he was carrying an aluminum pot of tea and a ceramic mug.

Flushing, Claire started, "But…"

"I made a contract with you, Dr. Rawlings."

"You did?"

"Indeed." He nodded, his eyes fixed on hers, tender, compelling. "Uh-huh. It's more of a personal contract. The bottom line is that I'm not going anywhere."

"Even after what I did?"

"I'm in this for the long haul. And you've come so far." He spoke the last words slowly, with emphasis. "Do you see it?"

Not really.

"And don't be embarrassed. There is a technical name for what happened, but let's just call it losing your cool."

"So you made me do that?"

"No. You made yourself. You just weren't aware of what you needed. A release. A clearing of your head."

"I was—I am—still so confused." She sighed. "And I'm meeting Glen later today." Her tone downshifted. "He's giving me a list. Of things he wants to keep. He wants to get this moving along."

Howard nodded sympathetically.

"I realize this is how things need to be." Her voice wavered. "Howard, I…I…just don't know who I am anymore. Other than MD, PhD…I've lost being a wife and…" She began to choke up but swallowed hard, holding back tears. "A mother." There. She'd said it out loud.

Howard spoke so very gently, as if it were only the two of them in the world, far away from the clanging of dishes and institutional lighting. "Remember: You are the one who told me about fetal cells remaining in your body for decades."

Her chin trembled as she nodded.

"You are still a mother, Claire, always will be."

"I'm not… Nothing…seems normal…"

"You have to trust me that you will get there again. Here is the hard part," he said softly. "You have to learn to walk sideways. Like a spider on a wall."

"What?"

He picked up his empty teacup and turned it upside down. "What would happen if I poured this pot of tea onto this?"

"It would splash all over, of course."

"But what if I put it like this?" Howard tilted the cup so it was not quite sideways but not upright either. "What if I pour now, Claire?"

"Some would get in, and some would end up on the table."

"Exactly. It's what I call walking sideways. Your goal is to get from here"—he inverted the cup once again so the opening was entirely inaccessible—"to here." The cup was now supported by his hand in an awkward tilted position, not quite upright.

"Most people live in a state where they are precariously off-kilter. Very few people are, let's say, fully upright." He set the cup upright and poured, slowly and deliberately. Claire stared at the tea settling into a smooth surface. "We just want to get you to where most everyone else is. Not necessarily great, but not awful either."

She looked dumbfounded. "But how do I get there?"

"Over time you will learn. To let go. Of old ways, old ideas that no longer serve your purpose. Find life's beauty again. It's the only way to allow healing."

She shook her head in disbelief. She felt like a bad student, the slow kid in advanced algebra. "Dunno how it applies to me. I can't let go of my kids... It's just wrong..."

"Hey. This is an allegory. It's not about your kids but being open to new possibilities." He continued, "With therapy and time, things will get better. You will see."

"Really?" Claire felt sarcasm rising in her throat like a vine on a trellis. "And when is that?"

Howard smiled. "That, my friend, is what we'll figure out together." He cleared his throat. "Or if you choose to see someone else..."

"Not gonna happen."

He touched the back of her hand lightly. "Has anyone used the word 'stubborn' and your name in the same sentence?"

She smiled. *Only Glen.*

"There's a decision here. One you have to make."

"And what is that?"

"You have to choose happiness. Daily, hourly, maybe even moment by moment. You have to find that the power is in you to do this."

Claire looked away. Was it possible? To choose little pieces, tiny crumbs of happiness for herself? Treetops were visible out the window. Swaying. Was *any* of this possible? Could she open herself to a wing's brush of happiness ever again?

"Right now, play hooky. Go for a walk. Get some fresh air. I'd come, too, if I wouldn't slow you down." He leaned heavily on his cane to pull himself up. "See you Monday. Our usual time? Turtle cove?"

"Turtle cove." Claire smiled. That's exactly what his office was. "Seven thirty sharp."

"And don't forget that dog of yours." Howard's eyes twinkled. "I miss him."

The weather was crap for early September; instead of clear and dry, it was overcast and gummy. Claire and Glen had agreed to meet at the spot on the lake that Claire now frequented with Gretchie, an inlet cut off from the main beach and not visible from the road. Pulling into the parking area, she could see two buoys knocking in the waves, drop-off markers. A *No Swimming* sign was posted at the edge of the sand, with smaller letters indicating unpredictable current. Claire parked and got out, circling around to let Gretchie out as well.

The weeds around the parking area were filled with the *chit-chit* of late season cicadas. Standing on the packed sand, Claire was struck as always by the beauty of the waves, the odor of the lake, like newly laundered linen. It reminded her of her childhood in Wisconsin when she and Vicki had collected shells, the colorless freshwater type that Claire found magical. If the girls were with her, now they'd do the same. Claire opened the passenger-side door and Gretchie sprang from the car.

The area, as she'd hoped, was empty. She walked past an abandoned child's play set. A lone swing with a black rubber seat and a rickety seesaw creaked in the wind. Beyond that, a rock jetty about fifteen feet long split oncoming waves in two.

"C'mon, girl." Claire slapped her thigh and unleashed Gretchie. "Run!"

Gretchie stopped only to nose a fish skeleton before sprinting with abandon, spraying sand in her wake. Claire imagined Lily and Andrea squealing, chasing behind. They would be five and a half and closing in on nine years now. Overhead, the sky moved with a motion that mimicked the lake's surface. G ended up in the shallow water, her feet immersed in small waves scalloping the sand.

"Hey you," Claire called.

Gretchie trotted back to Claire with a clamshell in her mouth.

"Drop it, G. Sharp." The dog did as commanded, then headed for a gull. Glen's car appeared minutes later. He parked and emerged. Claire felt the breath pull from her body. He was so handsome.

Truly. Gretchie beelined over and danced on her hind legs as she pressed her front paws into Glen's waist. He fell to his knees and wrapped his arms around her bobbing shoulders, pulling his face back from her abundant kisses. Claire swallowed back a lump in her throat. He grabbed a stick and heaved it down the beach, parallel to the water. Gretchie raced after it, tongue flapping like bologna—a ridiculous puppy in a grown-up dog body. Glen approached.

"Papers from my attorney." He held up a bulging plastic folder. "I'll just put them in your car?"

She nodded.

When he returned, they faced each other as the wind worked along their clothes, ruffling the hypotenuse of Glen's pants like sails in a storm. He followed Gretchie with his gaze. The buzz of boat engines could be heard on the other side of the jetty.

"Who would be out in this today?"

Claire smiled. "Fools."

A silence hovered between them like a bird deciding which direction to maneuver.

"Remember how we moved into our first apartment on the coldest day?" Glen offered first.

Claire nodded. "In the worst snowstorm ever."

"And your first anatomy exam? When you went to the wrong building?"

"The classroom instead of the cadaver lab? I had to go back at *night*."

"You were all spooked out."

The waves shushed against the hard-packed sand.

"Glen, there are things you never told me."

"Like what?"

"What you thought when we first met."

"Yes, I have."

"Not really. You said I was cute."

"You were."

"And my nose was crooked."

He nodded. "In a cute way."

"But what else?"

"I don't know what you want, Claire."

"I want to know how you felt beneath the surface. You could have had any girl on campus. Why me?"

"Because." He paused and looked down. "You were fierce and elegant and awkward."

"Really?"

"And I felt… I don't know." He met Clair's eyes with his own. "Smarter maybe, more alive for sure around you. Like you would always be a little wild and I would always be in for it—what I mean is, never bored." He continued, "But then there was this thing I didn't count on. How being a teacher feels mediocre next to being a doctor."

Claire managed to keep her mouth from dropping open. Had she known this all along and forgotten? Or was this an oversight on their part, never quite completing their own circuit of intimacy before life swept them quickly along?

"That's just bullshit, Glen."

"It's real for me." He looked away. He was difficult to hear, but she strained. "And now you're working on your PhD too. It's incredible, Claire, for you."

"I'm not in the program yet."

"I always thought if we had a son—sons—rather than daughters, it would be harder, you know. To prove myself to them. To live up to the difference between you and me."

"Glen, you were a great parent." Claire wouldn't choke on her emotion. He needed to hear this. "To our daughters."

His eyes glistened. He scuffed his feet in the sand. "You too, Claire. A wonderful mother."

Thank goodness Gretchie barked; it kept Claire's heart from falling through her chest. She zoomed between them, her ears flopping with joy. They both followed her trajectory, over to the parking area, then down to the edge of the water.

"Hey!" Glen called and then whistled. "Come back." He turned to Claire. "I don't like her near the water."

"Gretch!" Claire called. "Here, girl."

Gretchie raced toward them and, at the last moment, veered away.

"Glen, do you really want a divorce?"

He bit his lip before answering. "No… Yes… No… I don't know."

"Is it really too late?" Her voice shook. "For us?"

"I want us to try, Claire. I really do. I'm just not sure if I'm strong enough for you. For us."

She kicked at a pile of dried lake weed and rammed her foot into a rock jostled upright by hidden roots. Damn, now her foot throbbed, why did everything just hurt, hurt, hurt?

"The papers are in your car," Glen said. "You can—we can—think about it. Talk again in a few weeks?"

That seemed so terribly long to Claire. But before she said anything, Gretchie was between them with a stick in her mouth, holding it aloft as if offering it to the highest bidder. Glen knelt on one knee and buried his face in her neck. Then he stood up. "We'll touch base. Soon." He turned and headed for his car. "Be a good dog, G, okay?"

Claire wanted to follow him, to tell him that she was the weak one, not him. But he walked briskly as if more conversation would be too much. He started the engine and was gone. Claire waited until the taillights disappeared around the corner and then moved to her car.

"C'mon, girl." She opened the passenger-side door.

Nostrils quivering, Gretchie strained against the urge to chase down another interesting smell before jumping in when her ears shot up at honking overhead. Migratory ducks—a whole flock of them—were flying low and coming in for a landing, heralded by heavy wing beats and cacophony.

Claire bent into the car to pat the seat but hesitated, seeing the documents Glen had left, neat and contained in their case. She closed her eyes, taking a few slow breaths in and out. When she reached behind to grab for G's collar, her fingers grasped air.

Claire spun around. "Gretch, here, girl!"

With all the sounds in the landscape, there was clearly one absent: that of a large exuberant dog. Claire galloped toward the water. The wind surged, momentarily blurring her vision. She wiped her eyes. No dog in sight.

"Gretchie! Here, G!"

At the shoreline, the ducks landed and bobbed in the waves. Claire scanned the lake; it was all one color, muddy greenish-brown, without even a shadowy hint of where her dog might be. Just then a brown figure, barely distinguishable in the churning water, appeared about fifteen yards beyond the ducks.

That couldn't be G. It was farther than she had ever gone. Still, Claire stepped into the water, which veered in skittish insects around her ankles. The ducks rattled angrily. She squinted at the shape. A dog's head was cutting panicked Vs in the water. A blunt snout struggled at the surface and then vanished in a swell.

This isn't happening. Not now. Not Gretchie.

Claire ploughed through the water as far as her legs, heavy in sodden jeans, carried her, toward the spot where she could no longer see her dog, and then dove forward. The shock of the water over her head pummeled her like a cold fierce bite, knocking the air from her lungs.

She surfaced, searching. No dog.

She dove again, kicking off against a sharp boulder, this time lunging deeper, her eyes uselessly open in the murk. A full minute passed. Yet she wouldn't give up. Fifteen seconds more and she was grimacing against the pain in her lungs. She was not surfacing without her dog. Just as her oxygen became impossibly low, Claire's hand lit against something solid. A stick. No, it was furry. A leg! Push-pulling through the water with her remaining strength, she grasped Gretchie around her girthy middle and half swam, half waded back to land, slow as a turtle, under the bulk of her bloated and wheezing dog.

Claire fell to her knees and set Gretchie on her side. She was no longer coughing. Her chest did not move.

"C'mon, baby." Claire pushed downward on G's heavy rib cage. "You can do this, girl."

A wet sputtering sound, absolute music to Claire, filled the air as Gretchie's chest billowed. Within several seconds, she struggled to her haunches, looked quizzically around, and then sneezed.

Claire tried to stand, but G knocked into her full force, nuzzling and licking. Claire buried her face, sotted with dog kisses and tears, into Gretchie's fur.

"Oh God," she whispered. "Thank you, oh God!"

Gretchie engaged in a massive body shake, forming an aura of droplets around them both that splintered into primary colors, like glimmering shards of joy.

"We're okay, baby! We are okay."

Claire led Gretchie gently to the car and helped her into the concave well of the passenger seat. She found an old afghan in the trunk and wrapped it around her damp dog, tighter than needed.

"It's time, girl."

Gretchie poked her nose through the open-weave mesh.

"Let's go home."

Chapter 21

Moira

For two days, Moira couldn't leave her bed except to pee. She pretty much stopped eating and could barely hold a cigarette for the shaking of her hand. Something roared inside of her—a monster that was sucking her dry, sapping her energy. She suddenly hated this bed, this trailer, these ratty pajamas, this whole miserable life. She squished her cigarette out into an empty can of pineapple rings, Colly's dinner last night. The embers sighed as they drowned in a slick of juice at the bottom.

"Colly! Colleen! Come dump the butts!" Moira fanned the lingering smoke away from her face. Colly didn't respond. She must be outside somewhere. Moira's teeth ground with impatience. The entire world, it seemed, was against her.

How was this possible? Two jobs—menial, shitty-ass jobs—lost in the same week? Six double shifts in a row at the foundry and then pink-slipped? At least they'd closed the entire shift. But the animal hospital, even though she earned far less there, that's what hurt.

"You're fired, got it? We're letting you go."

That manager, a woman named Rosa, her face was stuck in Moira's mind. Who did she think she was, with hair like a fake red flame, acting better than everybody, dressing Moira down in the middle of the cage room, the smell of shite all over? Moira knew this type, a trashy woman rising above herself and willing to dump on people she thought lower than her.

"Found things stolen."

Rosa had to raise her voice over the off-kilter howl of a beagle awake enough from surgery to make a stink but not enough to keep from soiling itself. Other jobs, Moira had indeed taken things: small bars of soap, shampoo, and even toilet paper from the motel. Sometimes items from the customers who were foolish enough to leave things out. When she bussed tables, she'd grab a bread roll, take a little off the waitress's tips. But here? What was to steal here?

"Forceps. Syringes."

Syringes? Those were kept locked in a cabinet. Jesu. Like she was some druggie! Wasn't it obvious that the girl up front, the one with tattoos and piercings, who logged in the patients when they arrived, that she was their thief? Moira knew it instinctively, could read it in the girl's dark, angry eyes. She'd fought her Shelta down, even as it expanded into her vocal cords. There was a better way rather than carryin' on. She was slyer now, molded by bitter experience. She'd save her rage for something useful.

"Last pay is in the back room. Pick it up as you leave."

This Rosa followed Moira, escorting her out like a common criminal. But she was pulled back by that beagle, whose voice shifted a pitch, like it was in agony or something. The people in the waiting room would hear that. Maybe change their minds about this animal hospital. In the anteroom, Rosa's extra smock hung on a hook. She was a smoker too. Moira recalled a nice metal lighter Rosa owned, a silver Zippo with her initials engraved on it that Rosa snapped open like she was the queen of England. Moira reached into a pocket and found it and then slipped it into her own pocket. She turned around. A neat little envelope with her name in a cellophane window was propped on a small table. She opened it. Fourteen dollars and ninety-five cents. All the money in the world now.

It was a joke, really. Rent was due. Moira couldn't remember the last time she'd bought groceries. She almost doubled over laughing when two Siamese cats bumped against her legs, shattering her rage with ugly amusement. She'd always disliked cats. Sneaky tricksters. And these, in particular, the vet's own privileged brats, were favorites of Rosa's, who slipped them treats, trying to gain favor with the boss. Creamy with sinister brown masks—they should've been drowned as kittens. Moira held out her fingers as if offering a clump of tuna.

"Here, sweetie, sweet."

One cat, the smaller of the two, was foolish enough to approach.

"Enjoy this, my baby."

Moira cocked her leg back and then hauled off and kicked it behind the ribs. It didn't make a sound, just curled around her foot like a C, eyes popping with surprise. The larger one scattered as if vaporized, but the little one, the stupid one, looked up, as if asking for more. Moira kicked it again with the point of her shoe. *Reee-ooow*, it screeched before making off through the doorway. This all felt strangely good to Moira, tapping into a slow, angry churn deep inside, like a faucet that couldn't be turned off.

She jumped in the Buick with her anger packed tight inside like an overstuffed suitcase and headed home. Once she got to her trailer, she waded through the clutter, the wreck of a household, before getting into her boxer shorts and T-shirt and climbing into bed. One or two easy motions and she was done—folded away like a collapsible chair. Determined not to move, to let the world spin on without her.

But two days in bed made her restless.

"Colly!" Where was that girl? Moira hadn't heard her go out. "Damn."

Moira cinched a thin robe around her waist. Taken from a Red Roof Inn she once cleaned, but she never wore the robe except for dramatic effect. She shuffled from her bedroom and snapped on the TV, searching the channels for *General Hospital*. But even this wouldn't satisfy her today. In the kitchen, an empty box of saltines sat next to a jar of peanut butter and two soup cans licked clean. Her own hunger signals had been ignored for so long that they were lost to her body. Colly's painting stuff, cans and tubes and smears, were everywhere.

"Fookin' mess!"

Workin' like a fool at the foundry. Scrubbing animal filth. All of that for this child. *And this is my thanks?*

The rent notice lay crumpled on the floor next to a pile of carefully gleaned bones.

Colly needed to step it up. She was off playing, no doubt, near that lake. Moira sank on the couch trying to unsimmer her anger and counted the canvases propped lazily on the counter along the kitchen wall. Only two—a beach scene and a tree that Colly had been working on for what seemed like forever. Moira admired that tree, had encouraged Colly as she gradually developed it from a rough sketch, then filled it with life, from richly textured bark to handsome coloring.

"It's a maple," Colly had said. "You can tell by the leaves." She'd tilted it toward Moira for a good look. Each one of those carefully drawn leaves was shaped like a lovely open hand.

"That will get a good price for certain," Moira had said. She remembered at the time how Colly had beamed.

Now, she spotted something she hadn't seen before. An unusual figure in the roots. Could it be…? Not possible. An octopus! With swirling tentacles and a menacing expression. The gleaming eyes were something Moira had mistaken earlier for beetles in the soil. Mockery. Moira gritted her teeth. She heard Colly's voice, taunting in her fake Shelta, *No, Moira, I won't take care of you.*

The anger inside flashed from slow-burning embers into fury.

Stepping outside, Moira almost tumbled down the porch steps as the brightness of the sun assaulted her eyes. It was weirdly warm for October—what did they call that, Indian summer? And weirdly quiet. All the children, of course, were in school. She didn't know where to begin to look for that girl. It occurred to her that she had no idea what Colly actually did all day.

She spotted a half-hidden trail that led to the shore. Good as any place to start. A crow strutted and rasped angrily from the gutter of the trailer across the street. That creepy man's place. As she headed toward the path, the bird attacked, a black whir that flew like a small helicopter directly into Moira's face.

Caw! Caw!

"Get! *Blanog!*" Moira ducked, covering her head with her arm, and ran, fleeing the swooping attack. The bird pumped its wings near her head, then scurried away to settle on a low branch, keeping one sharp eye on her. "What the fook?"

It was certain now. The whole world was indeed against her. She stood in a fugue from the attack, never mind the heated air and the sun still smarting her eyes. She should turn around, crawl back into bed. Put a blanket on the bedroom window to keep even the tiniest splinter of light out. But that meant Colly would get off easy. No. It was time for her to come home and get to work. Moira set her jaw at a hard angle and followed the wave sounds through a thicket of trees. A low-hanging sycamore touched her with unwelcome fingers. Other things, branches with thorns, brushed into her ankles and she thrashed to escape them.

Arriving at the shore, Moira shaded her eyes with the flat of her hand against the glare reflecting off the white sand and water. She scoured the area, disgusted by it all: the seaweed-strewn beach, the froth on the waves like dirty soap bubbles. Peering closer, it looked more like the saliva from a rabid dog's mouth. Moira couldn't swim, hated the water really. Where was the charm? The smell of dead fish, the mocking gulls.

"Colly! Colleen!" she repeated, her voice graveled with anger. "Where are you?"

Moira soon tired of wasting her breath. Just as she turned to go back, a familiar low sound stopped her. Was that singing? And then a distinctive splash. This was behind her, just over the crest of a dune. She followed as the sound grew and Moira discovered a quiet pool of water surrounded by small trees. Here the sand was mud-colored. The air smelled like rotted tree trunks and all the things Moira most detested about beaches. In the midst of this damp and secret lair stood Colleen, kicking and wading happily, knee-deep in water.

Moira's stomach clasped into a fist, sickened by the sight of this girl's callous joy—the carefree din, the splashing and cooing at minnows—while Moira was in such dire straits. Colly raised her feet. Tar-black leaves clung to her ankles, the color and gleam of seal skin. In the next instant, as the sun ducked behind a cloud, Moira saw a changeling where a girl had stood seconds before.

Dear sweet Jesu! Colly, just like her namesake, had transformed. With her wild hair matted like kelp, green dye running down the sides of her face, she looked inhuman. Moira had but to shut her eyes for a second to see that image of a selkie, bounding through the surf toward the open sea, superimposed in her mind like a photo negative.

"Get your head straight." Eamon's voice echoed through Moira's head in his ugly mocking tone. The one that had made her cower, that had controlled her for so long. "Selkies aren't real." She blinked hard and Colly rematerialized.

Moira shook with fury. Now it was Colly's voice in her head. *Not taking care of you Moira, nah-nah-nah-nah…*

Moira scrambled back to the trailer and burst into Colly's room. She now saw in those chalk pictures nothing but secret maps, carefully designed escape routes. Moira rubbed her hands in fists over the paneling, catching a splinter along the thick of her hand. She'd only blurred the lines. Fizzing with rage, she tore the casing off Colly's pillow and rubbed harder with the fabric, this time erasing every mark.

She turned. Colly was in the doorway behind her, her legs muddy and shorts wet with filth. Moira stomped past her and into the living room.

"You." Moira pointed to the canvas. "What was that you said earlier? About taking care of me?"

Colly remained still, wide-eyed.

"From now on, we'll do things the hard way."

Moira pushed her way into the bathroom and unscrewed the single bulb from the fixture over the sink. The one small window was butted up against a tree so now there was no light.

"Moira?" Colleen spoke in a timid voice as she stepped into the bathroom.

Moira didn't respond. Instead, she rushed through the doorway and shut the door swiftly behind her and then locked it from the outside, leaving Colly in the room by herself.

"Let's see what twenty-four hours in a cave helps you figure out, missy."

The pounding that Moira had anticipated began, the shouting, the crying. Colly's tantrum carried through the trailer like an echo in a canyon. It was maddening. Moira ran a line of duct tape around the outer edges of the door. The yelling grew louder. She moistened the edges of a paper towel to make neat, little earplugs and then stopped.

No, this was ridiculous. Moira's thoughts congealed into a fist. She placed her face against the door. "Every minute I hear you pound, little one, is one more day in the cave. Got it?"

Bang! Bang! The pounding continued with increased ferocity. "Okay, now it's two. Did you hear me? Two full days until you're comin' out."

Silence.

Moira grabbed her cigarette pack. Down to three now. No matter, she needed one with urgency. She tapped it out onto her palm. Her right hand shook. But only a bit. She sat quietly. She managed to flick the stolen lighter with her thumb. It didn't work. She chucked it across the room where it dinged and bounced, becoming just another piece of the overall mess.

In the kitchen, she turned the radio to a country station. She needed simple noise. She raised the volume a little bit and then a little bit more, to drown out the commotion in her head—Siobhan, Eamon, and now Colly, their voices, their faces, all melding into one ugly cacophony.

She twisted the front burner on the stove to the on position. It clicked like an insect and then stopped. She turned the back burner on. Same thing. It clicked but no flame appeared. A low hiss joined the static of the radio. Damn pilot light must be off.

"Now where the fook did I leave the matches?"

Moira looked into the cupboards and saw nothing. She could ask Colly. Colly would know. That girl knew everything. She almost puffed with pride over how smart that child was. Maybe she'd been too hard on her. And then she berated herself. *Just like you to soften, Moira.* No, a lesson must be learned this day. Moira stood on tiptoe and ran her hand into each of the cupboards one by one. Nothing. And then she dragged a chair over to get a better look. All the while the cigarette dangled from her mouth, infusing cool menthol into her breath, like fresh air, clearing her brain.

A terrible restlessness came over Moira and it took a minute to realize she was actually hungry. Starving in fact. She'd go back to the A&W. Could almost smell the cheeseburger grease and the French fries. Besides, she was pretty sure they had matches at the walk-in part.

Leaving the trailer, Moira locked the front door and climbed into the Buick and drove off. There used to be stalls at the A&W, the kind you parked in and placed your order into speakers and they set a tray on your window. The good old days. She'd visited once, when she was a child. The whole clan filled the parking lot. Had Eamon been there? She couldn't remember. But Siobhan was, and they actually got along. Split a root beer float between them. When they were finished eating, they drove off without paying. It was a great time.

On the two-lane road, Moira hesitated. Had she left the burner on? No, she wouldn't be that forgetful. She'd bring Colly back a hamburger and root beer. Let her out of that selkie cave. Poor girl must be terrified.

But at the juncture of the road that would take Moira to the A&W, she veered in the opposite direction. Southwest. What if she just drove on tonight, right this minute—until she couldn't drive anymore? It was an intoxication, this idea of freedom. She pushed the Buick to sixty on the rural highway. The branches of pines lining the road reached toward her like open arms.

Chapter 22
Claire

Claire leaned across the kitchen table crowded with stacks of papers, several unwashed coffee cups, and other detritus from months of work. A fresh vase of delivered flowers with a note in bold letters that read **Good Luck with Your Presentation! Love, Vicki**.

"Kind of messy, all this work, huh, G?"

Gretchie eyed Claire knowingly, keen with the understanding that something was afoot.

Claire opened the folder titled "Radiologic advances in the detection of metastatic cancer" and ran her finger along a bar graph on the first page, stopping at the bold red rectangle that represented the patients responding to her protocol. While there was still much work to be done, the results to date looked promising. She hoped her colleagues and the committee members would see it that way as well.

It was already past noon and Claire needed to be dressed and on her way. The event, scheduled at a hospital in the suburb of Naperville—an hour west of the city—had been chosen for its potential for collaboration. It was only several minutes from her old life in Upton Grove. She grabbed the phone. Dialing, she gathered the materials for her presentation, which included transparencies for an overhead projector. Gretchie whined for a treat. Claire frowned and shook her head. The phone rang on the other end.

C'mon, Howard.

She needed one last bit of assurance before leaving.

An audience would be there. The thought tautened Claire's gut, dragged her back to that previous experience—the set and stage of *Chicago Live at Five!* where she still stung from the feeling of being psychologically flayed in public. But now, the only thing that stood between her and success was this final requirement. She'd considered going to Margaret Christner, to plead for a waiver of some sort that would get her out of the presentation. But no. That would feel as though Claire were somehow dishonoring her daughters. In turn, she wondered, would Lily and Andrea, in some small way, be proud of her despite her shortcomings, her stubborn willfulness, her serious flaws?

"Claire?" Howard started midconversation where they had left off last time, his deep tenor booming through the receiver as he discussed last-minute pointers. "Set out the pages in order, and then a quick greeting to the audience…"

Even though this was the hundredth reiteration, it was still reassuring to walk through every detail. She really couldn't be more prepared, right?

"Wish I could be there," he said. "Have that damn seminar of my own."

Claire sensed a twinge of nervous-parent anxiety in Howard's voice. Sheesh, he wanted this for her as much as she did. She had teased him the last time they met that she was his personal project, like Eliza Doolittle in *My Fair Lady.*

"Maybe, but I'm not that good-looking Professor Huggins, that's for sure."

"It's Higgins, Howard."

"Whatever. The point is that I believe in you, ma'am. You will be fine. Just remember to balance as you…"

"I know, I know." She'd smiled. "As I walk sideways. On walls like a spider."

She pictured his round face crinkling into a grin even as her brain conjured her tough-minded colleagues with disapproving frowns. What if her presentation went poorly? What if she failed?

"Just stay calm and focused, like we practiced. And where will my dog be this evening?"

Claire eyed Gretchie lounging on her side on the kitchen floor. She hadn't missed a single appointment with Howard, and it showed in this new belly-paunch from all of his slyly delivered tea biscuits.

"You know she's going to Glen's, Howard. I told you a million times."

"That's right."

It wasn't a necessary arrangement. But St. Mark's Hospital was only ten minutes from Glen's house. That's what Claire was now calling it, as if he alone belonged there. Maybe this was a dry run for custody arrangements, Claire thought wryly. Other than last night, when Claire called him to firm up the plans for today, they had conversed only twice in the month since meeting at the lake. Both spoke in careful clipped sentences, dodging deeper discussion. As if restraints were holding them apart. Yet so far, the divorce papers had remained untouched, as if something else was keeping them bound together, some kind of unseen force.

"I'll drop her off after three," Claire had told Glen. He wouldn't be home yet from work.

"Just let yourself in. She'll be fine. I haven't seen Gretchie in so long. I miss her." He didn't say he missed Claire. "And when you pick her up, we need to talk."

There it was. Claire caught her breath and nodded.

She went to her room to wrap up final preparations before leaving. She held up two suits, a light-weight taupe and a wool navy one with extra shoulder padding. She chose the warmer of the two as the weather was turning and there was a discernible chill in the air.

"What do you think, huh, girl?"

Gretchie wrinkled her brow and then dropped into a sphinx pose, with her haunches neatly lined up and forelegs extended.

"You are right." Claire nodded. "Pumps and the navy suit it is."

She struggled into the shoes, which pinched her toes—like strapping angry crustaceans onto her feet. She caught G's eye and pointed to them.

"You have no idea how lucky you are to be a dog."

She looked closely in a full-length mirror propped against the wall. Her stomach was flat—no, concave, as if she'd never carried babies. She still wasn't eating right. It was more about taste now. As if her ability to take pleasure in food had gone dormant.

Returning to the kitchen, Claire stuffed items into Gretchie's tote—in went her favorite canned food, and a new chewy, a complicated contraption with a braided rope and a rawhide bone. Not that she needed it. There were plenty of dog toys at Glen's house.

"No biscuits, sorry! Let's go, girl!"

Once on the road, Gretchie stretched out on the seat next to her. The vibration of the car soon soothed her into a sleepy trance. But she jumped up when they pulled down Crestview and sniffed the air greedily, her tail taut with anticipation. Claire's response was the opposite; her whole body tensed up.

It seemed like forever since this house had been her home. As she waited for the engine to settle completely before getting out of the car, she scanned the front of the simple brick bungalow—the nondescript brown shutters, the stiff angular hedge of yews.

On the porch, Claire unlocked the back door and entered. Gretchie remained outside, keenly nosing the perimeter of the backyard. In the small hallway leading to the kitchen, she encountered the parakeet cage and Butkus plumped up. Upon seeing Claire, he squawked. She couldn't help but laugh. How she missed that sound!

"You miserable, sweet tyrant of a bird."

The house was midafternoon dark. Part of Claire felt like an intruder, another part like a guest. She drifted throughout the rooms, noting that many things were now changed: ocean-blue walls in the living room, faux-leather furniture. And in the kitchen, the teapot wallpaper was gone, replaced by spackled patches awaiting a sanding and fresh coat of paint. The girls' room remained the same. Glen was true to his word to leave it untouched. Entering, she roved, exploring every nook with heightened senses. This room, Claire knew, was the one perfect thing that stitched her broken world together. Could just knowing it was here be enough?

Jay's dream catcher remained suspended over the crib. Claire leaned against the rail and examined the delicate weave before blowing a stream of air. It spun slowly. Lily would've loved such an item. Looking around again, Claire had a small revelation. She really had remarkable children. Lily, the very definition of sweetness, clearly took after Glen. And Andrea's huge personality had filled the room ever since she was a newborn, straightening her legs and kicking off her covers as if she needed to be on the move. And, man, could she yell. When she was hungry or needed to be changed. *I'm here, world, make room!*

For the first time, Claire allowed a sliver of forgiveness for having expected so much of herself. It was quite simply, how she was wired. So much like Andrea, her binary soul.

The sound of Andrea calling from beneath the water surfaced in Claire's mind. Why was Lily never in the dream? She squeezed her eyes shut. So much frozen in her memory shifted like polar ice in the spring. She needed to be careful or the images beginning to whir through her head might consume her.

"Count the clouds, one, two, three," she sang softly. "See the birdie in the tree…"

"If he has a broken wing…" A gentle masculine voice joined her own from the doorway. "He will never sing, sing, sing."

Glen! He entered the room. Fine wrinkles ran along his hairline. The gift of perpetual astonishment was still evident in his soft hazel eyes. She could smell his body wash, his damp masculinity. She could've doubled over from the ache deep inside.

"Hello, Claire."

She stepped back. Glen touched her arm to steer her away from backing into the rocker, the one covered with Mother Goose characters still blotched with stains from infant formula and dribbled pain reliever. Claire jumped at the contact and they both pulled back. A confused expression filled Glen's face and he looked away.

She was ashamed of herself. *He must think I don't want him near.* In truth, she was no longer used to the feel of soft touch on her skin.

He cleared his throat. "Tell me about your presentation."

She began awkwardly by describing the careful dosing regimen she'd worked out for patients. But emotion rose in her voice as she finished with how her research might provide hope for desperate patients, hope for their families.

"Listen to you, Claire. I just knew you'd make a terrific doctor."

Her eyes began to glisten. Hearing this from her husband—quite possibly her soon-to-be ex-husband, the one she still loved—hurt so much.

"Glen, I'm afraid."

He raised his eyebrows.

"Terrified, actually," she continued, "of this event."

He would get it, right? What a big deal it was for her to share that with him, her unspoken vulnerability?

"You will be great."

She appreciated that he said this, but wished he'd offered to come. As support.

Claire's gaze landed on the dresser top and the ziplock baggie that contained Jumpers's carrot. Against police procedure, Detective Hearns had arranged that they be allowed to keep it once the case was finalized on Andrea's death. Glen had brushed the ochre earth away and soaked it gently in dish detergent. The sight of it, restored to its bright orange, brought definition to their prolonged grief, their unspoken desperation.

Glen started to say something, and then stopped. He went into the living room.

She followed. They stood quietly for a moment, as awkward in each other's presence as adolescents on a date. He gestured toward the new furniture.

"I hope you don't mind, that old sofa was…"

"God-awful?"

He smiled. "Yes, and the chair…"

"That was G's chair!"

"I would never get rid of that. Just moved it. In the master bedroom now."

Outside, Gretchie yapped at a hapless squirrel. One that had probably grown accustomed to a dog-free backyard. Claire checked her watch.

"I need to go." She headed to the front door. "Glen," Claire said before leaving. "Take good care of my girl, huh?" A silly request since she'd only be gone a few hours.

Still, Glen smiled. "I will, Claire. You know that, right?"

"Yes."

"See you in a few." That simple phrase felt so strange and yet powerful. It would be nice to be with Glen again so soon.

She left, already missing Gretchie, even though she was in good hands, and grateful that she and Glen had reestablished what felt like feelings of generosity toward each other.

Bright lights illuminated the stage of St. Mark's Hospital auditorium. Claire stood at the lectern next to the overhead projector. Copies of the presentation had been distributed to the audience. She shivered at the chilly emptiness surrounding her and searched the faces frantically for anything that might resemble familiarity, but they melted into one shapeless mass. Finally, she met eyes with Margaret in the first row who nodded encouragingly. Claire flipped on the overhead projector and waited a moment before speaking.

"Thank you for coming." The mic squeaked, then boomed.

She pulled the carefully arranged stack of transparencies from a folder.

"I'm Dr. Claire Rawlings." Her voice expanded into the rows and people sat up attentively as she set the first plastic sheet on the projector. *Uh-oh.* The title page from a supporting paper. *Okay. Simple mistake.* She went on to the next one and then the next, fumbling through the entire pile.

My God, they're all the wrong ones!

"Shit," Claire mumbled too close to the mic. There were a few chuckles followed by restless crowd energy. She wiped her upper lip with the back of her hand and then reached down reflexively to touch her dog. There was, of course, only empty space.

"Um…"

Audible sighs from the audience.

Claire's blouse was beginning to cling under her arms and across her chest. She shuffled the sheets again as if they'd magically reassemble into the proper presentation—the one she realized that she'd left in a neat pile on the table at her town house. Two people slipped out the double doors in the back. She followed them with her eyes, imagining them disappearing down the flight of stairs on the other side. Downward, the same direction her stomach was heading. The door closed with a definitive thump. She couldn't allow this to happen. Not after everything. All the loss. All the shutting of doors in her life. She'd overcome so much to get this far.

"I'm just going to"—she cleared her throat—"walk through this with you."

She began slowly, desperate to regain footing, and then consciously raised the volume of her voice, to infuse it with what might sound like confidence. It took a minute, but the audience finally settled a bit. Making reference to the handouts, she sketched versions of graphs on each blank transparency while speaking, careful to emphasize key moments in the data.

Somehow, Dr. Claire Rawlings proceeded through her forty-five-minute seminar flawlessly. At least with no clearly detectable flaws. For a brief shining slice of time she felt as if the universe was on her side, and she wrapped up with a flourish. The immediate silence of her colleagues indicated they were impressed.

Once the Q&A section was completed, Claire stepped from the platform, drained and exhilarated, daring to believe she'd actually done a good job. Her relief was stupendous. Looking over the sea of colleagues, she spotted the back of a familiar head among the milling crowd heading toward the double doors. Glen. He must've felt her gaze because he turned and smiled.

She wanted to move toward him, but within minutes, she was surrounded.

"Excellent work, Dr. Rawlings." This compliment came from a white-haired gentleman next to a beaming Margaret. Claire couldn't recall his name but remembered he was a co-chair of the grant committee. Other presenters and audience members mulled and conversed. It was close to seven before everything wrapped up.

"Walk with me, Claire?" Margaret offered. "I want to show you something."

Margaret led Claire past the main lobby and through two

corridors to a newly constructed ward. A gleaming radiology unit was off to one side, private rooms to another.

"This wing is where patients might be treated with your protocol someday."

Just then an intern approached to engage Margaret. "Dr. Christner?"

Claire wandered to a large window where the lights of the suburb twinkled beyond the parking lot. She sighed, taking in the newness around her—the shiny floor, the smell of construction—and then ran her hand along the wall and smiled thinking of Howard. Spurred by the presentation, she'd indeed made one tentative step sideways along these walls.

A sudden disturbance in the vertical blinds startled Claire. A moth with wings shaped like a small pair of flat lungs fluttered weakly from a gap in the folds. Seeing this creature alive, beyond its season, momentarily took her breath away. Admiring its gypsum-white body, she drew close and whispered. "How on earth did you get here?"

The creature wavered toward the window and then disappeared back into the folded blind. Like a magician's trick.

Margaret was still engrossed in conversation. Waving, Claire mouthed her thanks. She left the hospital and was at the Upton Grove house in minutes. Gretchie galloped in ever-tightening circles around Claire. Glen stood near.

"You were amazing, Dr. Rawlings."

"You surprised me, Glen. By being there. Thank you."

"I wouldn't have missed it for the world."

The room was suddenly filled with the perfect tone of Glen's presence.

"Thank you again for coming." Claire's voice wavered. "For being there for me."

"I knew you'd be nervous if I told you."

"Ha! Like that was avoidable."

"Well, more nervous. I have a frozen pizza in the oven. Sit. Have a glass of wine."

"I have to drive."

Ignoring Claire, Glen disappeared into the kitchen and emerged with two ridiculously oversize glasses they had received as a wedding gift.

"Just one," Glen said. "You deserve it."

Claire sank into the new couch. It was really quite comfortable. They drank quickly, leaving a red velvety film in the goblets.

"They look lonely." Claire pointed to the empty glasses.

Glen poured more wine, which they once again both drained. He then grabbed another bottle from the kitchen and opened it unsteadily over the cocktail table in the living room.

"Careful." Claire cupped her hands as if to catch a spill.

He settled in the recliner across from Claire. "Do you know what I miss?"

She shook her head.

"Mr. Bubble."

Claire looked at him, startled.

"I bought a bottle once," Glen continued. "Just to smell it again."

Claire's heart caught in her chest. It was one of her favorite products in the world. She closed her eyes and was suddenly swirling a stream of it into water roiling from the faucet during Lily and Andrea's bath time. The frothy bubbles covered the water like insulation from which the girls, with Claire's help, constructed beards on their chins and then added bikini tops to their gleaming chests. Two little old men in girlie bathing suits. Eager to see themselves in the mirror, they often tried to stand while Claire admonished them: *Sit safely, ladies, puh-lease!* The whole time Gretchie snorfed through their soiled laundry with her flat nose, looking for dried tidbits of food.

This deliciously bright memory warmed Claire and she looked into Glen's eyes, which were soft and gauzy. "Remember the bathroom after?" she said. "The piles of suds?"

"And all the wet towels." He chuckled. "It was a million loads of wash after each bath as I recall."

A moment passed. And then Claire spoke, "Lily would be five and a half, Glen."

"I know."

Claire felt Lily's perfect shape against her chest and could see her rose-quartz eyelids droopy with sleep. She'd be tired after her bath.

"I'm sorry." Glen reached over and then dropped his hand. "I shouldn't have…"

"No. It's okay. You are right." She swallowed hard. "We need to talk about our girls."

Glen settled back into his chair. Claire could smell his tiredness. She, too, felt heavy. It was early, just past nine, but exhaustion, combined with the alcohol, was claiming them both. And then his eyes were shut and he was snoring lightly. Gretchie snuggled into the floor next to him and gave a satisfied wheeze.

Claire managed to lift herself off the couch and stumble into the master bedroom. She returned with an old floral blanket, which she tucked around Glen, and then pulled off his shoes one by one. He looked ridiculous with his black socks sticking out from under the pattern of faded peonies.

She stepped back.

There had been no talk of divorce tonight. And Claire found wonderment in how emotions can go underground and then be revived again like a dormant root system. Shadows in the room became images, but not scary ones. The drapes bunched at the edge of the window became a climbing rosebush. Cracks in the ceiling created some giant puzzle. And then her thoughts went beyond this room to the delicate wings of the moth that had visited earlier. And then to the rich memory of her girls after bath time, which now burned like a brilliant ember deep inside.

Claire kicked off her pumps and lay on the couch. She'd grab a quick nap and then leave. Closing her eyes, while drifting hazily to sleep, she returned, once again, to that underwater place, where Andrea called to Claire.

But this time, there was only silence.

Chapter 23
Jay

J ay hunkered at the end of his driveway, gathering stones. Some drunken teenagers had had fun the previous night fishtailing through the trailer park, knocking into the mailboxes. Now, on his knees, he piled rocks against the teetering pole to stabilize it.

"That should fix it," Jay announced to himself just as Moira's green Buick screeched by in reverse, practically smearing Jay into the gravel before lurching to a halt.

It was clear she hadn't seen him. But he saw her as she stopped to shift gears and light a cigarette with the cylindrical car lighter.

"Fookin' lighter."

He heard her through the open driver's side window even as he remained in a stunned crouch.

Once again, he caught a quick glimpse of that face. While it was just Moira's profile, he was now certain he had seen her before, but with a different child, not Colly, but a toddler. How was that possible? Wait, where was Colly? She wasn't in the back of that car, and yet when Jay turned toward the trailer across the street, he could see all was dark. The undercurrent that had been working within him since he'd met Colly was ratcheting up into alarm.

"Jesu..." Moira muttered through the unlit cigarette dangling from her mouth.

A mosquito sang in Jay's ear. He waved it away.

"*Dalon stk sudil!*" Moira gunned the Buick forward and disappeared.

Jay rose and stood frozen in the tornado of dust left in the car's wake. It was the same expression that had come from Colly when she'd cut her hand. What language was that? The tone and cadence reminded him of something vague and oddly familiar. Could it be the Shelta he heard as a child? They were Travellers? But that didn't fit. Not for Colly, at least. Jay shook his head, mentally working awkward pieces of a puzzle together.

It was as if a silent bell had been struck, but he still wasn't clear on its message. All his senses tingled as the murkiness of a several-years-old memory grew clearer: he now knew where he'd seen Moira's face before. That day with Claire Rawlings in the campground, when his car was broken down. The Traveller woman who had asked him to move his car. The certainty that he had felt at the time that the kidnapper was a woman once again rushed through him like an injection of adrenaline.

He closed his eyes and thought of the image on the picture that Claire had given him of her oldest daughter. While the features were now ruined, the spark he'd noticed about that child the first time he'd seen it, somehow remained tattooed on his brain. He did the math. Andrea Rawlings would be eight years old now.

Jay's mind dipped and weaved with possibilities, ugly possibilities, all leading him in an unimaginable direction. Andrea Rawlings was dead. They had proof. Jay bit into his upper lip, recalling what Claire had told him: a tooth, nothing more than a tooth and the ashes of her clothes. He needed to look in Colly's eyes to quell his rising panic. He needed to ask her again who Moira was to her. The sheer magnitude of what he was thinking—what it might mean—sent him racing across the street and onto Colly's porch. Facing the closed door, the trailer seemed different to him somehow, threatening. Like a wild animal in restless sleep. His internal alarm system was screaming, and his body moved as if on autopilot as it finally succumbed to his overpowering instinct.

Get to that girl.

He yanked open the screen and pounded hard on the metal security door common in trailer parks.

No response.

"Colly! Colly!"

He rammed a shoulder into the door. It cracked a half-inch or so along the jamb and then popped back into place. He was aware that there was commotion nearby. People out walking, sensing drama. Soon there'd be a crowd.

He pulled his hair from his face. *Calm down, man. Think.* A moth dive-bombed into his arm, marking it with a ghost of powdery scales. What if he was wrong and Moira pressed charges? He'd lose everything. But Colly might be in real trouble. Could Moira possibly be a kidnapper? A haunting image of Lily Rawlings's sweet face flashed through his mind. Could Moira be a murderer?

"Hey, man, whaddya doin'?" someone called from the road. A dog growled, low and angry.

Jay ignored the disembodied voice. No time to fuck around. In truth, he couldn't say what he was thinking then. He just knew he had to get to Colly. Every fiber of his being screamed at him that she was in there and in real trouble.

The trailer itself was eerily calm, with the exception of the faint strains of a radio inside set to a country-western station. Something was off, way off. Jay leaned closer to the door, trying to listen over the music. And that's when he smelled a faint, sickly odor. Gas.

He gave up on the door and leaped off the porch and into a sliver of dark alongside Colly's room. A hollow in the dirt kept him from being able to reach the window. He searched for something, anything to stand on. Stomping the weeds, he kicked away a plastic flamingo, bleached white from exposure until stumbling onto an old plastic birdbath on its side. He righted it and prayed that the base, weighted with sand, would hold. Hoisting himself by the slim window ledge, he managed to maintain a wobbly balance, knees bent, as if on a trampoline. The window was shut.

"Colly! Colleen. I know you're in there. Can you open the door?"

Two shadowy figures in the street became three.

"Get the manager," Jay called. "We need to turn the gas off—someone's in there."

He tried to hoist himself up higher. But it was impossible with such an unstable base. His palms, moist with sweat, had the slimmest of grips on the feeble sill.

Pressing his face to the filthy glass, he blinked to adjust his eyes in the murky dark of a bedroom. He searched, desperate. Nothing. Straining harder, he flattened his cheek against the pane. His pulse throbbed in his neck. Directly across from the window he saw what looked like movement in a bulge along the wall. Like a sea creature just under a wave. Must be a shadow. But no, the actual wall was moving. And then a small hand emerged between the seams of two panels, followed by the top of a head. Colly's head.

What on earth? The part in Colly's hair became visible and then her neck and the beginning of her shoulders. She was squeezing through the wall from a different room. He almost toppled over from the surprise.

"C'mon, Little Bird!"

Did she hear him? He couldn't be sure. But she kept struggling to pull herself through this gap in the now partially splintered wall. He called again but it came out as an inaudible rasp through his dry throat. He wanted to bang the window but wouldn't dare risk a shift in his grip. With visible effort she managed to twist sideways— *attagirl!*—and angle in such a way to crook her neck so her face was visible to Jay.

In this position, with her hair flattened and her bangs swept to either side as if she were running, he now saw something or, rather, someone else. A full-blown spasm wrenched through his stomach to his chest. But it wasn't painful. Instead, it flooded Jay with the familiar warmth of the feelings that he had suppressed for far too long.

He gasped as the great wheel of the universe, which had been slightly off-kilter for so long, clicked into place.

This was unmistakably Andrea Rawlings.

Tears welled in his eyes, but he held steady and took a deep breath. For the first time since he'd lost his mother and grandmother, maybe for the first time in his life, he was absolutely sure he was where he was meant to be, doing what he was meant to do. That there were no coincidences.

He let go with one hand and shakily tapped against the glass. She didn't move. He tapped harder.

"Keep coming," he yelled, wiggling the pane frozen by rust.

How could she not hear him? He cupped his hands and repeated his words.

She gained several inches by writhing and then curled her side body upward to pummel the panels with her fists. But they were secured by nails into the wall studs and would open no further to accommodate her torso and hips. She was able to just wave her right arm toward Jay. This simple movement let him know she could hear him, was with him in this. He could also read the exhaustion that was setting in.

Jay clenched his teeth. No telling how long the gas had been on in this small trailer. A timer, like a bomb, began in his head. *Tick, tick.*

He pounded at the window just hard enough to crack the glass, not wanting the broken pieces falling inside. Luckily, it spider-webbed into three uneven triangles. His legs quivered under him as the bird bath juddered. He wrenched out the pieces of glass, the last one cutting into the side of his hand like a deli meat slicer. He shuddered at the feel of it entering his flesh, but there was no pain, nor would he have cared if there had been. He tossed the broken sheets onto the ground where they shattered like frozen drops of rain, reflecting the twilight sky in a shimmering streak of silver. The foul odor of gas blasted him in the face.

"Little Bird. Come to me. Hurry. Please."

"I...I can't, Jay. I'm stuck..."

Jay tightened his jaw. Blood from his wound slopped onto his pants and the ground. He shakily managed his shirt over his head and twisted it around his hand. He didn't care if he bled to death, he just didn't want to scare Colly—no, Andrea! There was an air of impossibility around each action and the burning sensation that something terrible was about to happen soon.

He lifted himself as high as he could while keeping the tips of his boots in contact with the birdbath and stretched his arms through the ridiculously tight opening. It was just a bit bigger than a mailbox on its side. He momentarily doubted whether she would fit through even if he was able to reach her. But there was no other answer. Someone was talking to him from the road. Asking if he needed help or what. But they stood back, far away. The damn radio from the other room was louder now that the glass was gone.

"Hold on."

One of Jay's feet slipped from the birdbath. His left side listed hard downward. His weird position was slowing blood flow to his arms and upper body. Black dots lurked in his peripheral vision. Every movement, every sound had the quality of being observed through water. Jay waggled his head against the dimming.

"Git outta there, man. I called the utilities." The manager was somewhere behind Jay. "They're coming. You need to get down from there."

"The police," Jay barked. "An ambulance, now!"

"On their way. Get back!"

Jay counted in his head. Ten one thousand, nine one thousand— *tick, tick, tick.*

He could easily be undone by panic. But then, right then, Jay stopped. Closed his eyes. Recalling a powerful phrase he had learned from his childhood, he petitioned his dearest loved ones— his mother and grandmother—for their help. *Mitakuye Oyasin.* He then spoke their names for the first time since they'd passed—Grace and June. He thanked them, *pilámaya,* for leading Andrea to him. And then he enlisted Lily.

I need you now. She needs you. Pilámaya, too, for your light, your help.

He wasn't Catholic, but in his mind, he crossed himself anyway. He had seen it done a thousand times at the Catholic Home for Boys.

Exhaling deeply, Jay stretched his arms like an extension rod through the small window and turtled through up to his shoulders, groaning his way to his chest and upper abdomen. A sharp chunk of glass he'd missed punched a hole into his left arm. The tips of his work boots barely grazed the birdbath. Toppling would be disastrous now.

"Come to me, Little Bird." She was so close, yet a world away from his outstretched hands.

"Can't, Jay." She dropped her head to the floor. "I'm stuck."

"You can. Please try harder." He heard a truck pull up. A siren growing close. "You can do this."

"I...I can't." The resignation in her small voice almost broke him. But he drew strength from everything he knew to be true.

"Yes you can, Andrea."

Tilting her head, she looked at Jay with searching eyes.

"You heard me. Your name is Andrea Rawlings. I know your mother." Her face flashed with a mixture of disbelief and hungry reassurance. "You had a blond-haired, blue-eyed sister named Lily."

"Lily?"

"You were stolen by Moira." Jay strained further, beyond all physical capability, all the while fighting to keep his voice smooth and steady. "Your real mom and dad are good people who miss you terribly. I'm taking you home."

"Step back, please." A voice was coming from a loudspeaker at the road. "We are evacuating the area."

"What did you say?" She was clearly straining to hear over the radio, the commotion outside. The megaphone was stealing his words. Still, he continued.

"You are brave."

She made a fist and punched one of the panels from behind. Jay felt her effort throb through his own aching arms. He said another silent prayer, summoning every ounce of help and strength he could. He would not fail her. Or Claire. Or himself.

"Good girl. Keep coming." He was losing air in this position as the skinny edge of the windowsill practically sliced him in half, jagged bits of glass attacking from all angles. "Come to me. Push, Little Bird. It is important we do this fast."

He was growing dizzy and sucked air in uneven breaths. A numbing ache ran from his armpits. "Please."

He shook to revive his hands, which were white and numb. The cut hand had stopped bleeding. He feared they would soon fail him, that the birdbath would crumble. She bent into more of a tucked position, which brought her out all the way to her hips. He could see her spine, the fine ridges like a dragon's scales. Why hadn't he paid attention to just how skinny she was? A curtain of hair fell over the back of her head. There was almost nothing left of her, he could tell.

"No use," she whispered as her body went limp.

Jay's body, too, was failing; he'd have to drop down. His deadened arms were of no use. He began to shimmy backward, descend to the ground, sick with defeat.

"You are a warrior," he said. It would probably be the last thing he'd ever say to her. "My amazing Little Bird."

Just then she looked up; a wild expression stormed across her face.

Jay felt a life force like a gusting wind so strong it almost knocked him back.

A growl followed by a full-blown grunt boomed through the room. It was a primal sound filled with effort and strain, and, pushing with newfound strength, she burst through the wall with a mighty shove.

Jay strained forward to meet her. She was in his arms, finally! He grasped her firmly, pulled back, and dropping down with all the grace he could manage, yanked her through the open window in one fluid motion. It was a miracle, really. But their combined weight crushed the birdbath, which snapped beneath them. They piled onto the ground with one of his feet bent fully sideways. All his senses screamed pain. But he'd gotten her out. She'd probably scraped her legs and stomach awful coming through, but it didn't matter, she was with him. She was free.

The rotten odor trailed after them in a foreboding cloud.

"C'mon, c'mon, run."

Andrea rose and wobbled. Jay's ankle flared into a stunning pain, but he drag-pulled them both forward. They stumbled together like wounded animals toward the road, heading into a group of people who parted in anticipation. They were almost there, all the way to safety, when…

Bam!

The trailer blew like a tin can filled with firecrackers. The percussion knocked Jay flat with Andrea beneath him. He tried to roll to one side, but his head boomed as if in an echo chamber. His field of vision narrowed. Fireflies flashed in the branches overhead as if stars had descended from the heavens. The world spun in slow motion. Groaning, Jay craned his head enough to see only charred porch stairs against a fiery backdrop.

"Jay, Jay." He heard a girl's voice and then nothing except a hard thrum in his head, a distant sound, like a train coming. No, it was the sound of the world changing.

When Jay woke up in the ambulance, the first thing on his mind was Andrea. "Is she safe?" he gasped.

But then it turned to a darker thought. "Did she escape? That goddamn Moira?"

"Calm down, sir." One voice.

"What's he saying?" Another voice, farther away. No faces.

"Do you mean the little girl?" The first man again.

Jay began to flail like a fish. "She's hurt!" Jay raised his voice over the dull roar messing with his ears.

"She's okay. Scratched up but okay. A little groggy. She's in a different ambulance with the police. They're following us to the hospital."

"You're a hero, man, saving that girl from the trailer."

"The woman!" Jay again.

"You mean her mother?"

Ugh. Were they not listening?

"She was kidnapped!"

"Who? The woman?"

Jay fought to sit up. They didn't know anything.

"No. The girl!" He was yelling, pushing against some straps they must've put on him to keep him secure.

"Whoa. Whoa. The police. They're on it. You're pretty hurt. We gave you a little pain medicine."

What pain? And then it hit. A wallop from his ankle that raced like fire through his body.

"Oh, man." Jay lay back and moaned.

"Ten minutes, buddy. That's all. We'll be at Elmcrest Hospital in ten. Hang on."

"I need," Jay spoke through clenched teeth, "to talk to the police now. Now!"

A man's face came into view, hovering close to Jay. His eyes were grave, concerned. Jay could only hope he believed him.

"The police are on the radio. Want to know if you know where the mother is? The woman who rented the trailer?"

"That's not her mother! That woman kidnapped her. I know her real mother."

"Hang on, buddy. Just for a minute. Here. Can you talk into the radio?"

Jay tried. He saw the shape of it, the little perforations in the plastic case. He was able to say her name. Andrea. And then Moira's. His voice though, was coming from so far away. His head throbbed worse than his ankle. Vomit was rising in his throat. His message was garbled, all over the place and growing dimmer each second.

"Kidnapped at four years old. Sister Lily killed."

Gibberish, this all sounded like gibberish! But he fought to continue.

"A woman, Moira… Find her… She's dangerous…a criminal…"

He was a hot mess spewing information and they were goddamn slow on the uptake.

How to make them understand? It was maddening! He clenched his teeth, took a deep breath, and then spoke clear and strong.

"Hearns. Detective Juanita Hearns. Chicago. Call her, damn it. Call her!"

Jay could say no more. Was it enough? He strained forward. Even as he struggled to speak, the remembrance of his mother, his grandmother, and of Lily during the rescue warmed him like some type of internal glow. His intuition had not failed him, had never failed him. Hot tears sprang from his eyes.

"Buddy. It's okay. We'll be there soon."

Jay fell back just as the ambulance hit a massive dip in the road. The resulting torque amplified through his body, wrenching into his ankle. A vortex of pain concentrated with full force on the exact spot where bone was sticking out of skin. A wave washed over him and his consciousness was swept away.

Chapter 24
Little Bird

B y what magic was she now someone else? Andrea. This was what had come from Jay's mouth as he reached through her bedroom window to save her. The long, slow first *A* of it was wonderful. She had the urge to call for a pencil and paper, to write it over and over again. Andrea. It was a name; in fact, she might have picked all on her own. Then again, her mind was still so blurry. Wasn't Colleen who she really was? Could this all be some sort of trick?

She was only half here in this hospital room. The other half of her was still trapped in the trailer, shivering with fear in the dark. How could Moira have done this? Her eyes white with rage and never saying what was so wrong. She'd been caught for certain in her secret life, but Moira never seemed to care about any of that before. What had changed?

A cold object pressed into her chest. She twitched, just as she had done in the bathroom, no, the cave, when her heart was thrashing as she lay sideways on the cold floor tucking herself into a kidney shape. At the same time, her skin crawled with invisible bees working over her arms and legs with their feelers.

"Hello there. Again."

What? She tightened her brow and looked down. She was in a weird garment. The thing against her chest was a shiny stethoscope. A man in a white coat and a woman in a pastel-green uniform hovered next to her bed, drawing her fully back into the brightness of the hospital room. She had only seen doctors and nurses on *General Hospital*.

"I'm Dr. Grimes," the man said. He had on big, round glasses. "I don't think you heard me the first time." This was all so confusing. One minute trapped, then the next yanked from the grips of an explosion and now this place, even the smell was horrible, like germ-killing mouthwash. She wanted to cry but fought against it in front of strangers.

Dr. Grimes knelt next to her.

"I know this is scary…"

She drew her knees to her chest as a shield. Fear flooded her mouth, heavy and rough like wet felt. Her hands held onto each other as if glued.

"Can you tell me your name?"

"Where's Jay?"

The sheets in the bed smelled like the air in the room, only more intense, as if the vinegary atmosphere of the hospital had been baked into them.

"Is he your friend?"

She nodded, keeping her face locked on the wall closest to her bed. The painted cement blocks gleamed like perfectly stacked sugar cubes.

"He's in surgery."

"What!" She pressed upward against the bed, her hands starfished with tension, and swung around, eyes wide. She could still feel the strength in Jay's arms tugging her through the window.

"He'll be all right. I promise. It's his ankle."

"I need to see him."

"Soon. He'll be out soon. But right now, we're worried about you. Jay White told the police parts of a big story. We want to check it out. Can you help by telling us your name?"

A lump gathered in her throat. A few minutes before she would've said Andrea. But her head was clearer now and without Jay here to verify, it seemed somehow ridiculous. Had she even heard him right? And several hours before that she would've said Colleen. In truth, she was a mishmash of other people's names for her. Chimera, she wanted to say, a word she'd learned from *National Geographic*—a creature assembled from different places, none of which quite added up to a whole. She shook her head.

"Is it that you don't remember?"

She shook her head again. What now would she call herself?

"Okay." Dr. Grimes nodded solemnly to the nurse. "Kate wants to clean up those scrapes." She followed his eyes slowly down past the ties and snaps of the weird garment covered in faded asterisks like the pattern on the cracked countertop in the trailer, to the outline of her legs under the flowy material. Shifting to one hip, she just then realized that her shorts were still on. Her eyebrows rose in surprise.

"We let you leave your shorts on, remember?" Kate said.

"You were pretty insistent about that," added the doctor. She leaned forward and dug into her front pocket. The impression of the medallion against her thumb brought a brief moment of comfort.

Pulling the edge of the gown up, she was able to examine her skin on her legs, which was beginning to welt and colonize with amoeba-shaped bruises. This was nothing compared to the profound hurt deeper inside. She'd suffered worse scrambling down pine trees. She closed her eyes and leaned back, allowing Kate to approach.

Yet the darkness behind her lids was a dangerous place. It taunted her just like that phantom black spider spinning in small circles as she coiled herself against the terror of being locked in the bathroom. She was momentarily back in that tight space and almost screamed as she reflexively pulled away from a tangled mass of kelp fingers on her legs.

"It's all right," Kate reassured her. "It's only a damp cloth." She moved quickly yet gently. "Done now. You did a great job." Kate stepped back, and the doctor was once again near her side.

"Can you tell us," he asked softly, "what you remember about the explosion?"

Her head suddenly ached as she recalled Jay holding her and limp-galloping toward the road. Then came a flash and a boom and then silence for a few minutes.

"Where is Moira?"

"I'm sorry, honey," Kate said. "We don't know anything. The police will be able to help."

"I'm scheduling a CAT scan," Dr. Grimes said to Kate. "And where are Protective Services?"

"Should be here any minute." She lowered her voice as she continued talking to the doctor. They looked over a chart together, nodding and murmuring.

The sky outside the single window was deepening to Prussian blue. The door opened, and a policeman and an unfamiliar woman entered the room. The woman was heavy with blond hair that was too yellow, like when little kids choose the brightest crayon to draw the sun. The officer had a thick line of eyebrow that hid his expression.

The woman approached. "I am Mrs. Holder."

She looked a lot like the women she'd seen at laundromats with Moira—puffy, struggling with the weight of the baskets, but pleasant-faced all the same.

"I'm called a social worker. Think of me as a friend."

"Where is Jay?" She struggled to keep from whimpering and slipped her hand into her shorts pocket and fumbled until she found the medallion, then rubbed the edge with her thumb. "What's going on?"

"We'll find everything out soon, sweetie."

"Hello, little lady. I'm Sheriff Dobbs." The officer came close and kneeled down. "Can you tell me your name?"

"Little Bird."

"Oh. Is that a nickname?"

She shrugged. "Jay gave it to me."

"The manager at the trailer park told us he's your neighbor."

She nodded.

"Can you tell me about him?"

"He's my friend."

"Has he ever hurt you?"

She made a ridiculous face. But the sheriff didn't seem to notice.

"The lady you live with, Moira, I believe. Is that your mother?"

"No." Her head went light, as if it might fly from her neck. She was suddenly so very tired. Nobody knew anything. She rubbed her eyes with the heels of her hands.

"Can this wait?" Mrs. Holder stepped next to the sheriff. "At least a little while? This child is exhausted."

"One last thing for now." Nurse Kate again. "I need to swab your cheek."

Based on the expression she received, the nurse changed tactics. "I promise. One quick swipe, Little Bird." She winked. "Then we'll let you rest."

She opened her mouth, then turned away when Kate was done.

"Thank you," Kate whispered as she lightly rubbed her shoulder.

The window was lacquer black. This in and out of people, this waiting to hear about Jay, made her small, smaller, smallest, tamped down like a patch of nuisance weeds. She'd dry up, shrivel to nothing soon, and who'd notice? She'd grown up believing her parents had left her and now she was to believe something else?

If this was true, why hadn't they searched for her?

Time crawled forward. The room emptied, leaving her alone with Mrs. Holder. She noted the way the door swung, which direction people headed. Maybe she'd just sneak out that door. Wait for the opportunity and then be going the opposite way. Find a stairwell to sink into, search for Jay. *General Hospital* always had plenty of them. She just had to be patient.

In the meantime, she peered into the tin box on the tray table that Mrs. Holder had set near her side. It had a bunch of uninteresting stuff in it. A picture book. Like for a toddler. Some pencil stubs and a worn and thumbed-through and then ignored sketch pad with pages too thin for any kind of reasonable use. All of it tossed among a mess of crayons broken and peeled by some other lonely kid.

With each passing minute, her mind buzzed with fatigue, bringing forth things that sometimes came to her just as she fell asleep. She remembered now, being in the dark, packed into a space. Could barely breathe. But it wasn't the bathroom. And someone else was there. She caught her breath as a moment of clarity flashed: what had Jay said again…a sister, the thought unfurled like a precious bloom inside her. She was right then, in the trunk of a car, holding on to her sister's small hand.

Little Bird sobbed softly. This was too much. All too much. Clenching her fingers into balls, sleep was finally claiming her, under a curtain of confusion. And then the feel of skin against her own, the sudden yet faint image in her mind of a little blond girl, a sister, the idea of family, drew her bleary mind to fantasy. What if it were all true? Parents: her mom with blond hair and bright-blue eyes like her sister's, and her dad tall and handsome as all get-out. They would be on the porch of their little white house with raspberry shutters.

"What do you like to do?" her dad would ask, smiling.

"I like to climb trees."

"Me too. Cool." He would nod. "What else?"

"I like to untangle knots."

No, why would she say that? It was so random and untrue. But she could tell it didn't matter, nothing she'd say would bother her good-natured parents. Her mom would stroke her hair and her dad would wink.

This would all happen right on the porch swing. With a breeze filled with wild scents wrapping them in softness, and dog would be barking nearby—short, happy yips. Lily would be there too, on one of her parents' laps.

Little Bird's eyelids went heavy and she nodded off. But then a door slammed somewhere, a thick and percussive sound, and she shot up, alert with anxiety. Mrs. Holder looked at her with a worried face. Little Bird's eyes narrowed as tears flooded her vision. But she held them back. This was all so crazy. Jay getting an operation. The possibility of a family. Where was Moira? If she wasn't in the explosion, then where had she gone?

"Do you need anything, sweetie? I can get you more juice."

She hadn't touched the first cup offered however many hours ago. Before she could say anything, Mrs. Holder went to attend to a new policeman at the door.

Little Bird leaned toward the dark window. There were clouds in the sky, but a hint of the moon was there underneath like a coin under paper. If it were clear out, Jay would have a name for this, something like a shining water moon.

The phone rang. Mrs. Holder dashed to pick it up.

"Still nothing?" Her voice rose with worry.

Little Bird lowered herself to the floor. She'd sat for so long, her whole body was sluggish. She grabbed the bed to keep from falling. *Don't mess up*, she scolded her legs. *I need you now.*

Mrs. Holder motioned forward, the phone still near her face.

"Just going to the bathroom," Little Bird said.

In fact, she was dry as a bone. She'd studied the room. Mrs. Holder was in the blind spot now. Little Bird reached into the bathroom and turned on the fan and light switches. She took the ridiculous snap top off and put her own T-shirt back on. She then tiptoed outside the bathroom. Carefully closing the door behind her, she hid in the folds of the privacy curtain bunched several feet away, near the hall.

"What if they don't figure out...?" Mrs. Holder turned toward the window, absorbed in conversation.

Little Bird slipped quietly through the door of her room. The hallway was bright and she hesitated, blinking. She took two careful steps. She'd be around the corner, down a stairwell, and gone with a few more. She'd find Jay. But what if he wasn't all right? Her stomach lurched at that thought. No, Jay was a warrior. He'd be fine. He had to be. Her legs were good and steady now. She tilted forward, preparing for a quick breakaway.

A sudden yet gentle tug on her upper arm stopped her dead. She looked up. Behind Mrs. Holder's face, long thin ceiling lights glared overhead. Gleaming like sharp monster teeth.

"Oh, honey," Mrs. Holder's said in a tender voice.

Little Bird allowed Mrs. Holder to lead her back inside the room and help her into the bed. On the chrome tray pulled close, she saw the almost unrecognizable face of a frightened little girl.

She looked again into the crate. The crayons weren't as pathetic as she'd first thought. She poked around, moving colors into different corners without fully committing to any real interest in them. Slowly, she began to twin them with their opposites, green next to red, blue across from yellow and all the shades in-between. The rich, mellow odor of old crayons, so different from the plasticky new ones, made her want to use them. Suddenly, more than anything, she needed to draw.

Ignoring the sketch pad, she grabbed a bunch of stiff paper towels from a stack next to a pitcher of water and a plastic cup. She smoothed one out onto the tray table. Mrs. Holder nodded and smiled.

The moon belonged to Jay. The beautiful gas giants were hers, but they weren't real without a telescope, so what did it matter? She pictured a new planet in the sky. One close to the earth, but that no one else could see. Her own planet, dark and eerie. She worked somber blues and heavy purples in a circle. But this monster planet wouldn't fit on one paper towel. She opened another towel and ran her hand in a big bold circle, creating an outline that now swallowed the first. She filled the interior with continents frozen in place like the seas and craters on the moon, only shadowed with menacing shapes. It took a good ten minutes until she was satisfied. With a final stroke of a crayon, she gave the ugly planet a thin ring sketched in icy gray.

Mrs. Holder shifted in her seat, setting her fingers in a cross-hatched tent over her chest. She looked tired.

Little Bird steadied a pencil stub in her hand and paused before signing her work. She stretched toward the window again. The sky outside was losing its stars; lights on the horizon made it an unreal orange. Little Bird, that's what she'd write. But instead, her mouth filled with a soft round *A*.

Andrea.

She sounded it out. But somehow it didn't seem right. So she began to write Colleen, staying within the comfort of the looping *l*'s, but then dropped her pencil in abandonment, because both felt wrong. Tears came freely now, filling her cheeks and trembling chin as if running away from her eyes. These, she couldn't hide. Mrs. Holder came over to the bed.

"I know this is difficult," she whispered softly and took hold of Little Bird's hands. "The police are still trying to contact your parents."

Little Bird pulled away. This was all beginning to feel like a scam of some sort. How was this different from the lies Moira had told?

Jay's earlier words were nothing but a muddle of confusion. Who were these people that the sheriff, the doctors, Mrs. Holder thought they were looking for?

People who'd allowed her to be stolen, that's who.

Parents. Mom and Dad. The words slid around Little Bird and carried off through the hall. She wouldn't take ownership of them. They didn't belong to her. She shook her head to erase that stupid fantasy family on the porch of that perfect house. An embarrassment. She was a selkie, remember? A child of no one. She dropped all the crayons in the tin box and then shoved them onto the floor where they bounced and split and scattered like frightened mice. She then lifted her drawing up between her two hands and began to tear it, working one satisfying rip after another, each piece smaller than the one before, until a pile of shiny bits of a shattered planet grew on the tray table.

"Please, honey…" Mrs. Holder's eyes brightened with tears.

A sudden bellowing in the hall outside the door spun Mrs. Holder around.

"Take it easy, man…" It was possibly the orderly's voice. Followed by something about crutches. "Please, mister…"

"I need to see her."

Jay!

Spilling off the bed like seaweed pulled from a rock in high tide, she bolted past Mrs. Holder and yanked the door open. There stood Jay, all bandaged like the combat troopers she'd seen in old World War II movies, leaning heavily against a crutch.

"Little Bird!" Jay shouted and lowered himself as she ran toward him. She fell into the space he'd made for her in the crook of his free arm. He squeezed her against him and whispered into her ear. "*Tiyospaye.*"

She looked up, questioning.

His face beamed as he smiled. "Extended family."

Everything, the overbright hallway, the sighing Mrs. Holder, the orderly in his scrubs, all disappeared, and the world was now filled with Jay.

And nothing else was real. Nothing at all.

Chapter 25
Claire

The clock read 5:19 a.m. when Claire was startled awake by the shrill insistence of the phone. The sound felt like an invasion in the quiet house. She moaned, opening her eyes into slits, mildly irritated.

It rang again.

Who could be calling at this hour?

She lifted onto her elbow. A crimp in her neck brought her forward. She rubbed one eye and glanced around. It took a moment before recognizing her old living room wrapped in shadows. An empty wine bottle sat on a side table next to the chair where Glen was still asleep, sprawled like an overfed cat. Gretchie remained in a pile, plopped next to him on the floor wheezing in deep slumber.

Glen didn't move.

R-r-ring.

She leaned over the edge of the couch and lifted the receiver, leaving a moment of silence before speaking.

"Hello?"

Right then Claire changed her mind. She had no business doing this in Glen's house. When she moved to hang the phone up, a voice came on the line.

"Hello?" It was a woman. "Claire?"

The tone was clear and urgent. *Hearns!*

Claire bolted upright. "Juanita?"

"I'm being patched through by Detective Ferguson with the Michigan State Police. He's at Elmcrest Hospital near Benton Harbor."

Claire remained silent. Hearing Hearns's voice after so long scuttled all sense of context.

Juanita cleared her throat. "The detective asked me to make this call. He believes that they may have"—she hesitated, and then spoke boldly—"found Andrea."

What? Claire slumped in resignation. A vision flashed through her mind of a partial skeleton in a shallow grave, the bones singed clean, whitened with age. She glanced at her sleeping husband. His face. His hands. Peaceful. These words would now destroy that peace. "Dear God."

"Claire." Hearns was close to breathless. "You don't understand."

A thin cord of panic choked Claire. What was there to understand? She'd wake Glen and they would weep together over this terrible wound torn open.

"This child is alive."

What did she mean? The connection crackled. Hearns continued to speak but she became inaudible. Suddenly it occurred to Claire that this was some hoax, some cruel joke.

A man came on the line.

"Mrs. Rawlings? We will be running DNA testing against the records on file, but have good reason to believe that this little girl we have here is your daughter, Andrea."

"Repeat. What you have said."

This man was speaking gibberish. The time it took for neurotransmitters to flood Claire's synapses, to form a coherent network of thought and recognition, was only milliseconds. But in Claire-time, it was an eon, the equivalent to the melting of an ice age. She felt a sob rising in her throat but held it back.

He began again.

"Wait," she interrupted, "I need to get my husband on the line."

She stood. But she didn't move. It was as if her limbs were suddenly reviving after a cruel sleep-inducing spell and she was feeling them again for the first time. She set the receiver on its side and blinked. Then turned to the recliner.

"Glen." Claire's voice was a raspy whisper, not the volume required to truly wake someone.

He shifted and wiped his chin with the back of his hand.

"Glen." Louder this time, but still tinged with the sense that Claire's voice was coming from somewhere other than her own throat. She touched his arm.

Glen's waking was full of startle, a *Where am I?* expression flooding his face. He sat forward attempting to focus.

"Claire?"

She switched on a lamp and knelt slowly next to his chair because her legs were still unsteady.

"It's Andrea."

He searched Claire's face. "What?"

"Police." She pointed to the receiver. "They think they've found her."

If she could've crushed him with stones, it would not have been worse than the words she'd just spoken. He dropped his head into his hands.

"Glen." Claire had no idea how she managed to keep her voice steady. "They think our daughter is alive."

"What?" He pulled the recliner forward and leaped up.

Claire pointed to the kitchen. "Grab that line."

He rushed to the phone, almost tripping over the now-roused Gretchie, then lifted the receiver to his face, as Claire did the same in the living room. They stretched the cords to their extremes so they could see each other, but only barely. Neither would risk losing this line.

The detective began mid-story, not knowing that Claire had provided no information to Glen. "Jay White, whom we've confirmed through Detective Hearns knows you, has provided a positive ID based on a photo he says you gave him."

The detective continued to speak for several minutes, something about a woman kidnapper. An explosion. Jay and a rescue. But the words were a jumble.

All Claire could comprehend was the key point: Andrea, alive.

"What in God's name?" Glen pulled at his hair. "Jay White?

How could he possibly ID Andrea?" Glen shook his head in disbelief, the cord straining. At that moment, Claire detected the same panicked urgency as That Day when he had shown up at the gas station—insisting to the police, close to short-circuiting with fear.

"We have requested expedited DNA testing, but that may take a week at least…"

Hearns came on again. "Glen, they are doing a comparison of the old photo against a new one. But that, too, will take time."

His eyes grew large with disbelief at hearing this voice. Hearns continued, "So many things line up. The involvement of a woman Traveller. Andrea's age. We hope when you come she'll recognize you."

A woman! Claire fell to one knee.

Glen asked questions as they supplied information on the kidnapper, a name, Moira. Mixed in through all of this were directions to the hospital. Claire kept her focus on her husband. He stayed with them, getting more details. Claire didn't speak. Instead, she drifted from the voices.

She had heard Andrea calling through the deep. Claire began to fill with something remarkable, as if she'd just swallowed a glowing bulb. The possibility that she was a mother again was real. Everything now had the quality of water—voices, thoughts, the surroundings.

Andrea is alive. Andrea. Our daughter. Alive.

Words moved and shifted like sweet liquid, nectar. They were delicious and Claire savored each one. She closed her eyes.

"Until the testing proves otherwise"—she returned to the conversation as Glen said—"this is all coincidence."

Claire understood what he was saying. The possibility that this child was not Andrea was almost too much to bear.

"I'm sorry this is abrupt." A different voice spoke now. "I'm Dr. Grimes."

Claire was back again, in the moment.

"What is her status?"

She asked this as a question from one physician to another. It wasn't as if she was speaking about her daughter. She didn't dare to whisper the name Andrea. Those words were too potent right then, might somehow break this magical spell.

"She's shook up," the doctor said slowly.

"Does she remember anything about her past?"

"Doesn't seem to. I think we are dealing with amnesia, but I don't really know. She'll need a full psych eval—beyond that I can't say. We've never encountered anything like this before."

A thin blade of fear sliced through Claire, down the center axis of her body. She couldn't lose Andrea a second time. She was too dazed to absorb most of the information. All she knew was that she had to get moving to that hospital in Michigan as fast as humanly possible.

"This is…the whole thing…it's…" Glen interrupted.

"I know, Mr. Rawlings. Can you both come? Here? Now?"

"It is, I believe," Hearns spoke softly, "a three-hour drive. I will be coming too."

Time, time, time. It was what they didn't have. Andrea needed her mother. Now. Claire made a face at Glen, a pleading one. He locked eyes with her and nodded.

"We are leaving," Glen stated. "Now."

They hung up, and he grabbed Claire into a crushing embrace.

"It's her. I just know it," Claire whispered. And then they stepped back and stood at arm's length looking into each other's faces. Glen's eyes were soft and filled with fear and something he was now allowing—wonder.

"Let's go."

They dashed in different directions, grabbing whatever seemed to make sense—Claire's purse, Glen's keys. Claire forced one foot to follow the other to keep her grounded as her body seemed weightless. Gretchie wove between Claire's legs and then circled the room in high alert.

Glen raced back toward the master bedroom.

"My wallet."

"Your other shoe," Claire called. Within minutes, they were heading out. But Claire abruptly stopped at the door. "Glen, something's missing…"

"What?" He looked pained with urgency.

"We can't go yet…"

Of course. She grabbed the phone.

"Claire. Calls come later."

She held her palm toward him as she dialed, trying not to mix up the digits she knew so well. He sighed and cleared his throat as the phone on the other end rang. Once, twice, three times.

This is important, she mouthed. The machine started to kick on.

"Claire?"

"Thank God you answered."

"Is everything—"

"Howard. No time to talk. They think they found— No, they found Andrea."

She spoke quickly but with great precision. The hospital. Her daughter's condition. A rapid-fire rendition of every detail she knew and what she didn't. Thankfully, Howard heard enough to piece together what was happening. And he understood that, next to Claire and Glen, a child psychiatrist would be the most important person in Andrea's life right then.

"Just go. I'll be right behind. We can assess her there."

"Howard." Claire's voice shook. "Her status, her memory, I'm so afraid… Please. Hurry."

"She may not believe it's you without evidence, something tangible. Bring something of hers, a keepsake, a photo, a stuffed toy maybe?"

"Howard." Claire's voice vibrated at some weird frequency, as if she were out of body. "They say there is no protocol for this."

"Of course there isn't. How can there be a protocol for a miracle?"

Claire sprinted down the hall toward the girls' room. And then there it was. The layered light, darker near the floor and ceiling, softer near the windows, the same as it was five years before when she had crept through the house to check on Lily and Andrea. The memory of that early morning was stitched into her very skin like a birthmark.

There was no time to search through the boxes filled with items from the girls' childhood, stored on a high shelf in the closet. Each moment spent not driving to the hospital was time being stolen from a deposit that was running low. *Move, move, move* was all Claire could think. She grabbed the bag with Jumpers's carrot still on the dresser, along with a picture of Gretchie in a dog bone–shaped frame, taken when she was a puppy. At the other side of the room, she could see the shadowy outline of Butkus's cage and the silhouette of a bird with his head tucked beneath a wing. Silent for once! She returned to the living room where Glen nodded and jangled the keys. Gretchie paced at the door, clearly uncertain what to do with this new energy in the house.

"You call Vicki and I'll call the neighbors after we get there. Have them let G out."

Call their daughter's aunt…after we get there…sounded so ordinary, so matter of fact. Did not sound anything like a broken couple preparing to traverse into this amazing unknown. Just then, Gretchie reached her long legs onto Claire's thighs. Claire bent and ran her fingers through Gretchie's thick, short fur. "You, sweet love," she whispered, Gretchie's ears lifting, "are one perfect soul."

And then they were off, weaving through the neighborhood and the side streets.

Through the car window, Claire was startled by the beauty of the sky—the purple wisps of the stratosphere melting into different shades of melon-hued pastels. Was Andrea seeing this same sunrise? What did Andrea look like, how would she act? Was she smart? Funny? And what would she think of Claire? What would she look like to this girl? They said she was shook up. What did that mean? Why hadn't Claire asked more—she was a doctor, for God's sake.

Please—don't let her be hurt. Make her be okay.

Claire fought against her worries threading like beads on a string. God almighty, a woman. This was good, right? Less possibility of some terrible abuse. But what if she had actually become, in Andrea's mind, her mother? She'd gotten away, was still out there able to threaten her daughter. Claire bit the inside of her cheek. No. She'd stay focused in the moment until they learned more. She placed her hand into Glen's. Finally, they were flying onto the expressway. Heading east toward Michigan, crossing this great divide between their before and after lives.

The first time Claire saw her daughter was through a milky glass window and a half-open door. She was sitting at a table in a dirty shirt and cutoff jeans, hunched a bit as if trying to be smaller. Claire could only see her from behind. She had choppy hair, still the softest shade of brown mottled here and there with faded red streaks. Her feet, pulled free from stained tennis shoes, were visible beneath the table—the top one jammed into the bottom one, both bent into whiteness. Claire almost doubled over, as if tightened by a cord attached to her viscera. The social worker sat with her in the room. Claire had been told the woman's name when she and Glen arrived, but it was now forgotten. Other than blond hair and chubby features, Claire didn't bother to register her. Claire entered slowly through the doorway and then turned toward a slight shuffling sound. Jay! He was moving across the room on crutches, his leg in a cast.

Claire almost cried out. This was so incredibly strange. He smiled, concern creased into his face. He sat in a chair set a few feet away from the table.

"Andrea," the woman said. "Your parents are here."

Claire's daughter moved her head enough to glance at the social worker and then returned her gaze to the cinder-block wall. Claire caught her profile briefly and noticed the long, thin outline of her nose, her lunar-colored skin.

"I...I...should go," Jay said, moving to rise.

"No!" Andrea said. "Don't leave."

Claire and Glen circled around the table. Their movements were slow, awkward.

Claire tried to lessen the intensity of her focus on her daughter, but found she could not. A strand of hair dipped across Andrea's face, but not enough to hide the dark half circles under her eyes, which accentuated her preternatural paleness. Claire fought not to shudder at the scratches on her skin. That story was too large right then. A small dimple in her left cheek suggested whimsy in an otherwise somber landscape. She was beautiful, had clearly gotten her looks from Glen. Could she see her own face in his? Her aquiline nose and crystal-cut features? Claire detected the faint scent of rose-mary. No, it was pine—like forests, clean air, and rich, undisturbed earth. She trapped a gasp in her throat at the archipelago of bruises on her bare legs.

What had her little girl been through? Her expression was impenetrable. Was there a hint of recognition or warmth for her real mother?

There was none.

Glen reached across the table, trembling. Tears ran from the creases of his eyes to his jawline. Andrea drew back. Her eyes flashed between her parents.

"Your mother and father are thrilled to see you." The woman spoke again, clearly uncomfortable.

Each word lowered Andrea farther into her chair.

In all of Claire's fantasies, even the most outlandish, where her daughter was discovered on a desert island, or rescued from the mouth of a bubbling volcano, she was always happy to see both of her parents. Now, a cacophony of desperate thoughts banged like wind chimes in Claire's head. *This child*, she heard Howard's voice in her head, *needs something tangible.*

"Is there anything either of you can remember?" The social worker struggled to hold the anxiety in her voice at bay. "An identifying mark, perhaps?"

Claire fought against the blank screen that had become her mind. Searching the room, she caught her own reflection in the wavy glass. She must look ridiculous to this child with her closely cropped shade-of-death hair, and her eyes so sadly hopeful.

"There was a reddish stork bite, a splotchy birthmark on the back of her arm…" Glen offered.

"No," Claire whispered. "That was Lily, remember?"

"Is there anything else?" The woman's eyes screamed, *Come on, lady! You're her mother. There must be something else—think!*

But nothing materialized within the immediacy the situation required. How was it possible—to fail now, after all this time?

Claire reached into her purse. "I… We…brought something." She set Jumpers's carrot on the table.

Jay's eyes lit with surprise and recognition and then he shut them tight as if praying. Claire almost found herself doing the same thing. But she knew that if she closed her eyes, this all might disappear, that Andrea might not be there when she opened them.

The woman began to speak again. But Jay raised his palm and nodded to Claire.

"There's more. You can remember more."

She was there on That Day, piling the girls into the car, and then the girls were fighting over Jumpers, then Andrea was spilling crumbs on her dress from the Pop-Tart and Claire remembered how her head was reeling from the reaction and yet wanting, no needing, to get to her program because that seemed so incredibly important at the time and how long she'd suffered for that horrible, horrible decision, and also how sick she was and then finally, watching her girls sleeping in the back of the car.

"Maybe the dress." Claire's voice shook. "It was blue, soft, like denim, that material... What is it called...? Umm, chambray. That's it." Glen squeezed her arm. "Andrea." Her voice grew louder, clearer. "You had it on." She locked onto her daughter's eyes. "That day. When you were taken from us."

Andrea's posture remained taut, yet her expression softened, and Claire felt a momentary toehold on the face of this rock cliff. And then, just as quickly, Andrea turned away, giving her mother the back of her head, the way she'd done so long ago in the Taurus when Claire had handed her the Pop-Tart. This small gesture became a flashpoint, igniting in Claire a newfound strength, and her voice rose with excitement.

"My mother, your grandmother, made it for me when I was little. She used to sew little charms, religious objects, into the hems of my dresses...for fun or...or"—*don't stammer, Claire, not now!*—"or for good luck." The memory of her mother's hand, throwing stitches, the loving intention behind it carried her through. "That dress had a medal with the Madonna in it. It was no bigger than a dime."

She stopped. Enough had been said. Andrea sat frozen, still facing away. Claire dropped her eyes, fearing her disappointment would make this all worse. Just then, Andrea turned around and placed her hand, which was tightened into a fist, over the table. Slowly, and with great care, she unfurled her fingers so they opened like the blossom of a flower in the early morning sun. A small, oval item glinted in her palm, time-worn and discolored, and to Claire, unmistakable. The embossed outline of a veiled woman enshrined in stars.

The medallion!

Claire gasped. Something between a laugh and a sob escaped from her mouth. Her muscles lost all strength, and she couldn't move to grab her daughter. Instead, she placed her head into her hands on the table and sobbed, her shoulder blades pulsing like wings, releasing so much, so many years of pent-up sorrow.

Feeling the slightest touch on her elbow, Claire looked up. Andrea was closer, close enough to reach to her mother. Her daughter's eyes were shining, awash in this unimaginable moment. Glen, who ejected himself from the chair first, enfolded their daughter in a tender embrace, and she allowed it.

"Oh, Andrea," Glen whispered into her hair. "Oh, honey…"

A pulse of fiery energy raced through Claire, and she rushed to join them. The three of them were, for a few precious moments, a once singular organism, united again, as one.

Reading Group Guide

1. How did you feel while reading Andrea and Lily's kidnapping on That Day? What emotions did you experience?

2. The way Claire grieves the loss of her daughters is to become too busy to face all her pain, which in turn boxes Glen out of their relationship. Have you ever had an experience where you have done something similar, perhaps on a smaller scale?

3. Gretchie is a source of comfort for Claire after the disappearance. Have you ever had a pet that has helped you through a difficult time? How would you describe that bond?

4. Moira and Jay both have deep ties to their heritage. How do the Lakota and Traveller cultures influence the story? How do they shape these characters? How has your own heritage shaped you?

5. One of the key themes of *Little Lovely Things* is that people have the capacity to change and heal. Which characters do you view as changing in a positive way? In a negative way?

6. How do both Jay's and Moira's pasts influence their decision-making in the story?

7. Claire believes the light she sees on the day of the funeral is a sign sent from Lily. Have you ever experienced a strong sense of intuition or a sign? What did it feel like? Did it affect your decisions in any way?

8. Howard is able to draw emotions out of Claire that she actively avoids without his help. Is there anyone in your life who has played this role?

9. Andrea's imagination and creativity serves to keep her whole in a difficult situation. Do you believe that art has healing qualities?

10. Colly's relationship with Moira becomes more difficult as Colly grows older. How much does this impact the choices Moira makes?

11. The novel changes point of view each chapter. Was there a character you wished to return to more often than the others? Why?

12. The yearning to belong is universal to the human experience. Which character do you believe is most affected by this emotion?

13. Life can change quickly. Have you or has anyone close to you suffered tragedy and come through changed in a positive way?

14. Which characters do you find most relatable in the story? Why?

15. What do you think happens after the story ends? How does this family come together? Where does Jay fit in? Describe how you think each character will change from this experience.

A Conversation
with the Author

What inspired you to write *Little Lovely Things*?

There were many things, but one that jumps out at me was a brief newspaper article I encountered after my third child was born. For some reason, it stirred something deep inside me. It was about a kidnapping that occurred where the child was discovered as an adolescent many years later. There was no follow-up or closure to the story, which, in effect, left it to my imagination to create something larger.

This story deals with one of the greatest fears of motherhood—losing one's children. How did writing those emotional scenes affect you?

Because I am so profoundly connected to my characters, I had to force myself to separate when things became too difficult to write. I got in the habit of taking breaks—things like going on short walks—to recharge before returning to the emotionally rough scenes. Several times, I cried.

Which scene was the most difficult for you to write?

There were two scenes that were very difficult for me. The first is when Claire wakes, disoriented, after Detective Hearns tells her and Glen that Andrea is dead and visits the "snow angels" outside, imagining that the marks in the snow were made by her girls. It still gets me. Even now, my voice tends to tremble when I read it.

The second scene is at the very end, when Claire first sees Andrea after so much time has passed and so much pain endured. It really broke me up imagining how that would go. I love them both so much and wanted them to be together, but I also knew how tenuous the situation would be based on what had transpired in their lives. I am entertaining, at some point, writing another book that addresses their lives after the reunion.

We see both the Lakota and the Traveller cultures come into play throughout the novel. What kind of research did you do to help you portray those cultures accurately?

Plenty! Both cultures have incredibly interesting stories and languages associated with them. I spent a great deal of time studying Shelta and Lakota. Even though I used very little in the book, it helped inform my view of Jay's and Moira's personalities. My ultimate goal was to develop them as individuals, instead of simply casting them as representatives of their cultures.

Which character was the most challenging to write?

Moira. Jay basically presented himself to me fully developed, and I just followed the direction he provided. Both Claire and Andrea gave me difficulties at different times because they weren't always interested in cooperating with my desires! But it was the complexity of Moira's competing traits that made her the most challenging to pin onto the page.

Both Claire's and Jay's characters rely on signs and feelings of intuition to guide them throughout the novel. Do you believe in following your intuition in real life?

Yes! And then yes again! It's really interesting, because being educated in science, I've always been in the business of relying on the analytical side of my brain. When I started *Little Lovely Things*, I was determined to nourish my intuitive side more. Jay and Claire certainly emerged from this effort.

If you could pick a quality from each character to give to yourself, which would you choose?

This is easy! Claire has so many great qualities, but I would have to choose her determination. Andrea—hands down, I would love to have her feisty spirit and creativity. As for Jay, I appreciate his deep compassion and lovely soul. With Moira, I would probably go for a bit of her self-delusion. It might be helpful when I overthink things!

When you're not writing, what are you doing?

Oh man, what am I *not* doing? I recently quit my long-term career, so I am still adjusting to a new schedule as a writer. Aside from taking care of my family, I read a lot. I have many friends and love to socialize. I garden, paint, and cook, all of which inspire me creatively. I also am on a dragon boat team, which practices regularly and competes in festivals.

Acknowledgments

It's difficult for me to express my thanks to those whom I owe so much—the wonderful people who have supported me through the journey of writing and finalizing this book. You are all magical blessings in my life, as each and every one came along just when needed. (There are no coincidences!) Please know that you continue to inspire me in astonishing ways.

And while I'm no gymnast, my gratitude makes me want to express myself beyond the verbal—therefore, please imagine me performing backflips of joy and shouts of thank you to the professionals (my tribe of lovelies) who have had their hands and hearts in this work, whether at inception, throughout the process, or at pivotal moments: Anna Michels, Heather Karpas, Rachel Thompson, Sarah Miniaci, Sharon Green, Katherine Anne Connolly, Jane Ratcliffe, Doreen Erasmus, Andrea Robinson, and Kaitlyn Kennedy.

Never-ending cartwheels of gratitude and appreciation to my loving family—Jim, Patrick, Katherine Anne, and James. You are my very heart, without whose support I would never dream so big.

Moon bounces of special thanks to so many others who have lined my path with love and good wishes and unending support, including my sister, Mary Carol, and my dear friends Laura Blackburn and Doreen Erasmus—you have all saved me from myself more times than I care to mention! Finally, my mother, Lenore, who continues to guide me from heaven and, I'm pretty certain, is celebrating with an out-of-this-world martini.

About the Author

Photo © Frank Prosnotti

Maureen Joyce Connolly is a former owner of a consulting firm that helped develop medications for ultra-rare diseases. While she misses her old career, she loves being a full-time writer. Maureen received her bachelor's degree in physiology from Michigan State University and her master's degree in liberal studies from Wesleyan University. Her background and love for science and the natural world informs and inspires her writing. *Little Lovely Things* is her debut novel. She is also an award-winning poet, published in diverse outlets such as Emory University's *Lullwater Review* and *Yankee Magazine*.

Maureen appreciates good restaurants and preparing interesting recipes. She also enjoys painting, competing in races with her dragon boat team, and reading (of course!). Her favorite moments are those spent with her family.